# SMALL TOWN LAWYER

*Defending Innocence*

*Influencing Justice*

*Interpreting Guilt*

*Burning Evidence*

*Prescribing Doubt*

*Twisting Judgment*

This is a work of fiction. Names, characters, places and incidents either are the product of imagination or are used fictitiously. Any resemblance to actual persons, living or dead, events or locales, is entirely coincidental.

RELAY PUBLISHING EDITION, OCTOBER 2025
Copyright © 2025 Relay Publishing Ltd.

All rights reserved. Published in the United Kingdom by Relay Publishing. This book or any portion thereof may not be reproduced or used in any manner whatsoever without the express written permission of the publisher except for the use of brief quotations in a book review.

Peter Kirkland is a pen name created by Relay Publishing for co-authored Legal Thriller projects. Relay Publishing works with incredible teams of writers and editors to collaboratively create the very best stories for our readers.

www.relaypub.com

SMALL TOWN LAWYER - BOOK SIX

# TWISTING JUDGMENT

## KIRKLAND & HALL

# BLURB

**A murdered judge. An innocent accused. Justice comes at a deadly price.**

Small town defense attorney Leland Munroe isn't afraid to tackle cases others run from. But when a federal judge plunges to his death from a locked courthouse stairwell just before testifying, Leland is pulled into a deadly investigation. Every clue he uncovers drags him deeper into a dark web of deceit.

The FBI arrests Vinny Baptiste, a courthouse janitor with a troubled past and ties to the judge. It looks like an open-and-shut case—except Leland doesn't buy it. The judge had secrets of his own, and the evidence points to a far more influential suspect hiding in plain sight.

As Leland races to uncover the truth and defend an innocent man, the cost of justice grows steep. And the rural retreat that's been a safe haven in the past comes under threat from an unexpected direction.

In a system rigged to protect the powerful, can Leland expose the truth before the killer claims another victim…

# CONTENTS

1. November 17, 2023 — 1
2. December 1, 2023 — 10
3. December 8, 2023 — 26
4. December 11, 2023 — 43
5. December 12, 2023 — 53
6. December 19, 2023 — 64
7. December 29, 2023 — 80
8. January 9, 2024 — 92
9. February 9, 2024 — 104
10. March 6, 2024 — 119
11. March 28, 2024 — 130
12. April 18, 2024 — 143
13. May 9, 2024 — 155
14. May 9, 2024 — 167
15. June 14, 2024 — 183
16. July 8, 2024 — 194
17. September 18, 2024 — 205
18. September 20, 2024 — 214
19. September 27, 2024 — 224
20. September 28, 2024 — 235
21. September 28, 2024 — 241
22. September 30, 2024 — 251
23. September 30, 2024 — 261
24. October 1, 2024 — 275
25. October 1, 2024 — 287
26. October 1, 2024 — 299
27. October 4, 2024 — 312
28. November 27, 2024 — 323

*End of Twisting Judgment* — 329
*About Peter Kirkland & Daleth Hall* — 331
*Sneak Peek: The Bloodied Client* — 333
*Sneak Peek: Small Town Conviction* — 339
*Also by Peter Kirkland* — 351

# 1

## NOVEMBER 17, 2023

There's a fine line between curiosity and stupidity, and most days I tried not to cross it. That Friday was different.

I was walking out of a pretrial hearing at about 11:30 a.m., patting myself on the back for getting some evidence tossed, and I decided not to duck out of the courthouse by a side exit like I usually did. Instead, I trotted down the stairs to the second floor, wondering if Judge Ambleton's bailiff, Antoine, could tell me anything interesting about the trial happening in her courtroom. Maybe he'd let me watch. I was sure all the seats were full—the trial was on the news every night; nobody was talking about anything else—but Antoine had his ways.

He was standing tall beside the courtroom door with his hands clasped behind his back. As I approached, I gave him a nod, which he returned. Apart from the two of us, the hallway was empty. Extra security had made sure of that. The reporters were camped out front by the courthouse steps—I could hear the hubbub even though all the windows were closed.

The press had gathered because disgraced former prosecutor Patrick Ludlow, whose downfall I'd had a hand in, was looking down the barrel of thirty years in jail. Basking Rock was a small town, and nothing this exciting normally happened here. After federal corruption charges against Ludlow got dropped, the state brought similar charges against him. His attorneys had thrown up enough roadblocks to delay his trial for almost two and a half years, but his luck had finally run out.

And I wanted to see that for myself.

"Morning, Antoine."

"Morning, Mr. Munroe. You here to watch him beg for mercy?"

I chuckled. "That'd really be something, wouldn't it."

Antoine's expression told me he'd like to see that too. Three generations of Ludlows had controlled the justice system around here for close to a century. A new era was dawning, or so I hoped.

Antoine looked over his shoulder through the small window in the courtroom door. "Gonna have to wait a minute," he said. "If there's a recess before lunch, you go on in. Standing room only, though."

"You know who's testifying today?"

"That politician just got off the stand. White-haired guy. McCabe, I think?"

"Oh, I wish I could've heard that."

McCabe, a state senator, had gotten immunity on bribery charges in exchange for testifying against Ludlow.

"And before him," Antoine said, "it was that guy who went and ran against Mr. Ludlow a few years back."

"Oh, Tucker?"

"That's him."

"That must've been interesting."

Tucker had been a witness in a case of mine a few years earlier. He'd been called by the prosecution to testify against my client, but instead, thanks to a ton of legwork my private investigator and I had done, he blew the case wide open. On the witness stand, under oath, he'd told the world that Ludlow had blackmailed him to try to make him give false testimony. After that, Ludlow's life collapsed like a house of cards.

"You still got some good stuff coming up today, though," Antoine said. "I think the federal judge is next."

"Nicholson?"

"That's the name."

"Damn," I said. "Prosecution's starting with a bang, aren't they."

"Yes, indeed."

We shot the breeze for another minute. I wanted to see Nicholson testify, and not only for the pleasure of watching somebody destroy Patrick Ludlow. I had a trial scheduled before Nicholson in a few months, and I wasn't about to miss an opportunity to take the measure of my judge. I'd seen him on the bench before, but seeing him on the witness stand, I thought, could tell me things I had no other way to learn.

The noise level behind the door swelled. Through the window I could see spectators standing up. A recess had begun.

Antoine swung the door open, and I slipped in. A few men in suits passed me, heading out, and several more were going in the same direction. Phones had to be off in the courtroom, and people swarmed out during breaks to turn them back on and get a fix.

The courtroom was still crowded. Some spectators had gathered in clusters to talk in low voices, while others stayed where they were, probably to avoid losing their seats. I recognized a few people. My friend Ruiz, who ran the local prosecutor's office, was talking to somebody in the front pew. Ruiz wasn't prosecuting this case, since Ludlow was his former boss. The state had brought in a prosecutor from Columbia to handle things.

A man nearby stepped away from a conversation, and I saw, a few feet farther on, a woman's familiar gray hair. It was Laura, the secretary for my former boss, Roy Hearst. I called out to her.

"Oh, Leland! Hello there! Long time no see!"

We caught up for a minute. Before moving on in search of a seat, I asked, "Roy not interested in the proceedings?"

"Oh, you know how he is. This is too scandalous for him. He didn't even want to be in town for it—left a few days ago on a fishing trip."

I smiled. "Fishing off the side of a yacht, I assume?"

"Yes, indeed."

We said our goodbyes. As I made my way toward a seat, I wondered if Roy might have had the right idea. He avoided scandal, both to keep his reputation unsullied and to avoid making enemies of anyone whom scandal had brought low.

As I was detouring around some folks talking in the aisle, I heard a woman say, "My goodness, Leland Munroe! It has been *ages*!"

I turned and saw Shannon Pennington, our local true crime podcaster. She was fiftysomething, with the sort of perfect, caramel-blonde hair I associated with Southern female politicians.

"Shannon! I should've known you'd be here. Although is this really your type of crime?"

Her podcast specialized in South Carolina's more haunting or existentially disturbing cases of violent crime. She, unlike Roy, sought scandal out.

"Are you kidding me?" she said. "I've been here all day, every day. The former district solicitor's on trial for corruption! Who doesn't want to hear about that?"

"Well, you have a point."

"Anyway, great seeing you. I'll let you go find yourself a seat."

I said goodbye and kept going, begging folks' pardon as I maneuvered around them. I caught sight of Fourth—Dabney Barnes IV, the Lowcountry's media magnate—and switched directions. I had no desire to run into him. I didn't recall ever seeing him show up at a trial himself, and I was surprised for about half a second, until I recalled that Ludlow was a personal friend of his. I supposed he didn't want to entrust the reporting on this trial to anybody else.

I found a pew with an empty spot and sat down.

A bailiff whose name I couldn't recall was standing by the door to chambers. Another was watching the throng from his spot between the empty jury box and the empty bench. Normally, a courtroom only had one bailiff, but with a trial this high profile, I wasn't surprised that Antoine had backup.

At the defense table, silver-haired Ludlow and his phalanx of lawyers were huddled in an intense conversation. I had a clear view of them all, because the pew where Ludlow's family and friends had probably been sitting, the front row on the defense side of the aisle, was empty, except for the jackets and things that they'd left to save their spots. He was fighting for his life, and despite every bad thing he'd done—to me, to my clients, to the justice system itself—I felt a stab of pity for him. He was in his late fifties. If he got convicted on even half the charges, the actuarial tables suggested he could well die in jail.

The huddle of lawyers sat back, and one of them got up and headed for the door. Ludlow watched him go, and in the process, he spotted me.

Our eyes locked. His eyes narrowed, and I felt a sudden temperature drop. I kept my face in neutral, but the hairs on the back of my neck were telling me to get the hell out of there.

Only one other man had ever looked at me that way. Twelve years earlier, back when I was a prosecutor in Charleston, a gangland killer had given me the same cold stare after the jury came back with a verdict against him. I credited my continued survival to the fact that the man had died a few months later in a prison riot.

Maybe it had been a mistake to walk into this courtroom and let Ludlow see me gloating over his humiliation. I could've found out everything I wanted to know from the news and courthouse gossip. I could've gotten copies of the transcripts, whenever they came out, and read them in the safety of my home.

He was still staring at me like a cat—he hadn't blinked—when a man shouted in the hallway outside. Then somebody else shouted, and I distinctly heard the word "dead."

Ludlow glanced at the courtroom door and then back at me. He had no expression on his face. Nothing human, no concern or surprise.

He turned around to face the bench again and leaned back in his chair.

The noise in the hallway got louder. Someone in the courtroom said, "What's going on?" A couple of spectators got up and went to the door. Through the window, I saw Antoine's head shaking. He wasn't letting them out.

Walkie-talkies crackled to life. The bailiff by the jury box pressed on his earpiece, listening closely, frowning. Several more people stood up. There was a sense of impending chaos. I seized the moment to make my way to the door.

In the hallway outside, a woman spoke urgently to Antoine, and the only word he said that I could understand was "evacuate." He pointed down the hallway, swinging his arm in a hard, insistent gesture, and she went.

A few seconds later Antoine saw me through the little window, cracked the door open about an inch, and said, "I'm sorry, Mr. Munroe, but y'all are going to need to stay in there. We got an emergency here."

A pair of cops ran past, guns out, the handcuffs on their belts rattling with every step. I heard sirens out front. A lot of police cars, from the sound of it. Maybe an ambulance, I wasn't sure.

I lowered my voice and asked, "Somebody die out there?"

He gave a quick nod.

"Who?"

He looked around. Nobody was paying attention to us.

"I ain't tell you this," he said quietly.

"Course not."

"They say it's Judge Nicholson."

———

After an initial ruckus, the courtroom spectators—with a little help from Judge Ambleton banging her gavel—calmed down. We heard no gunshots; we smelled no smoke. Whatever had happened, people realized that we ourselves didn't seem to be in danger.

It was another hour before they started escorting us from the courtroom, five people at a time, with cops directing us straight to the main elevator bank and, from there, outside. By that point all the lawyers knew what had happened, because we were the only ones allowed to keep our cell phones with us in court. I'd turned mine back on about ten minutes in, and I wasn't the only one; under the circumstances, the judge was letting that slide. We still couldn't check the news—the courthouse was old, with thick stone walls and floors; the Wi-Fi was never good, and with this many people trying to get online, it was overloaded. Instead, in text after vibrating text, we learned from friends elsewhere that Nicholson's body had been found in one of the building's original stairwells, down at the bottom, as if he'd fallen over the railing.

None of us broke the news to the nonlawyers in the room, and we didn't talk about it with each other either. We all read our texts, clenched our jaws, and looked at the floor. The sudden death of a federal judge was a hell of a thing. Most of us had known him. The decent souls among us stayed silent out of respect, and the others, I figured, kept their mouths shut so as not to look bad.

As I walked to the elevator and rode down to the ground floor, I wondered how Nicholson had gotten into that stairwell. Two of the building's four staircases, at the front corners of the building, had been brought up to code and were in regular use. The back two hadn't been updated—they still had the low railings that folks built a hundred years ago—so they were kept locked, precisely to avoid falls. I'd glanced through the glass in the doors, so I knew what they looked like, but I'd never set foot in them myself.

I was baffled by how he'd gotten in there, and why. He had to have gone in voluntarily—he was a big guy, and security was tight; I doubted he could've been dragged in against his will. But somebody had to have unlocked the door for him.

And somebody had to have told him the stairs were there in the first place. He was a federal judge from Charleston, with no connection to Basking Rock as far as I was aware. You had to go to the back corners of the building to even know that those old stairwells existed.

The logistics were the only part I couldn't figure out. The rest was chilling, but obvious. As I stepped outside, squinting in the thin November sunshine, and dodged a reporter as she lunged at me with her microphone, I saw only one possible explanation for his death.

Some things could not be accidents. I did not believe in a world where a key prosecution witness happened to fall to his death on a cold stone floor, purely by coincidence, right before he testified.

## 2

## DECEMBER 1, 2023

I wasn't surprised that it took longer than usual to get through security at the federal courthouse in Charleston. Nicholson's body had been flown to his native Texas for burial, but his memorial service had been held the Sunday after Thanksgiving at Charleston's Grace Church Cathedral, and folks were still on edge. The FBI was investigating his death, and the FBI didn't investigate accidents.

After handing over their cell phones and going through the metal detector, my clients, the Learys—or rather, my eighteen-year-old client and his parents—and I rode silently up to our floor. I'd told them from the start not to talk about their case in hallways or elevators, and they took that so seriously that they didn't even chat about the traffic or the weather.

Cameron Leary was a tall, skinny computer nerd—smart, curious, mildly annoying, and devoid of any respect for established rules. He'd pulled a prank, or "made a statement," as he described it, that resulted in him being arraigned on multiple felony charges under the Computer Fraud and Abuse Act.

I'd told him how to dress for federal court, but he'd dismissed my advice as "idiotic constraints." He was wearing a fleece jacket over a T-shirt that said "Make Orwell Fiction Again." His way of protesting the draconian charges against him, I supposed. I didn't say anything. The judge wasn't going to see him today, so he could've worn a tutu for all it mattered. I was there for a status conference in chambers, and the law required the defendant to be present in the building while I did that.

"Here we go," I said, leading the family into the small, windowless conference room where they would have to wait. As I closed the door behind us, Mr. Leary said, "Terrible thing about that judge."

"Yeah, it really is."

"How does it… or does it…"

"Affect us? Well, it'll probably affect the schedule. They'll reassign us to a new judge—"

"I thought we already got put with a new judge," he said.

"What we've got today is a new magistrate," I explained. "They're like a lower level of federal judge. Normally, they handle the more straightforward pretrial issues, like what evidence is going to come in and what gets excluded. The judge handles the big pretrial stuff, if there is any, and the trial itself."

"Some pretty weird luck we've had here, with the judges," he said.

"Yep."

Our original magistrate had been sidelined with a medical issue. Our new one had only been appointed about a month earlier. She'd been at some big firm for twenty years, doing civil litigation and white-collar crime, but she had no judicial experience. I knew almost nothing about her. That was why I'd chosen to have this status conference in person, instead of staying home and doing it online. There was no substitute for being in a judge's chambers, getting a sense of their personality and looking for clues on how to deal with them.

"So are we just... starting over, then?" Mrs. Leary asked.

She sounded like starting over was more than she could stand. Most of my clients and their families felt like that at some point or other. Once you got sucked into the machine of the justice system, the wait for it to be over, plus the fact that you didn't know if it ever would be, was one of the hardest parts.

"We're not starting over," I reassured her. "I'm sure some of the things on our case schedule might have to be postponed, but they'll reassign us to somebody who's got enough room in his or her docket to not throw our schedule off too much. And it doesn't change anything for today, since it's the magistrate who handles status conferences, not the actual judge."

"Okay." She sighed and sat down.

The kid hadn't said a word yet. He was sitting at the table doodling on a napkin that he'd produced from his pocket.

"So, Cameron, how you been?" I asked.

He shrugged. "Well, this hasn't killed me yet, if that's what you mean."

"That's not something to joke about!" his mom said. "We'll get through this!"

There was fear in her voice. We hadn't discussed it, but it sounded like she shared my concern that an idealistic teenager facing decades in jail was a suicide risk. It had happened before. And Cameron was out on bail, with access to any number of methods for taking his life.

I sat down across the table from Cameron and said, "Look, you've got my cell number if you need to talk. I'll pick up day or night. You're stuck in the machine right now, and we're all here with you, trying to get you back out."

"I mean… thanks? But nobody's actually with me. I'm the only one who'd go to jail."

"Would you stop saying that?" his dad said, a little too loudly.

"What he means," his mom explained, "is you've got to stay positive."

"Yeah, if being positive works for you," I said. "But all you've really got to do is stay patient. This kind of mess takes a while to clean up. So in the meantime, just do whatever it takes to keep yourself sane."

Cameron let out a joyless laugh. "Oh, *I'm* sane. The problem is, it seems like nobody else is."

"Am I sane? Are we?" I gestured to his parents.

He gave a slightly embarrassed shrug, but he wasn't about to apologize. I didn't care. I knew it wasn't us he was mad at.

"You've got the sane adults on your side," I said. "More of us than you even know about. And we're here to hack your way out of an insane system."

I'd found out early on that explaining the law to him just made him argue with me, so I'd taken to using computer metaphors instead.

"How are you going to do that, when the whole OS is corrupt?"

I was glad I'd talked about this case with Terri, my private investigator. She was the only reason that I knew "OS" meant "operating system." Terri was tech savvy in ways I never would be, and she'd told me my best shot at getting Cameron to understand what we were up against and how I could help was to explain that the law was like the OS of our whole country, and I knew how it worked.

I shrugged. "Same way I always do. Find the bugs, and write the code to fix them."

That landed well. He nodded like it made sense to him.

My phone buzzed. Five-minute warning for the status conference. I had to go.

---

When I rounded the last corner before my destination, I saw LaRue, the federal prosecutor, in the hallway chatting with a vaguely familiar guy around my age. I couldn't place him, but I assumed from his navy pin-striped suit and their collegial vibe that he was a fellow lawyer.

I'd disliked LaRue on his own merits since long before he threw the book at Cameron, but lawyerly etiquette required a smile and a nod. He nodded back and said, "We were just discussing poor Judge Nicholson. Monty, this is Leland Munroe. He's actually from down there in Basking Rock."

As the two of us shook hands, LaRue explained, "Monty was Judge Nicholson's personal lawyer. And he was down there with him on the day, of course."

LaRue didn't need to explain that nobody in the legal field, not even a federal judge, would waltz into a courtroom and give testimony without getting advice and support from their own lawyer.

"Oh my," I said. "I'm sorry. What a shock."

With a bleak nod, Monty said thanks. It looked like Nicholson's death had hit him hard.

"Well, we've got to head in now," LaRue told him. "All I can say is, I hope they catch the guy soon and kick him straight through to death row."

"Amen to that," Monty said. He sighed and added, "Won't bring Nicholson back, though."

LaRue and I shook our heads, sharing his discouragement. We all knew that even when justice was done, it sometimes felt a little empty.

As we headed into the clerk's office to let her know we were there, I heard Monty's fine leather shoes clacking on the terrazzo floor. I remembered him now: James Montgomery, scion of a fine old family, wealthy from birth. When he wasn't hobnobbing with federal judges, he was on the local news giving opening remarks at some charitable gala or other. It was nice to see a silver spoon guy like that express a genuine emotion. I wasn't used to it.

---

Magistrate Vergala looked to be in her forties. With her height, her preppy look, and her right-to-the-point energy, she made me think of a killer field hockey player dragging her team to victory against all odds. From the family photos on the bookshelf behind her, it looked like she had three teenagers. Two of the photos showed beaming kids holding up trophies. Judging from what they were wearing, the girl was a gymnast and the boy did something in track and field.

Another framed photo showed her and, presumably, her family decked out in sunglasses and red-and-gold USC gear, all smiles, standing in front of what had to be the USC football stadium. I remembered from her bio that she was an alum.

With a computer science nerd as my client, a big sports fan was not my ideal pick for magistrate.

After the necessary platitudes regarding Nicholson's death, she said, "So, counsel, obviously there's going to be some rescheduling to do once this case gets reassigned, but in the meantime, I'd like to walk through and kind of organize this a little bit more."

"Of course, Your Honor," I said. "That makes sense."

"Is the existing deadline for any motion to suppress evidence still okay for both of y'all?"

That deadline wasn't until February. LaRue and I agreed that it was fine.

"Okay, then. So I'll look forward to that." She sat back in her chair with a look on her face like we were all set.

LaRue and I glanced at each other.

"And, Your Honor," he said, "if I may, I'd like to double-check with Mr. Munroe that we're good to go as far as the notices that my office was required to provide under Rule 12(b)(4)."

"Based on what you sent me last week," I said, "we are."

The federal criminal rules required LaRue to notify me of his intent to use certain evidence at trial, in order to give me the chance to object and move to exclude it. He was walking Magistrate Vergala through our conference by providing answers to the questions that she should've asked. With a newly appointed judge—one who didn't know the ropes yet—you sometimes had to do that.

"And, if I may," I said, "Your Honor, would I be correct in thinking that Magistrate Fletcher was not able to fill you in on the background of the case before he left?"

"That's correct."

I nodded. That made sense, since Fletcher had been wheeled out of the courthouse on a stretcher after suffering a heart attack.

"So, then, would it be a bad idea if we took a moment to fill Your Honor in on the basic outlines of the case?"

"We've got twenty-two minutes before my next conference," she said, "so go ahead."

She hadn't even looked at the clock before saying that. I made a mental note that this was a judge who paid close attention to time. Punctuality and efficiency were probably on the list of her top five favorite things in life.

"Thank you. So, my client, Cameron Leary, is a computer-genius kid, eighteen years old, but prior to this case he was already in his junior year of a computer science degree at Charleston Technical College—"

"So he started college at—what, sixteen?"

"Fifteen, Your Honor. His birthday was just last month. And like a lot of these science prodigies, Cameron's IQ is way ahead of his common sense. Candidly, Your Honor, his parents are not well off at all, and the reason he's able to afford my services is because last year, he won $75,000 in a national science fair for coming up with a way of using AI to diagnose thyroid cancer."

"My goodness."

"That's what I said too. Frankly, I don't understand much more of his invention than what I just told you. All I know is, it had something to do with algorithms for analyzing tissue samples. I brought this science fair press release in case Your Honor cares to find out more."

I took copies of it out of my briefcase and handed them to her and LaRue. I could sense LaRue getting irritated at the ticker-tape parade I was giving for my client. To avoid irritating the judge, too, I needed to cut to the chase.

"Anyway, Your Honor, that's his background. The reason we're all sitting here today is that this past January, Cameron found a security problem in the website of his student loan processor. He notified them, but they didn't take him seriously, so he reached out to a journalist, and—I don't want to waste Your Honor's time by getting overly technical at this stage, but essentially, what the indictment amounts to is allegations that my client took the journalist over to the back door of the student loan processor and opened it up to show him it was unlocked. So—"

LaRue chuckled quietly and said, "Your Honor, that's a cute story Mr. Munroe's told us, but it's missing some parts. If that were all that his client did, my office would not have brought charges."

"Well, it's missing parts because I'm not quite finished. I do apologize for the time it takes to explain this, but it's not what I'd call a simple case."

"Mr. LaRue," the magistrate said, "you'll of course have your turn."

"Thank you, Your Honor."

She looked back at me.

"So, speaking metaphorically so we can avoid going off into the technical weeds," I said, "the allegations are that Cameron showed the journalist the door was open, and then he went in and brought back a bunch of Social Security numbers and so forth to show him why that door ought to have been locked."

"I'm not a big fan of metaphors," the magistrate said. "Let's stick with plain English. Aren't the allegations that he hacked into the system, took the students' personal data, and handed it over to the journalist?"

LaRue smiled. "That's correct, Your Honor. He did that twice, actually. And that's the basis for the charges under the Computer Fraud and Abuse Act."

"Speaking as a former prosecutor myself," I said—I wasn't sure if Vergala knew that about me, and I wanted to make sure she did—"I question whether it's appropriate to bring two felony charges carrying a potential ten-year sentence against an overly zealous teenage whistleblower. But we can get into that later, at the motion-to-dismiss stage."

"Oh," Vergala said, as if I'd reminded her of something. "I assume y'all have had some talks about a plea. What's the status on that?"

"I offered a plea deal appropriate to the charges and the defendant's lack of a criminal record," LaRue said, "but Mr. Leary declined."

"Mr. LaRue offered six months in the federal penitentiary followed by two years of supervised release," I said. "We don't feel any prison time is appropriate, given Cameron's lack of any record and the nature of the crime."

"Obviously, Mr. LaRue's office has a different view."

"They do, Your Honor," I agreed. "Although he has yet to reach out to me with any type of plea offer relating to the new charges that he tacked on after we turned down that first offer."

She looked at LaRue with one eyebrow raised. I didn't want him to tell her his side of the story first, so I kept going.

"To give you a sense of the timeline, Your Honor, after we turned down that plea offer, Mr. LaRue did something a little unusual. He went back to the grand jury seeking a new indictment on additional charges. That's where the felony wire fraud counts came in."

The look she was giving him reminded me that part of her practice at her old law firm had been white-collar crime. In other words, she'd been a criminal defense attorney herself. She knew that retaliating against a defendant for turning down a plea deal was improper.

LaRue explained himself. "Your Honor, new evidence came to light, and in view of that, reindictment was appropriate."

"To be clear, Your Honor," I said, "there was nothing new about this evidence. Mr. LaRue's office seized all of my client's computer equipment—not just the devices identified in the search warrant, but everything they found—and it sat there in the evidence room for more than three months. He didn't even try to get a warrant to search the actual *contents* of that MacBook until two days after my client turned down the plea deal. So all that's going to be the subject of one of our motions to suppress—"

"Your Honor, frankly, I'm not sure why Mr. Munroe is trying to argue a motion that probably hasn't even been written yet, much less filed."

Vergala gave a brisk nod and leaned forward with her elbows on her desk. "Fair point. We'll cross that bridge when we get there. The hearing on any motions you may file would be on the first Friday in February, Mr. Munroe, not today. But, Mr. LaRue, I'm assuming that by that time there will have been some more discussion concerning a plea."

She was telling him, not asking him.

"Yes, Your Honor," he said.

"Good. And, since I don't expect to be seeing either of you until then, Merry Christmas."

———

From there, I drove to a pub on a side street near the private investigator's office where my son worked. The pub didn't look like anything special, so even in high season—which this wasn't—it didn't get tourists. I picked a booth according to my usual strategy: far from the door but facing it, a little out of the way.

When Noah walked in, I raised my hand in greeting. It was still weird to see my child show up to meet me wearing a suit. I wondered when the fact that he was now an adult would seem normal. Probably not until sometime after I wrapped my head around the fact that I myself was forty-seven years old.

Noah smiled as he sat down. "It feels wrong to have my back to the door. When do I get to sit where you are?"

"I guess when they install a booth where we can sit side by side. Then we can keep an eye on things together." I raised my glass of ice water to him. "Glad to see you've inherited my paranoia. Or did you pick that up from working as a PI?"

"Little bit of both, I guess."

He nodded to the waitress to bring her over. As she poured us each a cup of coffee, we placed our orders. We didn't need to look at the menu. Noah had pointed me to the shrimp po'boy the first time he took me to this pub, a few months earlier. He'd told me that's what he always got, and after a couple of visits where I did glance through the menu, I realized that nothing else ever sounded better.

After she left, we talked shop for a minute.

"Guy I work with is going to Miami over Christmas," he said. "To do a surveillance thing." He sounded a little disappointed that he hadn't been chosen for that.

"Is he? I guess that'll be nice for him."

"Yeah. I'm just stuck around Charleston, so far."

"Careful what you wish for," I said. "Not all work travel is fun. Terri once had to spend a week in some storage facility in West Virginia, looking through boxes of old files."

He laughed. "How's she doing?"

"Oh, fine. I don't see her as much, now that Squatter's too old to play much with Buster."

My Yorkie had loved running around with her rottweiler, but those days were in the past.

"Aww. Is he okay?"

I shrugged. It wasn't fun to think about how far past his prime my dog was. "You know. He's getting old." Squatter had been far from young when I found him several years ago, abandoned at the home I'd first rented when I moved back to Basking Rock. "Spends most of his time sleeping. But he's good. I got him dog beds for just about every room, so he can lie down whenever he feels like it."

"Poor thing," he said, taking a sip of his coffee. "I should've brought you a treat to give him."

"Well, I'll tell him you said hi."

"Good."

He looked at the dessert menu for a second and then glanced up like he'd remembered something. In a low voice, he asked, "How are things back home since the *incident*?"

Terri and I had taught him the cardinal rule that when you're out in public, you don't name the people or places that you're talking about. You never knew who might overhear. I was glad to see he was keeping that up.

"The courthouse thing?" We hadn't talked since Nicholson had died, so I figured that's what he meant.

He nodded.

I looked around. The place was noisy enough to provide some cover, and nobody was nearby. I relaxed a little bit.

"Well, one new thing is, Basking Rock's got FBI agents up the wazoo. You can't turn a corner without tripping over one."

He laughed. "Why— Oh, because this is federal?"

"Yeah. It's not local cops who investigate the death of a federal judge. Much to the annoyance of our town police. They're getting their toes stepped on big-time."

He smiled. "I mean, they've got to stay in their lane."

"You better not say that to their face."

"It's bad enough that it happened on their watch. I don't even understand that."

"I don't either," I said, "and I was there."

"You were? What, in the courthouse?"

I nodded. "Sitting in the courtroom where he was about to testify."

"Oh, man."

"Yeah. And security was tight as hell for that trial, plus he had people down with him. It's not like he came alone. So, yeah. I'm real curious how it happened."

"Is there *any* chance it was an accident?"

I shrugged. "I mean, sure, that's physically possible. And I suppose stranger things have happened on this earth. But with the timing of it, that'd be a hell of a coincidence."

He took that in for a moment. "Sure seems like a desperate move, though," he said. "And why *that* witness? Was that really the guy whose testimony was going to put him away?"

It clicked for me then that Noah really had grown up. A few years earlier, I would've had to spell out what I meant: Ludlow on trial, witness falls to his death right before testifying, therefore I suspect that Ludlow—a previously respected attorney who we both knew—

orchestrated his killing. But now, Noah connected those dots without my help. He took it for granted that seemingly normal people could sometimes do terrible things.

"I don't know," I said. "I haven't looked into it myself. But that's exactly what somebody's going to have to figure out."

After the waitress brought our sandwiches, quizzed us on our satisfaction thus far, and went away, I decided to go ahead and ask him a slightly radioactive question.

"You still in touch with the defendant's son?"

His eyebrows flicked up and down. He knew I meant Brandon Ludlow, black sheep of the Ludlow family. That kid was a sore subject between us, since a couple of years back, Noah's friendship with him had put Noah in the hospital and very nearly killed him.

He finished chewing a bite of his po'boy and said, "Not since I moved to Charleston. I mean, he'll pop up on my feed sometimes. But I haven't actually heard from him directly."

I nodded. A large weight had just lifted from my shoulders. "Well, let me know if you do." I paused to eat a french fry. "Or if you hear from anybody else connected with that family."

He looked at me, squinting like he was trying to read between the lines of what I'd said. After a minute he said, "You afraid of them?"

"I think cautious is a better word."

"Or paranoid, maybe?"

I thought of the empty pew behind Ludlow in the courtroom that day. Every jacket and scarf left on it signified a Ludlow ally who'd been in attendance but had left the room shortly before Nicholson was killed.

"Like I said, cautious." I took a slug of my coffee and decided to explain. "You know that defendant blames me for what's happened to him. So I've got a sense that I might be in his crosshairs. And if I am, then you could be too."

## 3

## DECEMBER 8, 2023

Terri, Ruiz, and I were in the diner near the courthouse in Basking Rock, having a late lunch and speculating about how the rest of Ludlow's trial would go. The TV was blaring. The lawyers who frequented this diner liked it that way; it made it harder for folks to overhear your conversation.

"I hope it doesn't run all the way to Christmas," Ruiz said. "I've seen jurors give up and just reach whatever verdict they can in order to get out of there before the holiday."

"Yeah, I know," I said. "You've got to give them enough time."

I pulled up my phone calendar to try to figure out when the trial might end. It had been scheduled to go until mid-December, but proceedings were suspended for almost a week after Nicholson's death.

"Oh, today's the eighth," I said. The date hadn't registered before. "You know this is the day John Lennon was killed? I can't believe it's been—what, forty-three years? Man."

Ruiz looked at me. "You know that off the top of your head?"

"It's the first news story I remember."

That murder—the first one I'd ever heard of—had come to me through the small TV screen in my mom's bedroom. New York at night, the stunned crowd outside Lennon's apartment building, police officers trying to move people back so they could close the ornate black iron gates at the entrance. White camera flashes, and the alternating red and blue from lights on the squad cars. A woman reporter who looked like she'd been crying said a man had shot Lennon as he was walking home with his wife. I'd turned to my mom and asked her questions that she had no answers for.

"Yeah," Terri said. "I remember that, too, actually. I didn't know the date, though."

"I keep track, I guess. He's the other musician I like."

She smiled. "Besides Tom Petty, you mean?"

I liked that she remembered that.

"Let me see that dessert menu," Ruiz said. He was the type of guy who thought a dessert should follow every meal, not just dinner.

As he was reaching for it, the TV on the wall switched to a "Breaking News" bulletin. A fresh-faced young man sitting at an anchor's desk announced that a courthouse employee, whose name the FBI had not yet released, had been arrested and charged with Judge Nicholson's murder. The diner's twenty-odd customers, including Ruiz and me, expressed our surprise with varied levels of profanity, and then the background hum of conversation resumed at about twice its previous volume.

Terri sipped her coffee, looking out the window beside our booth. The sky was gray—on rare occasions, the weather in South Carolina remembered that it was late fall—and the lamp over our table turned the window into a mirror, so I could see two of her. She was wearing her hair in a short Afro now, with a few golden stripes through the black.

She hadn't reacted to the news.

I cocked my head at her. "Did you know something about this?"

She shrugged and smiled at her own reflection.

"Oh my God," Ruiz said. "I thought you were friends!"

Terri laughed.

"I can just about believe you'd keep that from me," Ruiz said, with melodramatic humor, "but from *Leland?*" He looked at me, shaking his head. "That is a real betrayal."

She took another sip and set her coffee down. "I'd have told you if that case had anything to do with you." Catching the look on my face, she added, "Being in the courthouse when it happened doesn't count."

"Evidently not!"

"We're so out of the loop on this," Ruiz lamented. "I haven't heard word one from the FBI this entire time."

"Oh, I'm not surprised," Terri said. "All the local police have heard from them are things like 'Can the rednecks please get out of the way and let the *real* investigators work?' Some of my friends are mad about it, but I mean, it's the FBI. What'd they expect?"

Terri had been a cop for eight years, and she still had her finger on their pulse. But I was not interested in discussing the local officers' grievances.

"The murder charge is interesting," I said.

"You mean that it's not manslaughter? Yeah." She took another sip of coffee. I was getting the impression that she was using those sips as an excuse not to talk.

"Any idea who the guy is?" I asked. She didn't reply.

"I suppose we'll find out fairly soon," Ruiz said.

Terri drained half her cup and looked around like she wanted the waitress. I was now roughly 99 percent sure that she knew who the suspect was.

That surprised me. While it was true that she knew everything about everyone in Basking Rock—her roots here ran deep— nobody from here was involved in the investigation, and I couldn't think why somebody from an FBI office nearly two hours north of us would clue her in.

The waitress came, and Terri asked for her check. "I've got a few things I need to take care of," she said apologetically, once the waitress left.

We'd only been there for about forty-five minutes, and she hadn't mentioned anywhere she had to be afterward. Out the corner of my eye, I could see Ruiz giving me a quizzical look. I pretended not to notice.

"Well, I guess the two of us will stay awhile," I told her. "Maybe get dessert and hear some more surprises on the TV."

With a mix of humor and annoyance, Ruiz said, "I can't remember the last time I heard about a major local arrest on the freaking *news*. I think I might've still been in law school."

"I guess we've got to face facts," I said. "We're the redheaded stepchildren of the Charleston FBI." I looked at Terri. "Or at least, some of us are."

"The FBI's not the only way to find out what's going on," she said, and then she turned to smile at the waitress, who was returning with her bill. She thanked the woman and signed the credit card receipt. Ruiz and I kept quiet. Even if the whole diner was talking about the arrest, we weren't about to say anything meaningful in front of the waitress.

We said our goodbyes, and Terri left.

Ruiz picked up the dessert menu again. "I hate not knowing what's happening in my own damn town."

"Me too."

"You spend much time watching my dear old boss's trial?"

I smiled at his sarcasm. His dislike for Ludlow ran deep.

"Only that one day," I said. "You?"

"Oh, an hour here or there. I'm not wasting my vacation days on that." He signaled the waitress and added, "Problem is, Fourth isn't covering it with any particular accuracy."

"Of course not."

The waitress came over, and he ordered a slice of pecan pie. I did the same.

"I'd like to read some of the transcripts," I said, "if I could get my hands on them without having to find a time machine to shoot me sixty days into the future."

He laughed. We both knew it usually took about that long for transcripts to come back. Only parties to the case could get them expedited.

"More like ninety, I bet," he said. "On a case this high profile, which is for sure going to get appealed when he loses, that court reporter's going to triple-check everything before she turns it in. Why would you want them, though? Some kind of morbid curiosity?"

"I guess."

"I'm just glad to be rid of him."

———

Around dinner time, I was at my house staring into the fridge—it looked like my meal options were either a cheese sandwich or a bowl of cereal—when my phone rang. I went over to the coffee table, saw Cardozo's name on the screen, and picked it up. We'd been friends since law school, but we hadn't talked in a few months. He was a federal prosecutor, and we tended not to call each other much when I had a client that his office was prosecuting.

"Hey, how've you been?" I said.

There was wind noise on the line, like he was driving.

"How've I been? You mean since my most annoying colleague got confirmed by the Senate and came back as my new boss?"

I laughed. He'd never liked LaRue, and we'd both been dismayed back in the springtime, when their boss retired and LaRue got nominated to replace him as the United States Attorney for our district. I'd expected Cardozo to be the nominee, and although he'd never said so, he'd probably expected that too.

"I guess you've been having a blast," I said.

"Oh, yeah," he said. "When a guy like LaRue gets his hands on some real power, it only makes him a better human being."

"Oof. Yeah, I can imagine."

"You don't need to imagine. You know where his priorities are."

"I sure do," I said.

It sounded like he didn't approve of LaRue's decision to prosecute Cameron Leary, although I knew he'd never say so directly.

I heard a car door slam. He must've parked somewhere. I put him on speaker and took the phone back to the kitchen to make a sandwich.

"So I drove up the coast," he said, "and I'm on this little beach, nobody here but myself and a few seagulls, contemplating my next move. Hannah said I should call you and see if you can talk me off the ledge."

Hannah was his wife.

"What ledge?"

"Oh, the usual one for federal prosecutors who get bored with their lives. Private practice. White-collar criminal defense." He sighed. A gull squawked in the background. "No offense, but the idea of going into that line of work kind of nauseates me. The problem is, I don't see a lot of other exit ramps for a prosecutor who wants to get out of Dodge."

"No offense taken. I couldn't stand defense work, either, at first. You spend your whole career working to get bad guys off the streets, and now you're supposed to help them stay out of jail?"

He laughed. "That's encouraging. What a great way to put it. Now I'm thinking I might have to stay with LaRue."

"I mean, sure—why leave right when something interesting's about to start? Y'all just brought charges in that Judge Nicholson case, right? If I was in your shoes, I'd hate to miss that."

"Oh, LaRue's not putting me on that. I'm not his murder guy. He saves the good stuff for his friends. He'd have me cleaning the men's room if he could."

I made a sympathetic noise as I spread mustard on my bread, staying quiet for a minute in case he felt like telling me anything about the Nicholson case. I realized as I peeled off a slice of cheese that that was just a pipe dream. Lawyers knew what they could and couldn't talk about with each other, even those of us who were friends.

"Wouldn't it make sense to stay there until you find an exit ramp that you want to take?" I asked.

He sighed. "Yeah, that's got to be the better bet."

I heard waves crashing in the background. That sound was good for the soul: somehow it tied things together. Hearing it brought back every other time I'd heard it and every beach I'd ever heard it on. People on the other side of the planet were listening to the same sound right now.

An idea came to mind.

"Could you do the same thing in a different way?" I said. "Get into civil litigation, maybe, on the plaintiff's side, and go after some other type of bad guys?"

"What, you mean like personal injury?" He said that like he'd found something disgusting stuck to the bottom of his shoe.

"Yeah, maybe, or medical malpractice, product liability, I don't know. There's plenty of bad guys whose misdeeds aren't actual crimes, but they hit folks just as hard."

"Huh. I don't know. Anyway, Hannah told me it's fine if I want to quit and take a few months off. Said I could do some soul-searching. Her words, not mine."

"Yeah, that doesn't sound like something you would say."

"Right? Soul-searching! I can't do that. You start down that road, next thing you know, you're spending five grand on personal development seminars and saying affirmations to yourself in the bathroom mirror. I'd feel like a jackass."

I laughed. "Don't worry. I'd stage an intervention if it came to that."

"Thanks." I heard another gull in the background, and then he said, "Oh, dammit. I was gearing up to go back to work tomorrow, had some inspiring Shakespeare quote in mind—that 'once more into the breach' thing—and then I remembered that it doesn't necessarily end well."

Cardozo was way more cultivated than me. I didn't know what quote he was talking about.

"How's that one go?"

"It's something like—this guy's motivating a bunch of English soldiers to go back in there and fight somebody, and he says, 'once more into the breach, my friends, until we fill up the wall with English dead.' And then, obviously, people die."

"Yeah, that's not good."

"It's bloodthirsty, frankly. Maybe Shakespeare should've done some affirmations."

———

Around ten at night I was in bed with my laptop, researching a few points of law for my motion to dismiss in Cameron's case, when my phone buzzed with a text. *Can u do a video call now?* It was from Terri.

I texted back *Sure*, wondering as I did so why she wanted to be on video. Her next text explained *I'm with new client.*

I swore and got out of bed. By the time she called back, I was in the next room—my office—sitting in front of the bookcase containing all the old law books I never used anymore. I heard a little snort, which turned into snoring; Squatter was snoozing in one of his dog beds, under the table where my printer sat. I let him sleep. If the new client didn't like hearing my ancient Yorkie snuffling in the background, that was their problem, not mine.

I zipped myself into a fleece, which seemed less unprofessional than the T-shirt I was wearing, and picked up.

We said our hellos. Terri was sitting at a kitchen table next to a worried-looking older woman. The woman had dark eyes that stood out against her pale skin, and long dark hair with a few bright streaks of gray.

I'd been in Terri's kitchen, although not recently, and that wasn't it. The sleek lines and pink-and-blue color scheme made me think this one had last been remodeled when *Miami Vice* was on TV.

"Thanks for taking our call, Leland," she said. "This is Angie Baptiste. She's the mother of Vincenzo Baptiste, who was arrested today in connection with the death of that judge."

She had her work voice on, which I took to mean she and Mrs. Baptiste didn't know each other well. She'd also neatly avoided saying the word "murder," probably to avoid causing the woman any more distress.

"Not a problem," I said, in my own work voice. "How can I help?"

Mrs. Baptiste cleared her throat. "Mr. Munroe, thank you for talking to me." She wasn't from the South, that much I could hear.

"No problem."

"But please," she said, "tell me how to get him out. I can take out a second mortgage on my house. I got good credit. Whatever it takes."

When she paused, Terri said, "For background, Mrs. Baptiste's son—Vinny, that's what he goes by—is a member of the Basking Rock courthouse maintenance staff. Every staff member who was on shift that day was interviewed as part of the investigation, and during that investigation, Vinny hired me to assist him in looking into a few things."

She was letting me know that the son, not the mother, was her client.

"Oh, uh-huh," I said. "And are y'all calling because Vinny now needs legal representation?"

"Yes."

"Okay."

That meant there were things we couldn't say in front of the mom.

"So the problem we're calling about tonight is that Mrs. Baptiste hasn't been able to get in touch with Vinny. She was given a number to call, but they keep saying he's not done being processed. I've explained that that's pretty normal at this stage, but she's concerned. My own thought is that you may want to find out as soon as possible when his bail hearing is."

Mrs. Baptiste thanked Terri, and then she shot a nervous look back at the screen.

"I agree with you on both points," I told Terri.

"So when can he come home?" Mrs. Baptiste asked her. She seemed to find it easier to talk to Terri than to me. That, plus her forty-year-old kitchen, made me think that she probably didn't have much money or much education. Folks who had those things tended not to look so intimidated when they talked to a lawyer.

"So, Mrs. Baptiste," I said, "just to explain what's coming up, the next step that's going to happen is called the initial appearance. That's where the magistrate explains the charges against your son, and they'll also address bail. The initial appearance has to happen within forty-eight hours after his arrest. Now, he was arrested around lunchtime today, correct?"

They both nodded.

"And they would've taken him up to Charleston, because that's where they house federal…"

I stopped myself in time to avoid saying "prisoners."

Terri said, "Yes, that's where the federal detention facility is."

It was a state facility that had a contract with the feds, but that didn't matter. What mattered was phrasing things in such a way as to avoid using words that would make this woman more upset than she already was.

"Right. So the drive would've taken a good two hours, right there. The earliest his bail hearing could possibly be is tomorrow, but if he didn't even get there until late afternoon, he might not have been booked until after the cutoff."

Mrs. Baptiste had a deer-in-the-headlights look. I was dumping too many details on her.

"Anyway, long story short," I said, "I'll call them first thing tomorrow morning, but I'm expecting that his hearing won't be until Monday."

Mrs. Baptiste said something to Terri, who told me, "She'd like to know whether they need the bail money right then. Meaning on Monday."

"Uh, no. You don't need to worry about that."

Mrs. Baptiste sat back, looking relieved.

I didn't think bail money would come into it at all—there wasn't much chance a judge would grant bail on these charges—but since there was nothing she could do about that, I didn't see the point of hitting her with the hard truth tonight.

I decided to ask her some questions instead. That was allowed; the confidentiality owed to Terri's client, and my prospective client, only limited what information we could share with her. It didn't limit what we could ask her to share with us.

"Mrs. Baptiste," I said, "can I just ask—whereabouts are you from?"

She looked at Terri, confused. "Did he say where? Why's that matter?"

Apparently, the leisurely Southern stroll through a conversation was not her style.

"Just getting some background," I said. "Never mind. But tell me about Vinny. What's he like?"

"What's he *like*?" She looked incredulous. "You're asking me about his personality and when we moved here? Today my son got dragged out in handcuffs, they're charging him with murder, and you're asking me what he's *like*? He needs to come home, that's what he's like."

The fire in her voice made me sit up straight. I had misjudged her. On my laptop screen, Terri was looking at her with new appreciation.

"Absolutely, Mrs. Baptiste," I said. "I apologize. That came out the wrong way. I just wanted to get a better sense of who he is and what his story is, since I can't meet him immediately myself."

"So go see him tomorrow morning," she said. "Find out straight from him."

Even without hearing her accent, nobody could've thought she was from the South. I doubted whether a woman that refreshingly blunt could have so much as a single Southern ancestor.

"I'll do my best. And, Mrs. Baptiste, this is something I actually do need for the bail hearing. Could you tell me how long y'all have been living in the South?"

"Nine years. We moved here from Pittsburgh with my second husband, who was Vinny's dad. What's that got to do with bail?"

"The judge might want to know how deep your roots here are. It's about whether your son would stick around for trial or try to flee."

"Fine, but can we get a move on here? I just need you to help my son."

―――

After we got off the call, Terri texted to say *Can only talk for like 5 mins tonight. Going on stakeout. Call you in 10?*

I answered *Sure.*

I went back to my bedroom, partly worried for Terri—I didn't love the idea of her doing a stakeout by herself at night—and partly frustrated that I was going to have to wait to find out much about what she knew. If this case was garbage, if Vinny was obviously guilty and all there was to do was negotiate a plea deal, she wouldn't have called me. I'd finally reached the point—and she knew I'd reached it—where I didn't have to take on any paying client who walked in the door. For the first time since I'd lost my reliable old government job, five years ago, money was fine and looked like it would stay that way.

I sat down with my laptop and tried to keep reading the wire fraud case that I thought might help me get some of Cameron's charges dismissed, but I couldn't focus on it. My brain had changed channels, and I couldn't change it back.

Instead, I googled the new client, both as Vinny and as Vincenzo. He'd posted a few memes on social media, but that was it. His career was not the kind that showed up on the internet. And the FBI still hadn't announced his name.

My phone rang.

"Hey there," I said to Terri. "You going on stakeout? Everything okay?"

She must've heard the worry in my voice. "It's just somebody's sad divorce. Surveillance outside a motel. More sordid than dangerous."

"Oof. Man, if we wanted to see the shiny, happy side of life, we picked the wrong jobs."

She let out a resigned laugh. "I guess if the underbelly's there," she said, "you might as well know about it." Her car's engine got louder, like she was accelerating after a stop.

"Yeah. So what can you tell me about this Mr. Baptiste?"

"The main thing you should know for tomorrow, or whenever you meet him, is that he lied to the FBI—"

"Oh, that's not good."

"No, it doesn't set you up for a good relationship with them, does it."

"I find it makes them mad. What'd he have to lie about?"

A car honked, and she said, "Hang on." After a second, she said, "He's the one who let Nicholson into the stairwell."

"What—and he told the FBI otherwise, and then they found out?"

"Yeah."

I shook my head. The stupid things defendants did, including the frantic moves that innocent people sometimes made while trying to get out of trouble, were a large part of the reason I had a job.

"They catch him on camera doing it, or something?"

"No. Not that he knows of, anyway. A coworker he doesn't get along with apparently told them she saw him take the stairwell key. So he caved and admitted it."

"Oh boy. Any motive?"

"Not that he or anyone else has told me. And his life seems like it was okay—had a steady job, and he was about to finish some IT boot camp to hopefully start making better money. If I were on the other side, though, I'd be wondering if he got hired by Ludlow's people."

"Yup."

"Okay," she said, and I heard what sounded like her pushing the gear shift into place. "I've got to go. Time to document the death of my client's marriage."

"Fun. Can we talk more tomorrow?"

"No, I'm out of town. Maybe the next day."

―――

A little while later, I went to bed. Lying there in the dark, I thought through scenarios for Baptiste's bail hearing. I could see where this was going the way you can see a baseball right after it's been hit. You don't know exactly where it'll end up, but from the direction it's flying, you already know a bunch of places that it isn't going to land.

And Vinny Baptiste wasn't going to fly back home on bail. Even if by some miracle we got one of the few judges who wouldn't automatically refuse it on the grounds of the crime's severity—judges didn't like to let accused judge-killers walk free—there was another hurdle that I doubted we could overcome.

If Baptiste didn't have a personal grudge against Nicholson, then the prosecution's theory was probably that he'd been hired to keep a witness against Ludlow off the stand. The fact that he was a courthouse maintenance guy only made that seem more likely; a low-paying job with no prospects for advancement might well make a person more open to such offers.

Back when I was a prosecutor, if I thought I had a low-level hit man on my hands, I would've wanted to keep him in jail for his own safety. Granting bail would give his bosses the chance to off him before he could talk to me and tell me who they were. The best way forward in a case like that would be to hammer out a plea deal where he gave up his bosses in exchange for his freedom, and I made sure they were arrested before he got out. Every judge in the country would agree that was the best way.

No matter how many times I replayed the bail argument, that's how it went.

I was glad I hadn't told his mom that he wasn't coming home. This way, she might get a few more nights of good sleep before everything fell apart.

# 4
## DECEMBER 11, 2023

I didn't go see Baptiste right away. I agreed by phone to represent him at his initial appearance, since there wasn't time for him to get anybody else, but I also pulled up Monty's email on his law firm website and reached out. If I knew more about how the last hours of Nicholson's life had unfolded—what he'd been doing in the courthouse as he waited to testify—then I'd have something real to compare to whatever Baptiste told me. It would help me evaluate Baptiste's honesty, as well as his chances at trial. In short, it would help me decide whether or not to take his case.

Because I didn't want to get stuck. Once I agreed to be Baptiste's defense counsel beyond that initial hearing, I'd need the court's permission to stop. The closer we got to trial, the lower my chances of getting out of it. Baptiste would have to do something particularly stupid—insist on perjuring himself, ask me to tamper with evidence, adamantly refuse to follow my advice. Even if he stopped paying me, that might not be enough, unless I could convince the judge that it was financially catastrophic for me.

And that wouldn't happen. Business was good. Most judges would shrug and say I could survive one nonpaying client. And we all knew —although nobody ever said it out loud—that a lawyer forced to stay on some deadbeat's case could dial back his assistance to a minimum. After all, public defenders had fifty to a hundred clients at the same time. So I could give a nonpaying client one-fiftieth of my time and not bother bringing in any expert witnesses, and I'd still be in compliance with the rules.

But I didn't work that way. I felt duty bound to do a good job. So now that I had the means to pick and choose, I had to kick the tires pretty good before I took on a big case.

---

Monty's office, in a grand old building in the French Quarter, looked how I expected it would. Walking in a couple of hours before Baptiste's bail hearing, I saw lots of dark wood, columns on either side of the main doorways, plaster curlicues decorating the ceiling. My law office looked like a business; his was more like a historic monument.

The receptionist directed me to a waiting area with leather armchairs the color of tobacco stains. A stack of three or four magazines sat on the coffee table. The top one had a racehorse on the cover and featured articles like "Best Saddles for Young Equestrians" and "Life Lessons Learned from Training Thoroughbreds."

I was entertaining myself with ideas for magazines for folks with my background—"Life Lessons Learned from Fishing for Crawdads So We'd Have Food"—when Monty stepped into the lobby and invited me back to his office.

"Thanks so much for meeting with me on such short notice," I said as we walked down a wood-paneled hallway.

"Oh, you're welcome."

I'd told him up front what I was hoping to talk about, so I said, "I know it's a difficult subject. And I'm up against a little bit of a conundrum here."

"Yeah, I suppose you must be. I know everybody deserves representation, but…" I saw his jaw clench. He shook his head like he couldn't find the words to finish that sentence.

I got it. There was a big difference between believing in the abstract rules of justice and watching them be applied to the man accused of murdering somebody you knew.

"Right here," he said, and gestured me into his office.

"My goodness. What a view." Out the window we could see Charleston Harbor and the ocean beyond.

"Well, I certainly appreciate it," he said, stepping behind his big antique desk, which was positioned sideways, presumably so he could glance over at that view any time he wanted. "Can I get you anything?" he asked. "Coffee?"

"I never say no to that."

He hit a button on his phone and asked his secretary to bring us some.

As my eyes adjusted from the glare off the water, I saw that half of his office was taken up with a large, slightly faded Oriental rug. An antique, I figured—maybe an heirloom worth ten or twelve thousand dollars. Everyone in the Charleston legal community knew of his family; the Montgomerys had been wealthy since George Washington was a boy, and maybe longer than that.

Once our coffee was served, we got down to it. He walked me through the morning of Judge Nicholson's death. Monty had driven down separately, met the judge and his judicial clerk at the closest thing Basking Rock had to a Starbucks, and then walked with them to the courthouse, where they spent nearly four hours in a state of high boredom.

"You know how it is," he said. "Once you're through security, it's just easier to stay there."

"Sure, especially that day."

"Oh—were you there?" He looked mildly surprised.

I nodded. "I had a hearing that morning on another floor. Got there a half hour earlier than usual, because I knew security would be tight."

His eyebrows went up and down as if to say *so much for that*.

"Yeah," I said. "Obviously it wasn't tight enough."

"Nope." He crossed his arms over his chest and looked out at the water.

After a decent interval, I asked, "So why was it that y'all weren't watching the trial? Was it a Rule 615 thing?"

"Exactly."

Our state rules, like the federal rules, allowed a party to keep witnesses out of the courtroom until after they'd testified. The idea was to make sure they didn't embroider their own testimony in response to what some other witness had said.

"And I suppose he must've gone a little stir-crazy, sitting in the war room."

"Oh, we all did. But it's par for the course, isn't it?"

People waiting to testify, and parties during breaks in proceedings, sat in small, windowless conference rooms a few yards down from the courtroom door. It got old fast.

"And do you remember—" I shook my head. "I'm sorry. If this starts to seem like I'm grilling you, just say the word, and I'll knock it off. All I'm trying to do is get a handle on what happened and when, so that I can compare it to whatever this potential client tells me."

"You're doing your due diligence," he said, still focused out the window. "It is what it is."

"I really appreciate that you're willing to talk with me about this."

He looked back at me. "Well, and I appreciate that you've got some reservations about taking this guy on. In my practice I don't meet many criminal defense lawyers, but my impression is, with a case this high profile, most of them would jump in with both feet. It could make a man famous. After trial, whoever represents this guy might find himself on talk shows. Or maybe one of those legal commentators they put on the news." There was a bitter edge to his voice. In his shoes, I would've been bitter too.

"Yeah, I've got no interest in that," I said. "Maybe as a prosecutor I would've, but being known as the guy who gets killers off scot-free is not my thing."

He looked at me like he was about to ask a question, but then his puzzled expression vanished and he gave a thoughtful nod.

I had the sense that he'd been about to ask why I was in this line of work if I wasn't excited about freeing killers, but he'd stopped when he remembered that some folks needed to earn a living.

He, of course, was not one of those folks. When the sons of wealthy families went into the practice of law, it wasn't so much a job as a hobby or lifestyle. It gave them a different sort of power and something dignified to do with their time.

"Can I ask," I said, "do you have any sense of why His Honor went into that stairwell?"

"I do, yeah." He looked at me like he was appraising me, hesitating over a decision, and then he said, "You know what, you can go ahead and call him Nicholson. I don't mind."

"Thanks."

"Yeah. So, he liked to get his steps in every day. You know." He pointed to his Apple Watch.

It looked just like the one I'd bought to monitor my heart issues, except for one detail: his had a chunky band with a subtle sheen that made me think it was real gold. My watch was held on with a black silicone strap, the cheapest option available.

He let his arm fall back onto his desk and said, "Hindsight's twenty-twenty, but I guess too many people knew that about him. That and other things. With what you see happening these days… Let's just say that Nicholson was not always as vigilant as I would've preferred."

"That's unfortunate," I said. "I can certainly understand the need for vigilance."

"Yeah. And coming up on that trial, I had some concerns about your Mr. Ludlow."

"He's not my Mr. Ludlow."

He gave a quick smile that was more a grimace. "Your town's, I meant."

"I've had concerns about him for quite a while now, myself."

He nodded. "Well, it'll be a relief to see him put away. But a man like that doesn't go down easily."

"Not at all," I agreed.

"With the connections he has, and his assets…" He glanced at me with a hint of embarrassment. "Let's just say I know how that works."

I nodded.

"Although, unlike him, I don't have any personal friends in federal prison."

"Yeah, that's a whole other crowd he's got, isn't it."

"And that's the crowd I was concerned about. To the point that I suggested he ought to drive a different car than usual that day. I even rented it for him, so his name wouldn't be on it."

"That was a good idea."

I liked Monty's style. I'd seen a lot of trouble caused by naive optimists. Vigilance couldn't always prevent problems, but it made them a lot less likely.

He sighed. "Maybe. But unfortunately it wasn't enough."

"At least you know you tried."

"I tried a lot of things," he said. "I tried calling him when I heard a commotion in the courthouse, and they pretty much stopped everyone where they were."

"Yeah, that was something."

"I was actually in the men's room. They wouldn't let me go back to the war room or toward the stairs. So I called him a couple of times, but…"

While he looked out the window again, I took a sip of my coffee. It was a lot better than my office coffee. If we hadn't been talking in somber tones about his dead client, I would've asked what kind it was. Instead, I said, "One thing I've wondered: why was Nicholson's testimony so important?"

"Well, the trial's still ongoing," he said. "And on top of that, I've got ethical duties, so…"

"Understood. No, I get it."

We both knew that a lawyer's duty to keep his mouth shut about things his client had told him survived the client's death. And even without that, he wouldn't want to show any of the cards that were in the prosecutor's hand until after Ludlow's trial was over.

"Getting back to the day itself," I said, "once you were at the courthouse, how did Nicholson go about getting the key card?"

He winced. I'd seen plenty of people wince like that when they remembered one of the last moments where a different decision could've changed their fate or that of a loved one.

"That was my suggestion," he said. "He was getting a little antsy in the war room, so we went out and checked the stairwells to see if there was one he could use. One where he wouldn't run into any journalists, other witnesses, and so forth. The second one we checked was locked, so I figured if we could get in there and have it lock behind him, you know, it'd be more discreet. And safer, I thought."

"Yeah, that makes sense." I shook my head in sympathy. "Oh—am I hearing correctly? Y'all didn't actually have the key card?"

"No. The janitor opened the door for us."

"I see. And this janitor was the, uh, suspect?"

"Yeah—well, I assume. The janitor we met was a younger guy, maybe early thirties. Not White, maybe half-and-half. Or Hispanic, I don't know."

I nodded. That tracked. The TV news still hadn't shown Baptiste's picture, but Terri had told me he was twenty-eight and his dad was Haitian.

"Whereabouts did you meet him?"

"Well, it was whichever floor we were on—"

"Second floor?"

"I guess, yeah. And I want to say he was pushing a mop into an elevator. He had one of those yellow buckets on wheels, in any case, and a work uniform on, so... obviously a janitor. I thought maybe he could get us into one of those stairwells. And I went over and asked him, because—well."

He shrugged like it was obvious why he'd been the one to approach the janitor. It was. A good attorney's instinct is always to insulate his client, or as I sometimes thought of it, to stand between his client and the world.

"Okay, so *you* approached *him*?" That was good news from a defense point of view.

"Oh, of course. I mean, if some janitor came up out of nowhere, during that trial, and offered me a key—" He laughed.

I did too. "Yeah," I said. "That'd be a red flag right there."

"Right? I'd back away slowly..."

"Or not so slowly."

Our laughter died away. He turned and looked out the window again. "It should've still been a red flag," he said, like he was talking to the clouds.

"How so?"

"Ludlow's office was in that courthouse all these years. And that guy was a janitor, but he was still a courthouse employee."

"Yeah, fair point."

I actually hadn't thought about it that way. I was a little embarrassed that I hadn't. I made a mental note to find out how long Baptiste had worked at the courthouse.

"Did he see y'all go into the stairwell, do you know?" I asked.

He looked at me, perplexed, and then his face cleared. "Oh, no. I didn't go with Nicholson. I checked it out beforehand real quick, just to make sure it looked okay, but then I went back down to the war room. The janitor let him in, along with his clerk."

"Oh, and who's that?"

"Samantha Townsend."

"Right, I think I've seen her before, in court. He presided over a case of mine last year. Is she about thirty, blonde hair?"

He nodded and looked out the window again, squinting like he was trying to remember something.

"I assume she's been questioned?" I said.

"I would think so."

"She'd have to be, right?"

He gave a shrug like it hardly mattered now. His eyes seemed to be tracking something. I wondered what he was watching.

After another second or three, he said, "I actually saw that janitor a couple of times before I ever talked to him. I stepped out of the war room a few times, and I feel like he was there every time I did."

"Where? Same place?"

He shook his head, still looking out over the ocean. "No. I want to say by the courtroom door, once, and then another time over by the men's room. He was right outside when I came out. This is hindsight again, but was he following me? Looking for an opportunity?" He shrugged, swung his chair around to face me again, and said, "But he's a janitor, right? They're always in the hallways or the restrooms. So it didn't seem weird at the time."

## 5

## DECEMBER 12, 2023

In the bowels of the federal courthouse in Charleston, a guard let me into the room where Baptiste was waiting. He fit the description Monty had given: a light-skinned Black guy who could've passed for Hispanic, or maybe Middle Eastern. He was a good-looking kid, with enough bulk in his shoulders and chest to make me think he lifted weights. His face matched his age, but the touch of gray at his temples could've made Monty think he was a few years older.

He stood up and said hi, and we shook hands. For a guy who'd been in jail for several days, he looked pretty good. He was a little over average height, but he held himself with assurance—his posture made the orange jumpsuit he was wearing look like a mistake.

"Good to meet you," he said. "Thanks for coming." He had the same Yankee accent as his mom.

"Not a problem."

As we sat down, he said, "Thought I was going to have to handle this hearing myself." There was no resentment in his voice. Just stress and a touch of fear.

"No, course not," I said. "You called, I came."

"Yeah. Uh, is my mom out there?"

"I didn't see her, but it's early. I told her there wouldn't really be anywhere to wait until two p.m., and they won't let her see you privately, so she's probably not coming until closer to then."

That surprised him. "She can't wait in the courtroom until we get there?"

"No, up here it's not like in Basking Rock. Federal court's more formal. The bailiff doesn't open the door until the scheduled time, so she'd just be standing in the hall."

"Yeah, no. She's spent enough of her life on her feet," he said. After a second he added, in a voice that was somehow older and heavier, "And for this, I think she better be sitting down."

I nodded, but he didn't see it; he was looking at the floor. He didn't have the frantic disbelief about his situation that most of my clients did at this stage of the game. I wondered why. His air of resignation was something I associated with men who'd been through the grinder of arrest and court and prison before, but Terri had done a criminal background check for me, and he didn't have one.

"This is your first bail hearing, right?" I said.

"Uh, yeah," he said. "I never been arrested before. You know the county courthouse doesn't tend to hire criminals."

I smiled. I liked his deadpan tone.

He looked me in the eye. "I got a question to ask you. A couple questions, actually. How they charging me with murder when all I done is give the man a key card?"

There had to be more evidence than that. I was a believer in the old saying that a grand jury would indict a ham sandwich if the prosecutor asked it to, but if the grand jury was a vending machine dispensing indictments, the prosecutor still had to put his coin in first. The coin being a halfway decent story about why this guy was guilty. This key card thing didn't make the grade.

I shrugged. "We'll find out more as this proceeds. Did you appear before the grand jury, though?"

Appearing was optional. If he'd been there, though, he would've heard the evidence against him.

"Oh, hell no." He shuddered. No show of bravado, only fear.

"Good call. Why'd you stay away?"

He looked at me like he hadn't heard me right: could I be that stupid?

"I never advise people to appear," I said, "but a lot of them see it as a chance to tell their side of the story. They think if they can just explain what really happened, the problem will go away. And I don't usually get a chance to tell them that's not how it works, since most folks don't hire a lawyer until after the grand jury indicts them."

"Yeah. I didn't. Maybe I should have. I didn't call you before, because I'd heard that even if you have a lawyer, you can't bring him in there with you. That true?"

"Yup. It's just you, the grand jury, and the prosecutor."

"Okay, that's what I thought. And to me, that sounds like a setup."

"Yep. From a defense perspective, that's what it is."

"Could it have been any worse if I went, though? I mean, they still came out of it with murder charges."

"It could've been worse, yes. You could've said something in there that was bad for your case. Speaking of the charges, what's your understanding of them?"

"It's murder, right?"

"Yeah, and then one more. There's another felony count, for obstruction of justice, which they hit you with for lying to the FBI."

"A felony? Oh, man." He sighed hard and leaned forward, elbows on his knees, head hanging. He swore a few times under his breath, and then he sat back up. "That was—I don't know, I was just trying to stay out of trouble."

"Uh-huh."

He was shaking his head. "Feels stupid, saying that now," he said. "But in the moment… You ever been questioned by the FBI?"

"No."

"It's a bad scene."

"I'm sure."

"It was like a bunch of androids with guns, all trying to corner me. I was just, like—anything to get out of that room, you know?"

"I hear you. So, since the magistrate's going to ask, have you thought about how you want to plead?"

He looked at me the same way he had a few minutes earlier, like he was a little afraid I might be a complete idiot. "Not guilty," he said, as if he couldn't believe he had to spell that out. "On both. Who would — Does anybody plead guilty from the get-go? What's the point of that?"

The way he'd asked that hit me wrong. As if his decision was based on strategy: withholding his plea until the right offer came in. The truth was, it was a solid strategy, but my clients didn't usually strategize guilty pleas. Rather, they insisted on their innocence and asked me how they could convince the judge to make the charges go away.

"No, people don't generally plead guilty at this point," I told him. "But I still have to ask."

"Okay. I guess you've got to do what you've got to do. But I had one other question. I mean, this is a murder charge. Of a federal judge. So... is it even possible for you to get me home on bail?"

I didn't need to reply. He could see from my face what the answer was; it was the one he'd expected and feared. He looked away and closed his eyes. His face was taut. I realized he wasn't breathing. He was trying to hold himself together.

After a second he exhaled, and his shoulders slumped. "I got to tell my mom." He looked at me. "Can I see her beforehand, so we can talk?"

"Not anywhere private. You're going to have at least one guard with you. But I can try to get her into one of the conference rooms upstairs and tell her myself before the hearing. Does she check her texts?"

He nodded.

"I'll text her to meet me by the elevators. I'll explain the situation."

"Okay. Thanks." His fingertips started tapping a pattern on the table. He watched them tap, breathing deeply, an exhausted expression on his face.

The odd thing about him, I realized, was that he seemed to understand his fate. And accept it. Most of my clients didn't. At this stage, people who'd never been on the wrong side of the criminal justice system were normally still in denial. It took a longer conversation for them to even realize that the first hearing wasn't going to make the problem go away. And it usually took spending at least a week in jail before they really understood that they were going to be there for a while and started working on how to deal with that.

"I talked to her yesterday," he said.

"Your mom?"

"Yeah. Called her from the phone in the jail. I kind of knew how this was going to be—we see guys come in on murder charges down in Basking Rock. They come in for their bail hearings, and then they leave again in the same prison van. So I know how things go, but I couldn't tell her that."

"Course not. It's too much."

In South Carolina state court, judges almost never granted bail on murder charges. If he'd noticed that just from being a janitor at the courthouse, I thought—when janitors never watched hearings, never even set foot in a courtroom until everybody else had left—then he was the kind of guy who paid attention. The quiet observer type, who picks up on more than most people do.

Of course, maybe there was a simpler reason that he was resigned to his fate. Maybe he was guilty. Being arrested for a crime that you committed wasn't nearly as big a surprise as being arrested for one you had nothing to do with.

I couldn't ask him if he'd done it, of course. That was a cardinal rule of criminal defense. We didn't ask, because we couldn't put a guy on the witness stand if we knew he was guilty—not unless he planned to take the Fifth in front of the jury, which was never a good move. The ethical rules required attorneys to zealously defend clients even if we knew they were guilty as hell, but I personally could not summon any enthusiasm for keeping a murderer out of jail. I was not the right guy for that.

I was glad I'd only agreed to represent him for today's hearing. I preferred clients who I strongly suspected were innocent, or guilty ones who'd been overcharged. Somebody hit with multiple felony charges for what should've been a misdemeanor—there were plenty of those, and I could fight for a guy like that in good conscience.

But this was a murder being charged as a murder.

I checked my watch. The hearing was in forty minutes. The magistrate had decided to combine what was usually two hearings held a week or so apart, the initial appearance and the arraignment, into one. The arraignment was always later if the defendant was unrepresented, but if he had a lawyer already, they could be combined.

That was good. We'd get them both over with today, and I'd fight for bail, which would almost certainly be denied, and then, since there wouldn't be any more imminent deadlines for a while, Baptiste would have time to go find himself another lawyer.

"Anyway, look," I said. "I'll meet up with your mom before the hearing, take her aside, tell her she's got to be strong for you. There's nothing easy about any of this, but I know how to help mothers get through it."

"Yeah," he said. "If you can help her… thank you. She's been through enough."

―――

Magistrate Harris, a fiftysomething Black man with a law-and-order bent, got through the first part of the hearing at his usual high speed. He was big on efficiency. When he asked me the scope of my representation, I stood up at the defense table and said, "Mr. Baptiste has engaged me only for the purposes of this hearing. We will, of course, keep the court apprised of whether it's going to be me or different counsel going forward."

Out of the corner of my eye, I saw Baptiste turn and look at me. I'd made the scope of my work clear to him in my engagement letter, I thought, but I could feel his surprise. I kept my eyes on Magistrate Harris.

The clerk handed some papers up to the bench. Harris put his glasses on and scanned the cover page. "Okay. So, Mr. Baptiste, this portion of the hearing is your arraignment. I'm going to read out the indictment, which isn't very long."

He cleared his throat and said, "As I've already read the case caption into the record, I'll dispense with that part of the document and proceed to the counts charged. It reads as follows: 'The grand jury charges, Count One, Murder. On or about November 17, 2023, on the premises of the county courthouse of Basking County, South Carolina, the defendant, Vincenzo Alessandro Baptiste, within the special maritime and territorial jurisdiction of the United States, did with malice aforethought, willfully, deliberately, maliciously, and in a premeditated manner, as defined in 18 United States Code section 1111, effect the death of the victim, namely, His Honor Frederick Joseph Nicholson, who at the time of his death served as a United States District Court judge for the District of South Carolina, Charleston division.'"

He turned the page. "Count Two, Obstruction and Attempted Obstruction of an Official Proceeding. On or about November 19, 2023, within the District of South Carolina, the defendant, with the intent to avoid, evade, or prevent an official proceeding, to wit, the investigation into the death of the aforementioned victim, willfully gave false testimony, as defined in 18 United States Code section 1505, to the Federal Bureau of Investigation."

In the days following Nicholson's death, the FBI had questioned every court employee who'd been at the courthouse when he died. If Baptiste had called me then, to advise him on how to talk to the FBI, he could've avoided that felony charge and its potential five-year sentence.

"Mr. Munroe," Harris said, "have you discussed the charges set forth in Counts One and Two of the indictment with your client?"

"Yes, I have, Your Honor."

"And does he wish to enter a plea at this time?"

"Yes. He will plead not guilty to each count."

As Harris reiterated that to the court reporter, making sure the plea was properly entered into the record, I wondered why the indictment ended where it did.

It made no sense. For one thing, if the prosecutor had sold the grand jury on the theory that Baptiste was a hired gun working for somebody on Ludlow's side, there ought to have been a count for conspiracy. As a prosecutor I'd brought conspiracy counts in hired-killer cases, and federal law was no different on that. You didn't need to know who the other conspirators were in order to bring those charges; you could call them John Doe.

There also ought to have been some allegations for criminal forfeiture. A hired gun got paid for his crime, and the law, of course, didn't allow him to keep the proceeds.

I glanced over at the prosecutor. Alston Wilcox, a tall, skinny man in a navy suit and red bow tie, was leaning over, talking to a woman that I assumed was his paralegal. I knew of the Wilcox family—they were old money, like the Montgomerys—but I hadn't gone up against him in court before, so in preparation for the hearing, I'd run his name by Cardozo. I'd known he wouldn't be able to give me much intel; he never could on a case that his office was prosecuting. But he had felt at liberty to share that Wilcox was LaRue's right-hand man.

I hadn't needed more than that fact and the hint of disdain in Cardozo's voice to know Wilcox was bad news. Still, to clarify what type of bad news I was dealing with, I'd asked, "He a true believer, then?" And Cardozo had said yes.

True believers was what we called the prosecutors who seemed to genuinely believe that every last person they charged with a crime was not only 100 percent guilty but also a separate and inferior class of human being, deserving maximum punishment.

Guys like that had no self-doubt. It made them hard to reason with.

Magistrate Harris finished talking to his clerk and said, "All right. Now, is there discovery?"

Wilcox stood up. "Yes, Your Honor. There's some discovery that will be going out shortly. I also anticipate that the parties will be engaging in plea discussions. I understand that Your Honor has some availability on Monday, January 22, at ten thirty a.m., and I would therefore ask that the case be put down for a status conference at that time."

Harris looked at me.

With the holidays coming up, five or six weeks was a reasonable amount of time to wait. "I agree, Your Honor."

"All right," Harris said. He conferred with his clerk again, both of them looking at the black binder containing his calendar.

There was some back-and-forth about the length of the status conference and whether we could move it to the afternoon. I didn't much care what time it took place. I was still stuck on the lack of a conspiracy count or forfeiture allegations in the indictment. Did Wilcox somehow not think that Judge Nicholson's death was a murder for hire? What other theory could he possibly have in mind?

The Lowcountry was not a big place. Within any given social class, everybody knew, or at least knew *of*, each other. Ludlow was still on trial, but his family had wielded a lot of power for a very long time. Even if corruption charges did take him down, that dynasty wasn't going to fall; it could still pay to be in their good graces.

So I wondered, when it came to Ludlow, which side Wilcox was on.

They were both from old local families. Those families would normally be on the same side. And Judge Nicholson hadn't been one of them; he wasn't even from South Carolina.

If I was right about Nicholson's death and Wilcox didn't pursue that angle, then whoever had hired Baptiste would get away with it. The patsy would go to jail, while the man who ordered the murder remained free.

That wasn't something I wanted to see happen. Not even if the only way I could prevent it was by defending a killer in court.

Once the schedule for the status conference got figured out, Harris asked Wilcox where he stood on the question of bail. Wilcox unleashed a barrage of arguments against it, and I countered them as best I could. There wasn't much I could say; all of the things that courts consider weighed against granting bail.

After all, murder was the most serious crime, and a man accused of murder could be considered dangerous to the public. A man who'd only moved here from Pittsburgh nine years ago, and who had extended family in Pennsylvania and in Haiti, was arguably a flight risk. On top of that, he had no small children or elderly adults who needed him at home; nobody else's life would collapse if he lost his job.

Harris ruled against us.

I sat down, leaned over to Baptiste, and told him, "Well, you didn't get bail, but you got yourself a lawyer now."

# 6

## DECEMBER 19, 2023

In a windowless white room in the basement of the detention facility outside Charleston, Terri and I were waiting for Vinny. She'd driven over from wherever she'd been—I tried not to ask too many personal questions these days—and I'd come up from Basking Rock.

She was sitting on one of the folding chairs. I was pacing. I spent a lot more time at a desk than she did, so I liked to move around when I could.

"You got any Christmas plans?" she asked.

"Oh. I hadn't even thought about that. I guess it depends if Noah has much time off." I took my phone out of my pocket and tapped through to the calendar.

"Makes sense. I'm going to stay with my sister and my niece," she said. "Just warning you, so you don't plan on having me out hunting for murderers or trying to, like, hack into the Pentagon over the holidays."

I chuckled. I wondered why she wasn't spending Christmas with her boyfriend, assuming they were still together, but I didn't ask.

My calendar showed that the twenty-fifth was next Monday. Maybe Noah would come down for the weekend.

The door opened, and a guard led Vinny in. His hands were cuffed in front of him.

I gave the guard a nod. "Sir, would you mind taking those off him? I'm going to need him to be able to write some stuff down for me."

I had no such plans, but the cuffs were demeaning. The guard took them off and headed to the door, saying, "I'll be right outside."

"Thanks."

"Good to see you again," Terri said. "How you holding up?"

Vinny shrugged and said nothing. I'd learned that if my initial question got that quiet response, I shouldn't probe. A man in jail often didn't want to talk about it.

I popped a folding chair open and sat down. "What about your mom? How's she doing?" When I'd told her what to expect before we went into the courtroom for the bail hearing, her knees had almost hit the ground. She'd held it together, but it was a close call.

"I talked to her a couple of times."

It was clear he wanted me to move on, so I did. "They giving you internet access now?" I'd fought for him to get time in the jail's library so he could finish his IT boot camp online. He'd already paid for the whole course, after all.

"Yeah. Thanks. Ten hours a week, so it's going slower than it was, but at least it's going."

"Good. Gives you something to do."

Hopelessness flashed across his face. "Yeah, for whatever that's worth."

"It'll be worth something eventually," Terri said. "The question is how to get there. I tried to talk with that coworker of yours, Raylene, again a couple days ago. She wasn't answering my calls, so I went to the courthouse during their lunch break. She put her hand up in my face." She raised her hand, palm out: the universal sign for *back off*.

Vinny shook his head and muttered the swear word he usually employed in lieu of Raylene's name. I forgave him that. After all, she was the one who'd told the FBI that Vinny had taken the stairwell key card from the maintenance office.

Of course, that wouldn't have caused any problems if he hadn't already lied to the FBI.

"Yeah, unfortunately she doesn't have to talk to us if she doesn't want to," I said.

"I don't know if it's so unfortunate," Terri said. "I was just trying to get a read on her, but we already know she's not going to say anything to help you. She's got an axe to grind, for whatever reason."

"Her son's a loser," Vinny said. "High school dropout, does nothing but smoke weed and play video games. She complains about him all the time. Dude can't afford his own place, so he watches porn in his room—I overheard her complaining once that she could hear it through the door." His lip curled in disgust. "And then I walk in, with my steady job and my IT plans and whatnot—she saw me every day of the week, and I don't think she liked the contrast."

"Mm-hmm." Terri gave a slow, meaningful nod. "Especially since she and her son are White."

Vinny gave her a look that said *you got it*.

I felt the trapdoor of Southern history open. The resentment many poor White folks felt for their successful Black neighbors ran deep. I made a mental note that this coworker's hostility to Terri might not extend to me.

"Is she one of those victim mentality types?" Terri asked.

"Yeah."

"Some people don't like being reminded that they have a choice," she said. "Or their son does, in her case."

"Speaking of choices to make," I said, "I haven't heard from Wilcox yet about a plea deal, but with the conference coming up in January, I'm sure we'll be talking soon. So I'd like to figure out if we've got anything we can bring him."

"Is it weird that you haven't heard from him yet?" Vinny asked.

I'd noticed before that he tended to pick up on details that sailed right past most people. He struck me as the quiet, highly observant type. That wasn't common in men his age, and I liked it, but it did mean I had to watch how I said things around him.

"Little bit, yeah. Although it could be that holiday planning got in the way."

"Huh. Okay."

I didn't actually think that was what was going on. My best guess was that Wilcox wasn't proceeding on a hired gun theory, so he didn't think Vinny had any useful information to offer. That being the case, he was in no hurry to get a plea deal done. His best approach was to make us sweat as long as possible and then offer a bad deal at the last minute, when sheer desperation might make Vinny accept it.

But there was no point getting Vinny worried about that right now.

"So, that case we were talking about," I said. "The Ludlow thing. It's still going on—"

"Still?" Vinny was incredulous. "I think that's the longest trial that courthouse has had in the whole time I've been there."

"And that's how many years, again?"

"Seven. Since I was twenty-one."

"Uh-huh. Well, it'll be wrapping up soon. The jury went out yesterday. But you know the trial got continued for the rest of the week after Nicholson died, so it's been running behind schedule."

"Man, that courthouse must be mayhem at this point."

"Yeah, I'm sure. Haven't been there myself lately. Most of my work's here in Charleston these days."

"They've had the second floor kind of cordoned off," Terri said. "Access controlled. The other two floors are pretty normal now."

"They replaced that stupid camera yet?" Vinny asked.

He'd told us after the bail hearing that he couldn't prove where he was when Nicholson died because he'd been on the third floor, cleaning up near the stairwell door, and that was the one camera that didn't work.

"By the stairwell? I don't know," Terri said.

Vinny heaved a sigh and shook his head. He was looking off toward a corner of the room with an expression that I recognized. I'd seen it on a lot of people—my clients, crime victims, witnesses. I thought of it as the *if only* face, as in *if only* I'd done one or two things differently, I wouldn't be here now.

"You wishing you'd pushed harder to get it replaced?" I asked.

He shrugged. "Naw. Not really."

"No?" The set of scales in my mind tilted a hair toward guilty. An innocent man, I thought, would've wished the camera had been working so there'd be proof he hadn't been in that stairwell when Nicholson died.

"What I wish is, I wish I'd minded my own business," he said. "Kept my head down. I should've shrugged and said 'I'm sorry' when that guy asked me if there was a way into that stairwell, instead of going and getting him the key card."

"Yeah. Well… tell me, that wasn't the only key card for the stairwell, was it?"

"Oh, no. There were at least two that I know of. Both hanging on lanyards in the key cabinet in the maintenance room."

"And you took one that day?"

"Yeah, because I was doing the men's rooms on floors two and three, and those are at the back of the building. When there's a big trial, they don't like us using the elevators, and I wasn't going to walk all the way to the front stairwell."

"Okay. And was the second still hanging there when you took the one?"

He shook his head heavily. "I wish I remembered. I wasn't paying attention."

I thought for a moment. "Is that key cabinet kept locked?"

"Not the cabinet, but the maintenance office is. Staff all had cards to get in."

"And can you just grab the key card, or do you have to sign it out?"

"I mean, you're supposed to sign it out. But nobody ever does."

I sighed. "Okay. And when that guy asked you if there was a way into the stairwell—was it just that guy, by the way, or was he with anyone?"

"It was just him, seeing if there was a quieter place somebody could go."

"He mention who he was asking for?"

"No, but I knew."

"You knew?" That wasn't good. The scales tilted a hair further toward guilt.

"Yeah, because I saw what room he came out of. The war room for the next witnesses. He was in there with Judge Nicholson and some woman."

I figured he meant Nicholson's clerk.

"Blonde woman?" I said, just to confirm it was her. "Wearing a suit?"

"Yeah, they were all wearing suits. I mean, it's a courthouse. So it's suits, or some type of uniform, like mine… or random T-shirts and booty shorts and all that, for the criminals. You know how it is. Everybody's got to let everybody else know where they stand in life."

"Yep, I guess they do."

I thought of Cameron and his courthouse T-shirts. He thought he was dressing like a cool guy who didn't care about convention, but I knew he was dressing like a shoplifter who didn't respect the judge.

Terri spoke up. "Vinny, seems like you knew a lot about who was at that trial."

"Yeah," he said. "I mean, working at the courthouse is an interesting job." There was something defensive about the way he said that. Armor up.

"You ever think about going into the legal field?" she asked.

"You mean, like a lawyer? Oh, hell no. I don't want to be up in front of everybody, talking. That's why I like IT. You sit in some back room with the servers."

"I hear you," she said, smiling.

"And the courthouse is going to be hiring for that. They're doing an upgrade next year."

"I hope so," I said. "Reception's pretty terrible in there."

"The whole network is janky," he said. "However many years ago they put it in, somebody must've been, like, 'I can't handle these stone walls. Let's just give each floor its own router.' So I figured I'd get trained, and then when they start to redd up the system, they'll hire me."

"When they… what's that you said?"

He gave me a blank look. Then he got it. "Oh, redd up. Sorry, my bad. That's Pittsburgh for clean up."

Terri laughed. I saw it disarm him; he relaxed and smiled at her. She had ways of getting people comfortable enough to talk. "So, I hear you really want to keep on working at that courthouse," she said, leaning forward, looking fascinated. "You must like working there a lot."

"Yeah, I do. I guess I like… *watching*," he said. "And there's a lot to watch there. It's one of the reasons I like being a janitor. It's like you're invisible. You hear things. You see things. People just do whatever they're doing, like you're not even there."

I had a flash of something like double vision. On one side, Vinny was a quiet guy who picked up on things. On the other, he was a snake in the grass, spying. I couldn't tell which one was true.

"Yeah, working in a courthouse can be real interesting," I said. "You ever listen in on any cases?"

"Naw. We weren't allowed. But I knew what was going down."

"Uh-huh. You worked through the first week and change of Ludlow's trial, right?"

"Yeah."

"Just your regular shift?"

"Eight to five, yeah. Minus the hour for lunch."

"And you were probably there when they had the pretrial hearings, too, right? Those were in September and October."

He shrugged. "I mean, I wasn't in Cancún. Yeah, I must've been at work. I haven't been out sick or on vacation in I don't know how long."

"Okay. So do you remember anybody talking to you during that period? Anything beyond the usual where's the elevator or the men's room, or whatever?"

I was trying to skate on a very thin line. I did not want to coax him into confessing to the crime, but I needed to let him know that the door was open if he had any useful beans that he wanted to spill.

"Talking to me about what? You mean about that case?"

"Yeah. Or about Judge Nicholson. Or anything that stands out as… weird."

"I mean, *this* stands out as weird, right here," he said, cracking a smile, gesturing to me, or to our whole conversation.

I must've looked a little annoyed, because he said, "Naw, I'm messing with you, man. But what are you looking for? Something somebody said to me at work that's going to bust this case wide open?"

It sounded stupid when he put it that way, especially with the streak of sarcasm he layered on top of almost everything. But he was right; that's what I was looking for.

"Well… yeah," I said. "If you can think of anything."

"Man, that's some *Batman* shit, right there. What is this, a movie?"

I sighed, crossed my arms, and shut my eyes for a second. Vinny was entertaining and annoying at the same time. His banter would've been fun if we'd been out playing pool together, but it got in the way when I was trying to figure out what we had—if anything—to offer Wilcox in exchange for a plea deal. And it got in the way, I was pretty sure, of the truth.

I reminded myself that he was—or rather, he and his mom were—paying for my services. I owed him some patience, at least.

"Well, look," I said. "It might sound crazy, but I happen to know that Ludlow's got some friends who are not good people. Some of the ones I've had close shaves with are in federal prison right now."

Vinny nodded thoughtfully. He didn't look as surprised as I'd expected him to.

"But most of them aren't," I continued. "They're still walking the streets, and maybe the hallways of the courthouse during his trial."

"And that's why you're asking me about them."

"That's why I'm asking, yes. That man does not want to go to jail any more than you do, and he's got connections all across this state—"

"I think what Leland's saying," Terri interrupted, "is that if you could think through anyone you might've spoken with about the case, or even about any other case, and let us know, that might give us some leads or some ideas."

"Ideas about what?"

"Well, my main thing," I said, "is figuring out if you know anything, about Ludlow or anything else, that Wilcox wants to know. I don't think I've explained too well yet how plea deals work, but—"

"Oh, I know how they work." He sounded like he knew a lot, or thought he did. I looked at him. He didn't explain.

"How do you know?"

He sighed like an old man who'd seen too much. "I've... been around," he said. He was looking at the floor. He sounded like he was saying he'd been around a war zone or some other gate of hell.

"Mm-hmm," Terri said. The amount of sympathy and understanding that she managed to include in some of her *mm-hmm*s had always amazed me. It wasn't even a real word. I didn't know how she did it.

"I know you got to do this," Vinny told me. His voice was strained. He didn't like what I was doing.

"This... what?"

"Talk to that dude about a plea deal. That's your job, right? Or part of it?"

"Yeah, I mean, it's a step in the process."

"Kind of feels like you're playing poker with my life, though. Like, see if Wilcox goes for this—maybe that way I'll only get fifteen goddamn years in jail instead of a life sentence. Because those are the options, right?"

I hesitated—fifteen years was a little random, and in a federal first-degree murder case, a life sentence was not the worst-case scenario.

"Maybe," I said.

Vinny looked at me like he was pointing an antenna to scan for any thoughts that I was keeping to myself.

He found one. His lips tightened. "He could've asked for the death penalty, couldn't he?"

"Well, to be clear," I said, "he still could. The court's got to establish a schedule for that—"

"A *schedule*? Are you kidding me? A schedule for *death*?"

"Hold on, now. The rules are in place to protect you, okay? Federal law requires the court to set a deadline for the prosecutor to let us all know if he's going to seek capital punishment, and if he is, then we get our chance to argue why he shouldn't, and so forth."

For once, he had no comeback. The reality of prison, of being well and truly caught inside a system that they couldn't control, settled on people in layers, not all at once. I could see in his eyes that he was feeling the weight of a new layer bearing down on him now.

"So once that deadline gets set, the prosecutor's got to decide if he even wants to seek that penalty, and if he does, then he's got to run it by the attorney general to get his approval to even try, and then he's got to jump through a bunch of other hoops."

"The attorney general of the whole United States?"

"Yeah. Since it's a federal crime."

He nodded blankly, staring off toward the wall behind me. This whole thing seemed to blow his mind. Anybody would've felt that way.

"So, as I see it," I said, "the only thing that makes us even have to think about that at all is the fact that Nicholson was a federal judge. The rest of it—the fact there's only one victim, no torture or terrorism, no connection to gangs or organized crime—all of that weighs against it being a death penalty case."

His defeated mood seemed to lift. He looked at me, and before he even opened his mouth, I sensed he'd gotten a little bit of his spark back, somehow.

"Well, see what you can do, I guess," he said. "Tell you what. If you can get the attorney general of the whole United States to opt out of trying to kill me, my mom and I might give you a raise."

———

Ten minutes later, Terri and I walked out of the prison, heading for the parking lot, and I checked my phone. "Oh, Wilcox finally sent that discovery. Rachel says three file boxes came in." Rachel was my paralegal.

"File boxes? He sent it on paper?"

"I guess he's old-school. Or maybe he just likes to send it the slowest way possible."

"Whatever. As long as we get it, I don't care if he strapped it to a pigeon's leg! Can we go straight to your office?"

"Of course." I couldn't help but smile at the excitement in her voice. "You're like a kid at Christmas."

"Well, it feels like I've been waiting forever. You know, if this was one of your rich clients, I'd already have identified some suspects and interviewed half of their friends. But there were upwards of two hundred people in the courthouse that day, and I didn't want to waste this family's money doing basic legwork when I knew Wilcox was sending over a lot of what law enforcement found out."

We picked up our pace. The prison parking lot was big, and our cars weren't parked close by. We'd apparently arrived shortly before shift change; a lot of the cars I'd walked by on my way in were gone now. I was glad for that. I had some thoughts about Vinny, and a big, half-empty parking lot was a pretty good place to discuss them.

"You know, it's annoying," I said. "I can't figure this guy out. It's like there's two different— You know when you're driving, and you start getting out of range of your radio station and start picking up another one?"

"Sure, I remember that, back before satellite radio."

"Yeah. You'd get two different stations coming in and out, right? Like, your song cuts out and you hear the news from some other city—"

"And then half a second more of your song, and some static, and then five words of the news."

"Exactly. That's what he's like. For half a second he's a good guy who made a foolish mistake, and then it switches. He's genuine, and then he's hiding something—"

"Oh, he's definitely hiding something."

I looked at her. "Were you going to share that with me?"

"Once I know what it is, obviously. I'm still figuring that out." She was getting her key ring out of her purse. I saw her green Subaru about ten yards off.

"Why'd you bring him to me, anyway?" I asked.

"Well… I guess I thought, without you, he's the kind of guy who might fall between the cracks."

"How do you mean?"

"Well…" As we walked, she twisted her keys around and around in her right hand, thinking it through. I noticed her key chain was a souvenir from Miami. I wondered when she'd been there.

The keys stopped.

"So… I don't know this guy," she said. "He's not even from here. I don't know his people. I could absolutely, 100 percent, be wrong. But it didn't make sense to me that he did it."

"It didn't make sense?" I asked. "Or it still doesn't?"

She pointed her key at her Subaru and unlocked it with a beep. "Well, on his own, for himself, I can't see a motive."

"Right, but—our hometown defendant? Wouldn't he pay to get rid of a witness?" The parking lot was pretty empty, but I wasn't taking any chances by saying Ludlow's name.

"Sure, but he's not stupid." She opened her door and tossed her bag onto the passenger seat. "He's got plenty of friends and plenty of resources. So if he's looking for somebody to do that dirty work for him, why hire *that* guy? I mean, what qualifications does our client have for doing that?"

I had to laugh. I pictured a résumé: *Vincenzo Baptiste. Objective: Assassin for Hire.* From what I knew of Vinny, it would show no relevant experience.

"You see what I mean?" she said. "But at the same time, it's like he" —she tilted her head back toward the prison—"knows he's doomed. You're right about that radio-switching thing. He jumps back and forth from the channel where he's this smart, snarky, intelligent guy, to this other channel where he's got a target on his back and he knows there's no getting out of this. And just… *why?*"

I shrugged. "You've seen guilty men act that way before."

"Oh, of course. But usually, them being guilty makes *sense*. You can see the motive, or why that guy was the one. Just a second, I forgot to turn my phone back on." She leaned into her car and reached across the seats for her bag. The motion made her jacket ride up so I could see her little waist and the full curves of her hips.

I did not need to think about that right now. I'd gone down the wrong road with her at some point and found myself in a place where all I'd ever be able to do was look.

I turned around and checked out the prison instead. The American flag beside the entrance was hanging limp, like a bathroom towel. There was no breeze to lift it at all.

"Oh my God. Leland!" I swung around. Terri was looking at her phone, horrified.

She turned it around to show me a headline. Our local news website trumpeted "Ludlow Vindicated, Not Guilty on 34 Felonies."

I remembered the look he'd given me in the courtroom.

I'd cost him his job, his social position, and judging by the length of the case and the number of attorneys sitting with him at the table, probably at least a million bucks in legal fees.

He was not going to take that lying down. And now he was a free man, so he didn't have to.

# 7

## DECEMBER 29, 2023

Terri and I were sitting on the deck of Doug and Shannon Pennington's house as the sun went down, sipping tea, in my case, and a gin and tonic for Terri. Shannon had invited us to come by after their kids, who'd been visiting for Christmas, had flown home. We were there to find out what we could from her about the Ludlow trial. The trial transcripts wouldn't be out for months, and Shannon was the only person either of us knew who'd sat through the whole thing.

She was also the only person we knew who lived in Ludlow's old house. A quarter century earlier, he'd resided there with his first wife and their son. I couldn't help but wonder how different things might be now if his first wife hadn't died.

It was about seventy degrees, a little nicer than usual for this time of year. Shannon had stepped over to the outdoor kitchen area to get something from the fridge. The Penningtons had renovated their grand old Victorian inside and out; century-old trees framed the deep backyard. You could see neighbors from the front, but not from here. The land the house sat on had to be over an acre.

"Doug's going to be so sorry he missed you," Shannon said, putting a couple of things from the fridge onto a tray. "But on the other hand, he's got no interest at all in any of this true crime stuff, which I am just passionate about."

"I know you are," Terri said, in a *you-go-girl* tone.

"Did that verdict surprise you?" I asked.

"Oh my goodness, it sure did," Shannon said, standing at the granite counter, slicing up a lime.

"Me too. I'm trying to figure out where the prosecution messed up. Although I guess if you saw the whole thing and you expected it to go the other way, then..." I shrugged. "Maybe they didn't mess up. Sometimes juries get it wrong."

Shannon, coming back with the tray of tonic water and other fixings, said, "Well, I can tell you, it sure doesn't feel like they were watching the same trial I was. But then, maybe I was paying more attention to Mr. Ludlow over these past few years than they were."

"Oh, I'm sure that's true," I said. "We've got a better idea of what he's really like."

"Yes, we do. I was looking at it all through a very different lens, I guess." She set the tray on the low table in front of us and sat back down. "I do have to admit, though, that it got a little bit he said, she said at times. As far as, did this blackmail happen or did he really ask for this bribe."

"Oh yeah?" I said.

"Definitely. I mean, that Mr. Tucker came across real well at first, but once the defense counsel got up there..." She shook her head. "He made him out to be more of a sore loser, you know, because of how Mr. Tucker ran for Mr. Ludlow's job and lost. And so I guess the jury could've decided that that was why Mr. Tucker was up there saying Mr. Ludlow had done some bad things."

"Oof. I can see that."

If the jury discredited Tucker, I thought, that could have increased the value of Nicholson's testimony. A federal judge who, unlike Tucker, had no history of rivalry with Ludlow would've strengthened the prosecution's case.

"And the other witnesses, they got asked about plea deals and so forth, so…"

"Oh? About how many had plea deals?"

She looked thoughtful for a second and then said, "I'm trying to think of who *didn't*. I want to say that apart from Mr. Tucker, all of them said—not in so many words, but it was clear they were testifying so they could avoid going to prison themselves."

"Mm-hmm," Terri said. "So there was a credibility problem, I suppose."

I nodded. I'd polled enough juries to know that they tended to discount the testimony of witnesses who were testifying in exchange for a deal.

"But still," Shannon said, "even if that trial didn't go the right way, you know what—" Her voice cracked a little. "I just… I truly do feel blessed. I mean, what's happened with the podcast is more than I could have ever dreamed, and… This is going to sound silly, because I know in the fields that y'all work in, there's nothing special about being able to watch a whole trial from start to finish and really see how folks act in that situation, see our legal system up close. I'm sure to y'all, it's even boring sometimes. But it's not something I'd ever done before. How could I, back when I had my job?"

"Nope, you sure couldn't have," I said.

I vaguely recalled she'd been laid off or furloughed at some point a few years back, and since her husband earned enough for both of them, she'd decided to start a true crime podcast instead of looking for another job. Her show, *Carolina True Crime*, had taken off with astonishing success. Sometimes when I was looking for things on my phone, I tapped in the wrong spot and her smiling, airbrushed face popped up. Since I was a lawyer in South Carolina, the algorithms thought that I might want to listen to her.

She snapped open a bottle of tonic water and poured. "I'm telling you, it was just fascinating to watch it all unfold!"

"What part of the trial was the most interesting for you?" Terri asked.

"Oh my *goodness*," Shannon said, twisting the cap off a bottle of Bombay Sapphire. "Where would I even start? I got so much material out of that—it'd take me a week just to look through it all." She poured the gin and started mixing up her drink.

"Material?" Terri asked. "You mean—did you take notes?"

"I sure did. Every single day. Since they wouldn't let folks bring their laptops in, I had to use shorthand."

Terri's eyebrows went up. "You know shorthand?"

"Well, my mama made me go to secretarial school."

"Oh, she did, huh." Terri shot her a knowing smile.

"She did. And it's come in surprisingly handy, many times. You do *not* want to know how many notebooks I went through during that trial. They take up practically a whole drawer in my desk."

I froze to perfect stillness, like a cat that had spotted a mouse somewhere unexpected. This was the next best thing to trial transcripts, and I might be able to get my hands on it now, instead of having to wait months. With Shannon's notes, maybe I could put together the puzzle of that trial, and then I'd see the shape of the missing pieces—exactly where Judge Nicholson's testimony would have fit in the larger story that the prosecutor wanted to tell.

"I was planning on putting together a podcast episode about it," she said. "That was my thinking when I decided to attend the proceedings. And do you know what, Leland, I have to tell you, I actually had a card up my sleeve when I came over and said hi to you in the courtroom that day." She was smiling almost flirtatiously.

"Did you really!"

"Oh, it was nothing bad. I'm not a real sneaky type of person. I was just hoping I could get you to come on my podcast and talk about that trial."

"Oh my." I wondered how Ludlow would respond to hearing me talk about him on a true crime podcast. I didn't want to find out.

"Because I know, of course," she said, "that you can't talk about your own cases. And certainly not while they're going on. But since you weren't involved in that trial yourself, and you know Mr. Ludlow personally, I thought my listeners would really appreciate your insights."

"Why, thank you." I was silently plotting how to keep myself off her show without offending her.

She took a sip of her drink, leaned back in her chair, and sighed. "But *now*, though… Maybe all that time I spent was for nothing. At least as far as the podcast goes. Because I don't know how interesting that case would be for my listeners anymore, since that dang jury went and found him innocent."

"Well… not guilty," I said.

"Now that is true," Shannon said, raising her glass to me to signal her agreement. "That's absolutely true. A jury saying 'Well, we couldn't pin this on you' isn't the same thing as saying you didn't do it."

"Exactly."

"It's a disappointment, though. And they can't go after him again, can they?"

"Nope, it's one and done," I said.

"Because of double jeopardy, right?" She reminded me of some of the girls in my elementary school class—the ones who raised their hand for every question, happy to show off what they'd learned.

"Exactly right," I said. "I can tell you've done your homework."

"Well, I try," she said, looking very pleased.

"It sounds like you've got whole *notebooks* of homework," Terri said. "That is amazing, Shannon. Is there any chance we could take a look at—what do you think, Leland? The first week or two of the trial, at least?"

Nicholson had died on day six of the trial. I didn't want to home in on him by asking her for the notes from that day. Tipping our hand, letting a media personality like Shannon know what we were looking for, didn't seem like a good plan.

"Yeah, week one, week two, that'd be great," I said. "Did you happen to jot down any of the spectators' names? Especially the ones connected with Ludlow?"

"Oh, his bench was pretty full every day," Shannon said. "And I did write down the folks that I recognized, but there were a lot more that I didn't."

Basking Rock was a small town, but Shannon was from North Carolina originally. She hadn't lived here long enough to get to the point where she recognized practically everyone she saw.

"Yeah, his bench looked full the one day I did stop by," I agreed. "Anyway. What a shame."

I shook my head and looked off in the direction of the setting sun. After a second, I said, "I'd like to read through it all, actually, if that's okay. Especially the first couple of weeks, when the prosecution was presenting its case. Because, I don't know. I want to understand what exactly went wrong."

"Absolutely," Shannon said. "I can go get the notebooks for you when we're done with our drinks." She took a sip of her G&T and added, like it was an afterthought, "You know, the prosecutor who came down from Columbia especially for that trial, he talked about your poor Judge Nicholson right in his opening statement."

"Did he, now," I said. "Yeah, that was awful, what happened to him. Poor guy."

I'd kept my connection to the Baptiste case on the down-low as much as I could. Not a word to the press, and I'd made sure to leave the Charleston federal courthouse by a side door. Shannon must've been keeping an eye on the docket. Or maybe she had friends in that courthouse.

She was still smiling at me—I wasn't sure she'd stopped smiling since we'd arrived—and also, I sensed, watching me closely.

"So I just thought you might want to take a look at that part," she said. "In case it could help." Her head was tilted girlishly, and her perfect teeth were a very bright white.

I smiled back. My brain did a quick reset as I adjusted to the fact that Shannon Pennington was smarter than I had supposed.

———

That night, Terri and I sat on opposite sides of my office conference table. She was transcribing Shannon's notes on the opening statement, using a shorthand key that Shannon had written out for her. I was looking over the list my paralegal had made of every document or other item contained in the three file boxes that Wilcox had sent over.

"No interview notes yet," I said. "Just the *Brady* materials they've gotten so far, one folder that Rachel called 'miscellaneous media,' and a few of the investigative reports. Autopsy, crime scene, and so forth."

"Huh," Terri said, without looking up. She was engrossed in her work.

"Records of all the 911 calls from right after he was found," I said, flipping through the lists of numbers and call transcripts. "Man, there were a ton."

"Sure, with that many people on the scene, there would be."

I knew we wouldn't be getting any records of FBI witness interviews and statements until much closer to trial—maybe not even until it started. As a matter of pure common sense, the rules of criminal procedure didn't let defendants find out who was planning to narc on them until it was almost too late to prevent it.

What we did get early on, besides investigative reports, was copies of any exculpatory evidence the prosecution had—that is, evidence that tended to show my guy didn't commit the crime. Those were called *Brady* materials, after an old Supreme Court case. I was pleased to see that Wilcox seemed to define *Brady* materials pretty broadly. For instance, he didn't necessarily have to give me the lists that the FBI had made identifying everyone who was in the courthouse on the day Nicholson died, but he had included those. It made some sense to see that information as exculpatory. Every person in the courthouse that morning—or, at least, every person who wasn't under guard or stuck in a courtroom the whole time—was potentially a suspect. Knowing who they were would help me figure out who else might have committed the crime.

But the single-spaced list of their names and addresses was six pages long. Like Terri had said before, there had been over two hundred people there that day. The list didn't even say which floor of the courthouse each person had been on. It would require a ridiculous amount of legwork, far beyond what the Baptistes could afford, to investigate them all.

I put the list away and went to make coffee. When Terri was done with her transcribing, we could compare the list to Shannon's notes and see if we could narrow the pool down.

———

When I was halfway done with my coffee, Terri said, "Check this out! In his opening statement, the solicitor mentioned a bunch of witnesses who were going to appear and said what they were going to testify to. He didn't name them, but get this."

She read from her laptop screen: 'Ladies and gentlemen, you will hear, blah blah blah… from a federal judge who was presiding over a civil case involving Mr. Ludlow's real estate company—'"

"He has a real estate company?"

"You know how rich men are. They put their money in a lot of different baskets. Any idea what case that was?"

"No. I wonder why a real estate case ended up in federal court. I'll look on Westlaw, or PACER if I have to."

Legal databases had replaced law firm libraries early in my career. The one called PACER was a little clumsy to use, but it contained just about every document filed in every federal court case in the country.

"Sure. Anyway," she went on, "he told the jury that this judge who was going to testify would tell them Ludlow threatened him with blackmail if he didn't rule in Ludlow's favor." She looked up at me, eyes wide.

"Blackmail? Over a real estate case?"

"You think Ludlow wouldn't blackmail somebody to protect a big pile of his money?"

"No, if it was big enough, he absolutely would. Still, it's a little bold, isn't it, to try and blackmail a federal judge who's not even from South Carolina? Folks down here know what the Ludlow family can do to you, so a lot of us would fold right away. But Nicholson? That's a high-risk target."

"Yeah, that could go bad for him real fast."

"And I guess it did," I said, "if Nicholson was going to testify. But I'm curious what he had on Nicholson."

"Mm-hmm. It must've been pretty bad." She sat back, yawned, and rubbed her face. "Man, I'm too tired for this right now. I've got to get going."

"You'll be safe?"

She nodded. "I'm fine."

There'd been a time when I would've asked her to text me to say she was home safe, but I didn't do that anymore. It'd been almost a year since she'd told me she was seeing somebody. I didn't know how that had progressed. I'd never even asked his name, and she'd never told me. I'd backed off from most anything that went beyond our professional relationship, because I didn't want to intrude. And also, there was something pathetic about it, when I pictured her writing texts to me under his watchful eye.

Despite her words, she was still sitting there, now with her arms crossed, looking at her laptop screen like she was having a silent argument with it. A second later, she gave in. "All right, I'm just going to finish transcribing this stupid opening statement. I'm getting the hang of her shorthand, and there's only like two pages left."

She went back to her work. I flipped through the file folders in the second box that Wilcox had sent. According to the list Rachel had made, this was where I'd find a handful of reports about Vinny Baptiste.

There was one identifying half of a thumbprint found on the stairwell door as his. That didn't worry me; it proved nothing. He was a maintenance man who worked all over the courthouse, touching surfaces all day long. He could've left that print anytime, not just on the day of Nicholson's death.

There was an FBI background check consistent with what Terri had told me: that he had no criminal record. He'd never even been caught speeding.

Then there was a manila folder with several two- or three-page documents in it. The first one was a printout of a CNN story from quite a while ago—I checked the date; the article was from 2010. The headline said, "Manhunt Nabs Suspect in CEO Murder."

I remembered that. Some kid—the article said he was twenty-two at the time—had ambushed the CEO of a health insurance company outside of his Dallas headquarters and shot him dead. The killer was a good-looking kid whose name, the caption on his photo reminded me, was Primo Marconi. I flipped through the next couple of documents in the folder, scanning them to figure out what this stuff was doing in this box.

Four articles in, a more detailed story gave me the answer. "Jesus. Terri."

She looked up at me, concerned. "What?"

I slid the folder across the table, shaking my head. "You remember this?"

She looked down at the first article. "Oh, yeah. That was a hell of a thing, wasn't it."

"It was, yeah. And the reason Wilcox included that stuff is because that kid there, the killer, was Vinny Baptiste's big brother. Half brother."

"What?" She stared at me, then back at his photo. "Are you kidding me? How did I miss that? I ran good searches! Leland, I am so— I don't know how that happened. I'm so sorry."

I shrugged. "There's nothing to apologize for," I said. "The FBI's got databases that you don't have. And that kid's got a different last name —different dad, I guess. Doesn't look much like Vinny either. His dad must not have been Black. And that whole thing happened in a different state that must be, what, two thousand miles from Pittsburgh?"

"Yeah, but still. Jesus. I remember that whole thing. Didn't he get killed in prison?"

"Yeah, not too long after he was sentenced. And the reason these articles are in this box that Wilcox sent over is because the Texas prosecutor at the time, who got him put in prison, was—"

I leaned across the table, flipped to the page where his name was and pointed to it.

"Frederick J. Nicholson."

## 8

## JANUARY 9, 2024

Charleston Technical College, which Cameron Leary had attended until he was expelled shortly after his arrest, was a small campus whose main building—quaint, red brick, ivy climbing the sides—overlooked an artificial lake. Half a dozen modern buildings made up the rest of the school.

As I pulled into a parking spot, Vinny came to mind. I'd spoken to him briefly the previous week, and since then he'd left me a voicemail that I hadn't responded to. I'd been focusing on the Leary case, partly because we had deadlines coming up and partly because the revelation about Vinny's brother had put me in a tight spot. Maybe I *was* representing a callous killer. Maybe I was stuck.

As Noah and I walked to our appointment on campus, I finished up the conversation we'd been having in the car about Ludlow.

"So just humor me," I said. "Okay?"

"Sure. But I'm not that easy to find. I never told Brandon my address, and I'm not on my company's website—none of the PIs are."

"That makes sense. But still, keep your door locked."

"I always do. Man, do you think I learned *nothing*, growing up with you?"

I laughed. "Fair point." I glanced up at a sign we were approaching; we were going the right way. "Okay, new topic. For practice, tell me your story again?"

"It's not a story," he said. "It's true: I got an associate's degree in criminal justice, and the other day I noticed that they've got a program here where if you've already got an associate's, you can get a bachelor's in information technology in only two years."

I smiled. "Yeah, that part is true."

"There's no law that says I've got to actually apply for that program. I can just come for a visit, find out about it, and then change my mind."

I had wanted to get a look at the place where Cameron Leary had studied and worked. It was Noah's idea to get in by pretending that he wanted to study there and setting up a father-son tour. I couldn't tell him any more about Cameron's case than what had been in the news, but he knew that much, and he was outraged on Cameron's behalf. He'd taken a long lunch break from work to help out.

"You've nailed it," I told him. "You look like every other boy on this campus."

For added realism, after leaving work, he'd changed from his suit jacket and slacks into a T-shirt and knee-length cargo pants.

"It's perfect," I said, "except for the shoes."

He laughed. He'd forgotten to bring sneakers, Crocs, or similar student-bro footwear, so he had on the leather loafers he'd worn to work.

---

We toured the IT department alongside three other prospective students and their parents, checking out the classrooms in one of the generic concrete buildings. Noah asked smart questions about the campus Wi-Fi network and got a few answers, mixed in with sales pitches about the career prospects that five semesters at CTC would give him. I followed along, browsing the web on my phone.

While we were touring the student union, hearing about the twenty-four-hour gym and the discounts students got on laptops at the campus bookstore, I got an email from Terri. She'd read through the FBI reports that Wilcox had sent over in the discovery boxes and sent me her notes.

*2nd floor camera shows V going in that stairwell 11:52am, not coming out—must've come out on 3rd floor by broken camera.*

That was bad. I tried to think of another explanation for the lack of footage of Vinny coming out. The old stairwells also exited to the street, but I was pretty sure those doors had alarms on them.

I had some serious questions for Vinny, anyway.

I looked back at her email.

*Camera also shows V letting N and clerk into stairs together, 2nd floor, but she came out 5 mins later. Overall confirms their story. N's phone shows doing steps for 11 mins. Traces of his suit fabric on banister between floors 2-3, so fall was about 28 feet. Autopsy says landed on head/shoulders first. Subpoena phone company for full details re his phone?*

I forwarded her email to Rachel, asking her to work with Terri to put together a subpoena.

Then I caught up with Noah and the others. They were gathered near a plate-glass window, looking out at the college's tennis courts. A few healthy young people were hitting yellow-green balls back and forth down below, and the tour guide had obviously stopped there for a reason: it was the prettiest view of the campus we'd seen so far. This was the picture postcard we were supposed to remember when we were making the final decision on which schools to apply to.

Noah and most of the others were smiling. I tried to put myself back in that mindset—to forget about Nicholson falling to his death, as well as the darkness that became visible in middle age. I watched the slim, tanned tennis players and tried to see the world as it looked to college kids, when everyone was healthy and gorgeous and every day was another opportunity to flourish.

The guide took us back downstairs and directed us to the administration building, where each student had their own appointment with financial aid. As we walked over, Noah held his phone up to me.

"See that?" he said. "I'm on the campus network right now. Like he said, it's public. No password needed."

"They still haven't changed that?"

"I guess not."

---

The financial aid office, where Cameron had worked and where he'd hidden his laptop in his desk to let it run the code he'd written to hack into the system, was a fluorescent-lit open-plan space with eight or ten cubicles facing the waiting area. I paced around, listening for our turn and pretending to scroll through my phone. I was actually taking photos of the place so that I could look over them with Cameron and figure out what had happened where.

When Noah's name was called, we went over for our chat with an advisor. She was a fiftysomething Black lady, heavyset and friendly, with a nice smile. Her desk was decorated with family photos and several plants, small succulents with Bible verses printed in a windswept cursive on the pots.

After she'd chatted with Noah for a minute, she looked at me and said, "My goodness, aren't you lucky—you've got yourself a very hardworking young man here!"

"Why, thank you," I said. I glanced at the name tag on her ample bosom and added, "That's real kind of you, Miss Cherie."

"You're very welcome. And it puts him in a whole different category for loans and grants. Because he's lived on his own and supported himself for more than a year, we don't have to look at your income at all. He'll be evaluated just on his own income, which, generally, that's a lot more favorable."

She looked so happy for us that I felt a little guilty about our ruse.

"Well, isn't that great," I said. I didn't want to keep lying to this perfectly nice lady, so I turned to Noah. "You know what, you're a grown man now. Sounds like you won't even need my say-so on this. I'll leave you to it."

While they spoke, I wandered around the waiting area some more, taking a few more surreptitious photos.

I noticed a sign for the restrooms toward the back of the office, near a desk that was standing against a wall all by itself, without a cubicle. It looked like the setup that Cameron had described himself working at. To get a better image of it, I walked to the men's room with my video running the whole way.

Afterward, I drove Noah back to work, stopping at a Starbucks to get us both coffee while he went to the restroom to put his work clothes back on.

---

On my way home, I swung by Mrs. Baptiste's house to meet her in person. She lived in a white cottage in the next town up the coast from Basking Rock.

As she opened her red front door, I was hit with a smell of garlic and onions that reminded me I hadn't had lunch. Mrs. Baptiste was short and heavy, and she was wearing an apron, which she wiped her hands on as she invited me in.

"You're early," she scolded.

"I'm real sorry." I was pretty sure I wasn't early, but it seemed rude to check my watch. "I can let you finish cooking and come back—"

"No, come in, come in. You'll have to watch me cook, though."

"That's just fine. It smells wonderful."

She led me through a small, dark living room cluttered with knickknacks. It reminded me of my grandparents' house, except that instead of the plain wooden cross they'd had on their wall, Mrs. Baptiste's was ornate, with a finely carved and painted statuette of Jesus on it.

As we passed by it, heading for the kitchen doorway, I said, "Mrs. Baptiste, can I ask, did y'all raise Vinny in the Catholic church?" It wasn't a question I would've asked socially, but with any new client, I needed to gather as much background information as I could.

She stopped walking, turned, and looked at me like I'd just asked whether, by any chance, the Pope might be Catholic. It was the same *What are you, stupid?* expression I'd seen on Vinny's face.

"I'm Italian, born in Italy," she said, with a shrug that rippled all the way down her arms. "And Vinny's father was from Haiti. So what do you think?"

I smiled. "Sorry, I just wanted to make sure."

She made a dismissive noise and turned to head into the kitchen. I followed her.

"Can I ask, what's Vinny's relationship with his father like?"

"It was good. Not... *strong*, you know? Not like Vinny and me—a mother and son, it's special—but good enough. He died five years ago, though. Heart attack."

"I'm sorry. That must've been hard."

She shrugged. "Life's hard."

In the kitchen, eight or ten pans sat in the sink and on the counter beside it. She gestured me to a seat at the round Formica table, picked up a wooden spoon, and stirred whatever was in the big pot on the stove. I wondered who she was cooking for.

"So you were born in Italy, huh? But raised in Pittsburgh, or—"

"Yeah, from when I was seven, in Little Italy. It's a neighborhood there."

"Interesting." I wasn't sure what to make of the faint bitterness that had appeared in her voice when she talked about Pittsburgh. "Anyway, so, I talked to Vinny last week," I said. "He's doing okay, under the circumstances."

"I know," she said, tapping her spoon on the side of the pan. "I saw him yesterday. I go over most days."

"Oh, good. That'll help keep his spirits up."

"You know what'd keep his spirits up better, Mr. Munroe? If you got him out of jail. I was all ready to pay his bail. Went to the bank and everything."

"I did my best, Mrs. Baptiste, but it's up to the judge, and most of them won't grant bail in a murder case."

"*Murder* case." She dismissed that silliness with a wave of her hand and set a heavy lid onto the pot. "Vinny didn't murder anybody."

"Well, good." There wasn't much else to say to that.

"You want coffee?"

"Sure, thanks."

She trundled across the kitchen, took a beat-up silver espresso pot off the counter, and started unscrewing it.

"If you'd have got him out of jail," she said, "I told him, 'We'll just go to Italy.'"

In case I'd misheard her, I asked, "You'd go to Italy?"

Filling the bottom of the espresso pot with water, she said, "Yeah, forget all this. Get out of here. Why stay? I'm Italian from birth, so he's Italian too. We already got him his passport there, five or six years ago."

I was glad that hadn't come up during the bail hearing, although I supposed it would only have reduced Vinny's chance of getting bail from about 2 percent to zero.

To stop her from implicating her son in a plan to flee the jurisdiction, I changed the subject. "What is that you're cooking? It smells amazing."

"Busiate with shrimp and tomatoes. You got here too early for me to feed you," she said, filling the espresso pot's basket with ground coffee. "You should've come later."

"Yes, I wish I had."

"This is all for Vincenzo," she said, gesturing to the sink full of dishes and the food on the stove. I noticed the oven was on too. "I got a big freezer in the basement. I'm putting it there so he can eat it when he comes home."

I was glad, suddenly, that I'd arrived too early for her to feed me. Privately, I wasn't confident that her son was innocent. If I ever got to the point where I was convinced of that, maybe then I'd have the right to eat her food.

She put the coffee pot on the stove and said, "You want to see his room?"

"Sure. Does he still live with you?"

"Yeah. He's saving up. And he likes to help his mother out."

She took me across the house, down a hallway, and into an impeccably organized room with a tightly made twin bed. After the clutter of the kitchen and living room, it was like entering a different country.

"He a big reader?" I asked, looking at the tall bookshelf beside the window on the far wall.

"Oh, yeah. Reading and lifting weights, that's all he does. Go look at that. See what my son reads."

There was pride in her voice. I walked over and scanned the spines on the shelf at eye level. I couldn't understand them. "He can read Italian?"

"And he's learning Latin too. He's real proud of his heritage. Look at that."

She crossed the room, pulled a blue paperback off a shelf, and handed it to me. The cover said *Learn Latin with Cicero On Duties 1*. I flipped it open. On each page, the languages alternated: a paragraph of Latin, then English, back and forth. The part I looked at was talking about Socrates and Plato.

I stared at the thing in my hand, taking it in.

"Mrs. Baptiste," I finally said, "why's your son a courthouse janitor?"

She glared. "It's a good, honest job!"

"Absolutely, Mrs. Baptiste, yes, it is. My own mother cleaned houses for a living. I've got nothing but respect for that—"

"So why'd you ask that way?"

"Well… for one thing, my mother didn't speak other languages. I just meant—"

"What, is somebody going to pay him to sit around learning this stuff? Reading Cicero? Is that a job you can go get someplace?"

I couldn't help but smile. "No, I guess it's not."

She gave an eloquent shrug. If shrugs could speak, hers would've said *I rest my case.*

"He clocks in, does his work, clocks out at five," she said. "Comes home and…" She gestured to the bookcase. "This and the weights he set up in the basement, that's all he does. He say he wish he can be a cross between this…" She gestured at the bookshelf. "This Marcus Aurelius and Cicero, and then on the other side, Toussaint Louverture and that Dumas guy."

"Touss… sorry, who?"

"You know, the Haitian guy? A big, important general. Black, of course. Led some revolt to free the slaves. And Dumas, he's another Haitian general. His son wrote this book. It's real famous." She pulled a book off a lower shelf: *The Three Musketeers.*

"What? Wow."

"You don't know this?"

"No."

"You Americans. You don't know history." I had to laugh. She had a point.

"Seems like Vinny looks up to a lot of military men," I said, wondering if I could weave that theme into my opening statement. "He ever think about joining the military?"

"Oh, no." She gave a dismissive hand wave. "I mean, he thought about it, but he's all I got. He can't go die in… Iraq, Afghanistan, wherever they send them to die now."

I nodded.

"But he's doing good," she added. "At work, he earns sixteen dollars an hour, plus benefits."

"Sounds like it," I said. I'd noticed she was using the present tense, as if he still had that job and those benefits. Like most of the good mothers I'd ever met, she wasn't about to give up hope for her child.

I looked back at the bookshelf, scanning the authors' names this time, since most of the titles were in languages I couldn't read. Marcus Aurelius, one said. Julius Caesar.

"I guess when he told me about that boot camp thing he was doing," I said, "I assumed he was more of a tech guy."

"Oh, no. I mean, he likes that just fine, but the way he explained it to me was, the courthouse hires IT people, too, and they earn twice as much. And sometimes they can even read at their desk."

I came across a title that was in English. *The Stoic Life: Emotions, Duties, and Fate*. I pulled it off the shelf. It seemed to be some sort of guide on how to live right, based on a system of ethics from ancient Rome.

In law school, it had been drummed into us that character propensity evidence—in other words, evidence that tended to show someone was or was not the type who would commit the crime charged—was illegitimate. It wasn't admissible. It wasn't reliable. Officially, there was no such thing as a type of person who was likely to commit a certain crime.

That was why even evidence that the person had committed the same crime in the past wasn't admissible. The mere fact that a man had committed homicide or child molestation once, for instance, was not evidence that he'd done it on the occasion in question.

I'd known enough people, however, to know that there was such a thing as character propensity. Certain types of people did tend to commit certain types of crime. There were violent people and nonviolent ones. Principled people and greedy ones who'd do anything for a buck. Sadists and folks who carefully moved bugs out of their homes rather than stomping on them.

And I knew that you couldn't always tell. Some people were more complicated than others; they had sides you couldn't see.

Still, standing in Vinny's spartan bedroom, looking at these books, I couldn't square the man who'd lived here with the crime he'd been accused of committing.

# 9

# FEBRUARY 9, 2024

After canceling the meeting we were supposed to have about the Baptiste case in late January, Wilcox had called to reschedule for 10 a.m. on the ninth. I drove up and parked a few blocks from the United States' Attorney's Office, where he worked. It was sunny out, with fast-moving clouds, and warm enough that after a block I had to unbutton my blazer.

I was planning on visiting Vinny in jail afterward. I hadn't seen him since before the New Year—or really, since shortly before finding out about the connection between his brother and Nicholson. I'd been rationalizing that by telling myself that avoiding him would leave me conveniently unable to answer any questions that Wilcox might throw at me. "I'll have to check with my client and get back to you" was a time-honored escape valve for lawyers to get out of tricky conversations with opposing counsel.

But as I walked, I had to admit that that wasn't the reason I'd barely talked to Vinny over the past few weeks. The reason I was steering clear was that I couldn't get a read on who he was. He hadn't told me one word about his brother or the Nicholson connection. He was smart as hell; he had to know that that information mattered. I still had that double vision: thoughtful, quiet genius? Or snake in the grass? Or both?

I thought I knew a lot about people. Thought I was a good judge of character. But I'd never met a genius janitor before. I wasn't sure how much of what I'd learned by paying attention to normal people, and normal criminals, was applicable to him. And I couldn't get the answers I needed from a phone call. I needed to see his face.

Wilcox's office building was at the edge of the French Quarter, but apparently nobody had told the architect that. It was a generic box with none of the neighborhood's usual charm. It looked like the type of building where you might find a couple of dentists' offices and one of the less busy FedEx locations. Inside, though, the metal detector, X-ray machine, and phalanx of federal marshals made it clear that there was more to the place than that.

Wilcox's office was down the hall from the gray-on-gray modern waiting room. A secretary walked me over to it. I'd visited Cardozo there enough times to know that the lawyers usually came out to get their guests themselves, so I suspected that not doing so might be a power move on Wilcox's part. When she showed me into his office, though, I realized I was wrong. A pair of crutches leaned against the low barrister's bookshelf behind his enormous, antique-looking desk.

"Morning, Mr. Munroe." He gestured to a chair. On the wall above him was a large painting in a gold frame, which I vaguely recognized: George Washington up on a little stage before thirty or forty men in eighteenth-century finery, all gathered for the signing of the Constitution of the United States.

"Morning, Mr. Wilcox." I didn't offer my first name. From the way he'd set up his surroundings, I figured he'd prefer formality. As I took my seat, I noticed a full-sized grandfather clock standing on a fine old rug. I was glad I'd come into town instead of doing this meeting remotely. Seeing the effort Wilcox had put into giving the patina of centuries to a drop-ceilinged room in a 1980s office building, I had a better sense of who I was dealing with. "Quite a fine clock you've got there."

"Thank you. Yeah, that came down in my family, on the Calhoun side."

"Well, that's real nice." I wondered if one of the men wearing satin breeches in that painting behind him was a Calhoun. There'd been a vice president by that name around that point in time. I kept my mouth shut about the fact that the only thing that had come down in my family was my daddy's 1968 Oldsmobile. It had sat, with cinder blocks where the wheels should've been, in our front yard for my entire childhood, waiting in case Daddy came back.

"I'm sure you're a busy man," Wilcox said, "and I'm sure you've reviewed the discovery I sent over, so let me get straight to the point. I've charged this as first-degree murder, because that's what I believe it was. However, in the interest of sparing Judge Nicholson's family the pain of having to go through a trial, hearing all over again what happened to him and seeing some terrible photos, my office is prepared to offer second-degree murder and to recommend a thirty-year sentence."

I nodded, taking that in. It was obviously far better than a death sentence, and also better than the maximum sentence for second-degree federal murder—which was life in prison.

Still, there was no explaining to a man in his twenties that a sentence longer than he'd been alive was, all things considered, a decent deal.

I broke the few seconds of silence with a question. "Mr. Wilcox, would you be able to tell me what all you think really happened here? I'd appreciate that very much."

He chuckled. "It's funny, you know, that I can't ask you the same question."

I smiled. We operated under different sets of rules: I had a client whose confidences I was bound to keep, and he didn't. Of course, Vinny's confidences had told me nothing about what happened to Nicholson, but even if I could say so, Wilcox wouldn't have believed me.

With a shrug, I said, "Well, we didn't write the rules, did we." I glanced up at the painting. "Those who came before us wrote them, and we've just got to follow them."

"Yes, we do," he agreed.

"And I've got to put your offer in context for a man who's at least twenty years younger than either of us. I find that easier to do when I can explain to him how things look from where you're sitting."

He nodded like that was a fair point. "Well, I'll tell you what." He leaned back, rested his hands on his stomach, and looked out the window. After a couple seconds, he turned back to me and said, "It was a while back now, but I can't think of any place to start but the start. So here's how it looks to me: twelve years ago, your client was fifteen or sixteen years old, with a big brother he'd grown up with. Or half-brother. And I'm probably putting my own experience onto this, but I imagine, like any brothers, they fought sometimes, but they had each other's back, and the younger one looked up to the older boy."

I nodded like that checked out, although I had no idea of what Vinny's reality had been.

"But then his big brother…" He searched for the words and decided on "had a breakdown of some kind. And he went off and did what he did, which, from what I've seen, was totally unexpected—he had no prior criminal record. He seemed to be doing okay, and then out of the blue, he takes a bus across the country and he murders this man."

"I remember it. I mean, I'd forgotten, but it came back to me."

"Of course. It was a big headline. So he does that, anyway, and he gets caught, because he's not well and he's not making good decisions at all, obviously. And Judge Nicholson, in his previous incarnation as a Texas state prosecutor, goes full steam ahead: no plea offer, pushes real hard against the inevitable insanity defense—"

"Oh, did he?"

"He did. Not that a Texas jury would've necessarily bought that defense, anyway."

"No, I suppose that's a hard sell down there."

"Like it is here, although maybe even more so. Anyway, as a result, your client's big brother got sent to prison instead of to a mental hospital, and there he died, less than a year later." He sat back, arms crossed, as if he was done with his story.

I gave him a second and then asked, "And then what happened down in Basking Rock?"

He looked like that was self-evident, but spelled it out in case I'd somehow missed it: "A grudge met with an opportunity for revenge."

To kick the tires of his theory, I said, "Speaking of who might've had a grudge against the victim, do you happen to know what Judge Nicholson was planning to testify to in the Ludlow trial?"

With a mild smile, he said, "Well, I wasn't prosecuting that one, of course."

He hadn't said no. I found that interesting.

I remembered that it had been his office that had originally pursued charges against Ludlow, almost three years ago. They'd gone after him for a year or so and then withdrawn the charges. It had never been clear to me why the feds had done that, leaving the state to indict Ludlow instead.

Wilcox was pushing sixty. He'd been a prosecutor in the United States Attorney's Office for thirty-odd years. He had to know why the USAO had backed off of Ludlow. And if Judge Nicholson's utility as a witness had been apparent when the feds were investigating Ludlow, Wilcox would've known about that too.

But he wasn't going to tell me.

"Anyway, I can understand why you'd see my client as having a grudge," I said. "But where do you see the opportunity coming in? Are you saying Judge Nicholson walked into the Basking Rock courthouse that morning and my client just happened to recognize him? And decided to kill him then and there?"

He gave a microshrug, looking unconcerned.

I got the sense that the ball, in his view, was in my court.

"Well, obviously," he said, "there's a couple of different ways that could've happened. And, ultimately, as I'm sure you recall, don't we have to go with the one we've got the best chance of proving?"

"You do, yes."

He nodded. "So why don't you take that all back to your client and explain it to him. You know how it works. You've been behind my desk before, at the state level."

I appreciated the way he'd put that. He was respecting my seventeen years as a state prosecutor, instead of focusing on the shameful way that part of my career had ended.

"That is indeed how it works," I said.

"So tell him. Information has a price, and it's measured in years." Years off the sentence, in other words.

I agreed, thanked him for his time, and stood to go.

"You'll understand if I don't get up," he said, gesturing toward his crutches.

"Of course. I hope that didn't put too much of a damper on your holidays."

"Oh, it did. We went out to Vail over Christmas, and I took a fall on the slopes. Had to have surgery when I got back."

"Oof. That's rough."

"Indeed. But it is what it is."

I agreed, said goodbye, and left the USAO the same way I'd come in, avoiding the hallway Cardozo's office was on. I didn't want to tarnish his reputation among his colleagues. To have any member of the defense bar stop by for a social chat was bad enough, and my tainted reputation—which I suspected every lawyer in Charleston knew about—could only make that worse.

I rode the elevator back down to the street in a state of high excitement. A big part of the puzzle of this case had come together, and with that much done, I might be able to get Vinny to fill in the rest.

Wilcox, I realized, probably had made the same assumption I had: that Ludlow had to be behind this thing. He fully believed that Vinny Baptiste had committed the crime. That much was clear. But he didn't believe that an old, deep grudge had made Vinny Baptiste concoct a murder plot out of the blue one Friday morning in November.

And I didn't think so either. Whatever Vinny might be capable of, I didn't think he'd move that fast. He watched people, and he was smart. He was organized. He made plans.

What Wilcox seemed to think—and maybe he was right—was that Vinny's grudge had made him an easy target for Ludlow to recruit.

Find somebody with a grudge, point out an opportunity for revenge, and pay him a lot of money to do it; that was a solid formula. It often worked pretty well. And I figured Wilcox thought that was the most likely explanation here.

But he couldn't prove it. And unless we provided the intel that he'd need to go after Ludlow, he was going to prosecute the case on the theory that Vinny had acted alone. That way, he could put at least one of the responsible parties behind bars.

That was not okay with me. If that was what had happened, we needed to bring down the masterminds. They were more dangerous. And they could be dangerous for me and for my son.

I got back to my car and headed over to the prison. Whatever Vinny knew, if anything, the time to tell me was now.

---

In another white, windowless room, smaller than the one where Terri and I had talked to him, I met with Vinny again. He didn't look so good this time. I could tell he'd been in a fight, so I started there instead of going off on him about why he hadn't told me about his brother's connection to Nicholson. "What's with the black eye?"

He shrugged. "Lot of angry guys in here."

"I'm sure. You okay?"

"Yeah. I'm learning the rules." The acidic humor in his voice seemed like a good sign. I'd always thought humor was one of the best defenses against the curveballs that life sometimes threw right at your head.

"What rules have you learned?"

"Probably the main one is, don't go quoting Cicero to prisoners."

I laughed out loud. "Not the right crowd for that?"

"No. I might try Marcus Aurelius next, if I want this eye to match." He pointed to his unblemished right eye.

"I wouldn't recommend that."

"Yeah. But can you bring me any of my books?"

I shook my head. "Nobody can bring you books. Or mail you anything besides a letter. They're afraid of contraband."

"For real? All I can read is what's in the prison library? It's all, like, action novels and books about the Bible and…" He waved a hand, dismissing the rest as not even worth mentioning.

"No. You're allowed to have your own books, but they have to be new copies shipped straight from the bookstore to the prison."

He sighed.

I decided to get down to business. We didn't have unlimited time. "So, I met with Wilcox today. He offered a plea deal—"

"A plea? As in pleading guilty?" He sounded like he'd never thought it would come to this. His horror at the situation was quiet and deep.

"Yeah. Let me explain. He's charged you with first-degree murder, which can carry the death penalty, but so far he hasn't sought that. If he doesn't go that route, then the maximum sentence is life."

Before going on, I looked at him to make sure he understood. It seemed like he did. He was eerily calm. I thought he might be in shock.

"But he said that he's willing to drop it to second-degree murder, with a thirty-year sentence—"

That broke his calm. "But my mom will be— What's my mom going to *do*?"

I liked that his first thought was for her. "Listen," I said. "This was only his first offer—"

"How soon would I get out on parole?"

I wished I didn't have to get into that yet. "Well, there's no parole for federal crimes."

"No— What do you mean, no parole?"

"Congress abolished it I don't know how long ago. Thirty or forty years. But there is time off for good behavior. Every year of good behavior cuts fifty-four days off your sentence, so thirty years could come down to around twenty-five."

Almost whispering, he echoed, "Twenty-five."

"Yeah, but…"

I was going to let him know that he could get a better offer if he gave Wilcox information that helped trap Ludlow, but then another approach occurred to me—one that wouldn't open up a discussion of whether he'd committed the crime.

"When I was talking to Wilcox," I said, "something came up that I'm sure is hard to talk about, but I wish I'd found it out from you instead of him. He told me about your brother. Primo?"

He broke eye contact.

I gave him a minute.

When he spoke again, he still hadn't looked at me. "That's the gift that keeps on giving, I guess." He let out a small, bitter laugh.

"How do you mean?"

"How do I *mean*?" He looked at me like I was being unbelievably stupid again. "You read up on what he did, right? It was in the news."

I nodded.

"Okay. So he about killed my mom. She was forty-six years old, and she had a heart attack because of him. She had to leave her job because of all the publicity, and then she couldn't find another one. We moved down here, because back in Pittsburgh, we were *those* people. *That* family."

"That's hard."

"Yeah. And all that happened because Primo couldn't deal with his shit. He didn't have the courage."

I shook my head. I'd pulled Primo's case up on the web that morning and been reminded that he'd lost his father to cancer after their insurer refused to cover the cost of some last-ditch treatment that might have saved his life. After that, he fell apart. Quit his job, holed up in his apartment. A few months later, he hunted down the insurance company's CEO and took him out as the guy was heading from the gym to work.

Vinny was getting angrier with every sentence. "If he could've thought about anybody besides himself… I know he had it hard, but it's like he thought life wasn't *supposed* to be hard. Like, when has it ever *not* been?"

I had to remind myself how young Vinny was. I'd met plenty of folks twice his age who still hadn't figured out that they weren't entitled to spend life drinking margaritas on the beach. "You were still in high school when all that happened, right?"

"Ninth grade, man. And then tenth grade when he died. Fifteen years old, and all of a sudden, because of him, I'm all my mom's got left." He lurched out of his chair so fast it fell over, and he started pacing the room. I could almost feel the heat coming off him. "He cracked up. If I could never say his name again for the rest of my life, that'd be nice. But here he comes again, man. Here he comes."

For a few months or a year after committing murder, Primo had been a folk hero. He'd given voice to a rage against the insurance machine that millions of Americans shared.

But it didn't sound like he was any kind of hero to his little brother.

Vinny had stopped, over in a corner of the room. I could hear from his breathing that he was trying to calm down.

"Listen, Vinny," I said. "I know this is rough, but I've got to ask you some questions."

"Yeah, yeah."

"And I don't want to have to chase you around the room…"

I wanted him up close. I wanted to see the answers to my questions on his face.

"Whatever." He turned and came back to the table.

"So. Tell me what happened with your brother."

"You know the story, don't you? Don't tell me you didn't see it in the news."

"Yeah, I saw it. But I don't want some reporter's take on it. I want yours."

His jaw clenched, and he shifted in his seat.

Then he seemed to decide what the hell, might as well spell it out.

"He grew up kind of without his dad. I had a dad, he mostly didn't. Then his dad came back into his life, I don't know how, exactly, and they were getting to know each other. Which was good, I was glad he got to have that. But then his dad got diagnosed, some kind of cancer. He didn't tell me too much about what was going on—I mean, I was like, fourteen, and he was a grown man."

"Was he up there in Pittsburgh with you?"

"Yeah, his dad came back to town. Maybe for treatment, I don't know. Primo had him move into his apartment. He was taking him to appointments and everything. And then it got worse, I guess, and he didn't make it. You know the rest. It was in the papers."

"Primo tracked down the insurance guy?"

"Yeah. He lost his dad, so he went and made sure somebody else lost theirs too. I don't know." He spat the words out like they tasted bad.

To see how it landed with him, I said, "I remember, it seemed like for some people, Primo was kind of a hero."

"That's bullshit!"

"You don't buy that?"

"*Buy* that? Buy that a hero is somebody who takes a Greyhound bus to Dallas to hunt down some dude he never met? Because his *dad* died? People die! Get used to it! Man up!"

"I hear you," I said. "How old were you when your dad passed?" I knew the answer—it was in Terri's report—but I wanted to hear how he talked about it.

"Twenty-three. Five years ago this past Christmas."

"Tough time to lose a father."

"It's always a tough time. If you like him, anyway."

"Yep."

"Notice how I didn't get on a bus and go kill nobody, though?"

I couldn't help but smile. I was a big fan of humor in dark moments. Especially humor that had some bite. "Yeah, I noticed. More power to you."

I sat back in my chair and looked at him for a second. Nothing in what he was saying, or in the way he was saying it, fit with Wilcox's theory that he wanted Nicholson dead to avenge his brother's death.

I wasn't sure yet that Wilcox was wrong, but it didn't match what I knew. As a prosecutor, I'd worked on cases where somebody had murdered the person responsible for their loved one's death. Those people didn't talk like this. I'd never heard any of them ranting about the bad choices that their dead loved one had made.

But if Wilcox was wrong about the motive here, the only way I could convey that to a jury would be to put Vinny on the stand. Which meant I needed to get a better sense of how he'd come across. How he'd answer hardball questions like the ones he'd get from Wilcox.

"Vinny," I said, "I know Primo died in prison—"

He made a wordless sound that made me think his brother's death had eaten a hole in him, and it'd keep on eating deeper for the rest of Vinny's life.

"Whose fault was it that he died?" I asked.

"Whose *fault*? Himself! And the guy who killed him, obviously."

"Himself?"

"Yeah!" He spread his hands wide, palms up, like this could not be more obvious. "You go shoot somebody in Texas, what do you expect?"

"Uh-huh. What about the prosecutor?"

He winced like that was just one more pothole on a ruined road.

I leaned forward, put my elbows on the table, and said, "Listen, Vinny. Did you recognize Nicholson when you saw him that morning?"

I could tell from the hint of guilt on his face that he had, and that there was more to it.

"What— Did you know he was coming to the courthouse?" I said. "Before that day?"

"Yeah. Somebody told me, like, two weeks before."

"Who?"

"I don't know."

He looked absolutely genuine.

"You— How do you not know?"

"I got this freaking... *letter*? Like, in the *mail*." He said it the way Noah would have: as if letters sent by mail were some type of obscure ancient artifact.

"What'd it say?"

"It just— It was this, like, printout, of the judge's bio. And it had handwriting on it that said—I forget the exact words, but it was something about how he was coming to testify the week of... whatever week it was. Middle of November. And then the part of his bio where it said he used to be a prosecutor in Texas was, like, highlighted." He mimed the stroke of a highlighter across a piece of paper.

I couldn't believe it. I wondered if some *CSI*-style miracle might help crack this case. Handwriting analysis. A fingerprint. DNA in the saliva on the envelope flap.

"Where'd you put that letter?" I said. "Can I get it from your mom?"

He shrugged. "No, it was too freaking weird, man. I threw it away."

## 10

## MARCH 6, 2024

It was a sunny morning, 9 a.m., but when I turned onto the dirt road that led to the address Raylene had given me, the trees on either side were so gnarled and huge that they met overhead and covered everything in shadow.

A few days earlier, Vinny's coworker had finally agreed to talk to me. It was the second time I'd showed up while she was working. The first time, I'd seen her mopping a hallway on the second floor of the courthouse. She didn't give me the *back off* hand gesture that she'd used with Terri, but she made it clear that she didn't want to talk.

The second time, after walking the hallways and not finding her, I'd gone to the back corner of the courthouse where the maintenance office was. After I'd been loitering there for five minutes or so, she came out and scowled at the sight of me. She'd glanced behind her, making sure the office door was closed, and then hissed, "Sir, please don't come to my work!" She was a tired-looking White woman, midforties, so thin she looked malnourished.

"I need to talk to you," I'd said.

She'd stopped glaring at me and dropped her gaze to the stone-tiled floor. I'd had the sense that she was too tired to keep fighting. In an angry whisper, she told me her phone number. Then she dragged her yellow mop bucket around me and went on her way.

And now I was turning down the dirt road that she lived on. Fifty yards ahead, I saw the trailer she'd described on the phone. It was well kept, with a little wooden porch that the paint was starting to come off of. Pink paper hearts were hung in the front window, for Valentine's Day, I guessed.

The car in the driveway, a red Ford Escape, was a lot nicer than the house. It looked new.

I parked out front.

Raylene opened the door before I was up the steps and ushered me into her tiny living room. A baby about a year old was hanging onto the railing of its crib, practicing how to stand.

"Got my grandson here today," she said. "My daughter's at work."

"Cute kid. What's your daughter do?"

"Cashier."

"That's nice."

She gestured me to a chair but didn't ask if I wanted anything to drink. I didn't blame her. I was an intruder, not a guest.

As I sat, I said, "I don't want to take up too much of your time, Mrs. Andrews." I'd gotten her last name from Vinny so that I could be polite.

She shrugged like I was already wasting it. There was another chair, but she didn't sit. The baby started making a rhythmic singsong noise and bouncing up and down.

I went ahead and got started. "Can I ask, how long have you known Vinny Baptiste?"

"Since whenever I started working at the courthouse. Five years, I guess."

"And what do you think of him?"

She crossed her arms on her chest. "What do you *want* me to think?"

"I don't have a preference on that."

The baby's noise got quieter all of a sudden. I looked over. He was chewing on the railing of his crib. A line of drool dripped down the wood.

"If you put me up on that witness stand, you'll for sure hear what I think." She said it like a threat. I wondered if she realized that it wasn't up to me whether she was called to testify. She was the one who'd apparently seen Vinny take the stairwell key card and then ratted him out to the FBI. That made her a prosecution witness.

"Well, if you did go up and testify, what all might you say?"

"I ain't going up there, sir. Anyway, nothing you hear from me is going to help get him off."

Her vehemence about not testifying surprised me. The prosecutor ought to have told her he was likely going to call her, but with the trial not scheduled to start until late September, I supposed maybe it was a little early for him to have explained that.

I leaned back in the chair and said, "Well, it's my job to get him off, like you said, but I also have to figure out how likely that is. Which is why I'm here."

"That boy done lied to the FBI."

I squinted at her as if that idea were new to me. "Now, where'd you hear that?"

Her guard went up even higher than it was already. I looked away to give her a chance to relax. I smiled at the baby. He smiled back.

From where I was sitting, I could see Raylene's whole tiny kitchen. She didn't have a dishwasher. Unless they were tucked away someplace, she didn't even have a coffee maker or a toaster. But she had a new car in her driveway.

I looked back at her and said, as casually as I could, "Mrs. Andrews, how well did you know Solicitor Ludlow when he was working there?"

Her face froze. "That's got nothing to do with this," she said. "And the baby's got to go down for a nap now, so I think you need to leave."

———

Four hours later, I met the Learys in the lobby of the Charleston federal courthouse. Cameron was wearing another statement T-shirt—that habit of his hadn't changed—but the three of them were in much better spirits than the last time we'd been here. His dad shook my hand.

I'd negotiated a good deal for Cameron. In exchange for a guilty plea on two misdemeanors, LaRue had agreed to dismiss all of the felonies and not seek jail time. On the last felony, he'd agreed to a diversionary program—meaning that if Cameron could behave for the next year, LaRue would drop that charge and it would disappear from his record. We were there to complete the formalities for it.

In the war room upstairs, I took out the eight-page plea agreement that LaRue and I had hammered out and went over it with the Learys again. We'd already done that on a Zoom call, but I wanted to make sure everything was clear. Once it was, Cameron signed three copies of it: one for his own records, one for LaRue, and one for the judge.

He passed the copies over to me, and I signed them all with a flourish while he chatted excitedly about his education plans. Charleston Technical College didn't want him back, so he was looking at transferring to USC.

"That's a much better school," I said.

"I know! I thought the criminal charges and the whole expulsion thing would be a bigger problem than it was. I did have to talk to like four different people there and get a couple recommendation letters, but they said as long as it wasn't a felony, I was eligible."

"That's great."

A knock came on the door. It was LaRue. I handed him the documents, and he held them up against the wall outside so that he could add his own signature.

When that was done, I closed the door again and said, "Okay, Cameron. Just one more thing." I was looking at his T-shirt. It was black, with the word "Authoritarianism" inside a red circle with a slash through it.

"But—" he said.

"Cameron." I smiled. "I got you a good deal here. Could you just do me this one favor?"

"I don't have another shirt."

"My goodness." His mom sounded panicked. "Is this important? Should we go buy one somewhere?"

"Don't worry, Mrs. Leary," I said, swinging my briefcase up onto the table. "I heard this judge is a little old-school, so I came prepared."

The case had been reassigned to a judge emeritus who was about ninety years old and not a fan of informality. Monty had told me that. I'd reached out to him for intel, since I couldn't ask Cardozo for any type of guidance when it was his office prosecuting.

I unzipped my briefcase and pulled out a folded white shirt. "My son's about your size," I told Cameron.

He rolled his eyes. "Oh, come *on*! This is so ridiculous!"

"Go ahead and keep that T-shirt on underneath," I told him. "And you can take this back off the minute we leave the courtroom."

He shook his head in a good-natured way, acknowledging defeat, and put it on.

---

In the courtroom, Cameron hugged his mom, and she and his dad went to sit in the pews while the two of us went up to the defense table. LaRue was already at his table with the paperwork in front of him. I gave him a nod.

Proceedings began. Judge Asquith was tall and spry for his age. He recited the case caption and the statutes under which Cameron had been charged, speaking in an antique accent that had gone extinct soon after the advent of television. His white hair, with its sharp side part and sheen of pomade, looked like he'd gotten a haircut he liked in about 1955 and had seen no reason to ever try a different one.

I'd warned Cameron that Asquith might call him up to the stand. Most judges didn't do that at a plea hearing, but this one was of another era. Seeing Cameron up there, answering "Yes, Your Honor" when Asquith asked him if he understood the charges against him, I congratulated myself for having convinced him to put his antiauthoritarianism T-shirt out of sight.

"And do you understand, Mr. Leary, that the maximum penalty for each of the twenty-one charges against you under 18 United States Code section 1030(a)(2) is five years of imprisonment and a $5,000 fine?"

LaRue had charged Cameron with a separate felony for each of the accounts that he'd hacked into.

"Yes, Your Honor."

"And do you understand that the maximum penalty for the one charge under section 1030(a)(5)(B) is the same, namely, a five-year prison sentence and a $5,000 fine?"

"Yes, Your Honor."

That charge was the felony that LaRue had proposed a diversion deal on. It was for allegedly damaging the school's server by hacking into it. I had little doubt that I could've gotten that thrown out with a pretrial motion, since there'd been no quantifiable harm to the server, but resolving the whole mess on a plea deal spared Cameron the risk of a trial on the other charges.

"And do you understand that those penalties, if imposed, may run sequentially—that is, one after the other, for a total in this case of 110 years—and not concurrently?"

Cameron glanced at me. I gave him a micro-nod. He answered in the affirmative.

"And do you understand that by entering a guilty plea here today, you will be waiving your right to a trial by a jury of your peers?"

"Yes, Your Honor."

Asquith took several more minutes to make sure that Cameron understood all his rights and the possible consequences of his plea, and then he turned to face counsel. "All right," he said. "Now, pursuant to the

Due Process Act, I affirm that the government has a continuing obligation under *Brady v. Maryland* to produce all exculpatory evidence. Has that all been produced?"

LaRue jumped up and said, "It has, Your Honor."

"Mr. Munroe, any concerns in that regard?"

"None whatsoever, Your Honor."

"Okay." Asquith picked up his copy of the plea agreement. "Now, looking at this Memorandum of Plea Agreement that was handed up to me, which my clerk also printed out for me last night, and so I have read it, let me first get one point clarified: What provision of the rules is this being presented under?"

LaRue stood back up. "It's presented under Rule 11(c)(1)(B), Your Honor, of the Federal Rules of Criminal Procedure."

It was also being presented under Rule 11(c)(1)(A). I scribbled a note to myself to clarify that when it was my turn to speak. Monty had told me this judge was a stickler for precision.

"All right. So, in your view, Mr. LaRue, what is my role here under that rule?"

"Your Honor has two roles, one of which Your Honor has already begun to carry out, by addressing the defendant to determine that his plea is knowing and voluntary. And then also to apprise him that Your Honor is not bound by the sentencing recommendation of the United States."

Unlike plea bargains in state court, in federal court the judge usually had the discretion to tinker with whatever sentence the parties had agreed on.

"Okay. Now, does the applicable rule provide that I am to simply accept or reject this plea, as written?"

"It does not, Your Honor."

"Thank you. Now, Mr. LaRue, would my role be any different if you were presenting this plea agreement under either of the other subsections of Rule 11(c)?"

"Yes, there, Your Honor—and let me clarify, there is an element of this that's under Rule 11(c)(1)(A)."

"Yes, there is. I had noticed that. And I have no discretion on that element of it, am I right?"

"You are, Your Honor."

"And I evaluate that part under what's commonly called the interests of justice, correct?"

"Yes, Your Honor."

I almost felt bad for LaRue. Asquith was walking him through this like he thought LaRue was in need of a refresher on first-year criminal procedure.

"All right. And to ensure that it's clear on the record, what I'm looking at here on page four appears to be a diversion agreement on that felony charge we just spoke of, which was brought under section 1030(a)(5)(B)?"

LaRue confirmed that. The diversion agreement was the one part of our deal that was governed by Rule 11(c)(1)(A). Technically, it wasn't part of the plea deal; it was a stand-alone contract between Cameron and the feds.

"Now, as I read the indictment," Asquith said, "isn't that charge essentially duplicative of the twenty-one others?"

"Well, Your Honor, it does address the same actions on the defendant's part, but the purpose of that as a separate charge was to reflect the harm to the college's computer system."

"I see. And is that the harm referred to here in paragraph four of the diversion agreement?"

"It is, Your Honor."

"Okay. And it says here that that harm was assessed at $10,000. That seems to me a suspiciously round number. How was that valuation done?"

I kept my smile to myself. LaRue had insisted on putting that number in there, for no reason I could see other than to put something on paper that made the crime sound more serious. Even if Asquith was going a little overboard on the rules, that part of the deal had annoyed me, so I was going to enjoy watching LaRue get skewered for it.

He knew he was in trouble. "Well, Your Honor, given the difficulty of assessing precisely the, uh, monetary value of this type of damage, and in view of the need, or, I should say, the parties' wish, or counsels' wish, to avoid any unnecessary expenditures, such as the cost of engaging an appraiser or other expert in this type of valuation…"

He stumbled along in that vein for a few more sentences, until Asquith interrupted by asking me if I had agreed to the number.

To avoid throwing LaRue any farther under the bus than he already was, I said, "Your Honor, in the spirit of compromise, I believe each party made certain suggestions, and in order to resolve this case efficiently, wherever possible, the other party agreed to them."

"And was that $10,000 number one of Mr. LaRue's suggestions?"

"I believe it was, Your Honor."

It absolutely was, but I'd softened that point as much as I could. I knew I'd be up against LaRue again in future cases. Helping this judge humiliate him in open court would only make it harder for me to get my clients good deals in the future.

"Mr. LaRue," Asquith said, "does the United States government understand that before I enter judgment under a plea, I am obliged under Criminal Rule 11 to evaluate whether there is or is not a factual basis for that plea?"

This was getting out of hand.

"Yes, Your Honor," LaRue said. "It certainly does."

"That being the case, what was your factual basis for coming up with that number?"

"It, uh, the number is… what appeared to be reasonable, Your Honor, and proportional in light of the facts."

Asquith heaved a sigh and looked off toward an upper corner of the courtroom, shaking his head slightly, lost in thought. The look on his face was nostalgic, and something about his manner suggested that he was hearkening back to a bygone era when men were men and lawyers were not this stupid.

A few seconds later, he parachuted back into the year 2024 and said, "So, I'm of course not going to probe into the details of counsels' negotiations. However, it's apparent that what I have here is a plea deal where there's no factual basis for that $10,000 number. And the carelessness that's behind that choice of number, the flagrant disregard of your obligation to accurately present the facts, leads me to question the basis for any and all of the other factual assertions set forth elsewhere in this plea memorandum. So I'm going to have to say, this is not a deal that I can accept."

# 11

## MARCH 28, 2024

After three weeks of haggling, I left the latest meeting in LaRue's office and walked out into the sunshine, still without a deal. Unless I could somehow get all of the evidence tossed, every scrap of it, Cameron was going to trial on multiple felony charges. Transferring to USC wasn't going to happen. He was looking down the barrel of decades in federal prison.

I didn't know how the hell to tell him.

The big flowerpots all down Meeting Street were bright with tulips and daffodils. Their mindless cheerfulness bothered me. LaRue, as far as I could tell, was still angry about the way Asquith had treated him, and he was taking it out on me and my client because there was no way for him to take it out on the judge.

The fact that anyone would do that—play with a kid's life that way—instead of manning up and moving on from his mistake dimmed my view of the human race in general, and my profession in particular.

While I was standing at the corner of Queen Street waiting for the light, my phone rang. It was Cardozo. "I just got coffee in the kitchen and ran into LaRue," he said. "You *still* don't have a deal?"

"Nope."

The light changed, and I crossed, looking around to see if anybody was in earshot. Lunchtime was still more than an hour off, so there weren't too many people walking around. I jaywalked over to Washington Square, because the park was green and leafy and almost empty.

I told Cardozo why there was no deal. In fact, I unloaded my whole damn clip on his boss. If Cardozo now thought it was okay for us to talk about a case while his office was still prosecuting it, I figured I might as well say what I had to say.

After I finished, he was quiet for a long time.

"You know what," he finally said, "I think I'm done here. I've got a trial to wrap up, but then I may have to take Hannah up on that offer of hers."

"The soul-searching?" That term his wife had used made me crack a smile.

"Yeah, the soul-searching. Minus the searching, and the soul. All that's actually required is me walking out of here and not coming back."

---

When we got off the phone, I wanted coffee. There was a good café across from the federal courthouse on Broad Street, so I jaywalked back across and headed for it.

The aroma as I walked in did me good. The hiss of the espresso machines made it hard to think, which was nice too. Unlike most cafés, this one was full of men and women in pin-striped suits—being across from the courthouse, that's the crowd it attracted—so I fit right in.

I took a seat by the big front window and watched the steam rise off my coffee for a little while. That was as close as I ever got to meditation.

A basket of newspapers and magazines caught my eye. It had been a while since I'd read anything that wasn't on a computer screen or my phone. I went over, found a folded-up section of the Charleston *Post and Courier*, and sat back down. I scanned a few articles about new restaurants and bars—I'd grabbed the food section—and saw one I thought Noah might like. There was another one that looked good for a date, if I ever were to have a date. I took my phone out to snap photos of both articles.

As I did, a man said, "Leland! What brings you to town?"

I looked up. It was Monty, standing there in his navy pin-striped suit with a big to-go cup in his hand.

"Just work, as usual," I said. As politeness required, I added, "Want to sit down?"

He thought for a quarter second before saying, "You know what, sure."

I folded the paper up to make room for him. "How you been?"

He sat down and shrugged. "Life keeps on keeping on. You know how that is." He took a sip of his coffee.

"Yes, I do. Remind me, what's keeping on for you? I don't actually recall what your main practice area is. You do any particular type of litigation, or—?"

"Oh, no. I'm mostly a deal guy. Negotiating deals, papering them."

"Interesting." Nodding, I added, "That's not something I know a lot about."

In my first year at law school, I'd learned there were two main types of lawyers. Courtroom lawyers were litigators. The other kind, transactional lawyers, helped business deals get made and wrote the contracts that made that happen. After a professor referred to the two types as "gladiators" and "facilitators," I'd lost all interest in pursuing a career in transactional law.

"Yeah," Monty said. "It's certainly not the kind of law they ever show on TV."

I laughed. "So what type of deals do you do?"

"Some real estate, but mainly finance. So M&A, structured transactions, to the extent we do that down here…"

"Right, right." He didn't need to tell me that Charleston, South Carolina, population 160,000, was not a hotbed of major corporate legal work.

"But I've advised litigators handling white-collar defense, in cases where there's a financial angle… And that's all because I did my time in investment banking, before law school."

"Oh, did you?"

"Yeah, up in New York City. Four years. But who wants to live *there* forever, right?"

"I can't imagine getting through one of their winters."

"No, indeed. And everything's about ten times more expensive than it ought to be, if not more. It's like they've got a whole different currency up there. And nobody's got the time or inclination for—well, this!" He gestured to me, our table, the café.

"New York's not a friendly place?"

"Not real friendly, no."

We jawed for a while more about nothing in particular. As lunch got closer, the café filled up—on top of drinks, they sold sandwiches and soup—and the volume level went up several notches.

In a loud place, you can talk without being overheard. That's probably why we soon got around to the topic of Nicholson. I asked how the judge's family was doing.

"Well, they're… Mrs. Nicholson got a lot of support in the first month or so, lot of people reaching out. But that's fallen off now, so…"

"Yeah, that's how it is," I said. "After my wife passed, people were coming out of the woodwork for a few weeks. I had more casseroles in my fridge than I knew what to do with. But then…"

"Everybody's life goes back to normal."

"Except yours."

He nodded. "Yeah, I really ought to reach out to her again. Thanks for the reminder."

He'd finished his coffee by then. I could tell by the weightlessness of the cup; he was turning it around and around on the tabletop, fidgeting, and it almost fell over a couple of times.

"You know," he said, "I like to think that you and I have some common ground on… I guess, on the need to make sure that the full picture of what happened there comes out."

"Yes." I nodded. "I'd say we do."

I trusted that, as a fellow lawyer, he understood my situation. I couldn't talk about Vinny's case with him. But what he'd just said made it pretty clear that whatever Vinny may or may not have done, neither of us wanted him to take the fall for a crime somebody else had arranged for their own benefit.

"Okay," he said. "Well... then there's something that I probably ought to tell you." He'd slipped the thin cardboard sleeve off his cup and started meticulously tearing it apart.

"What's that?"

"I've been thinking about this. For a little while now, actually." He watched his fingers working on the cardboard. "And I've come to realize that it's something I am permitted to disclose. Because I learned about it from other sources than through my representation."

"Oh. Uh-huh."

We both knew that, although a lawyer's confidentiality obligations covered things he'd learned from his client, they didn't necessarily cover things he'd learned about his client from other sources.

He stopped working on the cardboard long enough to turn and look behind him. Nobody was very close by, and the café was still loud.

"Okay," he said, "as you know, I'm sure, he traveled down to your town with myself and his clerk. That is, we went in separate cars, but we all met up when we got there." He looked me in the eye. "I believe you know her name."

"I do." It was Miss Townsend, as I recalled. I was sure I could find her first name somewhere in my notes.

He went back to his fidgeting. "So, I came to learn that his relationship with that clerk was... untoward."

"Was it, now. Well, that's interesting."

"I thought it might be."

It went without saying that anybody in a sexual relationship with a murder victim, particularly an adulterous relationship, was automatically a suspect unless they had a rock-solid alibi. And to the best of my knowledge, Miss Townsend didn't have one. On the contrary, she'd gone into the stairwell with Nicholson.

With a little shrug, he said, "Now, I don't know what all you can do with that. Coming from me, it's secondhand information, after all. Textbook hearsay. But I have reason to be confident that it's true, and it didn't seem right for you not to know." He was making it clear, although I knew it already, that I couldn't call him as a witness about this. Even if he'd had direct knowledge—for instance, if he'd walked in on Nicholson and the clerk in a compromising position—I couldn't put a man's lawyer on the stand to talk about that.

But I could certainly use the clue he'd given me to find the evidence I needed.

———

That afternoon, back in my office in Basking Rock, I went out to the lobby to greet Lawrence Tucker. His testimony in a case of mine about two and a half years earlier had triggered Ludlow's downfall. I hadn't seen him since then, but he'd called the previous week, saying he "wanted to touch base" with me about "a case." He wouldn't get more specific on the phone.

Tucker was sitting in the waiting area with a black leather briefcase beside him. He still looked the same: tall, salt-and-pepper hair, could've played the president on TV. He stood up and hit me with a firm, businesslike handshake. As we went back to my office, he said, "Nice place you've got here. Good to see you're doing well since you left your last firm. How long have you been here, now?"

"Little over a year. Yeah, we like it well enough. How's the wife and kids?"

"Oh, doing fine, doing fine."

I took that to mean he and his wife had weathered the storm of the indiscretion a few years back that had cost Tucker his political career. If I had heard any gossip to the contrary, any whiff of divorce, I wouldn't have asked after his family.

Once we'd sat down, he reached into his briefcase, pulled out a thick binder, and set it on my desk. "I don't normally take this out of my house," he said, "but I really preferred to meet here."

"Uh-huh. And what is this?"

He opened the binder up and spun it around for me to peruse. It was full of printed-out news articles and photographs, with about a dozen colored tabs labeled with words like "Finances" and "Crimes." Everything in it was about Ludlow.

I'd known Tucker was a little obsessed with him, but now I needed to reconsider the "little" part of that.

"Huh. Interesting," I said, stopping on a page about the election where Tucker had run against Ludlow and lost miserably. Feeling his eyes on me, I turned that page quickly and flipped through to the tab labeled "2023 Trial." The first page was the headline about the not guilty verdict.

I shook my head. "That jury verdict, whew. I'm sure you and I feel the same way about that."

"'So the law is paralyzed,'" Tucker proclaimed, 'and justice never goes forth.' Habbakuk 1:4."

I remembered now that Tucker had a Bible verse for every occasion, and they were almost always pretty obscure. He seemed to like displaying how well he knew the book.

I looked at him, nodding. "I suppose that's about the sum of it."

"Yes, it is. I attended every day of that trial, and I was shocked by the outcome."

"Juries do the damnedest things sometimes."

"That's part of it, I suppose." Leaning back in his chair, he touched his fingertips together, tilting his head and looking at me like he was thinking about whether to make some type of business proposition.

After a second, he leaned forward like he'd decided in favor.

"So, I heard recently," he said, "that you're representing the young man who's accused of killing that judge."

"Hmm," I said, raising my eyebrows as if it were mildly interesting that he'd brought that up.

"I hadn't realized that before," he said. "I would've come to you sooner if I had."

"Oh?"

"Yes. You see that green tab there? The one that says 'Federal'?"

I looked down at the binder. "This here? Yes." I started turning the approximately two hundred pages between where I was and that green tab.

"Flip over to page 38 D," he said.

I hadn't noticed that the pages were numbered. As I turned, I said, "What's the *D* for?"

"When I find something that relates real closely to some information that I've already got," he said, "I put the new thing with that information. So if what I've already got is on page 37 of its section, then the new stuff comes in as 37 A, B, and so forth."

I looked at him in surprise and then looked right back at the binder. I didn't want my face to give away the fact that I thought he was either insane or some type of genius, and I was leaning toward insane.

Page 38 D appeared to be a travel itinerary, although not one printed off a website. It looked like Tucker might have typed it up himself. Under the heading "Flights," the first line said "12/23/23 1400 Gulfstream G400 JZI to EGE."

"What's this here?"

He leaned forward to see what I was pointing at. "Well, that's the date and time of the flight, and Gulfstream G400 is the plane. That's a twin-engine private jet, seats twelve. And then JZI, that's the private airport over on Johns Island. The destination, EGE, is another small airport: Eagle County, up in Colorado, right by Vail."

"Vail, the ski resort?"

"Yes, indeed. It's just another example of Ludlow's absolute lack of repentance or humility—you're aware of that, I'm sure?"

"I am." I didn't want to get into it, but I prepared myself for another sermon.

"It shouldn't surprise me at this point, should it. But four days after the verdict, he and his family hopped that jet to go spend Christmas there. At a cost, I might add, north of $6,000 an hour."

"Okay…"

He clearly thought Ludlow's vacation was shameful, but personally, I had a lengthy mental inventory of appalling things that Ludlow had done over the years, and taking his family skiing for Christmas didn't make the list. I'd never gone skiing, but I could understand splashing out on a family trip when you'd just managed to unexpectedly escape spending the rest of your life in prison.

"I should clarify," Tucker said. "Ludlow and his family only took up half of those seats. The others were occupied by a certain federal prosecutor you know, Mr. Wilcox, and *his* family."

I stared at him. Wilcox had told me he'd hurt his knee over Christmas, skiing in Vail. "They know each other from someplace? College?"

Tucker shook his head. "They both went to USC for undergrad and law school, but they were there about ten years apart. And I've never found that federal prosecutors from Charleston tend to get thrown together socially and strike up friendships with state solicitors from nearly two hours south. Have you?"

His tone was sardonic. We both knew that Wilcox and Ludlow normally would've run in different circles. The only reason I had a friend who was a federal prosecutor was that Cardozo and I had been in the same law school class, and then we'd spent nearly eighteen years working in the same town.

"It seems what brought them together," he continued, "is some real estate deals they were involved in about six years ago. Mr. LaRue was in on those too." He pointed to the binder. "There's some information about that at that red tab near the back."

I looked at it but didn't turn to it. I didn't need all the details yet. Absorbing what he was telling me was enough for now.

"Another thing to be aware of," he said, "is that I've been informed it was Mr. Ludlow who paid for the flights to Vail and back. To the tune of about forty grand."

I didn't have any $40,000 friendships. Most folks didn't. Spending that much to take somebody on vacation meant something other than friendship. Something like buying access. Buying an ally.

"Isn't that exactly the type of thing that got him charged with all those felonies?" I said. "And he's at it again right after his trial?"

"Can't teach an old dog new tricks," Tucker said with a shrug. "That's why my nickname for him is BB. As I see it, bribery and blackmail are his middle names."

I couldn't quite muster a laugh, but I flicked my eyebrows up and down to acknowledge his little joke. I thought it over for a second and said, "I suppose Wilcox could've paid him back."

"I suppose he could've." His tone suggested that it also might not be completely impossible for pigs to fly.

"Although if he was going to do that," I said, "why not just pay his own way in the first place?"

"That's what most folks would do, isn't it."

If Wilcox was in cahoots with Ludlow, I realized, then it hardly even mattered who had actually pushed Nicholson over the railing. Ludlow could've recruited Vinny, Raylene, or Nicholson's clerk. He could've tried to recruit all three of them, hoping one would take the bait. No matter which trail I followed, Wilcox would try to ensure it ran cold.

And nothing could be easier than for him to keep that covered up. All he had to do was not turn over that evidence. As long as he gave me *some* of the *Brady* materials, he'd look like he was complying with the law—even if he had boxes of other such materials that he kept to himself.

Shaking my head, I asked Tucker, "How'd you find all this out?"

"Well, Ludlow has friends," he said, leaning back and crossing his arms, "but so do I."

"I mean, I do, too, but this…" I gestured to the binder. My mental scales were tipping away from insane and toward genius.

"One of the many differences between myself and Ludlow," he said, "is that I'm a licensed private pilot. I've been flying out of JZI for almost thirty years."

"My goodness. So you've got a lot more friends there than he does, I'm sure."

"Well, he's got zero," he said with a laugh. "He's not a regular. Usually just flies out of Charleston International in a private jet. I guess he wanted to be more discreet this time, or maybe Wilcox did. You ever flown a plane, Leland?"

"As a pilot? No."

"Maybe you should. Flying small planes is… I don't like the word *club*, but it really is like a club that you didn't even know existed until you join it."

"Hmm. Well, I'm not much of a club joiner myself."

"Maybe you ought to be. There's a lot of really fine, upstanding people in that club. Not just the pilots, but the mechanics, the air traffic guys… all of us. And you know what? We help each other out."

## 12

## APRIL 18, 2024

My office smelled of fresh coffee and Terri's perfume, or whatever product she had on that gave her a faint scent of toasted coconut. We were going through the evidence I'd received the previous afternoon. Another box had come in from Wilcox. I was riffling through that while she looked at what Nicholson's cell phone company had sent that morning in response to my subpoena.

She made an interested noise, and I glanced over at her. My office was bathed in sunlight—it was a little past 9 a.m.—and it made her skin glow a bright, coppery brown.

I didn't comment on that any more than I had about her scent.

Still looking at the phone-company report, she said, "This gives us more data on time of death. And it's consistent with the autopsy—even narrows it down a little farther."

Based on crime scene forensics and the food he'd digested, the coroner had initially placed Nicholson's death somewhere within the hour preceding 11:53 a.m., when a courthouse visitor had glanced through the window of the ground floor stairwell door and spotted his body. Then he'd moved the start point up based on Monty's and Miss Townsend's estimates of when Nicholson left the room they'd all been in, so the window was about 11:35 to 11:53.

"Where's it narrow it down to?"

"Well, he was going up and down the stairs for about eleven minutes. The phone was counting steps and flights climbed. It stopped counting at 11:50, so if the phone was in his pocket, I'd say that's when he fell."

I nodded. The phone had been found shattered on the stone floor about twelve feet from his body. We'd worked together long enough that we didn't need to spell out what we were thinking: that he might've dropped his phone during a struggle, so it fell before he did.

"Of course, nobody reported hearing a struggle," she added.

I smiled to myself. I liked that we operated on the same wavelength.

"Courthouse was louder than usual," I said. "With the press outside and everything."

"Mm-hmm."

"Still, I guess that gives us a three-minute window."

"Does that help Vinny?"

"It might, if we can place him somewhere else in the courthouse based on some witness seeing him or on the security cameras that were working."

"I guess his phone wouldn't help."

I thought about that. "Not that I know of. All his GPS can do is tell us he was at the courthouse. Not which floor or anything."

"Right."

"I should talk to an IT guy. Or a cell phone guy. Get their take on it. But they're expensive as hell."

"Maybe your hacker kid would have some ideas. Or he might have a good teacher who wouldn't charge as much as an experienced expert witness."

"Yeah, I like that." I scribbled her suggestions down on the nearest Post-it.

"About the cameras," she said, "has Wilcox sent the footage over yet?"

"Some of it. And it looks like there's more here." I fished a flash drive out of the box. That was the format he'd sent the previous footage over on.

"Want me to take a look?"

"Thanks, but he can't afford you. I'll have Rachel do it."

Terri billed hourly, and I passed her fees on to clients. Rachel was salaried, so her pay was part of my overhead; it added nothing to the bill.

"Sounds good," she said. "Tell me if she sees something interesting."

"Yeah, I'll get her right on it. The only thing on her plate is pulling together the exhibits I'm using at Cameron's suppression hearing next month, but that can wait."

"They *still* didn't offer another plea on that?" She saw the answer on my face. "Why not?"

"Well, at first I thought it was just that LaRue was pissed off at me. But I think there may be more to it. There's something weird going on up at the federal prosecutor's office. You remember our old friend Mr. Tucker?"

"From the speedboat case? Mr. Pants Around His Ankles?"

I laughed. Tucker had inadvertently become a witness in my boat-crash case a few years earlier when police responding to the crash caught him and his mistress in a compromising position under a nearby bridge. "That'll be on his tombstone, won't it. Anyway, he came by here a few weeks back." I told her the upshot of my visit with him.

She was quiet for a little bit, her face serious. "Ludlow never stops, does he," she finally said. "Lord, how I wish the jury had put that man away."

"Amen to that."

"Wish I could pick Cardozo's brain. He must know Wilcox and LaRue pretty well."

"Yeah. Oh, did I tell you Cardozo resigned?"

"What?"

The astonished look on her face brought home, again, how different things were now. For the first several years after I'd come back to Basking Rock, we'd been pretty close. Not as close as I would've liked, but still. Back then, I would've called to tell her Cardozo's news within minutes of him telling me. She and I had been good friends.

Then I tried to make it more than that, and things got weird.

I put that out of my mind.

"Yeah," I said, "having LaRue as his boss was a bridge too far. And he didn't come out and say it until after he resigned, but he *hated* the way LaRue handled Cameron's case. Said it was absolutely un-American."

"Well, he's right. So what's he doing now?"

"Taking some time off. He's in talks with some plaintiffs'-side firm in Charleston that wants him to come on board."

"Plaintiffs' side? With *his* skills? He'd make a hell of a defense lawyer."

"Yeah, I think he'd rather work in a nail salon than do criminal defense."

She laughed.

"Oh, speaking of our friends up in Charleston," I said, "any luck getting Miss Townsend to talk to you?"

She shook her head. "I left her a couple of voicemails and got no response. Went to her house, and she slammed the door in my face. I did get a souvenir, though. A letter from her lawyer telling me to stop harassing her. It was pretty nasty—I might frame it and put it on my wall."

I chuckled. "We were never going to reel in a federal judicial clerk, were we?"

"No, she knows her rights better than I do."

"Well, it was worth a try." I thought things through for a second. "I guess my next decision is, do I give her a heads-up that I'm going to have to subpoena his texts if she won't talk to me?"

"If that wouldn't get her to talk to you, nothing would. But how much advance notice do you want to give her? Could she try to oppose the subpoena?"

"That's the concern."

I'd been wanting to get my hands on Nicholson's texts ever since Monty told me about the affair between the judge and his clerk, but I couldn't get them without a subpoena and a court hearing. And I couldn't get a subpoena without explaining to the court, on the public record, that Nicholson had been having an affair with a woman who was at the courthouse when he died—a woman who might, depending on what the texts showed, be a suspect.

If there were a way to get what I needed without dragging her name through the mud, I would've done it, but there was no way to get those texts without naming her in court, and there was certainly no way to prevent the press from being present at that hearing.

"I mean, she's got to know that if there's anything bad in their texts, you might get your hands on it," Terri said. "If she didn't want you to take that route, maybe she should've talked to us instead of literally slamming that door."

"Yeah, that's fair. I'll see about getting a subpoena. You did talk to her a little bit, right? What's your impression?"

"I talked to her for about thirty seconds a couple of times. Not enough to get much of an impression. She's a real good-looking woman, but she doesn't flaunt it. Classy, Ivy League, like you'd expect for what she does in life."

"Yeah. Sounds about how I remember her from Nicholson's courtroom."

"And nothing stuck out to me about her demeanor. I didn't see any flash of guilt or fear. But I was only with her for less than a minute, so take that for what it's worth."

---

That afternoon, in the basement of the jail outside Charleston, I'd been pacing for ten or twelve minutes when the guard finally brought Vinny in. I gave them both polite hellos and waited for the guard to remove the handcuffs, leave, and lock the door before I laid into Vinny.

"Tell me," I said, "how long have I been representing you?"

I could see that the anger in my voice got his hackles up. "Little before Christmas," he said.

"Yeah. Four months now. And I talked to your mom about your case even before that. And you know what neither of you told me?"

His slow blink and resigned shake of the head spoke volumes. *More than you even know*, his expression seemed to communicate. It made me wonder what other irritating surprises might be coming my way.

"You didn't tell me about your brother and how he was connected to Nicholson," I said, holding up one finger, starting to count.

"It didn't matter."

"And you didn't tell me about that letter you got." Two fingers. "And you also didn't keep it, for some reason."

"I don't hang on to things. Marcus Aurelius says the past is spent and done with."

"It's *not*, dammit! Vinny, if you really thought the past was over, you wouldn't be reading books by some guy who died two thousand years ago."

That got to him. He glared at me. "Man, did you drive up here just to give me crap? What's the deal?"

"The deal is that I can't represent you effectively if you keep not telling me important things. And on that note, today's problem is that

I got some more discovery from Wilcox, and do you know what he has that I didn't know about until this morning?"

He shrugged.

"Two things. Both of which I really needed you to tell me about before. First one is, they seized your laptop at home under a valid warrant, and what they found was you doing internet searches on Judge Nicholson ten days before he died, and looking up articles about your brother's trial."

"Yeah, because I got that letter. It made me curious."

The letter he'd thrown away. I took a deep breath. Venting that particular irritation on him wouldn't help any. "Fine," I said. "Anyway, the second thing he's got is video of you walking into that stairwell about five minutes before Nicholson's body was found!"

He sighed and closed his eyes. He radiated the sense of doomed resignation that I'd noticed and been annoyed about before.

"Vinny, let me tell you how this works. If this goes to trial, meaning if you don't take a plea, the first thing that happens is the prosecutor gets up and tells the jury a story about you. And I can tell you right now what he's going to say. He's going to talk about Primo. He's going to say your big brother got killed in prison, and you killed Nicholson to avenge his death—"

He gave a mirthless laugh and shook his head.

"Look, I believe you when you react like that," I said. "I actually believe you didn't blame Nicholson for that. But the only way the jury could possibly believe that is if I put you on the stand—"

"So put me on the stand."

"Okay, I'll do that. And then Wilcox will play the video I just watched this morning and ask you about it. The one where we see you go through the second-floor door into that stairwell, but we never see you come back out—"

"I went out the third floor."

"Great. The floor where the camera wasn't working, so we can't prove that you left the stairwell before he died—"

"I didn't."

I stared at him. "*What?*"

"I went in there, walked up the stairs, and out the corner of my eye—" He gestured to his right. "It was the color, man. The red. It caught my eye, and I looked over and saw him. And I just… freaked out."

I'd gotten Vinny's statement to the FBI in the first box of discovery that Wilcox had sent. That statement said not one word about this.

"Did you tell any of this to the FBI?"

He shook his head.

"And Raylene didn't, either, I guess."

"Oh, you know she would have, if she'd known. She'd love to take me down."

I let that pass. This was not the time to remind him that the cause of his predicament wasn't Raylene, but his own decision to lie to the FBI. Instead, I said, "The agents asked where you were at the time of the crime, right?"

"Yeah. I said I wasn't sure when the crime was. They kept going at me, so I said I wanted a lawyer and stopped talking after that." He looked at me like he wanted a pat on the head.

There was no use telling him now that Wilcox would make his failure to give that information to the FBI sound like even more evidence of guilt. So I gave him the pat on the head: "Well, that's good. But listen." I sat down at the table. "They've got this video. I know what they're going to say about it. So I need you to walk me through exactly what happened."

He looked tired. Exhausted. I understood now why he'd been acting, ever since I met him, like he thought he was doomed. Because he pretty much was.

He sat down.

"You always think you'll do something heroic in a situation like that," he said. "Or something honorable, at least. But then it turns out you're just average. No courage. Nothing." His shoulders slumped.

I felt for him, but I didn't need the editorial commentary. "Just give me the facts, Vinny. Step by step."

"Fine. Whatever. I went in with my bucket, to go clean the third-floor men's room, and on my way up the stairs, I saw—you know, the red. It caught my eye, and I looked over the railing. And there was…" He shook his head. "I mean, he was obviously dead. Guy in a suit, bad position, lot of blood. And I just… I actually thought it was the guy who asked me for the key card. They all wear the same type of suit, you know? And I was like, big mistake, man. That was a very, very big mistake. I was *not* supposed to let anybody into that stairwell, right? I wasn't even supposed to have the key card myself, technically, since I hadn't signed it out. But I did all that, and *now* look."

"And then what'd you do?"

"I got out of there."

"Where'd you go?"

"Men's room upstairs." He gave a bitter laugh. "Because that's where heroes go, right? That's the honorable place. Yeah. I dropped my bucket on the floor and went in a stall. I thought I was gonna—" He touched his stomach.

"And how long did you stay there?"

"I don't know, few minutes. Trying to un–freak myself out. Like, what am I going to say? I knew I had to tell someone, but what do I say? I let this guy into the stairwell, I knew that stairwell was dangerous, and now he's dead!"

He paused, stuck in the memory of it, so I gave him a little shove. "What'd you end up doing?"

He shrugged. "Bit the bullet. Finally. Realized I *wasn't* getting out of it, so I just had to go tell someone. But when I came out in the hall, it was already—you know, chaos. Cops stopping us from going anywhere."

I nodded. "I remember that."

"Yeah, so I was stuck up there with everyone else on the third floor for almost an hour. And by the time they let us out… What am I going to do, right? They already called the cops. The coroner's van was parked outside. It was too late for me to do anything. And my shift was over, so I just… went home."

I leaned forward, elbows on the table, and rested my head against the palm of my hand. It was my turn to shut my eyes in frustration.

I could put Vinny up on the stand, and he could tell the jury what he'd just told me, and maybe, despite the enormous stress of being on a witness stand fighting for his future, maybe his voice would ring as true to them as it had to me.

But even if it did, that probably wouldn't last. Wilcox would get up there and rip him to shreds. He'd make Vinny's sorry explanation of his bad luck and bad decisions sound like a half-assed, desperate lie.

I remembered something Terri and I had talked about more than once: people did stupid things, they made bad choices—and that was why we had jobs. I'd gone into the law, and she'd become a cop and then a

PI, thinking that our mission was to root out evil and keep good people safe. But it turned out that our missions were actually centered on basic human stupidity. Fixing the problems it caused. That was the foundation of everything we did.

We caught bad guys by following the trail of their mistakes. We helped good people by finding some way to save them from the consequences of their screwups.

Or we tried to, anyway. It didn't always work.

# 13

## MAY 9, 2024

Magistrate Vergala was not in a good mood. From the bench, she gave me yet another exasperated look. I was there to make a big ask: I had moved for her to suppress all of the evidence against Cameron Leary. He was sitting next to me, finally wearing a suit like I'd asked him to. His future was on the line. His parents were watching anxiously from the front pew.

LaRue's witness, the FBI cybercrime expert, was staring straight ahead, waiting for Vergala to rule on my objection.

"Your Honor," LaRue said, "this is essentially a relevance objection. But the Rules of Evidence don't apply in a suppression hearing."

That was true. The Rules of Evidence existed mainly to keep juries from getting distracted by irrelevant or inflammatory facts. A judge deciding whether to exclude evidence didn't need those protections.

"Of course they don't apply here," I said, "but surely the rules of common sense ought to. We don't need another disquisition about computer hardware from another FBI agent before we can determine whether there was a valid warrant here and whether the search of my client's dorm room and his laptop went beyond what the warrant permitted."

We had just spent over an hour listening to a different FBI agent testify in mind-numbing detail about how computer networks and the internet worked. Everyone in the courtroom had been informed that computers and phones had components built into their motherboards that were called network interface controllers, or NICs, and each NIC had a unique MAC address, which was transmitted to computer networks when you logged on and told the network what make and model of computer you were using.

"Your Honor, with all due respect to Mr. Munroe, this is a highly technical case, and my goal is to ensure that the record reflects what we need to know about the technology at issue. We're not talking about a search of somebody's pockets or their car. We're not…"

LaRue turned to look at the prosecution's table and pointed at the pile of stuff beside his chair.

"We're not talking about an FBI agent rummaging through my beat-up wheelie briefcase there," he said. "If we were, this hearing would've been over by now. There's plenty of case law about that type of thing, and we all understand what's allowed there. But this is twenty-first-century computer technology at issue here, and there's not a lot of precedent for this type of scenario. So to make sure we get the legal analysis on the warrant right, we need to get the technical details nailed down."

Vergala looked at me. "Mr. Munroe, aren't the allegations here that your client wrote some kind of software program to make his Dell laptop able to find and capture student loan account information, and then he hid that laptop in a desk at the student aid office so that it could connect to the Wi-Fi there and carry out that plan?"

"Those are the allegations, Your Honor, but I do want to make sure it's clear that the desk where he kept the Dell was the one that the office had provided for him to use. In other words, it was *his* desk. As I mentioned in my brief, during his sophomore year, which was last year, Mr. Leary worked part time for his college's IT department—"

I gestured to Cameron. Before I could go on, Vergala spoke up.

"And they sent him to the student aid office for a few days to straighten out some type of problem with the computer system there. I'm aware. I did read the briefs, Mr. Munroe."

"Of course, Your Honor. And, again, my objection to this line of testimony is that Mr. LaRue is taking up a lot more of the court's time than he needs to. We're past the two-hour mark now, and he's spent a lot of that time laying out minute technical details that really are not in dispute or even at issue here. I don't think we need to look at PowerPoint slides showing different types of NICs or know that a MAC address is a hexadecimal number in order to decide if the warrant was valid and if the search was properly done."

"That's a fair point," Vergala said. "And I appreciate your concern with the court's time, although I'm perfectly capable of managing that myself. So I'm going to overrule your objection. That being said, Agent Richter, I am going to corral your testimony if I find that I need to. So I would invite you to be mindful of not making speeches or going into more detail than you need to."

The FBI agent on the stand leaned toward the mike and said, "Certainly, Your Honor."

I sat back down.

LaRue leafed through a couple of pages of his notes on the podium and got back to business. "Agent Richter," he said, "can you describe what the defendant's software program did, in terms of how it worked?"

"Yes, I can. From the drawer where the laptop was hidden, it used a series of spoofed MAC addresses to connect with the Wi-Fi network of the financial aid office."

"Can you explain what you mean by 'spoofed'?"

"The program that the defendant wrote generated a random number in a MAC address–type format and sent that false MAC address to the Wi-Fi network in an attempt to log on. In layman's terms, that's similar to generating random passwords until you hit one that works so you can break into someone's account. Except, in this case, after it hit one that worked, it carried out certain operations within the compromised account, and then it closed out and went back to generating more spoofed MAC addresses to try to break into more accounts."

"And how many times did it try to break into student accounts?"

"In total, or per second?"

"Let's start with per second."

"Well, my forensic analysis showed that it was capable of generating a new spoofed MAC address and attempting to access the network on the order of fifty thousand times per second. But if the spoofed address succeeded in accessing the network, then the software carried out a couple of—"

"You know what, Agent Richter, I hate to interrupt," LaRue said. "But just to cross this point off my list of things we've got to make of record, let me ask you a different question, and then we'll come back to this. What did the defendant's software do after it managed to spoof a real MAC address and connect to the network?"

"Objection. Your Honor, I apologize, but that question's misleading."

"In what way, Mr. Munroe?"

"It suggests that my client's software is to blame for what happened after it connected to the network. And I don't think there's any dispute that that's not so. This network had a vulnerability that was inherent in the code that made it run, and what happened after any given computer connected to it was caused entirely by that code. And it's undisputed that my client didn't write *that* code. The details are in my brief, so I won't waste all of our time by rehashing them here, but—"

"I take Mr. Munroe's point," LaRue said. "I'll rephrase. Strike my question about what the defendant's software did. Can you just explain, Agent Richter, what the campus Wi-Fi network did if it detected a known MAC address?"

Richter paused. I had the impression he was trying to find a way to explain the problem without accusing the college of having made a big mistake with its network security.

"Well, for context," he said, "students on campus can access the internet through the school's Wi-Fi network. And, like any network, that one pays attention to who's logging in. So it looks at, among other things, the MAC address of the computer that you're logging in from. And, specific to the student financial accounts—which are part of what's called the *intra*net of the college, so like an internet that's closed to the public, meaning only students and staff can access it—anyway, if they detect what you referred to as a known MAC address, they recognize the student and present that student's home page to that student."

That was a lot of words for a simple problem. LaRue knew it, so he asked a question to sum it up: "So, based on your computer expertise, Agent Richter, is it fair to say that essentially the network identified each student's computer the first time they logged in, and after that, whenever the network saw that same computer again, it would make that student's internal campus home page pop up?"

That was a leading question, but I didn't bother aggravating Vergala with another objection. Both sides needed this information to get on the record.

"Yes, that's correct," Agent Richter said.

"And that home page contained what type of information?"

"Well, it had identifying information, such as name, address, and student number, right there on the main page. And then there were links to things such as their class schedule and financial aid documents, which in most cases would include their Social Security number."

I was glad to see that Vergala looked a little taken aback. It didn't take too much technical literacy to know that setting a system up that way might be a bad idea. As Cameron had told me in one of our first conversations, "I was actually embarrassed to be attending a college that stupid. I mean, I was like, what year is this—2005?"

"Okay," LaRue said, "now let's get back to the attacks that happened here. How many attacks did the defendant's software carry out per second?"

"Well, as I said, it was theoretically capable of generating a new spoofed MAC address about fifty thousand times per second. So think of that as trying fifty thousand random passwords. But if the spoofed address worked, meaning it got you into the intranet, then the software carried out a couple of operations, in terms of downloading student account information and so forth, which took more time. So, on average, when the software was active—which was only certain times of day; it wasn't programmed to be active 24-7—it came out to about thirty thousand times per second."

"Thirty thousand times per second." LaRue shook his head like he was dismayed by the scope of this thing. "And is this a type of computer hacking, or malicious software, that you've seen before?"

"It is, yes."

"And is there a name for it?"

"This method of hacking, which boils down to throwing a huge number of passwords or similar data at the wall to see if any of them stick, is called a brute-force attack."

"A brute-force attack. Okay. And do you have an understanding of why it's called a brute-force attack?"

He was repeating the term in order to make Vergala remember it. I didn't know whose job it was to come up with names for all the different ways of hacking into a computer system—I'd asked Cameron, and even he didn't know—but whoever it was, they obviously favored catchy, violent terms.

"My understanding is that it's— Well, the analogy is, say you're attacking a castle. You could do something stealthy, like sneak a spy in there or parachute soldiers in under cover of darkness. Or you could just use brute force, such as throwing thirty thousand cannonballs per second at it until the walls collapse. And this is that latter type of approach."

"I see. And in this case, how successful was the attack?"

"Our investigation found that seventeen student financial accounts were compromised over the course of three days."

"And is that a high number?"

"Well, it's seventeen young people just starting to build their credit and their finances. To me, that's a lot."

If we'd been in front of a jury, I would've objected on relevance grounds, just to have a chance to stand up and remind everyone that Cameron hadn't harmed anybody's finances. Here, I'd save it for cross.

"And does that number of compromised accounts tell you anything about the scale of the attack?"

"Well, as I think my colleague discussed earlier, a MAC address has twelve digits. So you could run this type of attack by guessing random combinations of twelve digits, but you wouldn't have a high degree of success, because the chances of getting all twelve digits correct is very low."

"And is that what happened here?"

"No. The first six digits in a MAC address identify the manufacturer of the NIC. So the way that this program was designed, it started with a known set of six digits that identified a laptop manufacturer that's probably one of the most popular types of laptops on campus, and then it ran guesses on the other six."

"So, statistically, how many times would it have to guess six random numbers before it got one right?"

"The number we use in the field is 2.824 billion."

Out the corner of my eye, I saw Cameron scribbling on his notepad. He was doing the math, double-checking the agent's testimony, but his numbers were more precise: $2,824,752,496 \times 17\ldots$

"And that's just to correctly guess one single MAC address?"

"Correct. So here, since there were seventeen compromised student accounts, you'd multiply that number by seventeen. So to make this a little more concrete, the defendant here essentially fired slightly more than forty-eight billion cannonballs at the city walls."

I glanced over at Cameron's notepad. After the equal-sign, he'd written 48,020,792,432.

"Billion with a *B*?"

"Yes, sir, billion with a *B*."

"Forty-eight billion. Wow," LaRue said, shaking his head like he was hearing that number for the first time.

I knew what he was up to. He was creating a pause to let that number keep reverberating in Vergala's mind. The worse she thought this crime was, the less she would be inclined to throw out the warrant. If it was a borderline warrant—and, in some respects, it was—then she'd err in favor of the prosecution.

I jotted down some notes on things that Agent Richter had said on the stand that ought not to be allowed in a jury trial. LaRue and his witnesses could get away with some shenanigans here that the Rules of Evidence would prevent him from repeating in front of a jury.

When it was my turn to cross, I didn't bother going up to the podium. I didn't need a place to set my notes, because I didn't need notes. This was a simple case, and I wanted Vergala to see that.

After introducing myself to the witness, I said, "Agent Richter, you were in charge of the computer forensics side of this investigation, correct?"

"Yes, that's correct."

"And a moment ago, didn't you mention a grand total of seventeen college students whose financial aid accounts were accessed?"

"I did, yes."

"And the access to each account lasted on the order of two or three seconds, correct?"

"That's correct."

"And isn't it true that your investigation showed that none of the data in any of those accounts was deleted or changed?"

After a micropause, he said, "Yes."

"To be clear, yes, that's true, not one single bit of data was deleted or changed in any of those seventeen accounts?"

"Correct, yes."

"And your investigation found that during the few seconds when those accounts were accessed, no transactions happened, correct? No money went out of or into any of these accounts?"

"That's correct."

"So it's true that none of those students had any money taken from their accounts during this alleged hacking?"

"Well, technically—"

"I'll rephrase." I didn't want him to go off on some tangent about potential future losses that Cameron's hacking might've caused. "So… you testified a minute ago that each of these alleged hacking attacks lasted two or three seconds once a given student account was accessed, didn't you?"

"I did."

"Okay. And whatever amount of money each student had in their account before the attack started, four or five seconds later, when the attack was over, they still had that same amount, correct?"

He glared at me. Then he leaned forward and said, "Correct."

While preparing for this hearing, it had taken me a good ten minutes to write and rewrite that question in such a way that he couldn't wriggle out of the answer. I was glad I'd put in the time.

"So no money was taken," I said. "Thank you. I have no further questions."

I wasn't glad for long. LaRue got up for a redirect. Standing at the podium, he said, "Agent Richter, did you just answer in the affirmative when you were asked if the amount of money in those accounts was the same a few seconds after the attack as it had been a few seconds before?"

"Yes, I did."

"And were you able to give a full answer representing the whole truth?"

"I tried, sir. But I was interrupted."

"Is there any further context that you think would make your testimony fully accurate?"

"There is, yes. What I want to make sure is clear here is that hacking into somebody's account isn't like breaking into somebody's home. If a burglar breaks in, but when he's gone your jewelry's still in your dresser drawer, he did not steal your jewelry. End of story."

"Uh-huh. I hear you. So, is there a nontechnical way that you can explain the impact of this crime on the seventeen student victims here?"

"There is, yes." Richter cleared his throat, preparing to embark on his monologue. "This crime," he explained, "is about taking somebody's information. Imagine if a burglar breaks into your home and takes photos on his phone of all your bank statements. Or imagine that he finds intimate photographs of yourself and your wife, and he takes good close-up photos of those. And then he leaves, without taking your originals. After the burglary, you've still got all those statements and those intimate photos. But the problem is, so does he."

Vergala's eyes widened. She nodded, and then she stopped herself—to maintain the illusion of judicial impartiality, I supposed.

"So does he," LaRue said. "So… does… he. Yes. And in your view, as an FBI computer hacking expert, what would that mean for the crime victim?"

"Well—can I keep speaking in a nontechnical way?"

"Please."

"What it means is, the cat's out of the bag. Permanently. You've lost your privacy. Your financial privacy, in my example, and your… well, your intimate privacy. The criminal who broke in has taken that from you, and you are *never* getting it back."

## 14

## MAY 9, 2024

We broke for lunch after that. As soon as I'd closed the door of the war room behind us, Cameron said, "She's not getting it, is she. He's got her on their side now. I need to— There's got to be — We need to make this thing *end*." I saw pure fear in his eyes.

To his parents, I said, "Could you possibly let us talk alone for a moment?"

"Oh! But…" His mom looked at him.

"It's an attorney-client privilege thing," I explained. "I'm sorry, but it's got to be just me and him."

"Okay. Cam, baby, we'll be right outside that door. You need anything, I'm right there."

He got ahold of himself enough to whisper "Thanks" and give her a nod.

Once they were back out in the hall, he said, "What do I have to do to get a plea deal that'll work? What's he want?"

"Listen, I know how you're feeling—"

"No, you don't!" He gave me an incredulous look. "If I get convicted on all this, I go to federal prison, right? But you just get in your car and drive home! How is that the same feeling?"

"I didn't say I felt that way myself. What I'm saying is that I've seen a lot of people go through this process, including the part you're at right now."

He calmed down a little—not much, but enough.

"This is one of the parts where things get very real," I said. "You hear some prosecutor tell your story in the worst possible way—"

"Yeah, I don't even recognize it," he said. "I mean, the technical details are mostly… about right. That's not the problem. The problem is, it's like he made a movie about my life, except he remade it as horror, or, like, a terror thriller—"

"That's a great way to put it. That's exactly what he's doing. Telling a story about a fictional character who's got your name, and who does some things you did, but he does them for terrible reasons and causes drama like you've never even seen. So, listen. It's my job to rewrite that story for the judge."

"Yeah, good luck with that. Anyway, I thought it was your job to get me a good deal."

"It's that too. But if I go try to get a deal out of LaRue now, either he keeps right on saying no, or he makes you an offer that sucks. Do you understand? This is not the time to fall apart."

"Oh, it's not? What, should I wait until she puts me in jail?"

"She's not putting you in jail. This isn't that type of hearing."

The mood he'd gotten into reminded me of the last time my laptop had gone on the fritz. Noah had pointed me to some instructions on the internet about what to do.

"Cameron, what's that thing called where you restart your computer in some special mode after it's been crashing?"

He was shocked. "Are you asking me for computer advice? When this judge is about to maybe ruin the rest of my life?"

"No, I'm just asking for the name of that... whatever that mode is called, where everything is shut off except what the computer needs to work on right then."

"What, booting up in safe mode?"

"That's it. Listen to me. Boot yourself up in safe mode, and just get through the rest of this hearing. After it's done, we'll be waiting on the judge's opinion for probably a few weeks or more. That's the best time to get a deal—when LaRue doesn't know which way this is going to go."

―――――

Back in the courtroom, I did a quick recross of Agent Richter.

"Now, before lunchtime, didn't you testify about a very dramatic hypothetical where a burglar could break in, snap photos of bank statements and so forth, and abscond with them?"

"Yes, I did."

"And wouldn't you say that the danger in that scenario is that those photos of the bank statements could end up just about anywhere?"

"That's one danger, yes."

"So the burglar could, for instance, sell them to identity thieves, or post them on the internet, or what have you?"

"Yes, he could."

"And that would be a terrible crime, wouldn't it?"

"I would say so, yes."

"But that's not what my client is accused of, is it."

"No."

"And isn't it true that you personally carried out the searches of both of his computers that you seized?"

"Carried out and oversaw them being carried out, yes."

"And y'all searched every nook and cranny of those computers, didn't you."

"I wouldn't characterize it as nooks and crannies, but…"

"Every file?"

"Oh, yes."

"Every email?"

"Yes."

"Y'all looked at every bit of data on those things?"

"Yes, we did."

"Y'all didn't have a warrant for any of that, did you."

He looked at LaRue. There was no objection to be made. "Not at that point, no."

"But still, y'all searched the heck out of those things. And you didn't find any evidence that my client ever posted any information about any of those seventeen students on the internet, did you."

"No."

"You found no evidence that he sold any of their information to anybody at all, correct?"

"We didn't, no."

"And no evidence that he ever offered any of it for sale, either, correct?"

"Not... No."

"Matter of fact, isn't it true that after those exhaustive searches, the only evidence you found about any of that information leaving his possession at all was where he shared it with an investigative journalist for the *New York Times*?"

"I couldn't speak to what paper—"

"Well, isn't it true that the man's email address ended in 'at NYTimes dot com'?"

"Uh, yes."

"And isn't it true that what my client sent to that one journalist wasn't the full records of those seventeen students, but one-page screenshots of their campus home pages with their names and Social Security numbers redacted?"

"We did find that he'd shared those, yes."

"And you didn't find that he'd shared anything else, correct?"

"That's technically correct, yes."

"Is there some nontechnical way in which it's not correct?"

He didn't answer.

"So it's clear for the record," I said, "you didn't find any evidence that he'd shared anything other than those redacted screenshots, correct?"

"That's correct."

"And as an investigator on this case, you've heard that my client's purpose in sharing those redacted screenshots with the *New York*

*Times* journalist was to act as a whistleblower to expose serious security problems with his campus's Wi-Fi, correct?"

"I've been told that's his excuse, yes."

"Thank you. I have no further questions."

———

It was another hour before LaRue finally put the agent on the stand who had obtained the warrant and led the team that carried out the search. He was a heavyset Black guy about my age called Agent Johnson. LaRue walked him through his credentials and then got to the point.

"Agent Johnson, can you tell us how you became involved in this case?"

"On January 10, 2023, I was asked by my supervisor to interview the head of IT at Charleston Technical College."

He stopped and looked at LaRue, waiting for the next question. Like most law enforcement officers, he knew how to testify: answer what was asked and then shut up. No elaboration, unless it was helpful to the prosecution.

"What did you do then?"

"I spoke to the head of IT, a Mr. Jeff Gorton, by phone."

"And what did he tell you?"

"Mr. Gorton told me that their monitoring had detected a pattern of failed attempts to connect to the Wi-Fi network. It was an extremely high number of failed attempts, and he explained that they weren't continuous; they were coming in what appeared to be random bursts six to fifteen seconds long."

"And did Mr. Gorton tell you what they had done in response?"

"Yes. He told me that he'd checked what's called the ARP logs and determined that these attacks seemed to be coming from a Dell laptop on the college's own Wi-Fi network."

Cameron's notepad bumped my elbow. Below the complex geometric doodle he'd been drawing ever since we got back from lunch, he'd scribbled *Hearsay?*

I wrote back *At trial. Not here.*

"And do you know how Mr. Gorton determined that?"

"Yes. As he explained, he'd observed that a MAC address corresponding to a Dell laptop had been on the network all weekend, but just prior to each attack—as I said, these attacks came in bursts—it disappeared."

"And did he explain what that meant?"

"Yes, he did. He explained that this Dell laptop appeared to be spoofing MAC addresses, which is to say, sending out false MAC addresses that misidentified which computer the connection attempt was coming from."

"Okay." LaRue paused to look through his papers on the podium. I could tell he didn't want to wade so far into the technological details that he lost the room.

"So, Agent Johnson, cutting to the chase, I don't believe anyone in this courtroom will dispute that Mr. Gorton did eventually find that laptop. Do you have an understanding as to how he did that?"

"As he explained to me, the defendant worked for him part time—for the college, I should say—and Mr. Gorton seemed to recall that the defendant had that type of laptop. So from there, as it states on the warrant, he looked in the desk that the defendant had been using and found the laptop hidden in a drawer."

"And did you seek a warrant to seize that laptop?"

"Yes, I did."

"On what basis?"

"On the basis that the information furnished by Mr. Gorton, including the ARP logs, gave me probable cause to believe that the laptop had been used—and, matter of fact, was still being used—to access student financial accounts in violation of the federal Computer Fraud and Abuse Act, among other statutes."

"And did you do so immediately?"

"No. I wasn't able to."

"Why not?"

"Because this whole conversation took place by phone, and before I was able to travel to the college and speak with Mr. Gorton in person, the laptop was removed."

"And did he tell you who removed it?"

"Mr. Gorton informed me that the defendant had come by and retrieved it. And not being law enforcement or campus security himself, Mr. Gorton didn't feel he had the authority to step in and prevent that."

"Okay. So, after the defendant came and got his laptop, did you then use a warrant to search for and ultimately obtain the laptop?"

"I did."

LaRue put the warrant up on the display and walked Johnson through it. He was thorough; he was making sure Vergala knew that on its face, this warrant was sound. He did the same thing as he questioned

Johnson about the search of Cameron's dorm room, establishing that Johnson and his team hadn't cut any corners. LaRue put up a photo of the dorm room and a floor plan of the hallway it was on, indicating which corner of the room they were in when they read Cameron his rights and how the search had proceeded through the space. It was textbook.

Except for one thing.

When I got up for my cross, I asked the clerk to put the warrant back up on the display.

"Agent Johnson, can you point me to where on this warrant it authorizes you to seize a Dell laptop?"

He squinted at the screen. "It's right there in paragraph three."

"Okay. And could you read out what it says about the computer you were looking for?"

He gave me a look. He knew what I was up to. "It says 'black Dell laptop.'"

"Thank you. And who or what is Dell?"

He looked at me like I was wasting his time. "That's who makes the computer. The manufacturer."

"Thank you. And during the search you just described of Mr. Leary's dorm room, you did seize a black Dell laptop, correct?"

"I didn't personally, but yes, my team did."

"Okay. But that wasn't the only computer you seized during that search, was it?"

"No."

"No, it was not. Because your team also seized a silver MacBook, right?"

"Yes."

"And those are manufactured by Apple, correct? Not Dell?"

"Yes."

A state cop might have waffled on that, feigning ignorance about exactly who made what, but Johnson was part of a cybercrime unit. He knew waffling would only make him seem dishonest. Instead, his strategy was to answer as briefly as possible, so that this line of questioning wouldn't last too long.

"So 'Dell laptop' doesn't refer to a MacBook, does it."

"No."

"Computer and cybercrime experts like your team certainly wouldn't read the words 'Dell laptop' and think they referred to a MacBook, would they."

"No."

"So can you point me to where on this warrant it authorized you to seize a silver Apple MacBook?"

There were two reasons I cared about the MacBook. First, that was the computer Cameron had used to forward a few pages of student financial accounts to the investigative reporter. There was no other evidence that he'd transferred the data to anybody. And second, if I could convince Vergala that the agents executing the warrant had gone beyond its scope, it'd be easier to convince her that they'd mishandled other aspects of the investigation.

Johnson said, "Paragraph six authorizes the seizure of 'other fruits and instrumentalities and evidence of the crime.'"

"So to confirm, we can both agree that this warrant doesn't contain the words 'Apple' or 'MacBook' at all, correct?"

"Not in so many words, but my team was relying on that catchall in paragraph six."

"Uh-huh. So put me in your shoes during the search, if you could, Agent Johnson. Let's say we've just arrived at Mr. Leary's dorm room on a warrant that authorizes you to seize a black Dell laptop that somebody reported might have been used to commit a crime. And you're also allowed to seize the fruits, which is to say the results, of the crime—so if this were a drug bust, you could seize the drugs and also any piles of cash you saw lying around, since cash is what a dealer gets from selling drugs. Correct?"

"Fruits isn't the only word on there." He was getting annoyed. That was good.

"Right, thank you, it's not. But just going through your logic step by step, can we agree that when you saw that silver MacBook in Mr. Leary's dorm room, you didn't think it was the fruit or result of some hacking crime allegedly committed on a black Dell laptop?"

He didn't answer.

"Can we agree on that?"

"Yes."

"Okay, so you weren't relying on the 'fruits' part of the warrant, then, were you?"

"No."

"Thank you. And next we've got 'instrumentalities.' Would you agree that that's tools of the crime, things that were used to commit the crime, that type of thing?"

After a pause, he said, "It can be."

"In a computer-fraud case, the computer somebody used to commit the fraud would be an instrumentality, wouldn't it?"

"Yes."

"And all its plugs and cords and so forth, correct?"

"Yes."

"And, let's say, if he hacked into something on the internet, then any router that he might have used to access the internet would also be an instrumentality?"

"Yes."

"And if he's accused of illegally copying data, then a USB key that he copied it onto, that'd be an instrumentality of the crime?"

"It would."

"And those things are instrumentalities because they're the instruments used to commit the crime, correct?"

"That's one reason, yes."

"Can you give me any other reasons?"

He didn't answer, so I looked over at Vergala. Before she could direct him to answer the question, he said, "Not as I sit here right now."

"So your answer is no. Thank you. Having walked through that, Agent Johnson, can you explain to me how anyone on your team could've thought that a silver MacBook was the instrument used to commit this crime, when the IT expert and his computer logs were clear that the alleged crime was committed on a black Dell laptop?"

"Again, the catchall also refers to 'other evidence.'"

"Well, let's just finish up this part first. It sounds like as you sit here, you can't explain why your team would've thought a MacBook was an instrument of a crime committed on a Dell. Is that correct?"

"Yes."

"Thank you. Now, what it actually says in paragraph six is 'other evidence *of the crime.*' Correct?"

"Yes."

"And when it says 'the crime'—now, the alleged crime that you were investigating when you executed that search warrant on Mr. Leary's dorm room was a so-called brute-force attack on the college's intranet, isn't that true?"

"Yes."

"And as you just agreed, the IT expert and his computer logs both said — Well, let me clarify. They both said that the alleged crime was committed on a Dell laptop, and then the IT expert, who had personally seen the laptop, said that it was black. Right?"

"Right."

"So how could a completely different computer be evidence of that crime?"

He didn't answer.

I'd made my point, and I'd knocked him a little bit off-balance. Now it was time for the kill shot.

"Agent Johnson, you mentioned talking with Mr. Gorton, the college's head of IT, and then finally going over to see him after the black Dell laptop in question was gone, correct?"

"Yes."

"And that was on what date?"

"January 12, 2023."

"And that's also the date on the warrant, correct?"

"Yes."

"And, to be clear, you hadn't received any other warrant relating to this case before that date, had you?"

"No."

"Matter of fact, you hadn't even sought one?"

"Not until Mr. Gorton informed me that the laptop had been removed, no."

"So all the conversations you had with Mr. Gorton about his ARP log and what he'd done to locate the laptop, that was all by phone, right?"

"Yes, it was."

"And I don't think Mr. LaRue got into this with you, but isn't it true that at some point after Mr. Gorton found the laptop and before it was removed, he asked you what he should do?"

"Yes. He's in charge of network security on campus there, and he was obviously very concerned."

"And he suggested instituting what's called a packet capture of the network traffic to and from that black Dell laptop, didn't he?"

"That was his idea, yes."

"So in plain English, he suggested using the technology at his disposal to intercept the data that was going in and out of that Dell laptop so that he could take a look at what that data was?"

"Again, he was in charge of security—"

"And he said if it was bad, he'd send the reports over to you, right?"

"Yes, because—"

"And you approved his plan?"

"I agreed that it would achieve his goal of knowing what was going on."

"And isn't it true that after talking to you, he carried out that plan?"

"He did."

"And he did so with your knowledge and agreement?"

"Again, I agreed that it would achieve what he was trying to achieve."

"But you didn't tell him not to do it, did you?"

"No."

"And as an FBI cybercrime expert, you're familiar with the fact it's generally illegal to intercept someone else's electronic communications, correct?"

"Well, depending on—"

"In your line of work, you're aware that under 18 United States Code section 2511, that's essentially wiretapping, and it's illegal for him to do unless you've got a court order that he's helping you carry out, correct?"

After a second, he said, "Yes."

"And when he carried out that plan, intercepted that data and then sent the results he'd obtained over to you, you reviewed those results and discussed them with him?"

"As part of my investigation, yes."

"And all of that was done before the date on that warrant, correct?"

"Yes."

"So it was all done without a warrant or any other court order, right?"

He took a deep, angry breath before he said, "Yes."

"Thank you. I have no further questions."

When I sat back down at the defense table, Cameron was staring straight ahead with no expression on his face. I'd told him about three thousand times that he had to act more formal and respectful than usual when he was in a courtroom—I'd had to repeat that advice quite a bit, since it didn't seem to stick—and I appreciated that he was trying.

I glanced at his notepad. Below the doodle, he'd written, over and over, in all caps, AWESOME! AWESOME! AWESOME!!!

## 15

## JUNE 14, 2024

It was nighttime when I got the email. I was in my office with Terri, slogging through courthouse security camera footage from the morning of Nicholson's death, which we had finally gotten the rest of in discovery, when my phone dinged. An alert popped up on the screen we were looking at. She read it.

"*Ludlow?*"

"Huh," I said. "Never got an email from *him* before."

I brought it up on my phone.

"Wants me to meet him tonight. At a little place up the coast."

She looked alarmed. "Tonight? Isn't it a little late?"

"He suggested meeting at ten."

She gave me a look. "Want me to tail you?"

"If I go?" I shrugged. "Maybe."

I sat back and closed my eyes.

After thinking on it for a bit, I said, "I have to go, don't I. To find out what he's got to say."

She nodded.

I sat forward and slapped my hands on the desk. "Well, let's get this wrapped up, anyway. So, who's on our short list?"

"It's easier to say who's not."

"That's for sure."

While I answered Ludlow's email with a quick "See you there," she turned her laptop so I could see the screen. She had three columns of names. First were the folks we were sure had stayed in the courtroom during the break in Ludlow's trial. Those names had come from Shannon Pennington's notes and my own memory. All of them were excluded as suspects. They could not have been in the stairwell with Nicholson.

Next were people who we could exclude even though they hadn't been in the courtroom during the break. The security cameras didn't cover every part of every hallway, but their coverage was decent; we had a lot of footage showing people who were somewhere else during the window of time when Nicholson was killed.

The third column had the people who either appeared on footage near the stairwell or were unaccounted for. They could've done it. They would've had to get into the stairwell first, but the key card Vinny had was not the only one; everyone on the courthouse's maintenance staff had access to the other. And Nicholson might even have let them in, if they knocked. I wouldn't have done that myself, but Monty said the judge was less vigilant than either of us.

This last list had thirty-one names on it.

"Lot of people to investigate," I said.

"I know. I wish he'd been wearing a good, old-fashioned watch."

"What, so the hands would be frozen at the moment of impact? Yeah, but watches probably haven't worked that way since before we were born. And even if they did, they can run fast or slow, so…"

"I know. I'm just wishing. If we could pinpoint the time of death, this list would get a lot shorter."

The autopsy had provided a time-of-death window going back one hour from the discovery of Nicholson's body, and FBI witness interviews had narrowed it down to about twenty minutes. His phone had recorded him going up and down the stairs, with occasional pauses, for eleven minutes, but there was no way to know whether he'd fallen while getting his steps in or while he'd been taking a rest. My subpoena to the phone's manufacturer had found that its step counter did not update in real time. The lag between taking steps and having them show up in the counter could be anywhere from a few seconds to five or six minutes. That meant we knew he'd walked on the stairs for *at least* eleven minutes, but there was no way to be sure it had been *only* eleven minutes. His phone couldn't help us narrow down the time of death any more than we already had.

---

Around nine thirty, I headed up the coast. I'd turned down Terri's offer to tail me; I didn't really think Ludlow would try anything. It'd be stupid to send somebody an email stating the time and place where you were going to take them out, and Ludlow was far from stupid.

And on the off chance he did try something, I didn't want Terri in harm's way.

The restaurant where Ludlow had said to meet was on the edge of a secluded beach. Beyond the restaurant's low, golden glow, which lit up a few yards of sand, the ocean was black.

The place was small and surrounded by palm trees—several tall, skinny ones that disappeared into the darkness overhead, and many more of the kind short enough to obscure my view in the front windows.

There were only four other cars in the lot. As I parked, I saw a No Swimming sign that warned of riptides. When I got out of my car, I heard the crash of waves.

Inside, Ludlow had taken a booth by a window. On the other side of the place, a couple was sitting at a table. There were no other customers.

I gave him a nod and walked over.

"Evening, Leland."

I sat down.

"Get you something to drink?" He signaled the waitress.

"Thanks." When she came over, I ordered a sparkling water and gave my standard excuse: "Can't do alcohol. Got a medical thing."

Ludlow nodded. He picked up his glass, which contained what looked like whiskey on the rocks, and took a sip. "How's your son liking Charleston?" he said.

"Oh, pretty good, pretty good." I hadn't told him where Noah had moved. I wondered who had.

"He could've done better in terms of neighborhood."

I'd certainly never told him what neighborhood Noah lived in.

I shrugged. "He likes it well enough."

"There's more violent crime around Dorchester Road than I'd be comfortable with, if it were my kid."

The hair on the back of my neck stood up. He was staring at me, his face blank. A stare like that, between enemies or strangers, was an open threat. And we both knew we weren't friends.

I kept my face as blank as his. "He can take care of himself."

"Still. Must feel pretty vulnerable walking around there at night, with that limp he's got."

I looked away—there was nothing to gain from letting Ludlow see that I felt like punching him—and pretended to check where the waitress was.

She was two or three yards away, bringing my water on a tray. She flashed a big customer-service smile, and I smiled back.

There was nothing behind my smile. The gears in my brain were whirling, in search of a solution. Ludlow was like a genteel, Southern crime boss: *Nice son you've got there. Shame if anything were to happen to him.*

The waitress set down a glass of ice and the bottle. She'd already popped the cap off. It was possible he'd asked her or the bartender to slip something into my drink. I decided not to take any chances.

"Interesting outcome on your trial," I said, nodding thanks to the waitress. I poured the water into my glass. "Were you surprised?"

He clenched his jaw but smiled. "Justice prevailed," he said. He raised his glass to that and took a sip.

"Is that what you call it when a witness gets killed before he can testify?"

He ignored that. Instead, he shared a platitude: "Tragic situation for the Nicholson family." His blank stare said he could not have cared less.

"It is, indeed." I picked my glass up and pretended to drink.

"The wages of sin," Ludlow said, with a shrug, "is death." A Bible quote; he'd always liked to hide behind those. His weren't as erudite as Tucker's.

"Oh? What exactly was Nicholson's sin?"

He shook his head, making a sharp sound with his breath, as if the sins were too many to be named.

"Well, if that's how it works," I said, "I'm surprised any of us are still alive."

With a solemn nod and steady eye contact, he said, "You've got reason to be surprised."

I was tired of his veiled threats. I was tempted to cut through the bull and call his bluff. But in Southern men, at least men of our generation, a blunt approach came across as weakness. We only resorted to that when we ran out of options or lost control of ourselves.

I leaned back, cocked my head, and appraised him for a minute. "I'm curious, Ludlow," I said. "Who is it that you serve?" I was proud of that insulting flourish—the insinuation that he was at some other man's beck and call. I expected him to be offended by that, but I was wrong.

"I serve a higher order," he said. The dead look in his eyes was gone. They were glittering now.

"A higher order?"

He nodded. "That's what I enforce." His tone was a little too fervent.

I chose my words carefully. "How do you enforce it?"

"With a great and mighty sword."

"Huh." I nodded, like I was thinking that over, and looked out the window. There was nothing to look at. Everything was black.

I had always thought Ludlow was driven entirely by his own corrupt self-interest. That would've been easier to manage, because a self-interested man was predictable. If he couldn't retaliate without putting his own money or power at risk, then he wouldn't retaliate.

But a zealot might do just about anything.

"Leland," he said, "you remember that time you came to the Victory Baptist prayer circle?"

"Oh." I looked back at him. "Yeah, I do."

About five years earlier, a friend, Henry Carrell, had invited me to the men's circle. It was a failed attempt on his part to help me restart my law career by getting me on the inside track with local business leaders.

"You should've kept on coming," he said. "Henry should have too."

"Oh?" I kept my voice light, but it was an odd thing for him to say. Henry, as far as I knew, had only stopped going to that prayer circle because he and his entire family had gone into the witness protection program and skipped town.

At least, that was the explanation I'd come up with for their disappearance. All I knew for sure was that Henry had provided testimony that had helped convict a man Ludlow had been close to.

"Yes, you should have," he said. There was fire in his voice. "The right people are part of that."

"I'm flattered you think I'm one of the right people."

"You're not," he said. "But you could've been."

I took that in with a slow nod. "And what would I have had to do to achieve that?"

"Let things happen the way they should."

I waited, but rather than elaborating, he took a sip of his whiskey.

"The way they should," I echoed back. "And what way is that, exactly?"

"There's a true way," he said, "and a false way. The true way is in line with a higher order. You've been fighting that."

"Have I?"

He nodded. "And that's how you lose things," he said. "Real important things." His stare had gone hard again.

I understood now how he'd gotten away with bribery and blackmail for so many years. The FBI could've rigged this restaurant up with cameras, and all they'd show was two middle-aged men talking at a dinner table. Ludlow didn't look threatening. He was leaning back in his chair, perfectly relaxed. I could've walked in wearing a wire under my shirt, and the recording would've been useless. Our conversation might sound weird, but that wasn't against the law.

He was threatening me and Noah, and we both knew it. We also knew that he was leaving no evidence of his threat. He could not be held accountable.

I wanted to get something tangible out of him. I crossed my arms on my chest and asked, in a defiant tone that I hoped would piss him off, "You think I can still avoid those nasty consequences?"

He didn't take the bait. With a placid smile, he said, "Well, the end of September's a little ways off yet. You've got some time."

---

Driving home, I called Cardozo, even though it was after eleven at night. I apologized for calling so late, and he said, "What, like I have to get up in the morning? I'm on my patio drinking a beer."

I told him about my conversation with Ludlow.

"I need a sanity check," I said. "The only thing I've got at the end of September is the Nicholson murder trial. So it's pretty obvious to me what he was getting at, but Elise"—my late wife—"always said I was a little paranoid."

"It's not paranoia if they really are out to get you," he said. "I've seen the files on Ludlow. Elise was a smart woman, but she looked on the bright side a little too much."

I sighed. "Yeah." We'd had this conversation before. Optimists, we agreed, didn't lock their doors. They lived for the moment and expected the best. Sometimes they got people killed.

"You tell Noah about this?"

"Oh, I texted him before I even left the parking lot. Told him to watch his back."

"Good call."

"When you were looking at those files," I said, "did you see anything about why your office let him slip through your fingers?"

"Oh, he was never going to prison on our watch." I heard him take a sip of beer. "Maybe I'll tell you why sometime."

"I know he's got friends there. Did I tell you about Wilcox and his trip to Vail?"

He said I hadn't, so I relayed what Tucker had told me. It was news to him, but he didn't sound surprised.

"That's something to keep in our pockets," he said. "Although it's not enough to bring him down. But if we ever do get enough, forget about my office. My old office, that is. They're… compromised. We'd need to share whatever we have on him with the Public Integrity Section of the DOJ."

"Never heard of them," I said.

"They're up in DC. They handle cases all over the country. Anything to do with fraud, bribery, and so forth in federal contracting, federal employees, that type of thing."

"They have jurisdiction over Ludlow?" Ludlow had spent his career as a South Carolina state solicitor. He'd never worked for the feds.

"If he bribes a federal employee, they do. That was a nice trip he gave Wilcox. And Wilcox is only two or three years from a cushy federal pension, so he'll squeal. He might be happy to take money from Ludlow, but he's not about to go to prison for him."

"I like this plan."

"This pipe dream, you mean. Unless you can dig up more on him."

I drove for a minute in silence. The highway was silver; the moon was full.

The quiet made me remember another thing Ludlow had mentioned.

"He actually said something about Henry Carrell," I told him. "I might've been reading too much into it, but it seemed a little sinister."

After a pause, Cardozo said, "Did he?" A veil had drawn over his voice, a guarded tone. Henry had turned State's evidence in a case of Cardozo's some years back, not long before he and his family disappeared.

"Yeah, he kind of implied that... I don't know, that there were some sort of bad consequences for Henry turning against him. I always thought the reason the Carrells disappeared was that they'd gone into witness protection." I knew Cardozo couldn't tell me anything about people in witness protection, but I figured it couldn't hurt to try.

"You know, the problem with witness protection," Cardozo said—his tone of voice was now in full press conference mode; I was going to have to read between the lines—"is the witnesses. They're human beings. I mean, picture what it'd be like to cut yourself off from everyone you've ever known, move across the country or the world, change your name. You can't call your parents or your sisters and brothers ever again. You can meet new people, but you can't ever tell them who you really are. So you're still alive, but your life is a lie."

"Oof. That's pretty terrible."

"Yeah, and most folks can't hack it. I can't even *tell* you how many cases there've been where the feds get some midlevel mafioso to testify against his boss with the promise of witness protection. And the feds do their job—they spirit him and his family away to a whole new life somewhere else—but a year or two in, he cracks. He comes back to see his mom one last time, or something like that. And they get him."

He was telling me what had happened to Henry. It was a punch in the gut.

After a long moment, I said, "Usually it's just the mafioso, though, right? Not his family?"

"Yeah. Not his family."

So Henry's wife and daughters were safe somewhere. At least he'd managed to get them out of harm's way, if not himself. I pictured them on a beach in California, or Australia—I remembered Henry saying once that he'd like to move there.

I didn't want to have to leave South Carolina. And I didn't want to share any part of the world with a man who was threatening my son.

"Ludlow needs to be in prison," I said. "We've got to take him down."

"I'm with you on that. But we need evidence. Good evidence. Better than what we've got so far."

## 16

## JULY 8, 2024

At the hearing on my subpoena for Nicholson's texts, Magistrate Harris was easy to convince. Forty minutes in, he ruled in our favor. I hadn't requested a hearing, because it was a straightforward legal issue; most judges would've decided it just on the briefs. But Wilcox had insisted on getting his day in court—he'd fought this one hard—so here we were.

Two journalists were also here, both sitting on my side of the gallery. I'd been dismayed to see them when I arrived, because there was no way to argue this motion without dragging Samantha Townsend—Nicholson's clerk—through the mud. But they had a constitutional right to be there, and the same constitutional right to splash her picture across their websites and repeat every sordid detail mentioned in our briefs. I silently cursed Wilcox for requesting a hearing and Harris for granting it.

The only other spectator was Monty. I'd realized when I saw him that this was the first hearing in Vinny's case since his arraignment six months earlier. Sometimes a victim's friends or family came to hearings religiously, like they were funeral vigils, a way of honoring the deceased.

Monty gave me a polite nod, but he sat on the prosecution side. That was normal. I didn't ever recall seeing a friend or relative of a murder victim sit on the defense side.

Afterward, as I was packing up my briefcase, I saw one of the journalists approach Monty. He stopped and talked to her for a moment, and before he could excuse himself and leave, the other one came to talk with him too.

I stopped paying attention after that, because I'd gotten an email I'd been hoping for.

It was from the court's ECF service, automatically notifying me that a decision had been filed. Magistrate Vergala had granted my suppression motion, tossing all the evidence against Cameron Leary. And since there was no longer any admissible evidence against him, she'd granted my motion to dismiss the indictment.

I hurried out of the courtroom. I needed to call Rachel and have her email me a copy of the actual order. And I needed to call Cameron.

---

At a nice Mexican place in downtown Charleston that evening, I raised my glass to the Leary family. "Here's to making it over the biggest hurdle. One down, one more to go."

The next obstacle was the inevitable appeal. LaRue had thirty days to file that. But the hardest part was over. As they all smiled and raised their glasses, his dad said, "Hear, hear!"

"Listen to this," I said, pulling out a printed copy of Vergala's opinion. "The first couple of lines are worth framing: 'The question raised on Defendant's Motion to Suppress is an ancient one: Should we eat of the fruit of the poisonous tree? And the answer, as always, is no.'"

"Yeah, hell no!" Cameron said.

As I'd already explained to them, LaRue was undoubtedly going to appeal, but Vergala had set the bar high. The appellate judge would defer to her factual findings—meaning her determinations about what had happened and when—and she'd nailed those down tight. As judges went, she was a hell of a writer. On the facts as she'd stated them, it was going to be hard for LaRue's appeal to succeed.

Sipping my sparkling water, I silently apologized to her for ever having thought that a sports nut was the wrong judge for my nerdy client.

---

After dinner, Cameron's parents went over to the bar so I could confer with Cameron without breaking attorney-client privilege. As they waited for their drinks, his dad said something I couldn't hear, and his mom threw her head back and laughed. It was good to see her finally looking relaxed.

I looked at Cameron and asked, "What's your T-shirt say this time?"

He opened his Hawaiian shirt like a pair of wings and displayed the message with a proud smile. It read "Libertarianism: noun. The radical idea that the government shouldn't control your life."

"Thank you for not wearing that in court."

"No problem. I busted this one out after you called this morning. Special occasion."

"It is indeed."

We sipped our sodas.

"Okay," I said. "Now, we've got a thirty-day clock ticking, and you've got to behave—understood?"

He cracked a smile. "You want me to spend all my time posting cat photos on Facebook, like some boomer?"

"Now, hold on," I said. "A lot of us Gen X folks are on Facebook too."

He laughed and apologized.

"What I want," I said, "is no headlines, and no weird new facts for LaRue to bring to a judge's attention. No hacking into anything, obviously. Just—I don't know, spend the thirty days learning another computer language, or something."

"I was doing that anyway."

"Good. And assuming he appeals, keep on learning Python or whatever, and stay out of anybody else's accounts, until this whole thing is all over with. Or ideally, forever."

"I learned Python when I was twelve."

"Of course you did. But you get my drift, right?"

"Whatever. Yes, sir, I do." He gave me a sarcastic military salute.

"Great. Oh, you know what, I've got a question for you. I don't know if this is really your wheelhouse, but do you know of any way to tell whereabouts in a building a person's cell phone is? I mean beyond GPS, like what floor or something."

"You mean a house, or—?"

"No, a bigger place. Like, say, a two- or three-story public building."

He thought about it. "Well, if it's got Wi-Fi that the phone can get onto, then yeah, maybe."

"Public Wi-Fi, you mean?"

"That, yeah, but also, if you've got a private Wi-Fi that the phone you're looking at is on, then that could work too." He started gesticulating, drawing structures in the air to illustrate his point. "It's got to be a big enough system to have different access points, or different routers." His waving hands placed several invisible routers in the air across our table. "Then you'd just look at the ARP logs to figure out which access point or which router the phone you're looking at was connecting through."

I stared at him. "Is it that simple? Really?"

He shrugged. "I mean, it's not simple. Not unless you're only looking for one phone and you already know everything about it."

"How do you mean?"

"Well, if there's, I don't know, a hundred people in the building, let's say that's a hundred phones. You've got to figure out which MAC address goes with which phone. And every smartphone's going to have at least three different NICs, each with its own MAC address, right?"

"Right, right." I nodded like I already knew that. "So... you took classes about that kind of stuff at CTC, didn't you?"

"Oh, of course. I already took all the IT courses except the ones that are reserved for seniors."

"That's great. So, I'm actually looking for a professor in that area who's good at explaining that type of stuff in plain English, like for beginners." I paused a second, then corrected myself. "Not just beginners. Boomers, even. You know anybody like that?"

He thought for about two seconds and then pulled his phone out.

My phone, which was sitting on the table, dinged. I looked at it and saw the contact card he'd sent me. Dr. Benjamin Da Costa.

"Thanks much."

---

When I got home that night, I sent an email to Da Costa and then sat in the armchair in my office, with Squatter snoozing on my lap, to look at my bulletin board for Vinny's case. It was a corkboard that took up a whole wall, and it was currently covered with photos of locations, witnesses, lawyers, Vinny and his family, Ludlow, and the stairwell, as well as Nicholson's family, his body, and his shattered phone.

A web of colored strings ran between the items pinned to the board, showing how they were connected. Pink string, for a good relationship, linked a snapshot of Vinny to one of his mom. A piece of black string, for a bad relationship, ran between Nicholson and Vinny's brother.

I used white string for connections that I didn't understand. Every string running to Ludlow's photo, even the one connecting him to Nicholson, was white. That one could've been black, since Nicholson had been planning to testify against him, but that was less important than the simple fact that I didn't understand yet what their dynamic was or what Nicholson had intended to say at Ludlow's trial.

Monty couldn't tell me because of client confidentiality, Ludlow obviously wasn't about to tell me anything that was true, and months earlier, Mrs. Nicholson had responded to my call by having her lawyer let me know that if I contacted her again, she'd go to the press and the state ethics board with complaints of harassment.

Squatter stirred on my lap, and I scratched his head. "Hey, Squats," I said. "Here's a bedtime story for you. That man over there is Judge Nicholson."

Squatter leaned hard into the scratching, and then he paused for a big yawn.

"There you go. Anyway, Nicholson got killed back in November, right before he was going to testify against that guy there. You know him, that's Ludlow."

Squatter made a rumbling noise, which I chose to interpret as a growl, and laid his head back down to rest.

"Yeah, we don't like him, do we. He ought to be in prison."

Even in his three-year-old mug shot, which I'd printed out from the internet when I was putting this spiderweb on my corkboard together, Ludlow had the false dignity of a politician. Collared shirt, necktie, strong jaw, blow-dried silver hair. Nicholson's photo, from the courthouse website, had a darker-haired version of the same look, but on him it didn't seem fake. He'd earned his gravitas.

I'd liked the guy. He'd been a fair judge, and a smart one. Between him and Ludlow, I had a strong preference as to which one I would've preferred to see fall off a tall staircase.

And the jury, I thought, would've liked him too. Most of the other witnesses had been politicians compromised by Ludlow's bribery, testifying against him as part of a deal to keep themselves out of jail. They were weasels, and I knew most jurors would have seen them the same way I did. Tucker didn't have that problem, but his history of running attack ads against Ludlow during the last election, when he'd been trying to win Ludlow's seat in the solicitor's office, would've made him seem biased.

I'd dug around, trying to find out if Nicholson had gotten a plea deal in order to testify, but there was no hint of that. And the fact that he'd still been on the federal bench, with no proceedings against him, was a strong clue that he hadn't done anything that would've made him need a plea deal.

Shannon had told me that the prosecutor's opening statement mentioned a judge Ludlow had tried to blackmail. Nicholson wasn't the only judge on the witness list—there were two more, both from state court in Basking County—and one of them had testified about blackmail. But I'd read Shannon's trial notes, and then the transcripts when they were finally filed. It was clear that with that state judge, the blackmail hadn't just been attempted; it was carried out.

And both of those judges had been removed from the bench. They'd been testifying against Ludlow to avoid even worse consequences.

But Nicholson hadn't had any whiff of scandal around him. No plea deal, no proceedings, and apparently he hadn't even given in to Ludlow's blackmail. He was the only untarnished witness.

Unless his life was sufficiently complicated for him to have more than one thing to get blackmailed about, what Monty had told me fit right in: Maybe Ludlow knew of the affair and threatened to expose it unless Nicholson ruled the way Ludlow wanted him to. And maybe Nicholson said no.

I was speculating, but that was the only story that accounted for all the facts I knew.

And if Nicholson had gotten up there and testified that he would not compromise his judicial integrity even in the face of public humiliation and possible divorce, he could indeed have changed the course of the trial. When it came down to it, most people admired integrity and courage. They trusted people who had those qualities. They believed what those people said.

I'd learned enough about jurors in my career to know that they loved witnesses like that.

And Ludlow had been a trial lawyer for almost a decade longer than I had. So he had learned that too.

I looked at Squatter in my lap. He was sleeping again. Whenever he woke back up, I decided, I was going to go replace that white string connecting Ludlow and Nicholson with a black one.

―――――

A little before eleven, my phone rang. It was Terri.

"Sorry to call so late," she said. "I just had an update that I haven't had time to reach out about until now."

"Oh, no problem," I said. "Let me run something by you first, though."

I shared my Nicholson theory. She liked it. She kicked the tires a little, running through a bunch of facts we knew to see if any of them were inconsistent with the theory. They weren't.

I also told her what Cameron had said about using the ARP logs of the courthouse routers to figure out where all the people we were interested in had been when Nicholson died.

"I love that," she said. "Absolutely love it. And, yeah, there had to be two hundred some-odd phones in the courthouse that morning, but most of them weren't near that stairwell."

"What was our short list, thirty-one people?"

"Yeah. Plus Vinny and Nicholson. Once you get the ARP logs, we'll at least be able to spot their phones, and maybe eliminate some. And who knows, maybe we'll even see when Nicholson's phone switched from the second-floor network to the ground floor, so we can narrow the time of death down a little more."

"You are way too excited about time of death."

I heard the smile in her voice as she said, "Oh, yeah. I'm like a kid at Christmas with this stuff."

I felt a surge of affection for her. I told myself to get over it.

"Anyway," she said, in a getting-back-to-business voice, "the update's about Raylene. I did a little digging on her car. Looks like she bought it a little over a week after Nicholson died. And she paid cash."

"Cash?"

"Exactly. And yes, it was new."

A car like that had to cost on the order of thirty grand. Of all the grandmas living in all the trailers in South Carolina, I doubted there was a single one who had the means to buy a car like that in cash.

"You got some evidence so I can ask her about that on the stand?"

"Of course."

"Well, that'll be interesting."

I moved a few mental chess pieces around. Come August, when I filed my list of exhibits thirty days before Vinny's trial was scheduled to begin, whatever we had about Raylene's car purchase would be on it. Wilcox would understand why—or if he didn't, he'd ask her. And as a result, he might decide not to call her; after all, the FBI had enough on Vinny without her testimony. So I would need to call her as a witness myself.

"You thinking you'll have to subpoena her?" Terri asked.

"Great minds think alike."

"All you'll get out of it is a witness you can impeach."

Impeaching a witness meant making the jury realize that the person on the stand was a liar or was biased in such a way that they couldn't necessarily be believed.

I sighed. "Yeah. And her lying doesn't exonerate Vinny."

"We could try to talk to her again. What we really need to know is who bought her that car."

"Yeah," I said. "And why. All she did was tell the FBI that Vinny took the key card. And that was true. Why would somebody pay her thirty grand just so she'd tell the truth?"

"You know," she said thoughtfully, "as a cop, I met a lot of people who didn't want to talk to me. They didn't want to get involved. Some folks don't want to narc on people they know, and pretty much nobody wants to sit in a room answering questions from a bunch of cops or FBI agents."

"That's fair. I wouldn't want to do that myself."

"Right? So, here's something to think about. Maybe she saw more than what she told the FBI. Maybe somebody wanted her to rat on Vinny but *not* mention anything else."

## 17

## SEPTEMBER 18, 2024

In my office on a sunny Wednesday morning, sitting in my most comfortable guest chair, Terri gave me the good news: Raylene had finally agreed to talk.

"You were right," she said. "She didn't just see Vinny. She was up on the third floor right before lunch, and she saw, quote, somebody else go in."

"Just—somebody? Come on. Who?"

"That's all she said. She called me last night, and it lasted maybe a minute at most. She asked if we could meet today or tomorrow at her parents' church up the coast. I'll confirm a time with her and send you the address."

"Huh. She afraid she's being watched?"

"She didn't say that, but that's what it sounded like. She didn't want us to meet at her place or here. I even suggested the Catholic church, since they've got those private rooms in the basement, but she said that would look weird, because she's not Catholic."

"Man," I said, shaking my head. "Small-town problems. Folks notice if you're at the wrong church."

"They notice a lot. And she knows it."

"If she wants to talk today," I said, "I'll cancel my golf thing—"

"You have golf things now?" She was smiling, and one eyebrow was raised. She knew golf was not my scene.

"I meet up with Roy sometimes. You know how he is."

"Oh, yeah."

My former boss had joked that he became a lawyer to support his golf habit. He played the sport better—a lot better—than anyone I'd ever met.

My phone buzzed. It was sitting on my desk, so I saw Noah's name pop up, and the start of a text message: *My apartment got broken*

"Just a second," I said.

I read the whole thing.

"Noah had a break-in last night," I told her. "Hang on."

I started typing a response. Then I thought better of it, apologized to her for the interruption, and gave him a call.

He picked up with, "I'm fine. Don't worry."

"Were you home when it happened?"

"No, I came back for dinner, but then I went out again. Had to go on a stakeout. It happened after that."

"Uh-huh."

"Weird thing is, they didn't take anything."

"Nothing? Really?" I tried to make my voice sound light. I knew he had a laptop, a TV, a setup for gaming—all the usual young-man-with-a-decent-job stuff. To break in and steal nothing, even though nobody was home to stop them, was more disturbing than a regular burglary.

"They left something, though. Hang on. I'll send you a picture."

A couple seconds later, it came through. The photo showed a piece of paper with something printed on it, lying on what looked like a pillow. I zoomed in to read the text.

It said, "The sins of the fathers shall be visited upon the sons."

I stopped breathing.

When I regained the ability to speak, I said, "Noah, um… can you get out of there?"

"Bruh. Are you kidding? I already did. I got home around seven a.m., found that, and bailed to my friend Zach's place."

"Okay, great. Is there… You think there's any chance they know where you went?"

"I mean, some? But not a ton. I drove to work first, so I could use one of our bug detectors to see if there was a tracker on my car. And I did a visual check, too, in the parking lot. Didn't find anything."

"Man, you're doing everything right."

With a hint of pride in his voice, he said, "Well, I didn't become a PI for nothing."

"No, you didn't. Anyway, listen, I don't know when it's going to be safe for you to go home. Things are not looking good. I can drive up there and help you figure something out—"

"Naw, I've got it covered. I'm going to Arkansas tomorrow."

"You're what?"

"I switched places with Zach. We work together, and they wanted him to fly to Little Rock for a couple weeks to look into something. He was bumming hard. Like, Arkansas was never on his bucket list."

I laughed. "Can't blame him for that."

He promised he'd check in regularly even while he was in Little Rock, and I let him get back to work. When we got off the phone, I filled Terri in and showed her the note.

"That is creepy as hell." She shuddered. "It's a good thing he's getting out of town for a while."

"Yeah. It's weird, though—he took care of it all by himself. I didn't even have to do anything."

"Well, he's grown up now," she said. "You raised him right."

"Or I just got lucky," I said. "Hope my luck holds out."

"Amen to that. Anyway, speaking of your luck, back to Raylene. She's already on your witness list, right?"

"Yup. Wilcox will have nothing to complain about there."

If I hadn't listed her, Wilcox could've tried to exclude her on the grounds that my failure to disclose her had hampered his trial prep. In real life, unlike on TV, surprise witnesses weren't allowed. Not unless you had a damn good explanation for why you couldn't have let the court and the other side know about them before.

"Good. And if what she says tracks with whatever Professor Da Costa sees in those ARP logs... I mean, if we can tie the person she identifies to a phone that was near the stairwell... my goodness. I mean, that's a slam dunk." She leaned back in her chair, smiling up at the ceiling like she was imagining something funny.

"What?"

"Oh, I'm just picturing what Vinny's going to say if Raylene, of all people, ends up saving his butt. He's spent a lot of time hating on her."

---

The weather at the golf course was perfect. Low eighties, bright blue sky, nice breeze. To our left, the ocean stretched off to the horizon. Fall and spring had always been my favorite seasons. They had all the best things about summertime, minus the sweltering heat. Terri had said Raylene couldn't meet until that evening, so I'd decided to catch up with Roy as planned.

He shaded his eyes with his hand so he could watch my ball fly down the fairway. "You actually are getting better at this! Marginally, maybe"—he looked at me—"but marginally's better than nothing, isn't it."

Friendly ribbing was part of the game for us. I put my club back in my bag. "I guess we both had to choose what to be, didn't we. Either a Mozart on the golf course or a Mozart in court. Can't have both."

He snorted. "Mozart in court, my God," he said, tipping his golf bag forward and heading down the fairway. "Whoever you are in court, I don't know how you stand it." He looked back over his shoulder, smiling. "If you ever want to come crawling back and handle my court appearances again, you let me know."

Roy was in business law. He negotiated deals and drafted contracts. When we'd worked together—or, rather, when I'd worked for him—he handled that and the golfing, and I handled hearings, court filings, and trials. Or, as I thought of it, the actual lawyering part of the job.

We walked along in pleasant silence for a while and, as usual, reached my ball first. His was another couple hundred yards down. I was picking which club to use when my phone rang.

"My paralegal," I explained. As I said hello, he pulled a three wood out of his bag and stepped away to swing at a few imaginary balls.

Rachel greeted me with, "Leland, something bad's happened."

"What is it?" I could hear from her tone that it was serious.

"There was— You know how Kenny's a police officer?" Kenny was her husband.

"Yeah?"

"He was at the scene of an accident a couple of hours ago."

I froze.

"It was that witness, Raylene Andrews. Her car went into the water over by the Sea Island Bridge. She didn't make it."

———

Roy and I finished the hole, but what little game I had was gone. I couldn't give him any details about the case, since we weren't in the same firm anymore, but I told him a key witness had just been in a fatal crash, and I alluded to Ludlow's threats. I also showed him the note that Noah had found on his pillow.

Roy grimaced when he read it. "Yeah, let's call it a day," he said. "To be honest, I think you and Noah ought to get out of town."

I nodded. I wasn't telling him or anyone about Noah's travel plans. Terri already knew, but I wasn't worried about that.

As we walked back to the clubhouse, I moved some mental chess pieces around, trying to see where things were going. No matter which way I moved them, I didn't like what I saw.

I left Roy at the clubhouse door and went to my car. There was a red SUV parked next to me, and it made me think of the fancy new car in Raylene's driveway. I felt bad for her. That thirty grand didn't mean much now.

But when Rachel had told me there'd been an accident, it wasn't Raylene who had come to mind. My heart had stopped for two people: Noah and Terri.

---

Back at the office, I called Cardozo, and then I called Terri.

She swore a few times when I gave her the news about Raylene. "I didn't tell you this," she said, "but the other night on my way back from Charleston, somebody sideswiped me."

"What the hell?"

"Yeah. They rammed into me twice, actually. Then a cop car came over the hill, and they, like, swerved off onto a side road."

I didn't ask why she hadn't told me at the time. It'd be weird to sound like I thought she owed me that.

"Did you report it or anything?"

"No. I didn't get a plate, or even a make and model. And it was about the most generic car imaginable. White or light silver, late-model sedan."

"And they definitely sideswiped you? Like, intentionally?"

"Well, the first time I thought they might be drunk. But they drove nice and straight after that. And then they did it again."

I was speechless for a second. Then I said, "No case is worth this."

She gave a resigned laugh. "Well, it's too late to get out of it now, isn't it." Vinny's trial was starting in thirteen days.

"Yeah, listen," I said. "You remember a few years back, when I had that break-in at my old house, and I took Noah up to Cardozo's cabin to keep him out of harm's way?"

"Oh, up in North Carolina?"

"Yeah, not too far from Asheville. I called him half an hour ago to see if I could get the key from him and hide out there for a while. His place is up in the mountains, but he's got broadband. I was thinking I could do the rest of my trial prep there—"

"That's good," she said.

"Yeah, but let me finish. It turns out he's up there already himself. And he invited you to come along."

I'd actually asked him if she could come. My exact words were, "I don't want her ending up the same way, in the water out by the Sea Island Bridge." He'd said yes with no hesitation.

But she was hesitating.

"This is just a safe place to stay," I said. "It's not like... There's nothing weird going on here. He's got four bedrooms and two baths. Plenty of room."

"Hmm."

After a second, when she still hadn't agreed, I stopped trying to act professional. I let loose with, "Terri, what's the point of me staying safe there if I come back and find you and your car got rammed into the water too?"

Over the phone line, I felt something like a temperature change.

"Okay," she said. "Let's go."

## 18

## SEPTEMBER 20, 2024

The place Cardozo called his "cabin" was a four-bedroom chalet-style house perched on a steep half acre of mountainside about an hour northeast of Asheville. A winding dirt road led up to it and several other houses set in clearings in the woods. In the living room, French doors opened onto a large deck with stunning views over the forest to the mountains across the valley. He had a hot tub out there, and a gas grill with more features than my stove. The first night, we'd cooked out on the deck and watched the sunset, but for our second night Cardozo had other plans.

"Got to show our faces," he said. "Folks like to know who's around."

"Thought you were a privacy freak," I said.

"Yeah, that doesn't work so well out here. You've got to know your neighbors. They can be real frosty otherwise."

"I'm sure," Terri said.

I nodded. We understood small towns, and this neck of the woods was so minimally populated that it was barely a town at all.

"Well, it'll be nice to stretch our legs," I said.

"Amen to that," Terri said. "And get a break from staring at Power-Point slides."

We'd spent the past nine hours making and editing slides of all the exhibits we were planning to use in Vinny's trial. If we'd brought our dogs, we would've had some forced breaks to take them for walks, but Cardozo's wife was allergic, so Noah had taken Squatter on his work trip and Terri had left Buster with her sister.

"Great. There's only one restaurant in town, but I think you'll like it. The food's good, old-school stuff."

"You know, Garrett, I don't want to cause a problem for you," Terri said as we were preparing to head out, "but I just want to check something."

*I don't want to cause a problem* was Southern for *there's a problem I need you to address.*

"Of course," he said. "What is it?"

"If things get weird on account of my... being an outsider, would we be able to jump in the car and get out of there real quick?"

He started nodding before she'd finished her sentence. "Absolutely. You just say the word. For perspective, there are a few Black families in town, and I've never heard a bad word about them. Attitudes out here seem pretty good. But anyway, that's part of the reason I thought we ought to put in an appearance. Make sure folks know that y'all are with me."

"Thanks."

"No problem." As he spoke, Cardozo screwed his eyebrows up. Something about Terri had caught his attention. I followed his gaze and spotted the diamond on her ring finger. I'd never seen it before.

It was a gut punch, but I kept my expression bland.

"Wait, you got engaged?" Cardozo asked. "Who's the lucky guy?"

"What? Oh, this?" Terri held her hand up, making what had to be a few thousand bucks' worth of diamond sparkle in the light.

I tried to look politely interested.

She snorted. "Oh my goodness, no, not at all."

"Still young and single?" Cardozo said.

I hadn't told him about the fiasco of my discovery, the previous year, that she was dating someone. To my mind, telling folks about the kicks I took would only make the kicks hurt worse.

"Well, I don't know about the young part," she said. "But as a woman, being obviously single can bring out the creeps. So I bought this on Amazon for about fifty bucks. I only wear it when I'm traveling. And since we're going out to eat…" She wiggled her hand to make the ring sparkle. "Time to bust out the cubic zirconia."

They both had a good laugh about that. Once I'd regained the ability to breathe, I laughed too.

---

We got into Cardozo's gray Volvo and drove six or eight minutes down to Linlandville, which he'd told us was home to about six hundred people. As we crossed the bridge, he pointed out the sights on the opposite bank of the river.

"We've got a campground down there—folks come stay in their RVs—and there's the convenience store. Couple churches, obviously, and the school."

The town only had about a dozen buildings, but from the number of steeples I could see, at least three of them were churches.

"I take it there's no synagogue," I said.

He laughed. "Yeah, we got used to that a long time ago. The girls like coming up here for that reason alone."

I heard Terri chuckle in the back seat. "I guess kids don't usually like church no matter *what* kind it is," she said.

"Yeah, that's fair to say." Cardozo turned right at the end of the bridge.

A block later, he turned into a lot beside a large, ramshackle building that looked like someone had built a family home 100 years earlier and then kept on adding rooms whenever they could afford to, using whatever architectural style was in vogue at the time. The main part was a white Victorian, but we parked beside a deep patio that was all varnished wood. The patio roof was held up by columns that were nothing more than tree trunks stripped of their bark.

The wide door was propped open, and the windows to either side were adorned with blue and red neon signs advertising different brands of beer.

As we got out of the car, Terri asked, "They got two different bands playing?"

We could hear rock music close by, and country a little farther along.

"Probably a band and a jukebox," Cardozo said, heading up the steps. "They've got a few different rooms in here, and they don't all have the same music."

"Little weird, but okay," I said.

He turned beside the door, made a chivalrous gesture for Terri to walk in first, and said, with a grin, "Yeah, it's kind of a weird place. Low-rent Southern Gothic. But that's what I like about it."

He wasn't kidding. The bar itself looked pretty normal, except for the trio of taxidermy deer heads hanging on the wall behind the bartender, and the noise levels were what you'd expect from a country bar on a Friday night. As Springsteen played on the sound system, the two-dozen people at their tables with fries and beer gave us a once-over. I felt self-conscious about my polo shirt and lack of facial hair. The male dress code here seemed to be T-shirts, flannel, and beards.

"Hey, Garrett," some mountain man called out, giving Cardozo a nod.

"Hey, Jarvis."

"No wife and kids?"

"Nope. Just friends tonight." Cardozo gave him a wave and led us through one of the doors that connected the bar to other parts of the restaurant. "For an actual meal, you go through to the dining room," he explained. "Or stay here, if you want to shoot some pool."

Small groups were standing around each of three pool tables, and more people sat here and there on furniture that looked like it had been sourced from several different yard sales.

"Yeah, maybe we can play after dinner," Terri said, slaloming around a red velvet armchair in which a man appeared to be sleeping. "If a table frees up."

We stopped to let a waitress with a tray of beer pass by. Next to us, a couple of women were crying and hugging each other on a beat-up Victorian couch. One of them said, "Honey, he does not even *deserve* you." Her friend answered, "I know. I *know*, but..."

We moved on.

"Didn't know you played pool," Cardozo said. "You any good?"

"So I've been told," Terri said. "I started... what, twenty years ago? I used to play for money, but then my friends stopped playing with me because they didn't like to lose."

I chuckled. "Sore losers. That's pathetic. I'll play you."

I didn't recall her ever mentioning that she played. There was a lot about her that I didn't know. In the half decade since I'd lost my prosecutor job and crawled back to Basking Rock to rebuild my life, I'd missed plenty of opportunities to connect with her.

For once, I didn't beat myself up about it. After all, there were good reasons I hadn't focused on her. It had taken years to drag Noah back from the brink of addiction and help him get launched. It had taken years to build my law practice and get solvent again. And what the hell would I have had to offer her, or anybody, if I hadn't done that?

I patted myself on the back. By focusing on my kid and my work, instead of flailing around in search of a girlfriend, I'd spared us both the indignity of some friend in a bar comforting her with the words *honey, he does not even deserve you.*

We passed into a large dining room with French doors that opened onto a cement patio. Out there, on the other side of a fire pit, a bluegrass band was playing while a few couples danced.

We got a table, ordered a basket of fried chicken and a bunch of sides to share, and watched folks dancing outside while the sun set behind them.

"You were right about the food," I told Cardozo. "I wouldn't have thought it'd be this good, in a place like this."

"Mm-hmm," Terri said. "Though I think this is the first time I've ever seen Leland look at a menu that had shrimp on it and then order something else."

I stopped gnawing my drumstick long enough to say, "I don't trust the shrimp this far inland. I wouldn't get sushi up here either."

She laughed. "Well, that's fair. You can make up for it when we're back in Charleston."

"Won't be long now," Cardozo said. "Week and a half, right? How you feeling about the case?"

I scanned the room to check our risk of being overheard. But folks talked loud in these parts, and they laughed even louder. With the sheer number of conversations going on, plus the band's jangly banjo and guitar, I couldn't make out anything being said at the other tables.

I relaxed and answered him. "Not great. I mean, the standard of proof's on my side, of course, but it's never good when the prosecution's got a real emotional story for the motive. And avenging your brother's death—that cuts deep."

Cardozo, dipping a piece of fried zucchini into a bowl of sauce, shook his head sympathetically. "And you don't think that's what happened?" he asked. "Ignore that if you don't want to tell me."

He respected boundaries better than most folks did. In the twenty-five years I'd known him, he'd never pried without making it clear that he would take no offense if I chose not to answer.

Now that he'd left the federal prosecutor's office, though, I could talk more freely.

"No," I said. "I genuinely don't. But I also don't look forward to putting my guy on the stand. Your friend back in Charleston does a hell of a cross-examination."

"He's not my friend. At all. But yeah, he's got decades of experience ripping people's hearts out on the stand."

"Yeah. And a twentysomething guy whose only courtroom experience is mopping the floor? I've trained him up as best I can, but…"

"You do have that other angle," he said. "With your ex-solicitor."

"It was a much stronger angle before that witness got… into her *accident*."

"Yeah. Well, to keep yourselves safe from 'accidents,' y'all just stay right here until the last minute, and then—did you book that hotel I told you about?"

I nodded. He'd recommended a Charleston hotel that had better security than most and was walking distance from the federal courthouse.

"And I swept Leland's car before we left," Terri said.

She meant she'd checked for tracking devices. There wasn't much point disappearing to the mountains of North Carolina if Ludlow could see where we'd gone.

"Swept it both ways?"

"*All* ways. Visual, RF, magnetic field detector, the works."

"She doesn't leave much to chance," I said.

"Good."

"You know what," I said, leaning back and looking at him, "I got a question for you. Since you don't work at that old job of yours anymore."

"Uh-huh. Well, I'll take it under consideration."

"Of course." I cracked a smile. "Ignore it if you don't want to tell me."

"I will," he said, smiling back.

"Any idea what was behind the decision not to prosecute that ex-solicitor of ours?"

"Yeah. I think he bought himself a friend. A couple of friends, actually."

"It's that simple?"

"It usually is," he said, chasing a mushroom around his plate. "Isn't it? People aren't as complicated as we like to think."

Terri chuckled. "You know, I used to work with a Catholic guy," she said. "He trained me when I was right out of the police academy. And he liked to say that of the seven deadly sins, only three of them accounted for about 95 percent of all crimes. And greed alone was more than half."

"That sounds about right," Cardozo said.

---

After dinner, Terri went to the pool room to get us a table while Cardozo and I settled the check. It didn't take us but ninety seconds to take care of that, but when we got to the doorway, I saw a twentysomething local boy in a ragged denim vest turn on her and say, "This here's *my* table. It ain't for the likes of you."

"Hey there, son," I called out, walking toward them at speed. "You in the habit of disrespecting retired police officers? Really? That your thing?"

"Dammit, Ryder," one of his friends said. "Get back here. I bailed you out last time, but I'm not doing it again!"

"She a cop?" Ryder asked me. Without waiting for an answer, he turned back to her and said, "Shit, ma'am, I'm sorry."

An older man in a cowboy hat pointed at Cardozo and said, "Yeah, and that there's her prosecutor friend."

"You fought the law, Ryder," another local said. "And the law won."

Their group cracked up. Ryder apologized to Terri again and slunk off to the men's room to the sound of guffaws.

I couldn't help but smile. I'd always liked watching groups of men use public mockery to shame each other into better behavior. To my mind, it was one of the foundations of civilization. It was a thing we did that most women didn't understand—they saw the unkindness of it, not the civilizing effect.

But Terri got it. I could tell from her stance and the look on her face that she knew the problem had been resolved. She pulled a pool cue off the rack on the wall, cocked her head at the mountain boys, and said, "Want to fight the law on this pool table here? I got a hundred bucks that says the law is going to win."

"A hundred bucks? Damn!"

They scrambled to take her up on it. Cardozo and I chalked up our cues, and three of the young men took their places around the table.

In twenty minutes, she obliterated them. We did our bit to help.

After the game, the pack of friends made Ryder empty his pockets, although he hadn't even been playing. They paid us the full hundred dollars in a pile of wrinkled fives and ones.

We drove back up the mountain, and I slept better than I had in a long time.

# 19

## SEPTEMBER 27, 2024

I woke up in the dark to a bone-shaking crash and the sound of splintering wood.

We'd been rained into Cardozo's cabin for the past couple of days. We'd gotten a ton of work done, and after wheeling his gas grill under the roof that covered about a third of his deck, we'd grilled steak one night and trout the next. We spent the evenings playing cards or board games and swapping our funniest stories. I'd been more relaxed than I could ever remember being, and I couldn't help but notice that Terri was relaxed too. The awkwardness between us was gone.

But something was wrong now. The rain was still pouring down, even harder than before.

I grabbed my phone. It was a few minutes before 6 a.m. I felt around for my bedside lamp and hit the switch. It didn't turn on.

I got up and went into the hallway. A beam of light swung around. It was Cardozo, in his bathrobe, with a flashlight.

"What happened?" I said. "Terri okay?"

"I'm checking. Come on."

As we crossed the dark living room, something hit the big plate-glass window, and it shattered. We threw our arms up to shield our heads as the wind and rain roared in.

I heard Cardozo swearing as I called out Terri's name.

"In the kitchen," she called back, shouting to be heard over the storm.

Cardozo veered left, toward the kitchen, and I followed. His flashlight beam showed that she was fully dressed and had gathered several bottles of water and a loaf of bread on the counter.

She yelled, "You've got a basement, right?"

"If it's not flooded," he yelled back.

I grabbed all the water bottles, the two of them got the bread, and we followed him to the stairs.

The basement had a few inches of water in it, so we sat on the steps. There were no windows anywhere nearby, nothing that could send an explosion of glass in our direction. I pointed that out, and we all relaxed a little bit.

The wind kept howling. The water covering the floor rose higher. We heard more trees crashing down. The sound was different when they fell onto a house.

"I hope the Careys are all right," Cardozo said. As time passed and we heard more trees hitting houses, and the metallic crunch of them crushing people's cars, he said the same thing about three or four other neighbors.

By eight, the water in the basement had risen to cover the first step.

"This feels like a hurricane," Terri said, a low thrum of fear in her voice. "But in the mountains? How?"

Cardozo and I shook our heads. We'd all seen the headlines on our phones a few days earlier—a hurricane was heading for Florida—but that was five hundred miles away.

From somewhere to the left, I heard a rumble so deep it felt like my bones were hearing it instead of my ears.

"Is that... a *landslide?*" Terri said.

"Probably," Cardozo said.

"We're from down at sea level," I said. "We don't understand these things." I was trying to joke, to lighten Terri's mood. It didn't work.

I typed a text to Noah to let him know we were okay, noticing as I did that my power was below 30 percent. Cardozo had tried several times but couldn't get a message through to his wife, and mine wouldn't send either. After another few trees crashed down, none of our phones had any bars at all. So they were useless, but I still cursed myself for not having charged the stupid thing.

By nine, the water had risen to cover the second step. Terri and I rearranged ourselves to let our host move a little higher.

By eleven or so, the noise outside had eased up. We wondered aloud whether the storm was over and decided to go take a look.

Cardozo's living room was destroyed. A tree branch lay across the couch, and a sea of broken glass covered the floor below where the window had been. Half the forest outside was gone. Looking down the hill, we saw fallen trees, dozens or hundreds of them, many with their dripping-wet root balls up in the air. Across the valley, an enormous scar showed where the side of a mountain had fallen away.

Between that mountain and ours was a brown lake that I didn't remember seeing before. A house was floating in it, swirling slowly, being carried to the left.

"Is that the river?" Terri asked. "Wait, where's the bridge?"

"Gone?" Cardozo said. "Or maybe submerged."

I went to look out the side door. A tree had fallen across my Subaru. Something else had shattered Terri's windshield. The glass was still in place, but it was white with a thousand cracks and cratered on the passenger side where something heavy had landed.

A little farther on, movement caught my eye. An old man in pajamas was leaning out a window at the side of his house waving something red—a dish towel, maybe.

"Hey, your neighbor down the hill might need help," I called to Cardozo.

I tested the side door; it opened fine. I looked up to make sure nothing was about to fall on me and then stepped out and yelled to the old man, "Morning, sir! You okay?"

"It's my wife!" he yelled back.

"She need help?"

"Yes!"

"Okay, be right there!"

Cardozo said, "That's the O'Haras. His wife's on oxygen."

"Oof. I hope she's got enough to last a while." I went to my room for shoes and blue jeans.

Outside, there was no more road. There were fallen trees, roof tiles, mud. I saw a child's stuffed animal caught in a bush.

It took the three of us more than ten minutes to cross the forty yards between Cardozo's place and the O'Haras', and another couple minutes to figure out how to get in, since the front door was about eight feet above ground level and the storm had plowed their car straight through the stairs. After a couple of options that Mr. O'Hara suggested turned out to be blocked by debris, I climbed up on top of their car and hoisted myself into the house.

His skinny, white-haired wife was lying on the couch. She raised a hand to say hi.

"So what's she need?" I said.

"That's her portable oxygen there," he said, pointing. Beside the couch I saw a plastic tank about two feet tall, with a strap on it. "She's resting to avoid using too much. It's only got probably another couple of hours left on it."

"Is that all the oxygen you have in the house?"

"Yep. Normally she doesn't use a tank, you know. She's on one of those concentrators. But they plug in, and with the power out, we don't have any way to charge it, so we hauled out the emergency one."

"I take it y'all don't have a generator?"

He shook his head. "Our son's getting one installed for us for the wintertime. Didn't think we'd need it this soon. We didn't anticipate the storm would be this bad."

I nodded, went back to the door, and yelled down to Cardozo, "You know if any of your neighbors got a generator?"

"Pretty sure the Andersons do. But they're farther up. Maybe a quarter mile."

I checked again with Mr. O'Hara how much oxygen was left, and then I did the math. We all discussed a few scenarios. The whole road, for as far as we could see, was in the same sorry shape as the part of it that we'd just crossed. There was no physical way to go a quarter mile uphill, see if the generator was working, and then come back and get Mrs. O'Hara and carry her up there before her oxygen ran out.

"I guess we just take her up there," I said, "and hope they've got what she needs."

"Between the three of us, we should be able to get her up there before her O2 runs out," Terri said.

We planned things out as best we could. Mr. O'Hara would stay in the house; the road was barely walkable for us, much less for him.

"I got some blankets and a few days' worth of food," he said. "And she made sure we had water." He gestured to the kitchen. About a dozen bowls and soup pots full of water were sitting on the counter.

He must've seen the confusion on my face.

"If the power's out at the source," he said, "that shuts our local water treatment plant down. The water stops coming out the faucets. With all the rain we had over the last few days, she made sure I got us prepared."

"Good call," I told Mrs. O'Hara.

Once Mr. O'Hara had helped his wife to the front door, I handed the backpack with her oxygen concentrator down to Terri, and then I handed down the tank that was attached to the long coil of plastic tubing that Mrs. O'Hara was breathing through.

Cardozo climbed up on the car so that the two of us could get her down to the ground. On the way uphill, we took turns carrying her while Terri carried her oxygen tank along with the concentrator and kept her company.

It took us nearly two hours to reach the Andersons' house. By the time we got there, I had a gash on my forehead from where I'd slipped and hit a fallen tree.

It looked like the Anderson place had taken damage similar to Cardozo's. Mr. Anderson, a big guy in his fifties, answered our knock and let us in when we explained ourselves. He'd powered up the generator that morning, he said, to keep their food from spoiling.

We apologized for the mud—we were all plastered in it up to our knees, and our hands and arms were dirty from the times we'd had to move branches or steady ourselves on something to climb around an obstacle—but he waved it off like it was nothing to worry about. After wiping down as best we could with a towel Mrs. Anderson gave us, we got Mrs. O'Hara situated in an armchair on the intact side of their living room and plugged in her oxygen concentrator.

Suddenly I was bone-tired. All three of us were. We went and sat on the deck, to avoid doing further damage to their real furniture, and Mrs. Anderson brought me some damp paper towels and a small first aid kit to take care of the gash on my head. After that I must've dozed off for a minute, because out of nowhere there was a plate next to me with a slice of bread and a piece of cheese.

Terri was still napping, but Mr. Anderson and Cardozo had a map laid out on the deck's coffee table. I picked my snack up and scooted my chair over to see what they were talking about.

"He's got a ham radio in his garage," Cardozo told me. "There's a few radio guys around here and in the next county, and they put their heads together to try to make a list of what roads and bridges are out. But based on their list, it doesn't look like there's any way out of here, for now at least."

"No way in, either," Mr. Anderson said.

I hadn't thought about that. After natural disasters, I had assumed rescuers came. But it was obvious, now that he mentioned it, that they needed roads and bridges to do that.

It was Friday afternoon. Vinny's trial was starting at half-past eight Monday morning, in Charleston, almost three hundred miles away.

"Are there any little airports nearby?" I asked. "Or someplace a helicopter could land?"

"There'd better be," Mr. Anderson said quietly, looking into the living room, where Mrs. O'Hara was sleeping. "Our generator runs on propane. We've unplugged everything nonessential to reduce the load and make it last as long as possible, but…" He didn't spell it out any further. We all knew what would happen if the propane ran out before we could get the older woman to safety.

We left Terri snoozing in her chair and followed Mr. Anderson through the house to the attached garage, where his ham radio setup was. At least from the inside, the garage looked like it hadn't suffered too much damage from the storm—just a broken window that he'd already covered with a sheet of plywood. Two folding tables arranged in an L shape held what looked like stacks of vintage stereo equipment and a small computer screen.

"I'd give you a little tour of my ham shack," he said. "Lot of cool stuff here. But we don't have time." He sat down, flipped a few switches, and slowly turned a dial. Static filled the room. He leaned over a microphone and started rattling things off like an auctioneer: "Mayday, Mayday, Mayday. Delta–Charlie–Five–Sierra…"

A minute later, when somebody answered, Anderson explained Mrs. O'Hara's situation and provided what sounded like our latitude, longitude, and altitude. "Gonna need a copter that can drop down a rescue basket," he said. "We're on the side of a mountain, and there's no place nearby that they can land. Over."

A crackly voice said, "What's your time frame? Can she survive twenty-four hours? Over."

"She ought to. We might have a little more propane than that, but not much. Over."

They went back and forth, and then the other guy asked him to hold on.

When Anderson leaned back in his chair to wait, Cardozo asked, "Who's that you're talking to? Local guy?"

"Yeah, I called in to the repeater. He's got a higher-powered system than mine. He's going to relay my message outside the area, see if we can find someone to come get her."

Something occurred to me. "How far outside the local area can you go?"

"Oh, no limit, pretty much. There's repeaters everywhere."

"Would a small airport have one of those? There's an airport outside Charleston called JZI—"

"Airport might," he said, shrugging. "Or, more likely, somebody that's part of that community has one. For whatever reason, there's some crossover between ham operators and pilots. Why?"

"I've got a friend who flies. And I've got a trial starting on Monday. Maybe it's wishful thinking, but I was wondering if he could somehow get us back home in time."

"Don't know where he'd land, though. What's a small plane need to land, fifteen hundred feet? Two thousand? Finding a flat stretch like that, around here, with no obstacles on it..." He shook his head.

I sighed. He was right.

"I mean, I can give it a try," he said. "But I've got to stay on this frequency until we get things figured out for Mrs. O'Hara."

"Of course."

"I'll check after that."

"Thanks."

While we waited to hear back, Terri woke up and checked on Mrs. O'Hara, who surprisingly wasn't too worried about her husband. "Oh, he'll be just fine on his own," she'd said. Terri also managed to clean up a bit more, making my own skin itch where the mud had dried. With three of us already hovering around the radio, she returned to the house to help Mrs. Anderson cobble together a meal for everyone.

It took most of the afternoon to arrange for a helicopter with a rescue basket. The voice over the radio said it would arrive the next morning, probably sometime between 9 a.m. and lunchtime.

Then Anderson started reaching out across the airwaves in search of Tucker.

Cardozo came back inside from a bathroom trip among the trees and said, "Sun's going to be setting soon."

"How long'd your walk up here take you, again?" Anderson asked.

"About two hours."

He whistled. "Y'all don't want to be doing that after dark."

"No, but we've got to tell O'Hara that his wife's okay."

"Sure, but this'd be a real bad time to break your ankle. One night of worrying won't kill him. We got sleeping bags and a foldaway bed. Y'all can stay."

———

Around eleven that night, Anderson shook me awake on the couch. "I got your friend on the radio."

We went back down to his ham shack, where Tucker's voice came through a cloud of static. "Leland! You just ride out that storm?"

"Seems like we did, yeah."

"Saw it on the news. It looks horrifying. Never thought a hurricane could get that far inland."

"I didn't either." No one did, or we'd have been warned about the danger.

"So, what do you need? Supplies?"

"Actually, if you're willing and able, we need a way out."

## 20

## SEPTEMBER 28, 2024

Early the next morning, Terri and I started back down the hill. Cardozo stayed behind so he could help Anderson get Mrs. O'Hara to the helicopter when it came.

A few more trees had fallen, and the mud had dried a little, but not enough to make it easier to walk. If anything, it was worse: less slippery, but stickier, like it was trying to keep you from moving ahead.

"You've got the directions?" Terri asked.

I nodded, patting my chest pocket, where two pieces of notebook paper were folded up and buttoned in tight.

After getting up at dawn, I'd spent an hour on the ham radio with Tucker. He'd reviewed maps of all the small airports and grass airstrips in the area and found a couple that were on the same side of the river as we were. Anderson had pulled out his big book of local maps and the list of washed-out roads and bridges. There was a grass strip a little over two miles away that looked like it might work.

I'd copied Anderson's maps with pencil and paper, using a highlighter to mark the lower points, which he thought might be flooded and impassible.

Tucker was giving us all day to get there. He'd told me he was borrowing a friend's Piper J-5 Cub, because unlike his own plane, it could take off and land in less than four hundred feet. His plan was to circle the field about an hour before sunset. If we were there and he could land, he'd pick us up. If we weren't or he couldn't, he'd drop supplies.

After about an hour and a half of careful walking, skirting crushed cars and climbing over toppled trees, we made it back to Cardozo's house. We needed our laptops for the trial, so I shoved them into the backpack Cardozo had told me I could find in his closet. We knew we wouldn't be able to wrangle our suitcases through the debris, and my briefcase would just throw me off-balance.

Terri went to the trunk beside the fireplace and took out a small axe. Cardozo wanted us to have it in case we needed to clear trees or branches off the landing strip.

We got some crackers from a cabinet and a half-eaten hunk of cheese from the dark, room-temperature fridge, and we took one of the water bottles. Everything else we left for Cardozo, since we didn't know how long he was going to be stuck.

Then we made our way across the muddy tree trunks to the O'Haras' place. We yelled for Mr. O'Hara a few times, and then I got up on top of his car to bang on the front door.

When he finally answered, he looked okay and was happy to see us.

"She's breathing fine on that oxygen concentrator," I told him. "And there's a helicopter coming to get her out of here today, before the generator runs out."

"Good, good," he said, smiling so hard I thought he might start to cry. "That's real good. Thanks. Y'all take care now."

He went back inside. We slogged and slipped and clambered on down the road. The going was too hard to talk much. I thought I ought to save my breath for when it was most needed, just like we had to conserve our food and water.

Within half an hour, the road changed. It looked like the mud had liquefied, swallowed a gray Ford Fusion and a red SUV, and then turned solid again, leaving about half of each car jutting out of the earth.

As we passed another house, a woman called out the window that her mother had died.

"I'm sorry," Terri called back. "We're going for help. We'll tell them you're here."

———

We thought reaching the first paved road would make it easier—it had to be easier to traverse than mud—but when we got there, we saw a mess of broken branches lying in a few inches of water, tangled up with a downed power line.

I saw the line first and put an arm out in front of Terri.

She swore.

"We can't touch any of that," I said. "Not so much as a leaf."

"Or that water," she said, staring at it. Her eyes were huge. "If that wire's live, that water might as well be a bolt of lightning."

We scouted a little bit to either side, and I pulled out my notebook-paper maps and studied them. We decided we had to backtrack ten or twenty yards, go down through what was left of the forest, and try to reach the road a little farther on.

We went back uphill a ways and cut between some bushes into the woods. The forest floor was a black sponge, soft muck with rivulets of water running down it like tiny waterfalls. The root balls of fallen trees were huge, some of them bigger than me, and the craters they'd left in the earth were deep and damp and loose.

"Let me get ahead of you," I said. "I'm heavier. Anything that holds me will hold you."

"That's mighty chivalrous of you."

"Yes, well, I figure if something happens, you're more equipped to find help than I am," I told her. She chuckled but let me pass, and we walked on in single file.

We made our way down the slope for another half hour. I heard the river in the distance but nothing else. No traffic, no voices. Not one bird was singing.

Between one step and the next, I felt it: a sound my bones could hear and a deep, slow-motion slide. The ground beneath our feet was not attached. I spun around, starting to fall, and saw terror on Terri's face. She was falling backward. The mountainside thundered as we went down. She slammed into me, and I hung on to her, trying to make us into a ball, because that seemed like the only safe shape. We wrapped ourselves around each other as a wave of dark earth churned over us, ramming mud into my nose and mouth, and then we lurched into something hard and the dark earth churned on without us.

We were caught in the root ball of a half-fallen tree. Terri was screaming "Oh my God!" over and over. I turned my head to cough up the mud and spit out what I could.

She fell silent. We looked at each other, both of us covered in mud, the mountain still shaking. I wondered how long this tree would hold.

I reached up and wiped some mud off her brow so it wouldn't end up in her eye. I heard a tree crash above us. I smiled at her. This wasn't a bad way to go.

She bent down and kissed me. I kissed her back, and between kisses we spat out mud, and we kept on kissing until we realized we weren't going to die.

———

Then we untangled, not looking at each other, and got back to work. The mountainside above us was a reddish-brown gash, with a few trees and houses up top where Cardozo's neighborhood still stood. Our part of the forest had fallen away. As we looked downhill, the asphalt road was about eighty yards off. I wrestled a long stick off the broken trunk of a nearby tree so I could poke the ground ahead of us as we walked, making sure it was solid before we took a step.

It took another hour to get to the road.

The town where we'd gone out for dinner only had six buildings now—I counted them—and they were up to their second story in brown river water. The restaurant was gone. The bridge was gone, or underwater. I wondered what had happened to the mountain men, the two crying women, the men Noah's age forking their money over to us at the pool table. I mentally wished them well and then put them out of my mind. There was nothing else I could do for them.

We stayed on the broken asphalt road, which sat on a spit of land about six feet higher than the river, and made good time for a while. We saw a woman's purse in the mud at the edge of the road, with a comb and a wallet a few feet away.

Something yellow caught my eye. Then I realized I was looking at a child about ten years old, wearing nothing but a pair of yellow shorts, tangled in a bush at the edge of the water. I climbed down to see if we could get him out, but he was gone.

Terri said a prayer.

Hours later, as we rounded the mountain, I saw a stretch of short grass a quarter mile off that had to be the landing strip. It was littered with broken branches, but they didn't look too big for us to move.

## 21

## SEPTEMBER 28, 2024

As the small plane rose higher, the ruined landscape unfurled below us. Broken bridges over brown rivers so wide they looked like lakes. Hillsides ripped away, and in the mess at the bottom, train tracks bent like paper clips. Whole towns had been reduced to piles of broken lumber, or in the valleys, to dark lakes with the roofs of a few houses poking out of the water. The sun was setting, and shadows of the mountains were drawing closed like curtains over it all.

From the back seat, Terri passed me our water bottle. I took a few slugs, gave it back to her, and devoured two of the protein bars Tucker had given me. The ziplock bag with the rest of them was on my lap. I held the edge of it in a tight grip, as if my safety might depend on having that food close at hand.

Ten minutes earlier, after Tucker landed on the strip, we'd unloaded the supplies that he'd strapped into the plane's two passenger seats. Some tarps, a four-person tent, a case of water, a few boxes of plastic-wrapped beef jerky. His wife had told him to bring diapers and formula, so there was a box each of those. We'd piled it all up on one of the tarps and then planted the bright pink plastic flag he'd brought in the ground so passersby could spot it.

I looked out the window. It was getting dark, and there were no lights on the ground.

Tucker's voice crackled to life in my headphones and, I supposed, Terri's too. "We should be in Charleston in around two hours," he said over the roar of the propeller and the rush of the wind. "We'll get you some real food there."

"Thank you," Terri said.

"Yeah, thanks so much," I echoed.

The fact that we could be plucked up from such devastation and restored to civilization in two hours was hard to take in. Out my window, I saw a white trailer on its side in the mud—it had been someone's home, but from here it looked like a crushed bug. If there'd been any people visible near it, I would've asked Tucker to fly lower so I could drop my protein bars down to them.

Something like a prayer rose in me: a sharp hope that the people who'd lived in that trailer had walked away to find help and were not dead beneath the waters.

Noah, I remembered, still didn't know we were okay. I hoisted my mud-caked backpack onto my lap, fought with the zipper—it was choked with what felt like dried clay—and found my phone. It was dead. Tucker's, I figured, probably wasn't, but I couldn't find Noah's number in my memory; I was too tired and too used to calling him by tapping his name on my screen. He would have to wait.

When I looked out the window again, we'd reached a point where the land below looked fine. The houses were intact, with windows lit yellow, and the trees were standing in their proper places. The storm had chosen one place to destroy and not another.

In my headphones I heard Terri murmur, "For we have walked through the valley of the shadow of death…"

I remembered that line from church as a child. I knew it didn't end there, but Terri had stopped speaking. She never got to the part that went "I will fear no evil."

I couldn't get there either. It would've sounded empty, like a greeting card. I turned to look at her in the back seat. She was gazing out the window, and in the red light shining from the tip of the airplane's wing, I thought I saw a tear on her cheek.

I reached back between the seats and brushed her fingers with the tips of mine. She didn't look at me—her eyes stayed on the land below—but she reached forward and grabbed my hand.

---

It was dark when we came in for a landing at the private airport on Johns Island, whizzing past the lines of blue lights on either side of the runway. We taxied into a big, well-lit hangar, and after Tucker had put chucks in front of the wheels of the little yellow plane and wiped the mud off the seats, we walked through the small terminal.

In our torn and filthy clothes, we got shocked looks from a few well-fed businessmen. Then a couple others came over to pump Tucker's hand and ask us how we were and what the situation was in western North Carolina.

One of the men peeled a few hundred bucks off the stack in his wallet and insisted, using Southern politeness maneuvers that I could not decently refuse, that I take it to go get me and Terri some new clothes. The other discussed with Tucker exactly where in the storm zone he could land his own plane and what supplies folks might need him to bring.

Then Tucker took us to the parking lot, threw some towels on the seats of his Mercedes for us to sit on, and drove us to our hotel downtown.

I used some of the cash to get us both T-shirts and shorts from the hotel gift shop, so we'd have something to sleep in, and then we headed for the elevator. Everybody else who was waiting for it chose not to get on with us, and in the elevator's mirrored interior, I saw why: we looked like we'd just crawled through a sewer. We got off on the third floor and headed for the showers in our respective rooms.

———

The next day, we bought suits to wear in court while Rachel drove up from Basking Rock to drop off our trial binders and a new laptop I'd had her put on my company card. I spent half the afternoon on the phone with tech support, getting the data transferred from my muddy old laptop to the new one. In the evening, after Terri and I had dinner in the hotel restaurant, my IT expert, Dr. Da Costa, came by to do some final prepping for trial. I'd rented a suite with a big office area. Terri, who was still exhausted from our ordeal, lay curled up on one of the beds while Da Costa got his laptop and big external display set up.

A feeling of unreality hovered over everything—to be clean and well fed inside a good, solid building seemed abnormal, a random stroke of luck—but I set that aside and got to work.

"I haven't had a chance to review any of what you sent," I told Da Costa. "We lost power before dawn Friday. So what'd you find?"

"I'll show you." He typed something on his keyboard and turned his laptop so I could see the screen. "These are the ARP logs for the Basking Rock courthouse on the morning of Nicholson's death."

The logs had arrived, in response to my subpoena, right after Terri and I had left for North Carolina. Rachel had sent them over to Da Costa. This was the first time I'd laid eyes on them.

"Okay…" I said. The information he was scrolling through made no sense to me. It was just columns of numbers and letters.

"What this shows is the MAC addresses and IP addresses of all the devices that were on the courthouse Wi-Fi network that morning. Since the courthouse set their system up with a router on each floor and Wi-Fi access points at the front and back of the building on each floor, we can see pretty much where each device was. Not exactly—there's some margin of error here—but it's still very useful. If a device moved around or changed floors, we can see that, too, because at some point during the trip it's going to connect to a different access point or a different router. And we can see when it did that."

"Wow." I was staring at the screen, trying to figure out how to present that mess of numbers to the jury.

"That's the raw data," he said. "Here's what I put together for the trial." He brought up a PowerPoint presentation, slid it over to the big screen, and started clicking through it. I nearly laughed with relief. Each slide showed a cutaway view of the courthouse's three floors and back stairwell, with icons of two cell phones—one red, one blue—representing Vinny and Judge Nicholson. The story the presentation told was where Vinny and Judge Nicholson had been at key points in time. One slide showed when Vinny let Nicholson into the stairwell by the second-floor door and walked away again; another two showed Nicholson's path up and down as he was getting his steps in. There was a slide showing where Nicholson stopped for a rest and one showing when he fell.

I pointed to the screen. "So that's Vinny? And we're sure he wasn't inside the stairwell at that point?"

"Well, like I said, there's some margin for error. What I can say for certain is that his phone was connected to the second-floor router via the access point at the back of the building, and then it switched to the third floor."

"So he went up the stairs? In that back stairwell?"

"Yes."

"Please tell me he wasn't there when Nicholson died."

"No, actually, it looks like it was right after Nicholson fell. And I mean *right* after, barely thirty seconds later. Here's the path."

He clicked something, and a video animation started playing on his slide. It had a digital clock running at the top, and it showed those two cartoon phones—the blue one representing Nicholson and the red one representing Vinny—moving through the courthouse. When it started, Vinny was on the second floor. Nicholson, in the stairwell, started climbing the steps from the second floor to the third. Then Nicholson's phone dropped to the ground floor.

Da Costa hit pause. "That's when he disconnected from the third-floor Wi-Fi and never reconnected to anything else. Which, to me, means that's when he fell."

"Wait, third floor? Not second?"

"Yeah, the access points all have a range—picture it like an invisible zone that extends a little ways into the stairwell. When you get close enough to the top of the stairs, you're closer to the third-floor Wi-Fi zone than to the second, so your phone switches to that one. When he fell, he disconnected from the third floor. And then the phone, obviously, broke when it hit the ground, so it didn't reconnect."

"Okay. And is that time accurate?"

The clock on Da Costa's screen said 11:50.32 a.m.

"Yeah. But that's the disconnection time. He would've fallen that whole distance in less than a second, so you can put the time he actually hit the ground at probably 11:51 and a few hundredths."

From the bed, Terri mumbled, "When I ran my tests, the phone disconnected on average eighteen hundredths of a second after it fell."

We looked over at her. She was lying on her side, her head on a big white pillow, with a corner of the quilt pulled over her. Her eyes were closed.

Da Costa gave me a quizzical look. "She did tests?"

"Yeah, right before we left town, she, uh…" I smiled, knowing the story was going to sound strange to him. "She talked to one of the courthouse IT guys, and she got a little help from another friend of ours there." It had been Ruiz, but I saw no need to mention his name. "Long story short, she managed to rig up some sort of bungee cord thing, using the same model of phone that Nicholson had, and she threw it over the railing I don't know how many times trying to figure all of this out."

"I dropped it," she murmured into her pillow. "I didn't throw it. And that bungee cord was twenty feet long. I wanted to make sure the phone was in free fall until the last quarter second or so, for the measurements to be accurate."

"When you say on average eighteen hundredths," Da Costa asked her, "what was the range?"

"Sixteen to twenty," Terri said, lifting her head so she could fluff up her pillow. "Pretty straightforward." She lay back down.

Da Costa typed away at high speed. I could see he was taking notes on what she'd said. "How'd you come up with that?" he asked her. "Do you have an IT background, or…?"

Terri cracked a big yawn. It lasted a while. When it was done, she said, "I'm a private investigator. I've got to have a background in a *lot* of things."

"And she does," I said with a smile before turning back to Da Costa's animation. "So who can you see on these networks? Was anybody else on the stairs?"

"Well, again, with this technique I can't place somebody in this back staircase with 100 percent certainty. What I can see is somebody's phone switching from one floor to another without the delay that there'd be if they were taking the elevator. And there's really no reasonable explanation for that, other than that they were in the stairwell."

"And do you see anybody else's phone doing that? At the back of the building, I mean?"

"Well, there were a lot of people in the courthouse," he said, scrolling through the columns of numbers on his laptop screen. "Although not nearly the two hundred-plus that you had mentioned."

Terri murmured, "You only see the phones that are on, though."

"Yeah," I said. "Most visitors have to turn their phones off at security. Or put them in airplane mode."

"Oh, okay. But Nicholson didn't, because he was a judge?"

"Right. And Vinny, because he was a courthouse employee."

"I got you. Yeah, there were several other phones at the back of the second floor. And there's one going from the back of the third floor to the back of the second, and then up to the third again." He pointed at a row of numbers.

"At the right time?"

"11:50, 11:51, yeah."

All I saw was code. Sequences of numbers, pairs of numbers and letters separated by periods.

"Can you tell anything about it?"

He grabbed some code out of the table and pasted it into the search field of some website on his other screen. After a moment, he said, "Well, it was an iPhone. Just a second." He opened another site and ran the search again. "Looks like an iPhone 15 Pro Max."

"Is that an expensive kind, or…?"

Terri started giggling. Without lifting her head from the pillow, she said, "Dr. Da Costa—"

"Please, call me Ben."

"Okay, Ben, Leland wouldn't know a nice iPhone if it bit him in the face. He carried this, like, 1990s flip phone, I swear to God, until… what was it, two years ago? And now he's finally got a smartphone, but it's this cheap, refurbished, like, factory-second Android thing—" She laughed again.

"That's true," I said, chuckling a little myself. "Any question I ask you about phones is probably going to be a stupid question."

"Not a problem," Da Costa said, smiling.

"Anyway, where was it? Are we sure this iPhone was in the stairwell?"

"Well, again, we're as sure as we are for Vinny's phone, and for the same reasons. It's on the third-floor Wi-Fi, then second floor, then back to the third, without any disconnection period to tell me that this person took the elevator."

"And was it in there after Vinny, or before?"

He consulted his rows of numbers. "Looks like it went in from the third floor," he said, "and that was about one minute before Vinny came in from the second floor. Then it came down to the second floor and was only there for six seconds before it went back up to the third. Assuming it went straight out the third-floor door—I mean, without lingering on the landing—then it left the stairwell twelve seconds before Vinny did. And there's actually about half a second of overlap, where they're both on the second-floor network."

I stared at him.

"Do you mean a half second where they were both in the stairwell at the same time?"

"Both in the stairwell within range of the second floor for half a second. That's what I mean. Then the iPhone went back up to the third floor. So, depending on how fast it was going up the stairs, there were maybe one or two seconds of overlap."

I pictured it as Vinny had told me. He'd said he'd gone into the stairwell from the second floor, something down below caught his eye, and he looked over and saw Nicholson's body. He'd never mentioned seeing or hearing someone, but I knew that the unexpected sight of a dead body tended to keep people from noticing anything else. And he'd been looking down, at the body, not up.

So he didn't see this iPhone person, but that didn't mean that the iPhone person didn't see him. I wasn't sure what to make of that, but it stuck in my mind.

## 22

## SEPTEMBER 30, 2024

It was a hot day, no sign of fall. Even at 8 a.m., as I walked into the Charleston federal courthouse with Terri, Rachel, and Da Costa, it was sweltering.

The three of them went up to Judge Jefferson's courtroom, Rachel pushing a cart full of binders and exhibits to get us set up. I took my briefcase and garment bag downstairs to meet Vinny.

One of the guards brought him out of the holding pen. When he saw me, Vinny looked taken aback. Lifting both his cuffed hands to gesture to the scabbed-up gash on my forehead, he said, "That from the hurricane?"

"This? Yeah."

"Damn. It got you, for real!"

I thought of the boy in the yellow shorts. "This is nothing."

Then I asked the guard, "Can you escort us to the men's room? He's got to put this suit on for trial."

In the courtroom, the prospective jurors filed in for voir dire. Judge Jefferson, a tall Black man in his fifties, presided. His clerk swore everybody in at once, and then Jefferson embarked on his version of the inspiring, patriotic speech that judges always gave at this point, to set the tone and make jurors aware of the importance of their service.

The last time I'd been before Jefferson, he'd been a magistrate, handling simple cases, preliminary hearings, and discovery disputes. But six months before Vinny's trial, he'd been elevated—that is, nominated and confirmed—to district judge.

Vinny found the fact that he was Black reassuring, so I didn't trouble him with my concern. Jefferson was smart, with a Vanderbilt law degree and a thoughtful, methodical cast of mind—all of which was good. He was a law-and-order guy, which wasn't ideal for defendants, but so was every other judge in South Carolina. I couldn't complain about that.

The thing that gave me pause was that this was Jefferson's first murder trial.

He'd gone from twenty years in private practice, litigating insurance-coverage and other civil cases, to being a magistrate. And now, with no experience presiding over any high-stakes criminal cases at all, here he was.

I didn't like my client being any judge's test case. But there was nothing I could do about it.

---

The jury panel was the usual. The forty people being questioned were mostly retirees, older stay-at-home moms whose children had left the nest, and a handful of plumbers, electricians, and healthcare workers.

A few Black people, a couple of Hispanics. As Jefferson asked them the basics—did they know anybody involved in the case, had they heard about it in the news, was there any reason they could not be impartial—nobody stuck out to me as being a clear winner or an obvious problem for us.

Jefferson excluded nearly a dozen people for knowing too much about the case already. Nobody wanted jurors who might share misinformation from the news or social media with their fellow jurors, and we certainly didn't want ones who'd already made up their minds. Three more were let go because they had past experiences with violent crime and said they weren't sure they could be unbiased.

Wilcox and I each got ten minutes to ask our own questions. It wasn't enough; it never was. I used my peremptory strikes to get rid of a few more—a man who'd given Vinny a judgmental look, a woman who seemed to find Wilcox fascinating, a man who radiated anger—and Wilcox did the same.

And then we were done. We'd chosen, with very little to go on, the people who would hold the rest of Vinny's life in their hands.

Jefferson called the lunch break and told us all to reconvene at one o'clock.

---

In the war room, with a prison guard standing outside the door, Vinny and his mom ate lunch together. It was the first meal they'd been able to share since his arrest ten months earlier. She'd cooked for him and brought it in three different Tupperwares. The room smelled like an Italian restaurant.

I wished I could leave them to enjoy each other's company without me, but I had to be there. If I hadn't told the guard I needed to spend the lunch break consulting with my client, he would've taken Vinny, who he called "the prisoner," back to the basement holding area to eat a sandwich by himself.

While they enjoyed their meal—Vinny raving about the food, his mom giving him hugs every thirty seconds—Da Costa chattered at me like a weird, hyperlogical kid. He'd never been in a courtroom before, and he wanted to share his observations. Court proceedings were, according to him, interestingly irrational. As I got to know him, I could see why he and Cameron had hit it off.

Da Costa's lack of court experience was why Vinny could afford him. And since he lived in Charleston, we could have him listen to all the testimony—just like the rich folks had their expert witnesses do—without needing to put him up in a hotel. I'd done what I could to prepare him for being raked over the coals on cross. I hoped it would be enough.

---

The prosecutor gave his opening statement first. He got to tell the jury the story, and I then had to convince them that his version wasn't true. Nobody had ever tried to quantify how much of an advantage that gave prosecutors, but it was palpable. I started every trial standing in the hole that the other guy had dug.

And once Wilcox introduced himself and thanked the jurors for their service, I found out that he knew how to spin a tale.

"I knew a man, ladies and gentlemen, called Frederick J. Nicholson. Forty-nine years old. A man who toiled many years as a prosecutor, making the streets safe for people like you and me. I'll put a picture of him up for you, so you can get a sense of the man."

A photo of Judge Nicholson appeared on the big display up on the wall and on the iPad-sized ones in front of every juror. It jarred me. I'd only ever seen Nicholson in black robes up on the bench, but this was a family photo showing him outside a football stadium. Blue sky, big smiles, everyone wearing the team's T-shirts. He had one arm around his wife and the other around both of his daughters.

"Yep," Wilcox said, with a tinge of sadness in his voice. "He had a good life. He was a married man, father of three. As you can probably see from those T-shirts, Judge Nicholson and his family were from Texas. They're wearing the blue-and-white colors of the Dallas Cowboys there. They only moved here to South Carolina eight years ago, when the United States government made him a federal judge here in our district. Mrs. Nicholson and their children are sitting in this courtroom today, right here in the front pew on the prosecution's side of the room."

He gestured to them, and I saw that Monty was sitting with the family. Mrs. Nicholson and her youngest daughter turned their faces to the jury—grave faces that seemed to be asking for help. The girl was still a child, eleven or twelve at the most. The son, who looked about twenty, and the middle daughter glanced at the jurors and then looked down, like they couldn't quite cope with the reality of what had happened and where we all were.

"Now, Mr. Nicholson—or, I should say, Judge Nicholson, because that's what he was at the time of his death—Judge Nicholson dedicated his life to the law and to the service of justice in this country. That path led him to be nominated by the President of the United States to become a federal judge, and the United States Senate confirmed him. Very enthusiastically, I might add, with a strong bipartisan vote. He served as judge right here in this district. Matter of fact, he served in the courtroom just down the hall." He gestured in that direction.

Then his arm dropped. He looked at the floor and sighed. This next part seemed like it was hard for him to say.

"Ladies and gentlemen," he said, still looking at the floor, "all of that came to an end late last year."

He looked up at them and continued.

"On November 17, less than a week before Thanksgiving, Judge Nicholson drove down to Basking County, about two hours south of here. He wasn't going for the reasons most folks visit the Lowcountry—not for the fishing, or the sailing, or any of that. He went down there with his judicial clerk, Samantha Townsend, and his lawyer, James Montgomery. He went in the service of justice, to give testimony as a witness in a court case down there. But, ladies and gentlemen, he never came back."

He looked from juror to juror, letting that sink in.

"The evidence you're about to hear will show that in the Basking County Courthouse, where he waited for hours for his turn to testify, a key card was used to let Judge Nicholson into a disused stairwell so that he could, as he would have put it, 'get his steps in.' In other words, exercise. But the man who provided that key card held a terrible grudge against Judge Nicholson. So he followed Judge Nicholson into that stairwell and pushed him over a railing, sending Judge Nicholson falling almost thirty feet to his death.

"The judge's family," he said, gesturing to them, "lost a husband and father. And they are here today to see justice done."

Monty whispered something to Mrs. Nicholson, who nodded. A few rows back, I noticed Nicholson's clerk. Like Mrs. Nicholson, she was dressed in black.

Wilcox started pacing.

"Now, in this trial, you're going to hear from a lot of witnesses. You'll see a whole lot of evidence. And I'll be the first person to tell you that a trial can be very technical, and it can be very dry. It's not like on TV.

We'll go step by step through every detail, and sometimes it can feel like a pile of facts so big it's hard to keep them all straight. The FBI and my team have had months to look through all these facts and figure things out, but you folks will only have a week. So, right now, before we all start looking at the evidence, I want to put it in plain English for you."

He turned to look at Vinny.

"As His Honor informed you earlier, ladies and gentlemen, this is the defendant, Mr. Baptiste. Before he was arrested for this crime, he worked at the Basking County Courthouse as a member of the maintenance staff." He turned back to the jury. "And let me tell you folks what led the FBI to his doorstep. It's real simple. I can count it out on one hand."

He started counting on his fingers.

"First off, the stairwell where Judge Nicholson died wasn't used by the public. Its railings weren't high enough for modern safety codes, so it was kept locked. That means the first question was, who let him into that stairwell? The FBI found out that courthouse janitors were allowed to use that stairwell if they needed to, and the key cards for it were kept in the maintenance room. The FBI then spoke to a witness who stated that shortly before Judge Nicholson went into that stairwell and died, Mr. Baptiste had gone to the maintenance room and taken the key card. So, of course, they went and talked to him."

He looked at Vinny again. Most of the jurors followed suit.

"The second piece of evidence you'll hear," Wilcox said, "is that when the FBI asked Mr. Baptiste where he'd been that morning and whether he'd provided the key card, Mr. Baptiste did something a little strange. He lied to the FBI. Faced with FBI agents investigating a murder, he chose to lie. He told them he didn't have anything to do with this. And he kept that lie going until he was faced with the fact that two different witnesses said he was the one. Only at that point did he admit it."

Wilcox spread his hands wide. "Who *does* that, ladies and gentlemen? Why would someone lie to the FBI? Well, you'll hear, over the course of this trial, what it was that Mr. Baptiste was trying to hide. For instance, number three…" He went back to counting on his fingers.

"You'll see time-stamped video footage showing Mr. Baptiste walking into the stairwell one minute before Judge Nicholson was pushed over the railing. And you *won't* see any footage of him walking back out of there before Judge Nicholson was killed. You won't see any such footage, because there isn't any. There is no evidence that Mr. Baptiste was anywhere but inside that stairwell at the time of the murder. You also won't see any evidence that anybody else was in that stairwell at that time. Judge Nicholson went into the stairwell with his clerk about twelve minutes before he died, but we have time-stamped video showing her coming out of it three minutes *before* he was pushed."

Wilcox started walking along the jury box, looking at the jurors.

"And now, on to number four. Because of the substantial evidence against Mr. Baptiste that I just described to you, the FBI was able to obtain a warrant to search his home and his computer. And what they found was that, two weeks before Judge Nicholson was scheduled to appear at the Basking County Courthouse, Mr. Baptiste ran some searches on him. He looked him up and read about him. He knew who Judge Nicholson was, he knew that the judge was coming to Mr. Baptiste's place of work, and he cared about that enough to be looking it up on the internet. And in a minute, I'll tell you why he cared."

He reached the end of the jury box and started pacing back the other way.

"So that's the state of it. Facts one through four show that Mr. Baptiste provided the card that got Judge Nicholson into the stairwell. They show that he lied about that fact to the FBI. They show that he went into the stairwell right before the murder. And there's no evidence pointing any other way: no evidence that he left the stairwell before the judge fell, and no evidence that anybody else *but* Mr. Baptiste was in there when His Honor was killed. Furthermore, they show that he knew Judge Nicholson would be coming to the courthouse that day and that he'd been reading up on the judge in advance."

He stopped and faced the jury. "And that brings us to fact number five, which is the *why*. Why did Mr. Baptiste do this?"

He nodded to his paralegal, and an old newspaper headline appeared on the display: "Suspect in CEO Murder Arrested." The article included photos of Baptiste's brother and the man he killed.

"I'm sure many of y'all remember this case from the news," Wilcox said.

Most of the jurors nodded. I could see surprise on some of their faces. They were wondering—anybody would—what this had to do with our case.

"I certainly remember it," Wilcox said. "On April 12, 2010, in Dallas, Texas, a young man by the name of Primo Marconi—that's a photo of him right there—hunted down and shot dead a health insurance executive who he blamed for his father's demise from cancer. Mr. Marconi was arrested and tried for his crime, and he was sentenced to life in prison for murder. Less than a year after he began his sentence, he was killed in a prison fight."

An article about that appeared on the display.

"What you don't see in these articles," Wilcox said, "is two crucial facts for this case. The first one is that Primo Marconi was Mr. Baptiste's big brother."

Two women on the jury gasped, and a man looked at Vinny in surprise.

"They were half-brothers. Same mother, different fathers, but they grew up together. They were close, until Mr. Marconi did the horrible thing he did and his life was cut short. And the other crucial fact," Wilcox said, "is that the prosecutor who brought murder charges against Mr. Marconi—charges that put him in prison, where he died—was Mr. Nicholson."

Everyone on the jury was staring at Vinny now.

"And that's the *why*, ladies and gentlemen. That was the grudge that Mr. Baptiste bore in his heart against Judge Nicholson: he held him responsible for the death of his big brother. If Judge Nicholson, back when he was a prosecutor, hadn't pushed for a prison term—if he'd recognized what some folks viewed as the brother's mental health problems and let him serve his sentence in a secure mental health facility, then Mr. Baptiste's brother might still be alive today."

Wilcox looked at the floor, shaking his head, and then looked back at the jury. "That's why Mr. Baptiste was looking Judge Nicholson up on the internet two weeks before the murder. That's why he was keeping track of Judge Nicholson's schedule and his movements. That's why he went and got a key card to let Judge Nicholson into a disused stairwell, and that's why he pushed him over the railing to die on the stone floor thirty feet below."

## 23

## SEPTEMBER 30, 2024

It was my turn. I stood before the jury, looking from face to face. All of them were paying attention. Two of them looked wary, like they thought I might try to trick them and they needed to be on their guard.

I introduced myself and Vinny—Vincenzo, I called him; in the formality and dignity of a courtroom, nicknames were out of place.

Then I said, "Mr. Wilcox just told us a very dramatic and compelling story. He told us about a tragedy that befell the Nicholson family, and that part of his story—the part about who Judge Nicholson was, and what was lost when he died—is absolutely true. Mrs. Nicholson lost her husband, decades before any woman expects to, and their children lost their father. And Judge Nicholson was a good man. I didn't know him personally, but as a lawyer, I had cases before him, and I can tell you that he was a good judge. His passing is an immense loss to his family, and to the legal community that I'm a part of, and to this country, which all of us are a part of."

A ray of sunshine came through one of the courtroom's high windows and hit my face, blinding me. I waited half a second—if nature handed me a dramatic moment while I was in front of a jury, I'd take it—and then stepped to one side.

"But the most important part of Mr. Wilcox's story—the part that you, as jurors, have been called here to consider and decide upon—isn't true."

"Objection," Wilcox called out. "Argumentative."

Opening statements were supposed to focus on evidence, not argument, but I doubted Wilcox actually thought that what I'd said was improper. He was just trying to break my flow and snap the jury out of the state of rapt attention that a good attorney could put them in.

Jefferson looked at me.

"The evidence supporting that will be in my very next sentence, Your Honor," I said.

He nodded. "Let's make sure of that, counsel. Overruled."

I didn't like His Honor's commentary. It played right into Wilcox's efforts to break my flow. And, worse, it could make the jury think I'd done something wrong.

"As the evidence will show," I went on, "the most important part of Mr. Wilcox's story is not true. First of all, the evidence will show that Mr. Baptiste never blamed Judge Nicholson for his brother's death. The only person he blames is his brother. You'll hear that directly from Mr. Baptiste. He'll tell you that he's angry at his brother for taking a man's life. He's angry at his brother for choosing to deprive that man's children of their father. And he's angry at his brother for inflicting so much pain on their mother, Mrs. Baptiste, by committing that heinous act. But he was never angry at Judge Nicholson for putting his brother in prison. He was angry at his brother for *deserving* to be put in prison."

I turned to look at Vinny so that the jury would look at him too.

"You'll hear evidence," I said, "that Mr. Baptiste operates by a moral code—a code that emphasizes discipline and personal responsibility."

"Objection," Wilcox said. "I apologize, Your Honor, but we're getting into propensity evidence here, which isn't going to be admissible."

"Not at all," I said. "This is about the lack of motive."

Jefferson thought about it. Then he nodded. "Overruled."

"As you'll hear," I continued, "Mr. Baptiste follows rules that I think we'd all agree are pretty sound. He doesn't drink or smoke. He's got no criminal record—his arrest in this case is the only brush with the law that he's ever had. He's been gainfully employed in a full-time job at the Basking County Courthouse since the age of twenty-one, and he helps support his mother by paying her rent for his bedroom in her home. And before all this unfolded, he was taking classes after work to become an information technology professional and get a step up in life. That's who this young man is."

I walked toward the jury box.

"So what the evidence will show," I said, "is that this so-called why that Mr. Wilcox spoke of—the reason, the motive—simply doesn't exist. It's a great story—I'd watch it if it were on TV—but it's not a *true* story. It's simply not what happened here."

Pacing alongside the jury box, looking at each juror in turn, I said, "You'll be able to hear that for yourselves when Mr. Baptiste testifies. But before we even get there, you'll also hear another absolutely critical piece of evidence. It's technical, it's dry, but it's objective. It doesn't come from anybody personally involved in this case. It comes from the phone companies that provided cell phone service to Judge Nicholson and Mr. Baptiste, and it comes from the automated records kept by the courthouse's internet service—which we'll be referring to as the courthouse's Wi-Fi, for short."

I turned and paced back up the other way.

"And what *that* evidence shows is that when Mr. Baptiste entered the stairwell, Judge Nicholson had already fallen over the railing and passed away. He had already gone to his reward. In short, Mr. Baptiste *could not* have killed him."

I heard some rustling from behind me and saw a juror glance in Wilcox's direction. To prevent him from objecting again, I added a quick, "That's what the evidence will show." The rustling stopped.

If Wilcox hadn't been so objection-happy, or if Jefferson had been better at keeping him in line, I would've said more. But I wasn't going to let him turn my story into a choppy mess or portray me as so desperate about the weakness of my case that I was willing to break the rules.

When I reached the middle of the jury box, I stopped and repeated, "That, ladies and gentlemen, is what the evidence will show."

---

When I'd concluded, Judge Jefferson announced a fifteen-minute recess. Wilcox and I had jointly requested a Rule 615 order to exclude witnesses from the courtroom until they were called to testify, so he informed the audience of that and ordered all witnesses to leave. I saw Monty and several others walking out. All of them were scheduled to testify the next day, but I supposed they'd wanted to see the opening statements.

Miss Townsend, Nicholson's clerk, was not among them. She'd been on Wilcox's witness list, but she wasn't on the schedule yet. I didn't know if she was going to be. We weren't required to call every single witness that we listed.

And, I recalled, she didn't work at the courthouse anymore. In the wake of my subpoena hearing, the media had gone to town on her. Dabney Barnes's news site ran her picture under the headline "Slut-storm? Federal Bimbo Has No Comment." I'd heard through the grapevine that she had resigned.

I didn't feel great about that, especially since we hadn't found anything useful in Nicholson's texts with her. Apparently, neither of them had been sloppy enough to create text evidence of their affair.

After the recess, Wilcox called his first witness. Jennifer Gonzalez, the Resident Agent in Charge of the Charleston FBI field office, was a sturdy-looking woman of about forty-five. Several of the female jurors perked up, looking more interested, after Wilcox had Gonzalez explain who she was. A female FBI agent who led an investigative team and ran her own field office was novel to them.

Wilcox walked her through her background, spending a lot of time on the training in murder investigations that she'd gotten at Quantico. It was the same training every new FBI agent got, and it was typically all they ever got, since there wasn't usually much need for FBI agents to conduct murder investigations. Most murders were state crimes, not federal; the FBI didn't get involved.

But Wilcox's goal wasn't to present a strictly realistic picture. His goal was to make Agent Gonzalez sound like a hotshot, and he succeeded.

"Agent Gonzalez," he said, "could you describe for the jury how your team became involved in this investigation?"

"Yes. At approximately twelve thirty p.m. on November 17, 2023, I received a phone call informing me that a federal judge from our district had died under potentially suspicious circumstances at a court-house down in Basking Rock. I spoke with the sergeant in charge, which is to say the lead local law enforcement officer on the scene, and then I immediately assembled my team and we drove down."

"And about what time did you get there?"

"Shortly before two thirty p.m."

"And what did you observe when you arrived?"

"Well, local law enforcement had secured the crime scene, and the coroner was on site with his team."

"So law enforcement was treating it as a crime scene at that point?" He knew the answer, but he wanted the jury to know it too.

"Our mandate, and any law enforcement officer's mandate, is to treat any potential crime scene as a crime scene until it's determined not to be one."

"And what does that entail?"

"Well, in many crime scenes the first priority is the physical safety of any victims, as well as officers and bystanders. But in this case, the victim was deceased, and there didn't appear to be any immediate threat to anyone else. So the priority was to preserve the scene with minimal contamination or disturbance of the physical evidence. Local law enforcement had already secured the boundaries of the scene, and they continued to control access after we took over."

"Can you explain what you mean by 'took over'?"

"My team took charge of the forensic investigation in the stairwell. Local law enforcement placed officers outside each of the stairwell doors, and it's my understanding that they also controlled the movement of people inside and near the courthouse, identified those on site, and so forth."

"Why do you say it's your understanding? Did you not see them do that yourself?"

"No, I did not, because I was in charge of processing the crime scene. Taking photographs and measurements, collecting the physical evidence, and so forth."

"Okay. And, with apologies to the family, at what point were Judge Nicholson's remains removed from the scene?"

"The coroner's team did that when we were done processing the scene, which was approximately two hours and forty minutes after we arrived."

"Is that normal procedure?"

"Yes. Only the coroner's office is permitted to move a victim's body, and on a properly managed crime scene, that doesn't happen until the scene has been processed."

"And to your knowledge, was any key card or any other means of physically accessing the stairwell found on the victim's person or anywhere nearby?"

"No. He did not have the means to get into that stairwell himself."

Wilcox nodded. "Did that tell you anything about how the incident had unfolded?"

"Yes. It told me that someone had let him into the stairwell and then fled the scene, taking the key card with them."

"Okay. Now, can you walk us through some of the photographs that your team took? I'd like to invite the family to look away at this point, or to depart the courtroom if they so choose."

Judge Jefferson announced a pause in proceedings, and Mrs. Nicholson left, along with her daughters. The son remained, looking stoically at the blank display, waiting to see what had happened to his father.

He flinched when the first photo appeared. It looked to have been taken from the second landing, about twenty feet up. Nicholson's body lay belly down, splayed in an unnatural position on the stone floor, with a pool of red around his head. Wilcox and Agent Gonzalez proceeded through dozens of photos. The blood spatter on the walls. The shoe that came off and landed six feet from the body. The shattered cell phone on the stone floor. The snapshots, one taken through a magnifying glass and the other not, of the tufts of navy-blue wool from Nicholson's suit, which had caught on the rough stone railing when Judge Nicholson started to fall.

"Agent Gonzalez," Wilcox said, "at what point did you conclude that the circumstances of Judge Nicholson's death were suspicious?"

"That had already been concluded by local law enforcement based on their knowledge and their observations. If his demise had not appeared suspicious to them, they wouldn't have reached out to the FBI. They called us because he was a federal judge and he'd been found in a locked stairwell that the public didn't have access to. In addition, at least on a preliminary visual investigation, no key card was seen on or near the body, which indicated that a third party may have let him into that stairwell and subsequently fled."

"I see. And what did you do to investigate that possibility?"

"We proceeded to interview all courthouse employees who had been present that morning, one of whom identified her colleague, Mr. Baptiste—the defendant—as having removed the key card from the maintenance room prior to Judge Nicholson's death."

"Did you find her statement credible?"

"Yes, I did. We had already taken the statement of Judge Nicholson's associate who actually received the key card from a courthouse employee, and he had described that employee's appearance in a manner that was very consistent with the appearance of Mr. Baptiste."

Every time she said Vinny's name, she looked at him. Nearly all the jurors followed her gaze.

"Okay. And did you investigate that further?"

"We did. I interviewed Mr. Baptiste on November 19, 2023, but he denied having provided the key card to anyone."

"And did that resolve your concerns?"

"No, it did not."

"Why not?"

"Because we had two eyewitnesses, one of whom didn't know the defendant personally but was able to describe him, and another who did know the defendant personally and identified him by name."

"You had two eyewitnesses identifying the defendant. Uh-huh." He looked over at Vinny; the jury did too. "And what were your next steps?"

"I interviewed the defendant again, this time accompanied by another team member, and we confronted him with the nature of the evidence against him. At that point, he acknowledged having provided the key card that was used to open the stairwell door."

"I see. And to clarify, who was this associate, and what was his role here?"

"Our investigation determined that Judge Nicholson had traveled to Basking Rock with his judicial clerk, Samantha Townsend, and his personal attorney, James Montgomery. We interviewed both of them and reviewed the available security camera footage, and we determined that Mr. Montgomery had been the one who interacted with the defendant, and that all four of them—that is, Judge Nicholson and his entourage, plus the defendant—had proceeded to the stairwell together. Miss Townsend went in with Judge Nicholson, but Mr.

Montgomery did not. After the defendant let them in, Mr. Montgomery went back down the hall."

"Went back down the hall in which direction?"

"His direction was consistent with going back to the room at the courthouse where the three of them had been waiting."

Wilcox nodded. "Was Miss Townsend still in the stairwell when His Honor was killed?"

"She was not. The security footage showed that she exited the stairwell after approximately five minutes. According to the victim's cell phone data, however, he was engaged in climbing up and down the stairs for approximately eleven minutes before he was killed."

"Okay, thank you. How would you characterize the demeanors of Miss Townsend and Mr. Montgomery when you interviewed them?"

"They both appeared to be very affected by Judge Nicholson's passing. They were also both what I would describe as cooperative witnesses. Neither of them appeared defensive, and they both volunteered information that was consistent with the facts as we understood them at that time."

"What about when you questioned Mr. Baptiste? What was his demeanor like?"

She paused for a moment as if thinking about it, though I was certain she'd prepared fully for this and knew what she intended to say. "He was evasive. I'd have to say squirrelly. Like he was hiding something."

"And did you ever determine whether he was, in fact, hiding something?"

"I did, yes. And he was."

"Can you explain that for the jury?"

"Mr. Baptiste claimed not to know anything about what had happened. He claimed not to have seen Judge Nicholson. I specifically asked him if he'd let anybody into the stairwell, and he said he had not."

"And was that true?"

"No. He was lying."

"What was he lying about?"

"All of it. The second time I questioned him, when he was faced with the evidence we had gathered, he broke down and confessed that none of that was true. He had seen Judge Nicholson, and he had let Judge Nicholson and his associates into the stairwell."

"So he'd lied about seeing the judge and lied about letting him into the stairwell—and was that all he lied about?"

"Obviously, when he claimed to, quote, not know anything about it, that was also a lie."

"And were Mr. Baptiste's lies important to your investigation?"

"Yes. They were critical."

"Now, when you say that he lied, are you basing that just on the fact that his story was inconsistent with other witnesses?"

"No, I'm not. I'm also basing it on video footage from security cameras at the Basking County Courthouse."

"Okay. Let's take a look at some of that now."

His paralegal cued up the footage, and for the next five minutes, we watched.

With the time stamp running like a stopwatch at the bottom right of the screen, Vinny escorted Nicholson, Monty, and Miss Townsend to the stairwell. He touched the key card to the lock. Monty opened the door and held it while the other two went in, and then he walked back down the hall. A few seconds later, Vinny followed him.

We jumped ahead, and Miss Townsend came back out of the stairwell. Wilcox called our attention to the time stamp on that: 11:45.

We jumped again. Vinny walked back up the hall carrying a bucket. He pulled out the key card and let himself into the stairwell. The time stamp said a few seconds after 11:52 a.m.

Wilcox motioned for his paralegal to hit pause. She did.

"Agent Gonzalez, would you be able to explain, just so the jury understands, why this footage is silent?"

"Security camera footage generally is silent, both to make sure the equipment complies with privacy laws in all jurisdictions where it's sold, and also because the sound quality in a public space doesn't tend to be that great."

"Thank you. And one more detail. Your team has reviewed all of the security footage from that morning pertaining to this stairwell, correct?"

"Yes, correct."

"So if I put this other footage here side by side, would you be able to explain that to the jury?" A second image appeared on the screen: a nearly identical hallway.

"Yes, that's the same area but on the first floor of the courthouse."

"Meaning the ground floor?"

"Yes."

"So we're looking at what exactly, here?"

"The security footage that shows the first-floor and second-floor entrances to the stairwell that Judge Nicholson died in."

"Okay. Thank you. And for the record, what's the time stamp on those?"

"They're both at eleven fifty-two a.m. and thirty seconds."

"Okay. Now, if I hit play, would you be able to explain what we're looking at?"

"Yes, I would."

"And, by way of explanation, could you identify the room that's on the other side of the hallway from this stairwell entrance?"

"That's the women's bathroom."

"On both floors?"

"Yes."

"Thank you.

He hit play. A woman walked into the second-floor bathroom, and another woman came out. Downstairs, the crowd was bigger. Three women came out, one went in, and then a woman in the hallway stopped short and looked at the stairwell door. She stepped closer, peered through the window in the door, and then turned, calling out, looking distressed. A man came to look, then another, and then a guard ran into the frame waving his arms. He looked through the door, stiffened in alarm, and whipped out his walkie-talkie.

"Agent Gonzalez, what are we seeing here?"

"The discovery of Judge Nicholson's body on the ground floor."

"And what are we not seeing?"

"The defendant, Mr. Baptiste. He went into the stairwell at the second floor approximately one minute before the victim's body was discovered, just before this clip started playing, but we still haven't seen him come out."

"And what does that tell you?"

"That either he's still in there, or he exited on the third floor, which didn't have a working security camera at the time."

"And since Judge Nicholson's clerk left the stairwell a few seconds after eleven forty-five a.m., have we seen anybody other than Mr. Baptiste enter it?"

"No, we have not."

"And have we seen anybody other than Mr. Baptiste pull out a key card and unlock it? For instance, to let somebody else in or out?"

"No, we have not."

"And as the investigator, what does that tell you?"

"Two things. First, that Mr. Baptiste is the last person we know to have entered that stairwell before the victim's body was discovered. And second, that he must've exited on the third floor."

"Uh-huh. And you spoke earlier about some fabric on the handrail that told you whereabouts in the stairwell Judge Nicholson was when he fell. Where exactly was that fabric?"

"On the part of the handrail that runs between the second and third floors."

"And was that an important fact for your investigation?"

"Yes."

"Why?"

"Because, as we just saw, Mr. Baptiste entered the stairwell from the second floor moments before Judge Nicholson's body was found, and he must've exited on the third floor. Which means that right before the body was found, Mr. Baptiste walked up the very flight of stairs that Judge Nicholson fell from to his death."

## 24

## OCTOBER 1, 2024

The next morning, I cross-examined Agent Gonzalez.

There was nothing to gain from talking about her investigation of Vinny. I didn't want to give her any more opportunities to talk about the evidence that pointed to him.

"Agent Gonzalez," I said, "I'd just like to go over what did *not* happen and what there's *no* evidence of. Now, this is real basic, but I want to make sure the record is absolutely clear: Mr. Baptiste has not confessed to having killed Judge Nicholson, has he."

"No, he hasn't."

"So this isn't one of those cases where somebody's confessed to a crime and then tried to retract that confession, is it."

"No, it's not."

"Thank you. And he's never confessed to having any type of altercation or argument or any kind of interaction at all with Judge Nicholson in the stairwell, has he."

"No."

"So you would agree, wouldn't you, that this isn't one of those cases where somebody's admitted he had some type of fight with the victim but denied that he caused his death?"

"Yes."

"Yes, you agree it's not that type of case?"

"Yes, I agree."

"Thank you. And isn't it true there's no DNA evidence linking Mr. Baptiste to Judge Nicholson?"

She paused, then leaned toward the mike and said, "That's technically correct."

"It's just correct, period, isn't it?"

"Yes."

"Because your team took samples from under Judge Nicholson's fingernails, didn't they?"

"We did."

"You took those to check if he'd scratched his assailant, as victims sometimes do, and those samples didn't match Mr. Baptiste, did they."

"We found no third-party DNA under his fingernails, no."

"So, to be clear, you ran DNA tests?"

"We did, but—"

"And there was no match to Mr. Baptiste's DNA?"

"No."

"And, looking at the other forensic tests you ran, you found fabric from Judge Nicholson's suit on the handrail, didn't you?"

"Yes, we did."

"And the location of that fabric told you where on the stairwell he'd fallen from, correct?"

"Yes, it did."

"But you found no fabric from Mr. Baptiste's clothes there, correct?"

"We didn't find any other fabric there."

"Or anywhere else in that stairwell, correct?"

"Correct."

"Okay. And your team was aware, weren't they, of the reason that Judge Nicholson was at the Basking County Courthouse that day?"

"Not when we arrived, but at some point in, I would say, the first few days of the investigation we were made aware of that, yes."

"Okay. So you learned that Judge Nicholson was there to testify against a local politician in a criminal corruption trial?"

"Yes."

"The criminal defendant he was there to testify against was a Mr. Ludlow, correct?"

"Yes."

"And Mr. Ludlow's trial had started at eight thirty that morning, correct?"

"Yes."

"A little bit more than three hours before Judge Nicholson died, correct?"

"Approximately, yes."

"But Judge Nicholson was killed before he could get up on the stand and testify against Mr. Ludlow, correct?"

She hesitated. I could tell she didn't like the way I'd worded that. "Correct."

"Okay. So, as an FBI agent, when a witness is killed shortly before he's supposed to testify against a criminal defendant, you don't normally chalk that up to coincidence, do you?"

"Objection," Wilcox said. "Hypothetical."

I looked up at the judge. "It's not a hypothetical question, Your Honor. But I'll rephrase. Agent Gonzalez, have you ever been called upon to investigate the murder of a witness?"

"Not often, but yes."

"When you say not often, that's because it's usually state law enforcement, not the FBI, who investigates murders?"

"That's correct."

"And on those unusual occasions when you've investigated the murder of a witness, you've considered whether the person they were going to testify against was involved in the murder, haven't you?"

After a pause, she said, "I have."

"And you do that because that person, the one they were going to testify against, would have an obvious motive for the crime, correct?"

"We investigate them when the facts point that way."

"And one of the facts that can point that way is motive, correct?"

"Yes."

"Okay. And isn't it true that Mr. Ludlow was charged with thirty-four felony counts for bribery, corruption, and so forth?"

"I couldn't swear to that number, but it sounds about right."

"And can you explain for the jury what makes a crime a felony, as opposed to a misdemeanor?"

"A felony is a crime that can result in a jail sentence of one year or more. Versus a misdemeanor, which carries a potential sentence of less than one year."

I heard Wilcox rustling behind me. We'd sparred over this in pretrial motions, and he knew where I was going.

"So," I said, "thirty-four felonies could mean thirty-four years—or more—in prison, correct?"

"Objection," Wilcox said. "This witness is a federal law enforcement agent. She's not able to answer questions about state sentencing law."

"Federal law defines felonies the same way state law does," I said.

Jefferson said, "Sustained."

At least the jury had heard the words "thirty-four years in prison." I hoped they remembered it.

"Now, you're aware, aren't you, that after Judge Nicholson died, Mr. Ludlow's trial proceeded to its conclusion without the evidence that Judge Nicholson was going to give, and ultimately, Mr. Ludlow was acquitted?"

"I'm aware of that outcome, yes."

"Okay. I have just a few more questions. I understand local law enforcement secured the scene before you arrived. Did they tell you how many people were present in the courthouse at the time Judge Nicholson died?"

"Yes. There were two hundred and fifty-six people present, not including Judge Nicholson himself."

"Two hundred and fifty-six people were in the courthouse when he died," I echoed back to her. "And how many of those potential suspects were you able to definitively exclude?"

There's a rule that you should never ask a question on cross that you don't know the answer to. I asked that one anyway.

I didn't know what her number would be, but I knew they hadn't questioned everybody who was there. Even a few potential suspects slipping through the net, much less dozens, would help convince the jury that there was reasonable doubt.

But she didn't give me a number. She said, "Oh, Mr. Munroe, bless your heart. I've been an FBI agent for eighteen years, as I believe I mentioned earlier, and that is not how a murder investigation works."

She had a maternal look on her face, as if I were a child who'd just done something foolish. And I had. A law enforcement witness—somebody who'd probably spent dozens or hundreds of hours testifying in court—was the last person I should've broken any rule of cross-examination with.

And she had the jury now. I could feel it.

I needed to wrap this part up and move to a strong note that I could close on.

"So you didn't actually eliminate everybody who could've done it," I said. "Thank you."

"Well, I can tell you, there were two old grannies in wheelchairs that we didn't feel the need to investigate, no."

I had to laugh. Not because she was amusing, but because acting defensive in front of the jury—acting like I couldn't take what she was dishing out—would cost me their respect.

"To sum up what you've said, there's no DNA evidence linking Mr. Baptiste to the crime, correct?"

"Not all crimes leave DNA evidence."

"It's a yes-or-no question, please."

"No, there isn't."

"And in your investigation, did you interview Mr. Ludlow?"

"I did, personally, yes."

"And how many of his associates did your team interview?"

"I'm not sure how you're defining associates."

"The usual way. Family, friends, colleagues, anybody he was ever in business with."

"We interviewed a number of them, but I can't give you an exact number."

"Did you interview everyone who was at the courthouse that day?"

"No."

"Did you interview every associate of Mr. Ludlow's who was there?"

"Again, I wasn't thinking of all these various people as associates, so I can't give you an exact number."

"As you sit there, under oath, you can't tell the jury that you interviewed every associate of Mr. Ludlow's who was there that day, can you."

After a second, she said, "No, I cannot."

"Thank you. I have no further questions."

On redirect, Wilcox led Agent Gonzalez back to the answer she'd been trying to give.

"Agent Gonzalez, you were asked how many people in the Basking County Courthouse your team eliminated as suspects. Were you able to finish your answer on that point?"

"No, I was not."

"To ensure the jury isn't misled, could you finish your explanation?"

"Yes, thank you. The defendant's lawyer asked a question that I found misleading. As crime scene investigators, we do not consider every person there to be a suspect."

"And why is that?"

"Because there are almost always people who physically could not have done it. Like in this case, most of the people in the courthouse weren't anywhere near that stairwell."

"And, going back to Mr. Munroe's definition of the word 'associates,' were most of Mr. Ludlow's associates near the stairwell?"

"No, they were not."

"Thank you. I have no further questions."

We broke for lunch.

———

A few minutes before one, a knock came at the door of the war room where Vinny and I were eating with his mom. I finally felt like I could eat her food in good faith. Her lasagna was incredible.

Opening the door, Terri said, "It's me."

I looked up. Noah was with her.

I greeted him with a worried, "You're back in town?"

"Hey, don't sound so happy about it," he said sarcastically. "I couldn't stay in Arkansas forever."

"I just— Things are still up in the air. You're not back at your place, are you?"

"No, still with my friend."

"Okay. Good."

"I'm glad you two came back from the dead," he said. "Terri was just telling me what happened. Whew."

"Yeah, it was something."

I turned to Vinny and his mom and introduced them all to each other.

"Noah works a few blocks away," I explained, and then I asked him, "Aren't you supposed to be there today?"

He shrugged. "I got my work done this morning and walked over just now. Told my boss I wanted to see your trial."

"Well, thank you."

I wished he could've stayed out of town, but the fact he'd come here meant a lot to me. For most of his teens, I'd been exiled to the land of the uncool. Watching me work had been nowhere on his list of priorities.

I looked at him again. There was something tight in his smile that told me he wasn't just here out of curiosity.

I checked my phone. We had about fifteen minutes until court was back in session. "You want to come get a coffee with me?" I asked. "The cafeteria's downstairs."

"Sure."

As we headed out, I told the guard outside the door we'd be right back. Leading Noah down the hall, I said, "Let's stop at the men's room." There was an older restroom around the corner, used by courthouse staff and the occasional visitor who happened across it.

We went in, and I checked the stalls. We were alone.

"What's going on?" I asked.

He met my eyes and then looked at the floor. "It's something I'm not supposed to tell you. And I really couldn't say it in front of Terri."

The word *supposed* made me think it had to be about his job. As PIs, he and Terri had ethical rules that they were required to follow.

I lowered my voice and asked, "Does it have something to do with this case?"

He nodded, and then quietly amended that to, "Well, maybe."

"Okay."

I thought about what to say. The rules of ethics mattered. The written rules for every profession had been thought through long and hard, and generally they made sense. I didn't want to lead my son into a cavalier disregard for that, especially not this early in his career, when he was still figuring out which roads to travel.

"So… let me tell you how I see things," I said. "Rules are important; you know I believe that. And the more important the thing at stake, the more important the rule. Still… Take the rule on homicide, for example. Thou shalt not kill, right? Pretty obvious. Nobody ought to do that. But even that rule's got exceptions."

"Oh, like self-defense?"

"And defense of others, yeah. And defense of your country, which is just defense of others writ large. If you see somebody being beat up, kidnapped, about to be raped, anything like that, you're allowed to use lethal force on their attacker just like if it was you being attacked."

He was nodding. He'd learned all that in his criminal justice degree.

"Of course, if you see somebody being slapped, you can't shoot the guy slapping him. Because what you do has got to be proportional, right? I mean proportional to the threat. You can slap the guy back, if you have to, but not shoot him."

"Right."

"Okay. So I would say there's no rule you can't break to save a human life. Or to save somebody from rape or kidnapping or any of that. But you only break it as much as you've got to. You keep it proportional."

He nodded slowly, thinking.

"I'll put my cards on the table about this case, so you can decide. I've got an IT expert telling me where everybody's phones were when that judge was killed, and he tells me there was somebody else in that stairwell. I don't know who it was yet, but that guy had a better shot at the judge than my client did. It seems my guy didn't go into the stairwell until after the judge was dead."

He looked at me in surprise. "Like, he's literally innocent?"

"I think he is, yes. I always thought it made a lot more sense that the guy who was on trial was behind it. He didn't want that judge to testify against him. And letting an innocent man go to prison for that murder is a real good way to cover things up."

His eyebrows came together. He was thinking it all through.

"So that's what we've got," I said. "You're the bystander watching something happen to my client. It's up to you to figure out if there's any use in breaking this rule, because maybe whatever you've got wouldn't even help him. And even if it would, it's your call whether this is worth breaking it for. If it is, then you're the only one who can figure that out."

We stood there for a minute, and then for two. He didn't say anything until almost three minutes had passed.

In a quiet voice, he said, "One of our clients is somebody's wife. We investigated him so she could decide whether to file for divorce. And in the course of that, I found out that judge of yours was cheating on his wife…"

He looked at me and saw that I'd already known that.

"… with his judicial clerk," he said. "But before that, or maybe at the same time, that clerk also had something going with the judge's lawyer. That's the guy whose wife is our client."

"Wait, Monty?"

"James Montgomery. Yeah. I took pictures of him with her at a resort down in Savannah. Telephoto pictures through the window of their room." I could tell from his expression what those pictures had shown.

"Jesus. When was that?"

"August of last year. About three months before Nicholson died."

## 25

## OCTOBER 1, 2024

Back in the war room, I asked the guard outside the door to take Vinny and his mom back to the courtroom, since he wasn't allowed to walk around on his own. As they left, Noah and I stepped in to talk to Terri. We had six minutes until court was back in session.

Without getting into the details of how I'd gained the information, I told her what we now knew about Monty. She jumped several chess moves ahead of me. "That's why he told you about her thing with Nicholson," she said. "He wanted to hurt her. He wanted us to think she might be a suspect and subpoena whatever we could, to put their affair on the record and humiliate her."

"Jesus. I told you he was at that subpoena hearing, didn't I?"

"Yeah."

"And he talked to the journalists who were there."

"Oh, I'll bet he did."

"Only for a minute, though."

"A minute in the courtroom, maybe. The rest was probably on the phone, off the record."

Noah nodded. "I read all the articles about that. Lot of what seemed like inside information, but his name wasn't in any of them."

Terri looked at him. I could see she was wondering why he'd read those articles, but she didn't say anything.

I looked at my watch. Four minutes.

"Have either of you seen him in the courthouse yet today?" I asked. "He's supposed to testify sometime this afternoon."

"No, but I'll look for him, if you can spare me," Terri said. "What do you want him for?"

"I don't want the man himself. I just need to know what type of phone he's got."

I pulled mine out—my cheap, factory-second Android, as Terri had called it—and swiped over to my notes from Sunday night's talk with Da Costa. "Okay, what we want to know is if it's an iPhone 15 Pro Max."

Noah started typing on his phone.

"Is that the big one?" Terri asked.

Noah said, "Yeah, and look." He showed us his screen. "It's got three camera lenses on the back, instead of two."

"Thanks," I said. "So, take as long as you need," I told Terri. "Rachel can take notes, and run my slides, too, if we get to them today."

"I'll help you," Noah told her. "One of us can check the front of the courthouse, over past the elevators, while the other one does this side."

She peered at him. "You already know what our target looks like?"

"Yes, ma'am."

"Huh. Okay." She turned back to me and said, "Send us his number. If one of us sees him, we can call him. Hopefully, he'll get it out to answer, and we'll be able to get a good look at it."

As I stuffed my papers into my briefcase to head back to the courtroom, they were strategizing how to approach the search. Noah said he'd check all the men's rooms. Terri brainstormed what to do if Monty wasn't here yet. One of them could go over to his office, she suggested. They traded ideas for excuses they could come up with to explain a visit there.

I hurried down the hall, pushed through the courtroom's big double doors—they were upholstered in brown leather, with polished brass studs; federal courthouses were designed to impress—and made it to the defense table just as the bailiff called out, "All rise."

———

The next witness was the FBI agent who'd led the team executing the warrant on the Baptiste home. Wilcox walked him through his credentials, and then they went line by line through the warrant. There was nothing wrong with it. Its scope made sense, and they'd only taken what it said they could take. The FBI screwed up sometimes, but not very often, and they hadn't screwed up here. As a result, I hadn't gotten one iota of the evidence against Vinny thrown out.

The agent's slide deck showing what they'd found on Vinny's computer was, unfortunately, very effective. He walked the jury through the PowerPoint, showing them that less than two weeks before Nicholson was scheduled to arrive in Basking Rock to testify against Ludlow, Vinny had gone down an internet rabbit hole, reading up on the judge, looking for photos of him, and finding old articles about his role in prosecuting Vinny's brother. Every search he'd run and every result he'd clicked on was listed in order of date, and then we looked at screenshots of the websites that Vinny had visited. Nicholson's official courthouse bio, his LinkedIn, his Facebook page.

Wilcox and this witness were trying to make Vinny look like an obsessive stalker, and they were doing a hell of a good job. As the agent testified, several of the jurors were shaking their heads. A couple of them shot disappointed glances at Vinny.

Beside me, Vinny sat stoically, watching the slides go by and occasionally closing his eyes like it was too much. Beyond him, Rachel wrote down the exhibit numbers shown on the slides. We would need all of those details if Vinny lost and we had to appeal.

There wasn't much I could accomplish on cross, but I did get the agent to admit that his team hadn't found anything violent: no searches on guns or any other weapons, nothing on how to hide evidence or how to kill a man. Vinny hadn't run the kinds of searches that—as the agent acknowledged—criminals these days so often ran before committing their crimes.

Those answers would help me build on my theme of what there was *no* evidence of in this case. I was itemizing every missing puzzle piece so that in closing I could show the jury how much of the evidence we all expected, from our life experience of watching TV crime shows, simply was not there. It was a decent way to try to raise reasonable doubt. Plenty of defense lawyers had used it on me when I was a prosecutor. Sometimes it even worked.

When I finished my cross and sat back down at the defense table, Wilcox stood up and said, "The United States calls its next witness, Mr. James Montgomery."

A young guy standing by the courtroom door—maybe an intern at the prosecutor's office—ducked out to go get Monty.

A minute later, Monty stepped into the witness box. He looked self-assured and serious in his navy pin-striped suit. He raised his right hand and swore to tell the truth, the whole truth, and nothing but the truth.

As Wilcox asked him his name, I touched my phone screen—it was in my lap—and glanced down. There was a text from Noah that I hadn't noticed; he'd sent it about ten minutes earlier, while I'd been crossing the FBI agent.

I discreetly unlocked the phone, glanced up at Wilcox to look like I was paying attention, and peeked back at the text.

It said *Yes! iPhone 15 Pro Max!*

I kept my face calm and looked back up at Monty.

"Mr. Montgomery," Wilcox said, "what was the nature of your relationship with Judge Nicholson?"

"I served as his personal attorney, starting in, I believe, the fall of 2016, shortly after I moved back to Charleston."

"And that was about how long after he was nominated to the judiciary, and confirmed by Congress as a federal judge?"

"A little less than a year."

"What did you do to merit so elevated a client?" Wilcox's tone was friendly.

Monty gave a quick self-deprecating smile. "I wouldn't use the word 'merit' myself. All I can say is, he reached out for advice, and evidently he appreciated what I told him."

"As a former prosecutor and a federal judge himself, he found you gave good advice?"

"I guess so."

"Now, was your relationship with Judge Nicholson only a professional one?"

"It was at first. But we knew each other for almost eight years, and I would say that by about a year or two in, we'd become friends."

"Okay. Now, before we go any farther, can you explain to the jury if there are any limitations on what you're able to speak about, in regard to Judge Nicholson?"

"Yes. As his attorney, I'm bound by a duty of confidentiality. I'm not able to speak, for instance, of any legal questions he ever asked me or any advice that I gave him. That duty survives the client's death, which means I'm still bound by it today."

"Thank you. I just want to make sure the jury understands what I'm about to say, which is, without getting into any legal questions or advice between the two of you, can you explain why you came down to the Basking County Courthouse with Judge Nicholson on the morning of November 17, 2023?"

"Yes. We all came down together for a trial."

"Thank you. I apologize, Mr. Montgomery, but to make sure everything's clear for the record, did you drive down in the same car with Judge Nicholson?"

"Oh, no. We each drove our own car. And so did his clerk, Miss Townsend."

The slight sloppiness of Monty's answer—making it sound like the three of them had come to Basking Rock in the same car—reminded me that he wasn't a litigator. He was a lawyer at the peak of his career, but he advised on business matters. He didn't go to court.

I let that thought percolate.

"Why did you travel down there that morning?" Wilcox asked.

"Judge Nicholson was giving testimony in a trial in the courthouse there."

"And what type of trial was that?"

"It was a criminal trial. He was testifying against the defendant."

"Okay. And again, without getting into any legal advice, were you traveling there with him as his lawyer, or as his friend?"

He thought for a second. "I would have to say both. Primarily legal, I suppose. But also to pass the time, because witnesses at a trial do a lot of waiting around."

"As you've just found out yourself today, I suppose."

He chuckled. "Yes, I have."

"Was this a routine trial that he was testifying in, or would you call it more high profile?"

"It was definitely high profile. There had to be about fifty journalists waiting outside with their microphones. That was actually another reason I decided to come."

"How so?"

"I didn't want my client, and friend, getting swarmed by reporters. If anybody was going to have to—I hate to say this, but—shove a journalist out of the way, I'd rather it be me than my client. Protecting his reputation was part of my job."

That was rich. Monty had to have known he couldn't orchestrate the public humiliation of Nicholson's mistress without tarnishing Nicholson in the process.

"Now, speaking of passing the time, was Judge Nicholson content to sit there in the—we call them war rooms, don't we."

"The room where we waited, outside the courtroom? Yes."

"War rooms," Wilcox said to the jury with a smile. "Take that for what it's worth."

Most of the jurors smiled back, and a couple of them chuckled. He was good at building rapport.

"So, was Judge Nicholson content to sit there in the war room all morning and bide his time?"

"Well, at first, he was. But we got there at about eight a.m., and Judge Nicholson was not someone who liked to sit around. He did enough of that at work."

Judge Jefferson smiled. So did some of the jurors.

"Would you say he was athletic?" Wilcox asked.

"Oh, yes. I played squash with him on occasion, and—" Monty's face cracked with a nostalgic smile. "I recall one morning where he'd beaten me three times before it was even seven a.m."

A juror laughed out loud.

Wilcox sighed. "Well, I know we're all sorry that he's gone." After a moment of silence, he asked, "Can you tell me, on the morning of November 17, did there come a time when Judge Nicholson got tired of sitting around?"

"Oh, yeah. He was tired of it by about nine. But he had to stay in the war room, because he wasn't sure exactly when he was going to be called to testify."

"Uh-huh. So, did that change at some point?"

"Yes, there was a recess at about eleven, and the prosecutor came in to inform us that Judge Nicholson wouldn't be going up until right after lunch."

"By going up, you mean up on the witness stand?"

"Yes."

"Okay. Once y'all got that information, what did he do?"

"Well, he said he wanted to get his steps in."

"And what's that mean, in your understanding?"

"We both have these smartwatches. Or had them." He held up his wrist and pointed to the elegant gold strap. "They count your steps, and you can set whatever goals you want. As I recall, his goal was twelve thousand steps a day."

"So you're saying he wanted to make progress toward that goal?"

"Exactly."

"How did he decide to do that?"

"Well, in Charleston he probably would've gone for a walk outdoors, but none of us were familiar with Basking Rock. So he mentioned that maybe he could use one of the staircases, walk up and down."

"Do you know how many staircases there are at that courthouse?"

"It's my understanding that there are four. One at each corner, I believe."

"And what did you think of the judge's idea?"

Monty grimaced. "I wasn't too keen on it."

"Why not?"

"Well, like I said, it was a high-profile trial. Journalists everywhere. And as a federal judge, he was relatively visible himself. I didn't want him getting accosted, basically."

"So what did you do?"

Monty looked down at his lap and shook his head. Sorrow came off him in waves.

"Do you need a moment?" Wilcox asked.

"I'll be fine. It's just… I had what I thought was a good idea at the time."

"And what was that idea?"

"I thought maybe one of the staircases might be less used or more out of the way. And I'd seen a janitor around, when I'd stepped out to the men's room or down to the café. The same janitor, in a few different places. So I thought I'd see if I could find him and ask."

"What did you ask him?"

"I went out looking for him, and he was right there, a few yards down the hall from our war room."

"He was right there waiting when you went out?"

I could've objected to that, but I didn't want to draw the jury's attention to it any further than Wilcox already had.

"He was."

"And is that janitor here in the courtroom today?"

"Yes, he is." Monty pointed to Vinny, and anger rose in his voice. "He's sitting right there at the defense table."

"I'll give you a moment," Wilcox said. I knew he was purposely drawing the jury's attention to Monty's anger. I'd done that in trials myself, to emphasize the injustice and the impact of the crime.

After waiting for Monty to compose himself, Wilcox continued. "Did you speak to him?"

"Yes," Monty said. "I told him Judge Nicholson wanted to get his steps in, and I asked if there was someplace he could do it that was out of the way, not a lot of traffic."

Wilcox nodded. "What did he say?"

"He showed me a key card that he had, on a, uh…"

He gestured to his neck.

"A lanyard?"

"A lanyard, yes. He just happened to have this key card with him." Monty let out a bitter laugh. "And he said he could let us into a stairwell that was locked. I said I didn't want to get him in trouble, and he said it wasn't a problem, but if we wanted, he could take us up to the third floor, because the security camera up there wasn't working."

So that was how Monty knew that camera was out of order.

"And is that what you did? Have him take you to the third floor?"

"No. I didn't want Judge Nicholson to spend too much time in the hallways and elevators—we didn't want to run into the press—so we just went in by the nearest door."

"Understood. And why did you think Mr. Baptiste suggested letting y'all into the stairwell?"

"Well, at the time, I thought he was trying to be helpful."

"Do you still think that now?"

"No, of course not."

"Why not?"

"Because I took Judge Nicholson over to that stairwell, and the janitor let him in, and about ten minutes later, he pushed him over the railing—"

"Objection!"

"—to his death!"

"Sustained," Judge Jefferson said uselessly.

I sat back down, annoyed that Wilcox had trapped me. I'd had to object—not doing so would leave the jurors thinking I was conceding the truth of Monty's statement—but by doing so, I'd given the jury a dramatic moment to remember once they were deliberating.

Wilcox spent another half hour establishing the facts he needed, and then it was time for my cross.

## 26

# OCTOBER 1, 2024

Standing at the podium, I gave Monty a nod and a polite but friendly, "Afternoon, Mr. Montgomery."

"Afternoon, Mr. Munroe."

"So, I don't have too many questions for you." I made my voice casual; I wanted him to relax. "I just want to ensure that the who, what, and where is real clear for the jury. I've got a floor plan here of the Basking County Courthouse."

Rachel clicked her mouse to bring up the exhibit on the big screen that hung on the wall. The image was one of the cutaways of all three floors that Da Costa had made.

I took out my laser pointer and aimed it at a door on the second floor. "This is what you referred to earlier as your war room, isn't it?"

"Yes, it is."

"Just around the corner from the courtroom where the trial was happening?" I slid the laser's red dot over to the courtroom door, and he confirmed the location.

"And I believe you just testified that Judge Nicholson waited in the war room with his clerk while you went looking for that janitor, correct?"

"Correct."

"That clerk was a Miss Samantha Townsend?"

"Yes."

"So, when you went out, you proceeded down this hallway here and met the janitor… where? Right about here?" I moved my dot around until he indicated it was in the right place.

"Okay. Then, after that conversation you mentioned with the janitor, where did you go next?"

"Back to the war room." I flicked my dot back there.

"And then, I believe you said, you personally escorted Judge Nicholson and Miss Townsend to the second-floor entrance to the stairwell, accompanied by that janitor?"

He took a second, like he had to compose himself. "Yes. I wish I hadn't, obviously, but I did."

"I understand. And that was this stairwell here, on the top left?"

"Yes."

"And you said the janitor opened the door with his key card?"

"He did."

"Okay, and did you go into that stairwell yourself?"

"No."

"Did you at any point that day go into that stairwell?"

"No, I didn't."

"You're saying you didn't? Okay. You let Judge Nicholson and Miss Townsend go in, and then you and this janitor walked away?"

"Yes. Or... I walked away. I couldn't swear to where the janitor went."

"Now, for the record, the jury has seen footage that I don't believe you've seen, because His Honor entered a routine order excluding witnesses in this case from this courtroom until after they've finished testifying. And that footage showed people going into and out of this stairwell."

I thought I saw a flash of nervousness on his face.

"And what the jury saw," I said, "is consistent with the testimony you just gave."

He relaxed.

"So thank you for clarifying that," I said. "And you testified, didn't you, that Judge Nicholson was an athletic man?"

"Yes. He was."

"Used a smartwatch to count his steps?"

He smiled at the memory. "Yes, he did."

"Was it the same kind as yours?"

His expression turned uncertain. He raised his wrist and looked at it. "It may have been," he said. "I don't actually recall."

"That's an Apple Watch you've got on, right?"

"Yes."

I heard papers rustling behind me at the prosecution's table. I figured Wilcox was probably looking in his binders for information about Nicholson's watch, to get a sense of where I was going with this.

"It counts your steps automatically?"

"Uh, yes, it does."

"And have you got an iPhone that it syncs with?"

"Objection," Wilcox said. "Relevance."

"I'll move on, Your Honor."

I was going to have to get the type of phone he had on the record another way.

"Now, Mr. Montgomery, didn't you try to call Judge Nicholson from the Basking County Courthouse shortly after he died?"

"I did. Shortly before I learned of his death, yes. I called three times."

"Do you happen to recall what time it was when you placed those calls?"

"I do now. I had forgotten, but in preparation for this trial, I went back and looked at my phone records for that month. And I placed the first call at eleven fifty-four a.m."

"Okay, eleven fifty-four- a.m. Thank you. And what phone did you use to call him?"

"My cell phone," he said, with a slight gesture toward his coat pocket.

"Was that the same cell phone you've got with you right now?"

"Yes, it was."

I made my voice slightly bored, so my question wouldn't seem important. "And is that an iPhone 15 Pro Max?"

"Yes."

"Okay. Now can I just ask, and I apologize to the Nicholson family for this, but it's necessary. On that morning of November 17, 2023, when you went to the Basking County Courthouse with Judge Nicholson and Miss Townsend, his clerk, you were already aware, weren't you, that the two of them were having an extramarital affair?"

"Objection," Wilcox said. "Relevance."

"Apologies, Your Honor," I said, "but may we have a sidebar?"

Jefferson granted that, and the two of us went up to the bench. The court reporter stood up and brought her stenography machine over to record our argument, and Jefferson hit the button to turn the white noise machine on so no one else in the courtroom could hear us.

"Your Honor," Wilcox said, "evidence concerning any alleged affair that the murder victim may have had with Miss Townsend is completely irrelevant. We've got her on video leaving the stairwell at least five minutes before he was killed, and other evidence, including witness testimony and her phone records, confirming she was talking on the phone at the time he was killed. And even if this were relevant, which it's not, it's highly prejudicial. Mr. Munroe is dragging the name of a dead man through the mud and essentially inviting the jury to improperly conclude that this affair may have had something to do with the man's death."

"I hear you," Jefferson said. "Mr. Munroe?"

"This goes to the witness's credibility, Your Honor," I said.

He cocked his head like he wasn't sure he'd heard me right. "Explain to me how the victim's affair has anything to do with this witness's credibility." He sat back, arms crossed over his chest. He was not a man who liked nonsense, and I could tell that's what he thought this was.

"Happy to, Your Honor. Now, first off, I'm not at all trying to implicate Miss Townsend in any of this. Her affair with the victim is not the point of my intended line of questioning. It's a puzzle piece that I need for my client's defense. My expert witness, who'll be on the stand probably the day after tomorrow, is going to put the puzzle together."

"Your IT guy?" Jefferson asked.

"Yes."

"What's his technical expertise got to do with this affair?"

"Alleged affair, Your Honor," Wilcox said, glancing at the stenographer. The jury was never going to hear what we were saying, but it would be in the trial transcript, so he wasn't about to let my statement pass unchallenged.

"Alleged, yes. Mr. Munroe, I am not inclined—"

"If I may, Your Honor, I'd like to finish my explanation. It's, admittedly, somewhat of a complex issue."

"Go ahead," he said, irritated.

"Your Honor," I said, "are you familiar with the fact that every cell phone, laptop, and so forth has what's called a MAC address?"

"I'm not, no," Jefferson said.

"Well, at the risk of oversimplifying what's going to be some technically complex testimony, every device has a component in it, an electronic part, that's involved in connecting to Wi-Fi networks. And that part essentially broadcasts a number, similar to a serial number, to the Wi-Fi networks that it connects to. That number's called a MAC address. And each Wi-Fi network keeps a record of every MAC address that connected to it, and when it connected, down to the hundredth of a second, and on some networks the record also tells you where in the building the device was."

Wilcox gaped at me. "What on earth does any of that have to do with this alleged affair?"

"I have the same question," Jefferson said.

"Judge Nicholson's affair with Miss Townsend isn't the point," I said. "It's just the first link in the chain—"

"A chain of what? Where are you planning to go with this, and what's it got to do with this witness?"

Jefferson was fed up. I had to show my cards.

"Your Honor, the point is that this witness was having his own affair with Miss Townsend. And then he found out she was seeing Judge Nicholson. And then he went into that stairwell with Judge Nicholson. A minute ago, he denied that he ever went into that stairwell, but the IT records will show that he did. And only one of those two men came out of there alive."

Jefferson stared at me, speechless.

Then he turned to Wilcox. "Counsel, is there any truth to this, to your knowledge?"

"No, it's— This is an absolutely ludicrous—"

"If Mr. Wilcox had known," I said, "anything he had on it would've been exculpatory for my client, so he would've been obliged to disclose it as *Brady* material."

"Yes, he would've," Jefferson said.

"So I'm sure this is news to him."

I was giving Wilcox a dignified escape route. Whether he'd known about Monty's affair or not, he could take the off-ramp I was providing to avoid looking bad in front of the judge.

He took it.

"This allegation is absolutely new to me, Your Honor," he said. "And for the record, I'm not conceding that there's any truth to it."

"Understood," Jefferson said. "Mr. Munroe, explain to me how your expert plans to put this all together."

"Well, my technical expert is going to explain two things. First, that the Wi-Fi network at the Basking County Courthouse shows that my client's phone didn't enter the stairwell until about one minute *after* Judge Nicholson died. And second, it shows that an iPhone 15 Pro Max, the same make and model of phone that this witness just testified he used that day, entered that stairwell from the third floor, where there was no functioning security camera, right *before* the judge died, and it passed through the area where Judge Nicholson fell from, and then it went back up and out on the third floor."

"That is ludicrous," Wilcox said. "We've got camera footage of him returning to the war room."

"What we've got is footage of him heading toward the war room. There wasn't a camera pointed at the war room door. And there's nothing ludicrous about the records of that courthouse's Wi-Fi network. Those records are kept automatically, and they say what they say. They provide evidence that this witness was in the stairwell at the time of the murder, and this line of questioning, if I'm allowed to pursue it, will show his motive for killing Judge Nicholson. I can't think of anything more obviously relevant than that."

"Your Honor," Wilcox said, "Mr. Munroe's own explanation shows why this should not be allowed. He's got the right to present whatever defense he needs to present, but he's essentially saying that this line of questioning is a fishing expedition for highly personal and embarrassing information that, even assuming it's true, won't even be connected to the victim's death unless this expert gets on the stand at the end of the week and says what Mr. Munroe claims he's going to say. Because there is literally *no* other evidence that this witness was in the stairwell at the time. So that should come first. Call the expert, and then *if* he establishes where the witness was, maybe then we can talk about this alleged affair."

"There's some sense in that," Jefferson said.

Wilcox kept talking. "I would submit, Your Honor, that under Rule 611(a)(3), he doesn't get to embarrass my witness with this kind of highly personal matter, and he doesn't get to confuse and potentially poison the jury against him, unless he's laid the groundwork and showed how it's relevant. Mr. Munroe can recall this witness when it's time for the defense to present its case in chief. Put the expert up first, and if Your Honor is satisfied that he's laid the groundwork, then he can call Mr. Montgomery back to the stand."

To my horror, Jefferson was nodding like that worked for him.

If Monty got off the stand without answering any of my questions, my chances of getting what I needed from him might go up in smoke. I didn't know how corrupt Wilcox was. If he gave Monty a heads-up about what I was planning to ask him, Monty might take a sudden vacation outside the jurisdiction. I couldn't put my son and his private eye photos on the stand, and nothing else I had on Monty was even close to strong enough to convince Jefferson to put the trial on hold until he returned. So the trial would proceed through the remaining witnesses, and the jury would go to verdict without ever hearing that Monty had been in the stairwell when Nicholson died.

"Your Honor," I said, "if you do decide to postpone this line of questioning, I'd like to remind Mr. Wilcox that this is a confidential sidebar, and nothing I've said ought to be shared with anybody, and certainly not with this witness."

"Of course not," Jefferson said impatiently.

"Right, of course not," I echoed, turning to Wilcox, looking him in the eye. "Because even inadvertently letting this witness get a sense of what I'm planning to ask him might be construed as witness tampering."

He wilted a little. I didn't need to tell him that witness tampering was a federal felony.

"Mr. Wilcox is not going to be tampering with any witnesses." Jefferson still sounded irritated. "Correct, Mr. Wilcox? Let's make it of record for the transcript." He gestured to the court reporter.

"Correct," Wilcox said.

"Of course," I said. "Thank you. And if I may, Your Honor, just one more point before we get back to my cross. As I mentioned, I've actually got two lines of questioning here. Mr. Wilcox has objected to the first one, about the affair. The second one relates to the MAC address of this witness's phone. So just to tee up what we'll be hearing later from my expert, what I would propose is that Your Honor allow me to ask a very short line of questions that should lead to us getting this witness's MAC address on the record. I'll need to consult real quick with my expert, and once I've asked those questions, I'll end my cross and we'll move on. Then, in a few days, I'll ask Your Honor to let me recall Mr. Montgomery, after my technical witness has laid the groundwork. In other words, if my expert shows that it was this witness's phone in the stairwell, then, and only then, I get to ask him about the affairs."

Jefferson looked at Wilcox. "Counsel? Any objection to that?"

"Yes, Your Honor, absolutely. This is— What he's proposing to ask the witness is— There's a privacy interest here, and there's been no subpoena for this information, no—"

"There's no privacy interest in the witness's MAC address," I said. "His phone essentially broadcasts its MAC address to every Wi-Fi system it comes near. The courthouse Wi-Fi system right here probably has it in its logs right now. And it's been nearly fifty years since the Supreme Court stated the bright-line rule that there's no reasonable expectation of privacy in any information that a person voluntarily turns over to third parties. *United States v. Miller* in 1976 and *Smith v. Maryland* three years after that said so. And this witness's phone, like yours and mine, turns this information over to every Starbucks he walks past."

"You could've subpoenaed this," Wilcox said. "This eleventh-hour—"

"No rule required me to do that. Mr. Montgomery was on your witness list. We all knew he was going to be testifying, and I do *not* need a subpoena to ask your witness a question on the stand."

Jefferson nodded. He was coming around to my side.

Wilcox kept at it. "Your Honor, this overreach—"

I turned to him. "Why are you fighting this? I have the right to ask your witness any question relevant to my client's defense."

Jefferson said, "I'll allow it."

---

After the sidebar, Jefferson briefly addressed the jury, explaining what sidebars were—an opportunity to discuss an objection and ensure that the Rules of Evidence were followed—and that they should not be concerned about them. While he did that, I walked past the defense table and leaned down to Da Costa, who was sitting in the front pew.

"What questions do I ask to find out his MAC address?" I whispered.

"Well, first... You know what, hand me your laptop."

I turned to grab it off the table and gave it to him. He pulled up a web page for me, and I walked back to the podium with it.

Monty was staring daggers at me.

"Mr. Montgomery," I said, "I've just got a handful of questions for you, and then we'll be done. Do you have your cell phone up there with you?"

He glanced at Wilcox but got no help.

"Yes," he said into the mike.

"Could you please get it out?"

He pulled it out of his coat pocket and held it in his hand.

I looked at my laptop screen. "Okay, and could you go to Settings? That icon should look like a little gray gear."

"I'm sorry," he said, giving the jury a puzzled smile. "Is that a question, or…?"

"Yes, I'll be asking the question as soon as you get to a certain point in your settings. Could you go to the gear, and then tap where it says 'General'?"

He looked at Jefferson, who asked him to proceed.

"I'm happy to bring my phone records in," Monty told me, "if you're asking me to establish when I called Judge Nicholson. Unfortunately, I made those calls so long ago that they don't show on my actual phone anymore."

"Thank you, but this will take less time," I said. "Could you please tap that gray gear and go to 'General'?"

He did what I'd asked.

"Now, could you tap where it says 'About'? And then scroll down to where it says 'Wi-Fi Address.'"

"Okay," he said.

"Is there a number there? It should look like several sets of two digits, with colons separating them. Do you see that?"

"I do."

"Could you read me that number?"

He read it.

"Thank you. I have no further questions."

I closed my laptop and walked back to the defense table. In the front pew, Da Costa's mouth was wide open in amazement. He looked at me and gave me a nod.

## 27

## OCTOBER 4, 2024

Three days later, on Friday morning, Da Costa walked the jury through his new PowerPoint. For an hour and a half, we watched three cell phones move through the Basking County Courthouse: the blue and red ones representing Nicholson and Vinny, and the black one he'd added, labeled simply "iPhone 15." He gave a tutorial on MAC addresses and Wi-Fi systems. It was accessible—he didn't use overly technical language—but it was dry; some of the jurors looked like they were struggling to stay focused.

When he testified as to what each of the three cell phones' model numbers and MAC addresses were, one juror raised an eyebrow, and two more exchanged looks. I took that as a sign that they remembered what Monty had said on the stand about his own phone. As for the other jurors, I saw no trace of recognition on their faces. There had been two and a half days of testimony since Monty had stepped down from the stand, and much of it had been gruesome; the coroner had spent a full day testifying, with photos, about Nicholson's cause of death. That kind of thing had a way of making people forget what had come before.

After Da Costa returned to his seat in the front pew beside Vinny's mom, I asked for a sidebar. The court reporter brought her machine over, and the judge pressed his white noise button.

"Your Honor," I said, "as we discussed on Tuesday, Dr. Da Costa has now laid the groundwork for me to recall Mr. Montgomery."

Wilcox countered with, "Your Honor has discretion under Rule of Evidence 611(a) to deny Mr. Munroe leave to recall this witness, and it's the position of the United States that leave should be denied. Mr. Munroe made it very clear the other day that his intention is to essentially harass and embarrass this witness with questions about an alleged extramarital affair, and on what grounds? All we've heard is that a certain model of iPhone, which happens to be one of the most popular cell phone models in the country, appears to have been present in the rear of the courthouse. Dr. Da Costa testified himself that he couldn't place it in the stairwell with 100 percent certainty."

"He also testified about the phone's model and MAC address," I said. "And those matched what Mr. Montgomery testified to about his own phone."

"Your Honor, all Mr. Montgomery testified to is that he's one of the millions of people who happens to own one of those phones. Given that nearly two hundred and fifty people were in the courthouse at the time of Judge Nicholson's death, I'd be surprised if there weren't twenty or thirty other iPhone 15 Pro Maxes in there too. And as for this so-called MAC address, Mr. Munroe, has your expert performed any type of forensic analysis of Mr. Montgomery's phone?"

I stared at him. "You mean, did we get a subpoena, serve it on Mr. Montgomery, overcome whatever arguments his lawyers might make, impound his phone, and get it into Dr. Da Costa's lab for analysis in the last—what's it been—sixty-five or seventy hours since Mr. Montgomery testified? No, we did not. But that doesn't matter, because Mr.

Montgomery read out his MAC address under oath on the stand. We don't need computer forensics to establish a fact that's already of record."

"Your Honor, it's improper to put technical evidence in through a lay witness. Mr. Montgomery has, to my knowledge, no technical expertise—"

"It does not take technical expertise to read out a number that's automatically displayed on the screen of his phone. You might as well suggest that he's not qualified to look at the back of his phone and read off the serial number."

Jefferson leaned back in his chair and asked, "Have we established that the witness read off the correct number? I seem to recall seeing several different numbers or strings of letters and numbers here and there in my own phone settings."

"Yes. As Dr. Da Costa testified, MAC addresses have a certain format, which is called a hexadecimal format, where you see six sets of two digits each, with colons between them. And that's the format of the number that Mr. Montgomery read off to us on Tuesday."

Jefferson embarked on some back-and-forth with his court reporter, asking her to read back what Dr. Da Costa had said about that and then to find the number Monty had read out on Tuesday.

It took her a minute. She read it back.

He nodded. "Mr. Munroe, you may recall the witness and proceed."

———

Monty took the stand after lunch. I gave him a smile. My first few questions were softballs; their only purpose was to help him relax and to remind the jury of what he'd previously said about how events unfolded on the morning of Nicholson's death.

Mrs. Nicholson and her children were in the front pew on the prosecution side, where they'd been every day since the trial began. I knew how my next questions would make them feel, and I wasn't happy about it. But there was no other way to put the truth in front of the jury.

"Okay," I said. "Now can I just ask, and I apologize to the Nicholson family for this, but it's necessary. On that morning of November 17, 2023, when you went to the Basking County Courthouse with Judge Nicholson and Miss Townsend, his clerk, you were already aware, weren't you, that the two of them were having an extramarital affair?"

I heard Mrs. Nicholson gasp. Monty looked past me, in her direction. A flurry of movement behind me told me that somebody was probably comforting her.

Monty brought his gaze back to me and heaved a sigh. His face looked grim with responsibility. "Yes," he said. "I was aware of that unfortunate fact."

"Okay. I'd like to show the jury a photograph now."

With a few mouse clicks, Rachel put a photo of Miss Townsend up on the display. I'd asked Terri to look for the most beautiful picture of her that she could find, and she'd found a good one on Instagram. I was telling a story of jealous rage, and I wanted a photo that would help the jury believe that.

"Mr. Montgomery, is this Miss Townsend?"

"It is, yes."

"And did you know approximately when her affair with Judge Nicholson started?"

He hesitated. In an apologetic tone, he said, "I believe that may be getting a little too close to what I mentioned on Tuesday, about my duty to maintain Judge Nicholson's confidentiality."

"Understood. Let me put it another way." I locked eyes with him. "Did you learn of their affair before or after August of 2023, when you were in Savannah having your own extramarital affair with Miss Townsend?"

The flash of shock and fear on his face was satisfying. I enjoyed it for a second while Wilcox yelled, "Objection! Assumes facts not in evidence."

"It goes to the witness's credibility, Your Honor."

Monty looked to the judge for help. He found none.

Jefferson said, "If you're able to lay the foundation, Mr. Munroe, I'll allow it."

"Thank you. Mr. Montgomery," I said, looking him in the eye, "are you married?"

"I am."

"And did you travel to Savannah, Georgia, without your wife, in August of 2023?"

His eyes flared with anger, but he kept his voice calm. "Did I— I'm sorry, I'm not understanding what this has to do with—" He looked at the judge again.

"Please answer the question," Jefferson said.

Monty kept looking up at him, frozen. Something about his body language reminded me that as a transactional lawyer, he probably had little or no courtroom experience. He was no gladiator. He didn't even know the rules of the game.

I almost felt sorry for him. Almost.

"Your Honor, permission to treat Mr. Montgomery as a hostile witness?"

That meant I could ask him leading questions.

"Granted."

Monty turned to look at me with a thousand-yard stare. Outside a courtroom, a look like that was a threat of physical violence.

I appreciated, not for the first time, the way a courtroom served as a container, a limiter, a place of forced peace. Because we had courts, bailiffs, judges, and rules, many conflicts were resolved with mere hostility, when they otherwise might've ended with somebody dead.

"Mr. Montgomery," I said, marshaling the facts Noah had shared with me, "isn't it true that on or about Friday, August 25, 2023, you visited Savannah, Georgia, and stayed at the River Walk Inn?"

His glare flickered with a trace of fear. Including specific facts in a question tended to make a witness think that you had evidence of those facts, and that if the witness lied, you would present that evidence with a humiliating flourish. Sometimes that was true. This time, it was a bluff.

A litigator would've been familiar with that tactic.

After a moment, Jefferson said, "The witness will please answer the question."

Stalling, Monty said, "Could you repeat it, please?"

"Isn't it true that you visited Savannah, Georgia, on or about Friday, August 25, 2023, and you stayed at the River Walk Inn?"

Monty leaned toward the microphone. "I did visit Savannah. But—"

"You did. Thank you. And isn't it true that on that occasion, you met Miss Samantha Townsend at the River Walk Inn?"

"Met her? No, I did not."

I'd used the wrong word. "Met" had several meanings, and a contract lawyer like him would have no trouble finding at least one that he could disagree with.

"Isn't it the case that you saw Miss Townsend in Savannah?"

I thought I saw a flicker of desperation in his eyes, but then he screwed up his face like he was trying to remember.

If he testified that he didn't remember, there was nothing I could do. I had no evidence I could use to contradict him.

Noah had described to me some of the photos he'd taken. I went out on a limb.

"Mr. Montgomery, would you be surprised if I told you that security camera footage from the River Walk Inn, taken shortly after ten p.m. on the night of August 25, showed you and Miss Townsend going into your hotel room together?"

His face spasmed with anger.

"And would you be surprised that the footage showed you had your arm around her shoulders and your hand on her left breast?"

"That has nothing to do with this!" he yelled.

"Were you jealous when you found out your girlfriend was sleeping with—"

"Objection!" Wilcox said. "Your Honor, Mr. Munroe is blatantly harassing this witness with highly personal—assuming it's even true, it's a highly embarrassing personal matter—"

"Order!" Jefferson said. "Counsel, and Mr. Montgomery, this is a court of law, and y'all need to show some respect."

"Absolutely, Your Honor," I said.

Wilcox and Monty apologized too. I could see from Monty's face that he was calming down. I doubted he'd let his anger take him over again.

And if I couldn't get a rise out of him, I might not get any more truth out of him either.

Standing at the podium, I looked at my binder, pretending to review my notes. I turned a page, buying time to think.

All Monty had to do to get out of this was pretend he didn't remember any Savannah trip last August, or didn't remember who he'd seen there. I had no receipts, no security camera footage, nothing to prove him a liar. The judge and jury would see that I'd been bluffing, and Vinny would be the one who paid the price.

I looked up at Jefferson on the bench. "Your Honor," I said, "may I propose that, given the level of emotion that was brought out by that line of questioning just now, we try a more dignified approach?"

Jefferson looked interested, so I went on.

"Under Rule of Evidence 614(b), a United States District Judge has the discretion to question a witness himself. That's particularly appropriate where it helps clarify the facts in a more efficient manner. So may I suggest that Your Honor question Mr. Montgomery, perhaps simply asking yes-or-no questions, to clarify the sequence of events—namely, when he was involved with Miss Townsend and when he became aware of her involvement with the victim in this case?"

Jefferson looked open to that. "Any comment, Mr. Wilcox?" he asked.

"No, Your Honor."

"All right." Jefferson turned to look down at Monty, and Monty turned to look up at him.

I doubted Monty had ever been grilled by a federal judge. It wasn't a pleasant experience. Litigators had to get used to it.

"Mr. Montgomery," Jefferson said, "Mr. Munroe referenced a trip to Savannah, Georgia, this past August. Did you take that trip?"

After a second, Monty said, "Yes."

"And did you encounter Miss Samantha Townsend on that trip?"

"Yes."

"And on that trip, were you intimate with Miss Townsend?"

Monty broke eye contact and looked down.

"Mr. Montgomery," Jefferson said, "I would remind you that you are under oath."

Monty nodded. He still wasn't looking at the judge.

"Please answer the question," Jefferson said.

"Your Honor," Monty said, "I'm going to have to invoke my right to remain silent."

I was electrified. He'd just admitted that further testimony would incriminate him. I glanced at the jury. They looked confused.

I wasn't worried about that. I could use my closing statement to explain what they needed to know.

Jefferson said, faintly incredulous, "Are you pleading the Fifth?"

"Yes, I am."

Jefferson raised his eyebrows—it was exceptionally rare for a witness to take the Fifth, especially one who wasn't the defendant or a coconspirator—and called a recess.

When court reconvened, I stood up and announced, "Your Honor, ladies and gentlemen of the jury, the defense rests."

Wilcox stared at me. There were still three more people on my witness list, including Vinny himself. Trial was scheduled to run through the following Tuesday.

Wilcox asked the court for an overnight recess. I figured he needed time to completely rewrite his closing argument. As for me, I only needed to cut the last few paragraphs and add a compelling explanation about Monty incriminating himself.

"Your Honor," I said, "I certainly don't object to a brief recess—an hour might be appropriate—but I'm prepared to close today."

As I'd told Vinny during the recess that had followed Monty's testimony, we now had everything we needed. When it came to reasonable doubt, it didn't get much better than having your technical expert place somebody else at the scene of the crime, getting the jury to understand what that guy's motive might've been, and then having him take the Fifth.

"Do I really have to let them destroy my life like that?" Vinny had asked. "They've had me in jail for almost a year. Don't I get to speak in my own defense?"

I winced. "Well, you can testify if you absolutely want to," I said, "but there's no way to do that without giving Wilcox a chance to rip you to shreds. And once you're up there, you can't get down until he's done with you. So you don't want to get on the witness stand unless there's no alternative. I mean, look at what happened to Monty."

He laughed, shaking his head.

"So how about this instead," I said. "I do my best to get you a not guilty verdict today, and then you can tell your story to a reporter. With Wilcox nowhere nearby."

He took that in, then gave a slow, deliberate nod. "You know what? Yeah," he said. "Because Marcus Aurelius talked a lot about what he called prudence. Which is just good judgment, I guess. And if what you're saying isn't prudence, then, man… I don't know what is."

## 28

## NOVEMBER 27, 2024

The sun was shining, and I was on a forty-foot sailboat with Terri and Noah, heading for the island where Terri's grandmother lived. It was the day before Thanksgiving, about seventy degrees. The blue-green water was calm, and a flock of pelicans had just flown by.

Terri and I were sitting on a bench at the back of the boat, leaning against the rail. Squatter was snoozing in his dog carrier, which was sitting next to me with the strap over my shoulder for safety. A few yards ahead I could see Noah in the small polished-wood cabin, sitting on the cooler of bottled drinks that we were bringing. He'd gone over there to feed a dog biscuit to Buster, who was crated, she'd explained, because on a previous trip he'd leaped into the ocean. Now Noah was talking to Bala, the old guy that she told me she always hired to take her out to the island.

"I can't believe you wouldn't let me bring my potato salad," I told her. "I haven't made it in years, but it's good, I swear."

She laughed. "No! We're going to my nana's house. Just, no."

"Is Nana the only one who's allowed to make potato salad?" I joked.

"It's my aunt who makes that, actually. If anybody else brought it, that'd be an insult to her."

"I guess I've got a lot to learn about your family."

"I guess you do."

Noah came out of the cabin and made his way back to us, hanging on to the rail and watching for water on the deck. "Bala says we're not likely to see any seals," he told us. "I know we hardly ever see them from shore, but I thought there might be some out here."

"Didn't know you wanted to see them," I said. "Did I not take you to the zoo enough when you were a kid?"

He laughed, taking a seat on the other bench. "Is once 'enough'?" He pulled a bottle of soda out of the pocket of his hoodie and opened it. After taking a sip, he said, "You can't hear anything but the wind, up in the cabin. And we're far from home, so you've got no excuses anymore."

"Oh, is that right? I've got to tell you, have I?"

He'd been pestering me about Vinny's case since it had ended, about seven weeks earlier, with a not guilty verdict.

"Yes, you do. I demand it as payment for my services."

"Man, you've gotten real bold since Terri gave you that ethics lesson."

She'd guessed how I came by the crucial information about Monty—or, rather, she'd figured it out; guessing wasn't something Terri did. She'd talked to Noah and explained that he shouldn't have disclosed that Monty's wife was considering divorce, since the wife was his client and that was her secret. As for the rest of it, though, she'd reassured him that telling me about Monty's affair was the right thing to do.

"Okay, okay," I said. "Tell you what, though. Go get us something to drink first."

He went back to the cabin and returned with a bottle of fizzy water for me and some kind of spritzer for Terri.

I cracked my bottle open, took a sip, and told him how I'd gotten Monty to read out his MAC address.

"Then, once Da Costa testified," I said, "and placed him in the stairwell, I called Monty back to the stand and hit him with questions about his affair. He tried to finesse the first few, but then, when it was clear which direction things were going, he took the Fifth."

Terri smiled. "That never goes over well with a jury."

"Right? He's basically telling them he's guilty."

"Yeah, that's *way* the heck beyond a reasonable doubt," Noah said. "Is that why he got arrested?"

The FBI had walked Monty out of his home in handcuffs a few days before Halloween. We'd all seen it on TV.

"Maybe partly," Terri said. "The main thing was probably putting Dr. Da Costa in touch with the FBI. I'm sure that, plus Monty's testimony, was all they needed to get a warrant."

"Wow." Noah raised his soda bottle to me, and we all took turns clinking. After a moment, he said, looking downcast, "I can't believe that judge died over an *affair*, though. That's just sad."

"Oh, he didn't. Not entirely, at least."

"What?" He looked at me like I wasn't making sense.

"Well, you saw Ludlow's perp walk yesterday, right?"

"I heard about that," he said. "Didn't actually see it."

"Terri got me a copy of the warrant," I said.

She smiled and shushed me.

"Terri *didn't* get me a copy of the warrant," I said. "I just magically know what he got arrested for. It was murder and conspiracy. When he's formally charged, we'll be sure—"

"Why'd they arrest him without charges?"

"Probably they were afraid he'd flee the jurisdiction before the grand jury could be convened. So we'll know more once the grand jury comes back—but if you want my take, Monty must've turned him in. I'm assuming that was in exchange for a plea deal."

"Wait, so Ludlow planned it—"

"And used Monty to carry it out, probably by threatening to reveal his affair or whatever else Ludlow had on him. It just so happened that Monty's best opportunity—or his last opportunity, at any rate—was at the courthouse that day." The letter Vinny had received was still a mystery. Ludlow might have sent it, trying to hedge his bets in case Monty got cold feet. Or maybe Monty had hoped Vinny might take matters into his own hands. In any case, Vinny didn't bite.

"As soon as you two told me about their affair, I could see it all," Terri said. "Monty must've gone and knocked on that third-floor door, and when Nicholson saw him through the window, of course he let him in. They were friends. Or he thought they were."

I took another sip of my water. The island was coming into view in the distance. It was still just a blue shadow.

I'd been wondering if Monty had hesitated—if the reason Nicholson wasn't killed until right before he testified was that, until then, Monty couldn't bring himself to do it. Maybe something that morning had pushed him over the edge. Jealousy, from Samantha Townsend's presence in close quarters with the two of them. Or a threat from one of Ludlow's people.

Or maybe I was just being sentimental. Maybe Monty was a good actor, a good liar, and I had been fooled.

Cardozo had been wondering the same thing, though, when I talked to him about it. For whatever that was worth.

Noah was leaning back against the rail with his hands behind his head and his elbows out. "What ever happened with that hacker guy?" he asked.

"Oh, they appealed," Terri told him, "but we won there too."

"You did? Awesome."

"Mm-hmm. Game over for the prosecution."

"Yeah, he's a free bird," I said. "He's heading to USC in January to finish his computer science degree."

"Good one, man," Noah said. "Nice job."

I nodded. "Could've gone either way, though."

"A lot of things could've," Terri said.

"Yep." As I watched the horizon, a few examples came to mind. The fact that I was with her now, sailing out to meet her family. Winning both my big cases this year. My son being all grown up and, it seemed, successfully launched. There'd been a time when I wasn't sure if he'd survive his teens.

And only two months ago, that long moment where I'd thought that Terri and I were going to die when the earth was ripped out from under our feet.

None of those things *had* to turn out the right way. But all of them did. If Terri's family's Thanksgiving tradition involved making everyone at the table take turns talking about what they were grateful for, I might need awhile to say my piece.

I felt Squatter starting to move around in his dog carrier, and I bent down to see how he was. He looked more alert than usual. The sea air was probably doing him good.

"You know what," I said, sitting back up, "let's see if we can go a day or two without talking about work. No more murder or crime. It's Thanksgiving. Tell us what we're going to eat."

"I like that," Terri said. "Get away from all that morbid stuff for a minute. Okay, now, the first thing, Squatter's going to love: pork like you've never tasted before."

"I am so there for that," Noah said.

"And then for sides, oysters—"

"Oysters?" he said, surprised.

"Do you see this ocean around you?" she asked. "Yes, oysters. And then okra, cornbread, and pineapple pudding. And rice. A whole lot of rice. And the pies that I'm helping Nana make tonight."

"Can I help?" I asked.

"No," she said, laughing. "You've got to learn your place here."

I smiled and looked back at the island. If I had a place there, that was good. Very good.

A seagull wheeled in the sky ahead, and we sailed into the blue.

# END OF TWISTING JUDGMENT
## SMALL TOWN LAWYER BOOK 6

*Defending Innocence*

*Influencing Justice*

*Interpreting Guilt*

*Burning Evidence*

*Prescribing Doubt*

*Twisting Judgment*

PS: Do you enjoy legal thrillers? Then keep reading for exclusive extracts from **The Bloodied Client, Small Town Conviction,** and **Small Town Trial**.

# ABOUT PETER KIRKLAND & DALETH HALL

**Loved this book? Share it with a friend!**

**To be notified of the next book release please sign up for Peter's mailing list, at www.relaypub.com/peter-kirkland-email-sign-up.**

## ABOUT PETER

Peter Kirkland grew up in Beaufort, South Carolina. As a kid, Peter loved history and learning about his area. One year in school, he was given a project to research a few South Carolina law cases and the precedents they set and their effect on people's lives. This research project lit the flame for his passion for law and creating a more equal justice system since. Soon after this, Peter began reading legal thrillers voraciously and enjoyed the legal maneuvering and justice found within. As an adult he has continued researching the law and understanding the system and its effects on individuals. A few years ago, he decided to try writing his own legal thriller.

Now a full-time writer, he uses his research, passion for justice, and real case studies to bring together courtroom dramas with deep, rich characters, and gripping twists and turns.

New to the industry, Peter would love to hear from readers.

## ABOUT DALETH

Daleth Hall grew up in Ann Arbor, Michigan, raised by a handicapped single mother who instilled in her a deep love for truth, justice, and the written word. By the age of three, she was already reading and writing, thanks to her mom's guidance. After discovering that a creative writing degree wasn't enough to pay the bills, she followed her brother into law school and has spent the past 17 years as a trial lawyer. Early in her career, she worked high-stakes criminal cases—from murder to federal corruption—until a colleague's close call with an ex-client escaped from prison and tried to hunt him down convinced her to switch to civil litigation. Despite the shift, Daleth remains active in criminal justice, serving as a bilingual court interpreter and working pro bono to overturn wrongful convictions. In addition to her legal career, she writes gripping legal thrillers, plays, and short stories.

Daleth would love to hear from readers who can contact her at Daleth HallWriter@gmail.com

facebook.com/AuthorPeterKirkland
goodreads.com/peterkirkland
bookbub.com/authors/peter-kirkland
amazon.com/Peter-Kirkland/e/B0942NYRL9

## BLURB

*A teenage girl is charged with the unthinkable…*

The crime? The brutal murder of her own parents. The prosecution's argument seems airtight. But small town defense attorney Maggie Gallagher senses something isn't right…

Months earlier, Zoey Conrad had already faced her worst nightmare when two men broke into her room. In the terrifying struggle that followed, one intruder ended up dead. The judge declared it self-defense and dismissed the charges, allowing Zoey to rebuild her life in their small town. But now, with her parents found murdered under disturbingly similar circumstances, the evidence against Zoey quickly piles up.

Maggie knows Zoey and she wants to believe the girl is no killer. Yet the more she learns about the twisted life the Conrads led, the stronger her compassion for Zoey grows. But the deeper she digs, the worse things get. Especially since Maggie's own son has gotten personally involved.

As the prosecution builds an ironclad case and the clock ticks down, Maggie must race to expose the truth. If she fails, Zoey's fate is sealed—and an innocent life could be shattered forever.

Get your copy of *The Bloodied Client* (Maggie Gallagher Legal Thriller Series, Book 2)
Available January 15, 2026
(Available for pre-order now)
www.peterkirklandauthor.com

---

## EXCERPT

**Chapter One**

You expect warning signs before a disaster. Sirens. Gunshots. Clouds rolling up on your perfect blue sky. But I was sure my sky was all blue, no clouds, no sirens. Nothing out of its place—at least, that I could see.

The Dunlaps were in for a quick probate issue—Emily Dunlap and her son Ken. Emily's husband George had passed on unexpectedly in a car crash, and I could see that her grief was still raw. She looked past me, not at me, as I talked through our business. My office had a nice view of the old courthouse, but I doubted she noticed it in her state.

"Mrs. Dunlap?"

She focused her gaze on me to show she was listening. Ken gave me the nod, so I went on.

"Most of the estate was in both of your names: the house, the business, your Atwood Lake cabin. There's no paperwork you need to worry about to transfer those assets. Same goes for—"

Ken cut in. "His retirement account?"

"Yes, that as well." Emily was back to staring past me, and I found myself frowning as I went on. "All his accounts were in both of your names, with the exception of this one." I held out the statement for her to see, but she didn't look at it. Ken reached out instead. Was he a little too eager? I thought back to an old case I'd once prosecuted, a son who had stolen his mother's estate. Sold it all out from under her while she stewed in her grief.

Ken smiled. "Uh, Ms. Gallagher?"

I realized I was holding onto the statement, clutching on tight as he tried to take it. But he wasn't the kid from that long-ago case, and Emily wasn't that sad, helpless mother. She had her sisters and cousins to lean on, and Ken was a good kid as far as I'd seen.

*You're not a prosecutor anymore,* I reminded myself. *And not everyone is a crime waiting to happen.*

I let go of the statement and cleared my throat. "It's an investment account, and it's just in your husband's name. Same goes for your Lexus, and your son's truck. I've prepared an order for the court to sign, to transfer those over. You should be through probate by the end of this month."

Ken let out a tight breath and sagged with relief.

"So we give this to the judge, and that's it? We're done?"

I could sense his fatigue, so I offered a smile. "I'll take care of that part. You're essentially done. All I need from your mom today is her signature here." I'd prepared applications to put the titles for the Dunlaps' two houses solely in Emily's name. Now I passed her a pen, and she signed them without reading.

"So that's all you need?" She seemed relieved too, glad to be done with this and with my office.

"That's all," I said, then searched for some words of comfort. "Your husband did a great job securing your future. He made this easy as easy could be."

Emily laughed then, a soft, broken sound. She blinked, then she stood. "Yeah. That was George."

The Dunlaps filed out and Auntie El bustled in, in one of her trademark loud floral blouses. I'd thought about asking her to tone down her wardrobe—we were a law office, not a car lot—but clients liked her. She put them at ease. And she cheered me up too, a bright splash of color to pep up my day.

"So sad," she said, when the Dunlaps were gone.

I sighed. "I know. How old was he, sixty?"

"Sixty-one, far too young. Damn those drunk drivers." Auntie El set about straightening my desk. I winced, thinking back to Dad's drinking days, all the times I'd had to confiscate his car keys. There'd been a few times I hadn't caught him fast enough, and only by God's grace had he come home okay.

Auntie El stepped back, done with her straightening. "You have Edie Endicott coming by later. She has some more questions about her 'divorce.'" She did bouncy air quotes, and we both groaned. Edie had been coming every week for a while, testing the waters on her maybe-divorce. "And you've got the Batchelder custody hearing, so you'll want to get down to the courthouse by four."

"Get me their file," I said.

Aunt Louise fetched the file, and she freshened my coffee. "You ever wish you'd get a splashier case? Like when Troy was charged with killing Coach Schafer?"

I shuddered at the memory. "That case was messy in a lot of ways. Don't forget, it started when his son almost died."

"But it was exciting. You live for a challenge. I've known you all your life, so don't act like you don't."

I thought again of the Dunlaps and their dull probate case, and how I'd flashed back to the Mulligan fraud. Had some part of me wished for a monster to fight? I did love a challenge, no doubt about that. But Troy's case had been awful. Folks had been hurt. I shuddered, remembering how hard it had been on Troy and his family.

"No one gets traumatized in probate court."

"But does it stir your soul?"

I swiveled my chair around to look out the window, at the old courthouse with its closely-cropped lawn. No one heard cases there anymore, not since the new courthouse went up down the road. But still, when I looked at it, I always sat straighter. It reminded me why I did what I did.

"My soul's fine," I said. "Now, go on, get." I put on my "gruff sheriff" voice to show I was joking. Auntie El huffed, hands on her hips. Then, with a shake of her head, she went out, grumbling the whole way about stubborn people. I watched her go, smiling, then got back to work. I was fine with these types of workaday cases, and finer still with leaving at five. No long nights holed up in my office, desperately digging for contradictions in witness statements. No tossing and turning, losing sleep over whether I'd done everything I could to save my client's life. With these cases, I could rest easy—and have time to relax. I'd made it home every night last week to a hot dinner, and I expected this week to play out the same.

Get your copy of ***The Bloodied Client*** **(Maggie Gallagher Legal Thriller Series, Book 2)**
**Available January 15, 2026**
**(Available for pre-order now)**
**www.peterkirklandauthor.com**

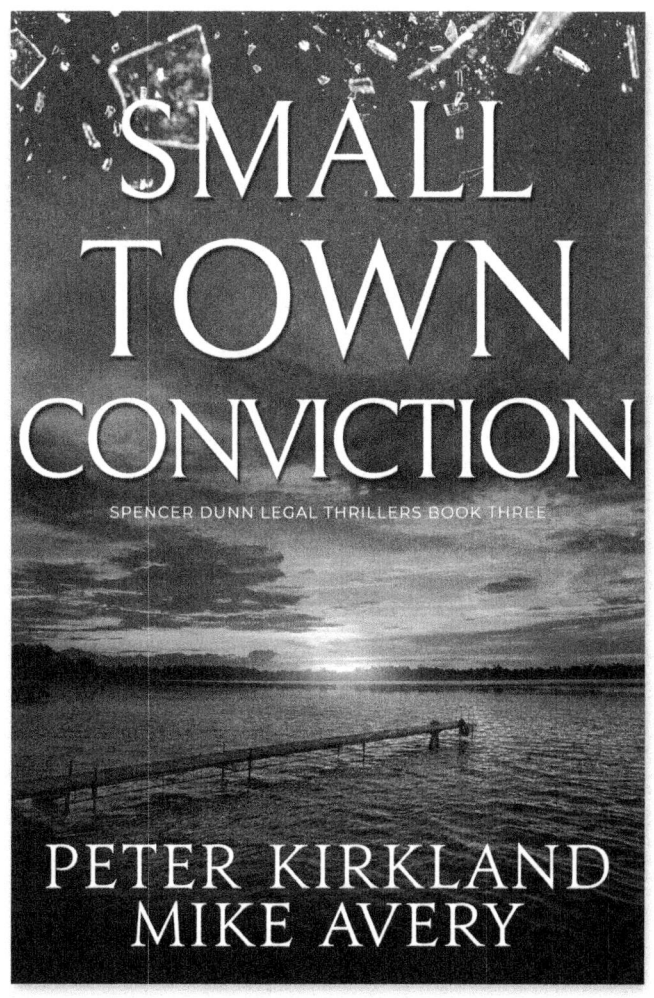

**BLURB**

**One small town. One deadly weekend. Three shocking crimes…**

A local business owner is shot and disappears under mysterious circumstances. Another man goes on a hit-and-run rampage. And a horrifying day care incident sends innocent children to the ER. At first glance, the events appear unrelated. But as he investigates, local attorney Spencer Dunn begins to think otherwise.

When Spencer digs beneath Autumn Harbor's idyllic surface, he uncovers a dark thread weaving the cases together—a thread that leads straight to Jack Butcher, the flashy civic leader whose shiny public persona masks a rotten core. For years, Butcher has operated from the shadows, untouchable… and Spencer is determined to change that.

With pressure mounting and his own family under threat, Spencer races to connect the dots before his innocent clients are convicted. But the truth is more twisted than he ever imagined—and Butcher will do anything to keep it buried.

Now, with the impact of past and current cases coming to a head, Spencer must put more than his legal skill to work—or he may become the next casualty.

Get your copy of *Small Town Conviction*
**Available February 26, 2026**
**(Available for pre-order now)**
www.peterkirklandauthor.com

———

**EXCERPT**

### Chapter One

"It's a miracle those kids didn't die." Alastair shook his head in grateful disbelief.

"They would have, if your client hadn't had that Narcan ready and waiting," I said. "Pretty reckless, keeping heroin in the house where you operate a day care."

"She says the drugs weren't hers, that she didn't know anything about them."

"If that's true, why did she have the Narcan?"

It was Monday, and I was eating an early lunch near the courthouse with my boss, who was also my father-in-law. He'd been in court that morning, representing Cathy Silver. Children at her day care center had found packages of heroin in a playroom cupboard and torn them open, ingested some of the powder, and had to be rushed to the hospital after she gave them a dose of Narcan.

It would have been an upsetting story in any case, but my wife and I had a new little girl at home, a four-year-old we were hoping to adopt. To put it bluntly, Alastair's case freaked me out.

"I don't know," Alastair said. "Cathy hasn't told me much, other than to deny any knowledge of the drugs. Even though she's lived in Autumn Harbor her whole life, the judge denied bail on the grounds that she presented a threat to the safety of the community."

I nodded and looked down at the Reuben I'd ordered. I loved sauerkraut. Whenever I was in New York, I'd get a hot dog slathered in it from a street vendor. Thinking about those kids in the hospital, however, made its tangy aroma smell more like rotten eggs. I pushed my plate away.

"I don't know what's going on in our little town," Alastair continued. "Had you heard about Joe Murrell, who runs We Love Your Junk?"

"We Love Your Junk?" I asked. "Please tell me that's a secondhand store and not some sort of adult business."

Alastair gave me the side-eye. "It's the local waste haulage company. Anyhow, the owner's gone missing. Didn't show up for work on Friday or Saturday. Then there's your new client."

Roy Pelletier, an accountant, had been driving through town Saturday night and hit a pedestrian. Rather than stopping, he'd fled the scene and led the police on a high-speed chase before finally slamming into another car. Accountants could be reckless just like anyone else, of course, but Alastair was right—that was a lot of weird incidents in a short period.

"I guess it's all good for us criminal defense lawyers," I said, though my stomach was still uneasy. "I'd better get going," I added. "I need to talk to Roy before the hearing." I didn't know Pelletier well, but I'd been introduced to him at Whiskey Business, my wife's bar and restaurant, and we'd exchanged pleasantries a time or two.

I met him in the lockup next to the courtroom where he was due to be arraigned at two. No other prisoners were present, so we could talk privately through the bars of the cell. He appeared to be wearing the clothes he'd been arrested in. They were filthy.

"Before we go in front of the judge, I need you to tell me what happened Saturday night," I said. "Anything you say while we're talking about your case is covered by the attorney-client privilege." A friend of his had dropped off a check for the retainer at my office that morning. "That means I can't repeat it without your permission, except to others in my firm and anyone else we might hire to work on this with us. You do need to know, however, that if you tell me you did the things you're charged with, I can't put you on the stand to deny them."

He nodded and said he understood.

"I'm jumping ahead a bit, but I can't help wondering," I said, "how'd you get so dirty?"

"I guess I was dizzy after I hit the other car. I opened my door to get out, but I stumbled and fell on the ground. I tried to get up, but I kept falling. Finally, I decided to sit where I was until help came."

"How long did you feel dizzy?"

"A couple of minutes. The cop helped me to my feet after he took care of the other driver, and by then I felt better."

"What did you tell the officer?"

"Nothing. He took a good look at the situation and then read me my rights. I thought the smart thing to do would be to keep my mouth shut."

"Good call. Okay, let's back up to how this all started—before the first collision. Can you walk me through the whole thing?"

Roy wiped sweat from his forehead. "I was out for a drive, and I must have hit something … someone … at the corner of Myrtle and Main. It was dark, and the streetlight was out. I didn't see anyone, but I heard a loud thump on the passenger side. I panicked and hit the gas."

"Why didn't you stop to see what had happened?"

Roy was a few inches shorter than I was and had to look up to meet my eyes. "I know I should have. I can't tell you why I didn't. Maybe it was, like, adrenaline? I wasn't thinking. My foot just stomped on the gas, and I shot out of there."

"Where had you been going before the collision happened?"

He shook his head. "Nowhere. I was just driving around to pass the time."

"Do you have any outstanding tickets or criminal charges that you were afraid would come to light?"

"No."

"Had you been drinking? Was your auto insurance in effect?"

"Of course I have insurance, and no, I hadn't been drinking. There's no question about that. You don't have to take my word for it—the breath test they gave me at the station came back negative."

Many hit-and-run drivers left the scene because they knew things would get worse if they stopped, whether due to preexisting legal issues or their impaired status at the time of the incident. It seemed that Roy simply fell into the category of people for whom shock triggered flight.

"Anyway," Roy said, "right after that, I mean, like, a couple of seconds, I noticed a car coming up fast behind me."

"Did it have lights and a siren on?"

"No. I had no idea it was a cop. It scared the you-know-what out of me, and I kept accelerating, trying to get away. I was flying. It couldn't have been even a minute before I smashed into another car that was pulling out of a parking space. That's when I realized I couldn't just keep going."

"What happened then?"

"Like I said, I fell getting out of my car. The guy who'd been chasing me flashed a badge, told me to stay where I was, and headed over to the other car to check on the driver. I guess he, the driver, was hurt, because after a little while an ambulance arrived, and they put him on a stretcher and took him away. Then the cop came back to me and got me on my feet, read my rights, and arrested me."

Roy told me he was an accountant who worked for a number of people and businesses in town, that he'd lived in Autumn Harbor ever since he'd graduated from college, and that he'd never been arrested or even gotten a parking ticket. That was all good from the standpoint of bail, but it made me wonder if there was more to the accidents and high-speed chase than met the eye. I didn't want to get surprised by whatever that might be in the courtroom, so I made him go through everything one more time, giving me every detail he could. He insisted there was nothing else to the incident and said he had just panicked.

I left Roy in the lockup and waited in the courtroom for his case to be called. After the judge disposed of a few minor matters, the clerk called my case, and the bailiff brought Roy before the bench and released his handcuffs.

"Roy Pelletier," the clerk called out, "charged with violations of Section 2252, hit-and-run, Class C; Section 2413, driving to endanger, Class C; Section 2414, refusing to stop for a law enforcement officer; and Section 751-B, refusing to submit to arrest."

Judge Barbara Robinson was on the bench, wearing her trademark purple rhinestone glasses. She was known for her independence and unpredictability. I'd appeared in front of her several times, usually with decent results but sometimes with a very bad outcome. "Is your client prepared to enter a plea, Mr. Dunn?" she asked.

"Yes, Your Honor."

The clerk read out the charges again, one at a time, and Roy pleaded not guilty to each one.

"I'll hear you on bail," the judge said.

John Stanford, the prosecuting attorney, stood. "We're asking you to set bail in the amount of $100,000, Your Honor. The defendant is charged with a hit-and-run accident that caused injuries, then leading the police on a high-speed chase in an attempt to escape, resisting arrest, and finally a second collision causing a concussion and several broken bones. He poses a flight risk and is a danger to the community, and a significant bail is required."

Roy was as pale as a ghost, and I winced. A hundred thousand was probably quite a bit more than he could raise. I'd had other cases against Stanford. He was a young lawyer with little understanding of human failures. I hoped the judge could see that.

"Mr. Dunn," the judge said.

"Your Honor, I know it's unusual to call a witness at an arraignment, but I notice that Officer McElroy, who arrested my client, is in the courtroom this afternoon, and with the court's indulgence, I'd like to ask him a few questions before you set bail."

"Very well," the judge said, "but keep it brief, Counselor."

The officer took the stand and was sworn in, and I moved to stand in front of him in the witness box. "Officer McElroy, I just have a few questions for you. First, the car in which you chased my client wasn't a police car, was it?"

McElroy looked briefly at the prosecutor, then back to me. "No, it was my private car."

"So it wasn't equipped with lights and a siren or any police department markings, was it?"

"No, sir."

"Where did you find Mr. Pelletier after the second accident?"

"He was sitting on the street next to his vehicle."

I nodded. "Did you give him any instructions?"

"Yes, I told him to remain where he was."

"And he did, didn't he?"

"Yes."

"When you returned to him, you placed him under arrest?"

"Yes, sir."

"He didn't resist in any way, struggle with you, or attempt to flee, did he?"

"Not at that point, sir."

"No further questions."

Stanford stood. "Officer, what car were you in that evening?"

"Like I said, my personal car. It's a bright yellow vintage Ford Mustang. Very distinctive."

"To your knowledge, had Mr. Pelletier ever seen that vehicle?"

"Many times. We know each other. He does my taxes, and he's often complimented me on my car. He knew who was chasing him."

That came as a surprise to me, and I stifled a burst of irritation at my client. Why hadn't he told me that when we spoke before the hearing? I got quickly to my feet. "Objection, Your Honor. The witness can't know what was in someone else's mind."

"Sustained," the judge ruled.

"Nothing further," Stanford said.

I got up again. "Just one or two questions on redirect, if the court please."

The judge looked unhappy about the time this was taking. "Proceed. But just one or two."

"Officer, it was nighttime when this incident occurred, was it not, and the streets were dark?"

"Not completely dark."

"You had your headlights on?"

"Yes."

"So someone in the car ahead of you, looking at your vehicle in his rearview mirror, would mostly just see your headlights? It would've been very difficult, maybe impossible, to see the vehicle itself, wouldn't it?"

McElroy smirked. "As you said, Counselor, I couldn't know what someone else could see."

What they could see wasn't exactly the same thing as what they knew or had been thinking, but I didn't want to test Judge Robinson's patience by pressing the issue. I was confident she had gotten the point, and, grudgingly, I had to admire the officer's wit in trying to turn the tables on me. "No further questions."

"You're excused," the judge told McElroy.

"Your Honor," I said, "before addressing the question of bail, I'll move to dismiss the charges of refusing to stop for a law enforcement officer and resisting arrest, the former on the ground of lack of scienter—the defendant had no reason to know it was a police officer chasing him—and the latter on the basis of the officer's testimony. Once my client knew that McElroy was a law enforcement officer, there was no resistance."

One of Judge Robinson's pet peeves was overcharging by police and prosecutors. She liked to get directly to the nub of the issue. She looked at Stanford. "I think it will sufficiently serve the interests of justice for us to try the defendant for the hit-and-run and driving-to-endanger charges."

Stanford looked like he had something to say about that, but given Judge Robinson's demeanor, he swallowed it. "No objection, Your Honor."

"Very well," the judge said, "the counts for refusing to stop and resisting arrest are dismissed."

"Thank you, Your Honor," I said. "Given that, I suggest that bail in the amount of $5,000 would be sufficient. Mr. Pelletier has lived in this community ever since he finished school. He has no prior record and is well known here. He has an accounting practice and does the taxes of many local citizens. Given his ties to the community, he cannot be considered a flight risk, and given that we're essentially dealing with automobile accidents, I don't think it would be fair to consider him a risk to the community."

Judge Robinson didn't hesitate before saying, "Bail is set in the amount of $10,000, and the defendant is ordered to surrender his driver's license to the clerk's office and to refrain from operating a motor vehicle until this matter is resolved." She set a date for Roy's next court appearance, and the clerk called the next case.

The guard took Roy back to the lockup, and I followed.

"Can you post that?" I asked.

"No problem. Can you call my friend for me? He'll bring cash to the jail."

Roy gave me the friend's name and number, and I agreed to call him.

"If he shows up quickly, you should be out before dinner," I said. "We'll talk again in a couple of days."

Get your copy of *Small Town Conviction*
**Available February 26, 2026**
**(Available for pre-order now)**
**www.peterkirklandauthor.com**

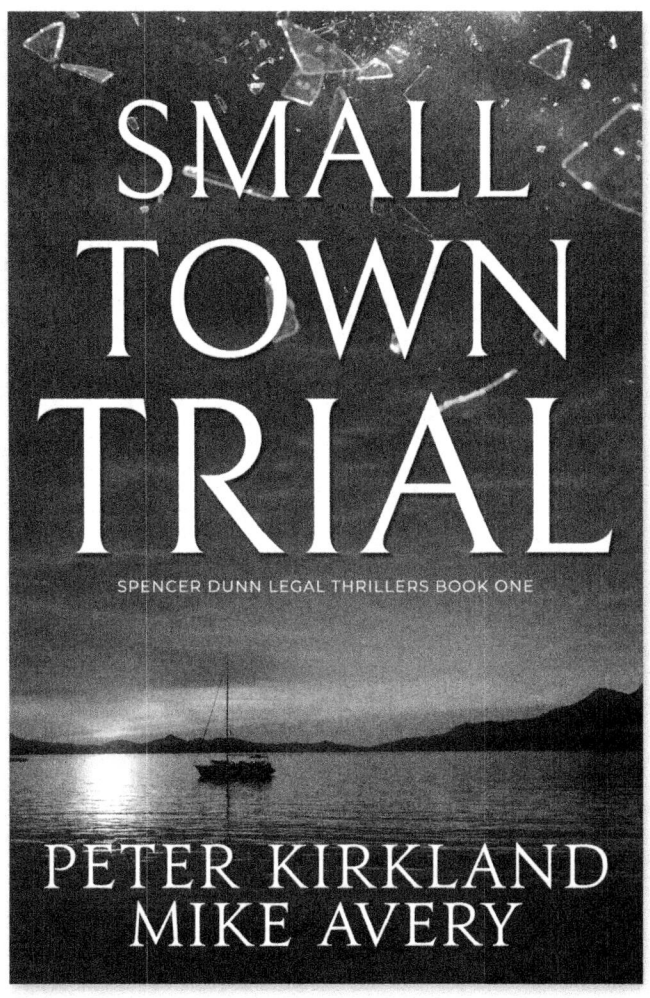

## BLURB

*Murder on a placid lake… Can Spencer Dunn keep his head above water?*

When beloved mayor turned state senator Carlton Osborn is found dead on his boat, the local police suspect foul play. The only suspect is pregnant nineteen-year-old Amber Vega. And the only lawyer willing to take her case is Spencer Dunn. The hotshot attorney is eager to restore his reputation after a humiliating loss in court. But this case may be more than he bargained for....

Amber was caught red-handed on the boat with Osborn's body, and the police are determined to pin the murder on her. Even worse, she was having an affair with the senator, and was caught in a vicious argument with his wife. But the more Spencer digs, the less the story adds up. Something smells fishy, and it's not just Osborn's corpse!

Spencer will stop at nothing to uncover the truth, and he doesn't know the meaning of the word "quit". But if he can't unravel the mystery, prove Amber's innocence, and uncover the real killer, he might be the next one to find himself sleeping with the fishes...

**Grab your copy of *Small Town Trial* (Spencer Dunn Legal Thrillers Book One)**
**Ebook**
**Paperback**
**Audiobook**
**www.peterkirklandauthor.com**

---

### EXCERPT

**Chapter One**

One juror is all it takes. Every lawyer knows this, even the bad ones. Hell, *especially* the bad ones.

It was subtle but unmistakable. Juror number seven's lower lip quivered, and her eyes moistened every time I referenced the plight of the single mother: cast aside, emotionally blackmailed by a cruel ex-husband, beaten down by an unfair system. She felt it; she knew. Some of the others in the jury box seemed less sympathetic. Or maybe they were bored. It was difficult to tell. Perhaps their minds were already made up. I rested my hand on the exhibit shelf directly in front of number seven. Her own hands were shaking and tearing at a tissue in her lap as I spoke.

"So, you see, ladies and gentlemen, it is not as simple a matter as my colleagues for the prosecution would have you believe. As you were instructed when the trial began, for the crime of criminal restraint to occur, there must be both action and intent. In legalese, actus reus and mens rea."

I took a moment to look into a couple of jurors' eyes. It was hard for me to give this case my all when I thought it should never have been brought... but it had, and my client had agonized over it every day since.

"It means guilty actions and a guilty mind. The Maine family code stipulates that for what took place to be a crime, the noncustodial parent not only must take the child out of the state—that is the action—but he or she also must intend to take them somewhere where they cannot be found. In other words, the children are hidden away. That is the guilty mind, the intent. Do we have that here? Has the prosecution produced a single shred of evidence that even suggests that my client intended to conceal her children in a secret location in an attempt to deceive their father and keep them from him?"

I had no difficulty sounding sincere, at least. Shannon Maroney wanted nothing but the best for her kids, and she played by the rules. Which was more than I could say for some of my clients.

"No! We do not. We have absolutely none of that intent here. Not a scintilla. Not even a hint. First of all, my client was the rightful custodial parent when the trip north began. More importantly, these phone records," I continued, shaking the stack of papers in the air, "introduced as evidence and acknowledged by the prosecution, prove that my client notified, or attempted to notify, several people of the children's exact location, including Mr. Maroney. And we heard testimony from some of them: the girl's music teacher, several parents of school friends, Mr. Engel, the boy's karate instructor. They all knew that Ms. Maroney and the children went to Canada to visit family, and that the visit involved an unplanned excursion to the family cabin. They were also informed that Ms. Maroney's father suffered a heart attack and had to be airlifted from that remote cabin to a hospital in Ottawa. We showed you copies of those reports: the Life Flight and hospital reports. I ask you, ladies, and gentlemen. If you were going into hiding with the intent to never be found, would you tell a half dozen or so friends and acquaintances exactly where you are? And would you attempt to inform the children's father as well?"

A few of the jurors shook their heads at this, including number three, a thirtysomething man who'd spent most of the trial looking at his smartwatch.

"In fact," I continued, pointing to the prosecution's table, "we are here for only two reasons. Firstly, Ms. Maroney's travel itinerary had to be changed through no fault of her own. Hasn't that happened to all of us? Secondly, we are here because Mr. Maroney thought it would be easier—or crueler—to file a complaint than to pick up a phone and reach out to any one of those people who knew exactly where his children were. He knew the names of the parents. He knew their routines. He took the kids to music lessons and karate practice. Why not call up the music school and ask if they had heard from his ex-wife? Or any of the parents who were notified—had to be notified—that the girl's birthday party needed to be canceled? But no. Let's beat the poor woman who's stuck in the wilderness, whose father was dead for all she knew, let's drag her into court. That'll make her regret getting a divorce. That will be a nice payback. And I submit that the prosecution, by bringing this matter to trial, is only enabling that sadistic behavior."

Okay, maybe that was too much. But I was right, and I was pissed. My client was being legally assaulted by a vengeful ex-husband. And a misguided and overzealous prosecution was the weapon he chose. Why? I had no idea. Some DAs just get a bug in their britches, I guess. Or maybe the Fathers for Equal Rights lobby were big donors. Either way, it should never have come to this.

"In conclusion, ladies and gentlemen of the jury, I'm afraid we've dragged you down here for nothing. We're wasting time that you could use for better purposes. You have been shown conclusively that, while my client did indeed take her children out of the state, Mr. Maroney was informed of the expected plans. And we have likewise demonstrated that while the plans may have changed, there was never any intent to deceive Mr. Maroney or to keep him from knowing the whereabouts of his children. We have, in fact, proven that the opposite is true." I raised the phone records again. "Ms. Maroney is innocent of this crime because there *is* no crime. Truth and reason leave you no choice but to find the defendant not guilty. Thank you for your service here today."

Whatever Perry Mason effect I hoped to create was ruined by the sound of my left hearing aid throwing feedback into the otherwise hushed courtroom. I must've brushed the stack of papers I was holding too close to my ear as I lowered them histrionically. One juror covered his own ears; another jumped in her seat, startled. I looked at the floor to conceal my red cheeks as I retreated to my seat at the defendant's table.

As was my habit, I attempted to get a furtive read of the jurors' faces as they filed out of the box and through the door to the deliberation room, hoping to get a sense of what they were thinking. Granted, for all my bluster during closing, this wasn't exactly the crime of the century, and my client would probably never face real prison time if found guilty. But this case bothered me more than most. I'd represented all kinds of clients back in New Hampshire—some innocent, many guilty—but none of them were being railroaded like Shannon Maroney.

One of the jurors stopped just before exiting and turned to look straight at me. He was pulling at his right earlobe. I wondered, did he also wear hearing aids? Or was he judging me, wondering why someone my age would have a hearing problem? It was only a matter of time before the good people of Bar Harbor learned the truth. Spencer Dunn got beat up by the son of one of his clients—an innocent man now sitting in a cell in Concord, New Hampshire, doing eight to fifteen. In retrospect, my ability to hear properly was a small price to pay for such bad lawyering. Would that get out too? Bar Harbor's newest transplant was a washed-up attorney on the run from his failures, his demons.

"What now?"

"Huh? Oh. We wait."

Shannon Maroney put her hand on my right forearm, pulling me out of my thought spiral. "Do you think they will really do it? Will they, could they, find me guilty?"

"They shouldn't. I meant what I said up there. This is one of the most ridiculous cases I've ever defended. Let's grab a coffee. The clerk will call me when the verdict is ready."

Forty-five minutes later, we were back in the courtroom watching the jurors enter and take their seats. This time, none of them looked at me or my client. That could be a bad sign. Then again, a short deliberation was usually good news for the defendant.

"Ladies and gentlemen of the jury, I understand you have reached a verdict."

"Yes, Your Honor," the forewoman replied, standing.

"And your decision is unanimous?"

"Yes, Your Honor."

*Unanimous.* My gut fluttered at the word. No matter how large or small the case, the impending verdict always evoked a nervous reaction. It's an experience shared by most trial attorneys. But I've often felt that the suspense hits me harder than most. Maybe I just take these things too personally.

"Excellent. Please hand the verdict to the clerk."

The clerk took the sheet and gave it to the judge, who scanned it quickly and snapped it back to the clerk without any hint of what it contained. I made a mental note never to play poker with Judge Dickenson.

"Please read the verdict, madam clerk."

"In the case of the State of Maine versus Shannon Jean Maroney, the court finds the defendant not guilty of the crime of Criminal Restraint by Parent, as defined by section three-zero-three of the Maine Family Code."

"Thank you, clerk, and thank you for your service, members of the jury. Please remain seated. This matter is not yet closed."

*Not yet closed?*

"I wish to offer my remarks on this matter, which we have all been a party to these last few days."

Judge Dickenson's tone was serious. This was the first case I'd argued before the man—hell, the first case I had in the whole state of Maine. But I could tell a lecture was coming.

"Ms. Greathouse, Mr. Carter, far be it for me to suggest frivolousness on the part of the Hancock County prosecutor's office. I like to believe the best of our public servants."

"I'm sorry, Your Honor?" The man at the prosecution table shot to his feet.

"Sit down, Mr. Carter. I'm not looking for a rebuttal. Now, since we have what I believe was the correct verdict in this matter... It was very obvious that Mr. Maroney—are you in the gallery, sir? Yes, you, Mr. Maroney. I'm talking about you. Mr. Maroney, as an aggrieved ex-husband, clearly embellished the circumstances of his children's supposed disappearance at the hands of his former wife. He made remarkably little effort to find them. One wonders if he was even trying to find his kids at all. I agree with defense counsel. This complaint smacks of retribution and a misuse of the law. I am also inclined to admonish the prosecution for bringing us to this point."

"Thank you, Your Honor," I said.

"Sit down, Mr. Dunn. As I was saying, Ms. Greathouse and Mr. Carter, I would be remiss if I did not take this opportunity to reacquaint you with our mediation process. This matter could have been adjudicated with much less fanfare and, I would add, less jeopardy to a mother who has demonstrated a willingness and desire to do the right thing for both her children and the law."

**Grab your copy of *Small Town Trial* (Spencer Dunn Legal Thrillers Book One)**
**Ebook**
**Paperback**
**Audiobook**
**www.peterkirklandauthor.com**

Printed in Dunstable, United Kingdom